Valentine and the Mobsters

Terry Hornby

Valentine and the Mobsters

Print ISBN: 978-0-6458491-6-5

Electronic Edition published in Australia in 2023 by Terry Hornby

More information may be gained upon contact with the author at hornbywriting@gmail.com

Typeset in 11pt Garamond

Cover design by Nicklas Reiniger and BookCoverZone

Also by Terry Hornby

Valentine and the Devil
Valentine and the Undead
Valentine and the Mobsters

Dedication

To the Maroochydore Library writing group.

Every second Friday a bunch of us meet at Maroochydore library and write our hearts out. We talk books and writing, and we talk about demons, love affairs, cosy mysteries, movie scripts with stagecoaches, aliens and good food recipes. It is a great group, sponsored by the Queensland Writers Centre

Thank you for your company, let's do it some more.

And above all, thank you to Glenda, the light of my life.

Chapter 1

The cell had four bunks, two up and two down, all attached to the side walls. Three of the bunks were occupied which led me to believe the last top place was mine. None of the occupants made eye contact with me, never a good sign. I stayed where I was, not taking that final step into my new home.

One of these guys was the key, the one who set the tone, the one who told the others what to do. I dismissed the man on the top bunk, he sat with legs over the side and swung them back and forth. Maybe nerves, maybe keen for exercise. The guy underneath him lay on his back, arms by his sides with eyes in a fixed stare at the space above him. Could have been trying to check leg-swinger's butt out through the mattress, but I doubted it.

That left contestant number three, a big, beefy type on the lower bunk under the only other vacant space. He had fleshy arms with his prison-issue sleeves torn off to show the world his muscles and tattoos. The muscles were impressive, but the tatts were straightforward. Burning skulls just never go out of fashion, no matter the planet.

The guard behind me gave me a little push with his baton, "In you go, sweetheart, daddy has to shut the door now. Nighty, night. Don't let the bed bugs bite." I took a step forward so the cell door could slide shut behind me. Yes, these doors slid shut, they weren't on proper hinges but seemed to glide back and forth on a hidden track. Jails have little differences, sort of a spotter's hobby of mine. Our friendly guard sauntered off to do whatever prison guards do in their idle hours.

I still hadn't said a word and showed no emotion or facial reaction since I entered the cell. Joining a jail full of society's malcontents wasn't the time to be upbeat and friendly.

Lardo on the bottom bunk broke wind as the cell door shut behind me. Leg-swinger's eyes flicked between him and me even while he kept his face on the opposite wall. This confirmed my opinion of him as a bit player in our little drama; he was staying out of the way but needed to follow the action. He was doing what survivors always do, see which way the wind was blowing. The other guy on the bottom bunk stayed very still, almost rigid. He was definitely an observer and not a prime mover.

This meant Big and Beefy was either the main contender or one of the others was the puppet master thereby manipulating Big and Beefy. I thought the chance of this was very low, which meant Mr. Tatts was the man to watch.

And respond to. Goodie.

We all wore prison clothes, prison shirt, prison pants and soft slippers, not shoes or boots. The chances of doing irreparable damage by a vicious slippering were slim. This was a pity because a good pair of boots, coupled with some iron or steel toes and heels, can do wonderful damage. Done it myself a few times, ribs tend to crack under a good kickin'. Been on the receiving end once or twice which is ... not so good.

But we were in slippers so no go with the heavy-handed treatment. But on Gamma 5 a wiry little monk had taught me unarmed combat techniques. He eventually tried to kill me, an action all too frequent in any new acquaintance I make. He showed me how to deliver a barefoot front kick which was both brutal and damaging. Keeping your toes curled up and out of the way is an important part of the action, otherwise you can hurt yourself. A tip for young players.

I stepped into the cell and gave my target a vigorous snap kick to his cheekbone. It depressed quite satisfactorily as his head snapped to one side. I was pretty sure he did not have a broken neck. Pretty sure, but not positive. You can't have the customers dying on opening night.

Leg swinger stopped his movement and gripped the sides of his bunk with renewed intensity.

"Hey!" His voice started and stopped abruptly, but I was interested in his body movements. Was he going to jump into the fray or crawl into his shell? I also kept half an eye on the guy still prone on the bottom bunk, the one who hadn't given me any clues as to his allegiances. Both these customers were very still. Not the still before a fight but the tense stillness when you want the bad man to go away.

Leg swinger swallowed a couple of times before squeaking again, "You killed Lennux..."

I moved over to the comatose body of my victim and checked his pulse. I was hoping the body symmetry was enough like mine to have a heart in the same places. Under his neck, I felt the slow beat of blood, fighting its way through his body fat and general sludge. It seemed he was still alive. By grabbing his left arm and heaving mightily I was able to drag his unconscious body to the edge of his bunk. As he teetered on the edge, I gave a slight push and he rolled quite loosely onto the hard floor with a wet little splash.

I took up his position on the bottom bunk and lay back with my arms under my head. I may have hummed a tune.

Leg Swinger slid himself to the floor and made sure he was pressed hard up against his bunk. I turned my head to get a good look at him and his bunkmate. This standing guy was thin and pasty in a twitchy sort of way, he looked like he needed some good meals, fresh air and sunshine and a whole lot of peace and quiet. Or more drugs.

I gave them both my best smile, "How're you doin'?"

"Is he.... Is Lennux, ...dead?"

"Don't think so, but I've been wrong before."

"Are you...," more pauses. Leg Swinger was big on twitchy pauses, "Are you just going to leave him there?"

I flicked a glance at our unconscious cellmate, "Yeah. Why?"

"He might need help?"

"Probably does."

"Well," he swallowed again and flicked his eyes about the cell, looking for answers. "Do you want me to, like, get some help?"

"Knock yourself out."

The circus began. Leg Swinger called out for a guard, yelling about needing medical assistance. In a short time, our uniformed turnkey strolled up and stuck his nose between the bars on the door.

"What happened here?"

"Guy fell off his bunk," I said. There was a moment of pause while the turnkey thought that through.

"He fell off the bottom bunk?"

"Yep."

"Looks pretty badly hurt." There was a bit of foot shuffling as he fidgeted with the decision-making process. "I'm calling for backup."

We all remained quiet. I whistled an aimless tune while the guard called in his report over a small communicator clipped to his belt. Leg Swinger climbed back onto his top bunk but left off his exercise routine, the guy on the bottom slowly sat up and swung his feet onto the floor making sure he didn't get entangled with his bunkmate. I tried to tense up in preparation for a fight without appearing to quiver too much. This is not easy, so I gave up and instead turned my head to face him. A little character study seemed called for.

He was of medium build with pale blond hair and a face lined with struggle. His eyes slowly rose from our comatose companion to me.

"You're in a lot of trouble," he said.

I stayed silent, just looking at him. Like most people, he couldn't let the silence remain unfilled. If he hadn't started the talking it would have been fine to remain quiet, but now he had committed himself to being responsible for our little social interaction. He jutted his chin forward before speaking, a sure sign of stress, "He was here for you, you know."

I scratched my neck and cracked a few knuckles, filling in the time.

"You're in a lot of trouble, man," he repeated.

"You said that," I pointed out. My eyes roved over the underside of the top bunk. I could see bits of mattress poking through the slats making up the base of the bunk. Pretty fancy accommodation for prisoners, imagine having a bed **and** a mattress. I could be very comfortable here.

The guard had been watching our little drama unfold and decided to enter the fray with his own observation, "A lot of trouble. Mr. Calcout won't be happy about what happened to Lennux."

"Not my fault he fell off his bunk," I felt I had to maintain some sense of innocence. "Is Calcout the Head Jailer?"

A medical team arrived before we could continue our little chat. We were told to move to the back of the cell and face the wall. I turned my head to look over my shoulder and received a shove in the back to remind me of my place.

A new, darker voice joined the conversation, "Prisoners will keep their faces to the wall when instructed to do so!"

Another shove interrupted my meditations, "What happened here?" The new speaker had one of those gravelly voices that doesn't like coming out into the fresh air too often.

"Guy fell off his bunk," I replied.

"You're Valentine, right?"

I started to turn around, a big smile on my face, "That's right, pleased to meet you..."

I had obviously offended the etiquette of prisoner-guard dialogue because my warm greeting was interrupted by gravel voice saying, "Shut up, prisoner!" He underlined his statement by pushing me hard against the wall. I could smell his breath as he leaned into my shoulder and brought his mouth close to my ear, "Now we all know what happened here. I'm not going to waste my time investigating and recording the issue because you will be dead by evening. Do you hear me? Dead!"

He relaxed his grip and allowed me to return to a more vertical stance, one with a lot less face and hard surface contact. I resumed my study of the wall, behind me I heard a few groans as the team lifted Lennux, probably onto one of those beds on wheels I had seen in Sick Bay. After the clanking noises had died away, we were instructed to turn around but remain against the wall.

In the cell with us were our original guard and another character who stood glaring at me in silence for a few moments. This must be the owner of the dark and broody voice. I gave him a wink, don't know why, it just happened. The lads tell me I have a habit of doing inappropriate things at precisely the wrong time. I can't help myself.

This was just such a moment, the newcomer responded to my cheery wink by punching me in the stomach. Did a good job of it, too, a short travel distance of fist combined with transference of body weight onto the leading foot. I felt his entire mass impact my stomach as his fist attempted to say hello to my backbone.

Chapter 2

My lungs emptied all the air, spots came and danced around my eyes and my brain said, "See what happens when you mouth off!" Then it shut down in disgust and left me on automatic pilot. This was a bad thing because my normal reaction to getting hit is to hit back.

Which I did, I swung an elbow into the new guy's face and gave him a decent clip on the nose. Blood spurted everywhere, he fell back and the onlookers shouted in astonishment. And then, of course, I entered a world of hurt as two guards took out heavy truncheons and proceeded to beat the living snot out of me.

After a while, it felt like years but was probably only a few moments, I found myself lying on the cell floor with lots of body parts sending in damage reports. I seemed to have gained another loose tooth as well as blurred vision and a massive headache. Kidneys and ribs still seemed intact although my arms were on fire. A good habit when receiving a beating is to get your arms in front of the more delicate bits of the body, the downside is the arms tend to cop a real hammering. Just another tip for young players out there.

"Got anything else you want to try, Valentine?" asked gravel voice, now with overtones of blood nose.

"No, I'm good," I groaned.

He turned to my cellmates and said, "Get him on his feet and down to the mess hall. And then stay away from him. Mr. Calcout will want to see him over lunch."

From my prone position, I watched their boots turn and walk out the door. They had good boots, I like boots.

After a few moments of nothing, I felt hands under my arms as my cellmates tried to heave me to my feet. Good luck with that, boys, I thought. I am a very big and horrible man, these two guys looked like a stiff breeze would blow them over. I let them struggle with my inert body mass for a few moments, Leg Swinger was doing most of the grunting, but his mate was turning a good shade of red. I pushed them out of the way and dragged myself up the wall to a vaguely vertical position, the beating was too short to do lasting damage so all I had to do was put up with the pain for a bit longer and it would start to recede. It was just pain, nothing to it. All part of my job description.

Bloody Magic, bloody NightWatch, bloody horrible men who kill my friends.

Because that was what had brought me here, someone killed a friend of mine. A copper teaching me how to be a better copper, better than my normal pile of rubbish. I don't like people who kill my friends, I don't have that many to spare.

"Are you all right, Mr. Valentine?" Leg Swinger was giving me a deep and concerned expression.

"I'm fine, nothing that alcohol and loose women can't fix." I stood up a bit straighter and pushed the pain away, time for the next step in my grand plan. My grand plan consisted of finding who was behind the death of my friend and then killing them. Not a lot of detail but I'm still new to the whole planning concept.

Being thrown into jail wasn't part of the overall scheme but the authorities on this world took a dim view of the way I interrogated a prisoner of theirs, probably understandable since I had killed him. Honestly, some people.

Step one of my plan was locating a key player in the criminal fraternity on the planet. Since I had been thrown into the clink, I would have to modify my plan. Perhaps I could locate such a person in a prison? Would such a person exist? Why is planning so hard? My boss makes it look easy.

"Take me to the mess hall. And who are you guys?" I said.

Leg Swinger shuffled his feet and stammered "I'm Amadi. Thief."

I grunted and swung my glance to the other member of our happy band, the quiet one. Him I watched carefully.

He pursed his lips, shrugged his shoulders, and said "Babajide. Arson."

"Do you guys always introduce yourself with your special life skill?"

"It's what we do in prison, Mr. Valentine," said Amadi. "When you meet someone new you give your name and your crime." He did his foot shuffle again, "So, uh, what's your crime?"

I took a step towards the cell door, all body parts seemed to be functioning so I kept walking out of our happy home. "Bit of variety. Violence, theft, killing, general mayhem. I guess I'm an all-rounder, never got to specialize." I kept walking and turned right out of the cell door and along the walkway. I was demonstrating real leadership to my buddies who had fallen in behind me with that little dance step you do when someone moves off unexpectedly.

"Uh, Mr. Valentine, you're going the wrong way," said Amadi.

I stopped and turned around, "What?"

He gestured over his shoulder, "The mess hall is that way, next floor down."

"Lead on, Amadi, Thief," I commanded. "Take me to the Warden of this fine establishment. What's his name, something like Calcout?"

Babajide stopped me with a hand on my arm, I turned to face him with a gentle query in my raised eyebrow. My gentle query asking if he wanted to lose that hand. He dropped his arm and said, "You don't understand, Mr. Calcout isn't the warden, he's not even one of the guards."

I stood there trying to project a deep and thoughtful manner, which is a hard look for me.

"He's a prisoner. He runs the whole jail. You don't want to cross Mr. Calcout. Biggest gang boss in the region."

This was the guy whose henchman I had just beaten up, a key player.

My cunning plan was working.

We strolled down an exposed walkway overlooking the floor below. Along my left was a row of cells each with a door giving access to this walkway; above my head was the ceiling of what I assumed to be another walkway.

I stopped and leaned over the rail to look around, also to intentionally cause my two buddies to stumble into me. They muttered some apologies for their clumsiness. Poor sods seemed to have little experience with someone who played these little games, it confirmed my suspicion about their status in the pecking order. They were one step above bottom feeder, innocent bystanders and victims-to-be.

You had to like them.

The cell block extended above my head for some distance before finishing in an austere ceiling with embedded light sources. It all looked clean and spotless, quite unnatural to me. Our clothes were of simple but robust material, the floors appeared to be regularly scrubbed and there was a strong sense of order about the place. I didn't like it at all.

"Uh, Mr. Valentine?" came a little voice behind me.

I turned to Amadi, "What?"

"We probably need to keep moving, Mr. Valentine. Mr. Calcout won't like to be kept waiting."

"Why do you call me 'Mr.'?" I asked.

He gave me the open-mouth fish look I get sometimes when a person's mind tries to process my question in relation to the surroundings. "Because....um...."

"Because we don't know who you are," chimed in Babajide. "Even though we are both due for release tomorrow we want to show you some respect in case you are someone important."

"Rest easy, lads, I'm nobody. Keep with plain 'Valentine.'" I turned back and kept walking, thinking over the whole concept of respect in a prison. "So, you guys get out tomorrow? Why were you in the cell with me and ugly? Don't they have a nice safe place for non-violent types like you two?" I had some experience of living in confined spaces for long periods with unpleasant people. Unpleasant and violent people from whom I had learned a thing or two about getting along in a dangerous world.

"We wondered the same thing," replied Babajide. "They probably wanted two witnesses to give Lennux an alibi for whatever they had planned for you. Credible witnesses."

"What makes you two credible?" I asked. "I mean, you are criminals. No offense but doesn't that mean you may be a little dishonest?"

Amadi stiffened. "I stole to support my family. My father has a small store that is struggling. His brother, my uncle, is the family leader and has chosen to forge relationships with unpleasant men. My uncle told me we could keep my father's store open if I agreed to do some tasks for his friends."

I had heard this story before. Sometimes it was even true. "Uh-huh," I said. "You're just a poor young man led astray by low types. I think I know this song. You have a heart of gold and wouldn't hurt anyone, and you only stole to help out others. Is there a sick brother or sister in there somewhere? Usually is. How about a long-suffering mother with worn-out hands and careworn features?"

"My mother is dead, Mr. Valentine," said Amadi. "I have no brothers or sisters and only one cousin, Emilii. She is still a child."

I shrugged, no reason to doubt him. Or believe him.

Babajide chimed in, "Amadi is an honest man, Mr. Valentine."

"Apart from the whole 'being a thief' thing," I replied.

"His uncle can be quite...demanding," said Babajide.

Amadi coughed and said, "I would prefer my family not to be discussed. Please understand, Mr. Valentine, both of us would be believed because we are not a part of the criminal tapestry of this world."

"Criminal tapestry?" I said. "Sounds colourful, are they all sweetness and light then, your villains? Calling criminal gangs a 'tapestry' almost makes them sound gentle and harmless."

"They are neither gentle nor harmless. They traffic in blood and pain," said Amadi. "My father has kept our side of the family out of his brother's clutches but at the price of my service."

Babajide said, "We are almost there, Mr. Valentine. We will leave you at the end of this walkway."

"Sure," I said. "Well, it's been nice talking to you blokes. Look me up if you are ever in the city and we can talk about our prison days. Relive some of the high points."

We came to a set of stairs leading down to the floor below, my companions stopped and said," We wish you well, Mr. Valentine. Undoubtedly, Lennux was placed in our cell to hurt you. We do not know you, but you have treated us with consideration. By removing Lennux from the prison population you have helped a little. His violence will not be missed. You may have made many enemies but please know we are not among them."

This was a strangely moving little speech from my two recent acquaintances. Calling on all my personal charm, I grunted. "Sure," I said, "no worries. See you around, fellas." Charisma, I've got buckets of it.

Descending the stairs, I came to a large open space with rows of tables set up, I could recognize a mess hall when I saw it. Most of the tables were occupied by fellow prisoners, they were chatting and doing the things people do while waiting for a good feed.

At the bottom of the stairs, I almost tripped over another prisoner, a little bloke who was standing there in casual conversation with three large, brutal looking men. Summoning all my people skills I politely asked him to move by saying, "Out of the way, Shorty."

I could tell I had transgressed a hidden law of the prison, the social temperature dropped and my two erstwhile companions at the top of the stairs moved back even further to get away from the consequences of my social impropriety.

"Let me guess, short stuff, you'd be Calcout?" I asked.

"I am Mr. Calcout," replied the little guy, leaning into the honorific, "and you are in a great deal of trouble." He turned to one of the slabs of meat beside him, "Tell Shaqir." Big and burly lumbered off into the crowd and Calcout turned back to me with one of those looks which sums you up and finds you wanting. I've received a lot of them over the years.

I felt a bit of diplomacy was called for, "So, you're Mr. Big?"

Chapter 3

He backed up a pace, I took the opportunity to step onto the floor of the mess hall and have a good look around. This wasn't hard to do because Calcout only came up to my waist. How he came to be a top boss escaped me, he must have hidden depths.

At this point I realized why he had backed up. It was to give his remaining bookends a bit of swinging room. The thug on my right launched a punch at my head which started from deep space while the guy on my left launched a sidekick at my malnourished stomach.

It's good when we start talking in a language I understand.

I leaned back a little and let the haymaker swing past my nose while turning to one side and catching the outstretched foot of my second dance partner. I gave him a smile and a wink before grasping his foot by ankle and toe and twisting hard in an attempt to turn it a full circle. There was a snap as some bit of him broke and he fell to the floor making the mewling noises we all do from time to time.

The puncher backed up a bit more, his eyes flicking to his downed partner. He didn't go into a panic. Not good, he seemed to be an experienced nasty man which could mean I was in for a long workout. Hey ho, it's a man's life in the NightWatch.

I stepped over his buddy, I may have put some weight on his knee. Some behaviours are just instinctive, when a guy goes down, I like to keep them down. It saves the trouble of putting them down again.

We squared up in a small ring with Calcout giving me a smug grin, the rest of the prisoners had formed a large circle around us with enough space to do the dance. Calcout's smirk annoyed me, I tried to think of a clever witticism until sudden pain erupted in the back of my head. Down I went, I found myself examining the floor from close up. I was on my hands and knees in front of Calcout, the guy had really tiny feet. Someone had given me a real wallop on my poor, misunderstood noggin.

Calcout trod on my fingers to catch my attention, "Allow me to introduce you to Shaqir." He grabbed my chin and twisted my head to see the biggest, hairiest man in the world. He was shirtless with large quantities of black curly hair matting his stomach, chest and shoulders. Bits of it even came out of his nose. Gross. From my groggy position, I could even see the backs of his hairy hands as he cracked his knuckles. Yukky.

Calcout squatted down, took my chin in his fingers and looked into my eyes, saying, "You just put Shaqir's brother into hospital, he has a broken cheekbone and a possible fracture of the skull. Shaqir wants to discuss the poor life choices you have made and, I must confess, I am looking forward to seeing you hurt." The little squirt stood up and I was left on my hands and knees in front of his prison-issue pants. The back of my head was painful, the earlier blows from the guard were still ready to pop up and remind me of past mistakes.

This was not going to end well, I thought. I might even die here.

What I needed was a weapon, maybe a big gun or a knife. Best of all, a hammer.

I pulled my feet under me and reached forward to grab Calcout by his ankles. I pushed erect and heaved the little guy up in a large arc, like chopping an axe into a tree. I spun and brought the surprised form of Calcout around in a beautifully wide swing, his entire body was horizontal and picking up some decent speed as he flew through the arc. He was certainly screaming.

I leaned back a little to make sure he hit Shaqir about head height. To be honest, I would have settled for any contact that gave me an advantage in the fight that was to come. Maybe the little guy would stun my erstwhile opponent for a few beats and so let me try some other dirty, underhand street fighting technique.

Calcout hit Shaqir squarely on the head. In fact, both their heads collided with a meaty thwack. Meaty with a hint of crack in it. Calcout's head flattened, and stuff came out his nose as I let go of his ankles. Shaqir's eyes lost focus and he stood erect for a moment before falling directly onto his knees, probably doing some more damage there. After holding this motionless pose for another whisker of time he fell forward onto the hard floor, his nose doing a fine job of cushioning the blow. We all heard it smoosh across his face.

I staggered back and looked at the carnage around me. Calcout seemed to be dead. Shaqir may have been dead. In any case, he wasn't going to give me any more grief for a while. I rolled my shoulders and let my gaze swing around the room like I meant all this to happen.

There were a lot of mouths hanging open as the assembled criminals of this world took in the shattered form of their previous employer before they began to look at me, the initiator of it all. The gang didn't look happy with me.

"How you doin'?" I said to the assembled multitudes.

At this point, I had given myself up for dead. I was about to be pummeled by all and sundry until I was just a jam smear on the floor. Couldn't happen to a nicer guy.

Thug number two took a step towards me, his little piggy eyes ablaze with indignation and anger. "You're a dead man." Thugs are not strong on verbal diversity. He waved the gang forward to finish me off by saying the old favourites, words I have heard many, many times, "Get him!"

Generally, at this point, I end up on the losing side of a thumping but there was something different about the mood of this crowd. Rather than gazing upon my unblemished visage with toothy grins they were staring at thug number two with looks of apprehension.

Perhaps my reputation as a freestyle brawler had preceded me. Perhaps they felt shy over engaging me in a spot of the old rough and tumble. Or perhaps it was the little red dot floating over the face of thug number two. I joined the rest of the guys in watching it drift over his forehead, slide down his cheek and then dance a little on his shirt. Quite colourful.

"There's a....," said one of the gang. One of the boys was trying to be articulate, how cute. "Lendo, there's a red dot on your shirt. An aiming dot."

Lendo looked down at his shirt, saw the dot and went a paler shade of prison white. He turned his gaze up and over my shoulder to somewhere above my head. The rest of his boys did the same until we had one of those ridiculous situations where everyone is looking at a certain spot - except you.

A familiar voice drifted down from above, the voice of an angel, "Why aren't you dead yet, Val?"

I turned to see a group of men leaning on the railings overlooking the mess hall. One held a blaster with an aiming dot pointed at my recent debating partner, Lendo.

The bloke on the end spoke up, "We're getting jack of shooting guys who want to kill you, mate."

I smiled, "Good to see you, too, Teddy Boy."

My release from prison flowed smoothly, mainly because the man standing beside Teddy Boy was Sergeant Frenzek. He was the aide to one of their top-ranking coppers, the late Captain Boaths, a man I had called friend. My murdered friend. Frenzek had some serious pull around the constabulary, and no one was going to give him a hard time over the paperwork for my transition from threat to society to law-abiding citizen.

This planet had a regulation that allowed any prisoner to be released into the custody of a senior police official. Frenzek had that sort of rank, not the sergeant bit, that's reasonably ordinary – heck,

I'm a sergeant from time to time. No, Frenzek got his influence from his membership in an elite unit. This unit was responsible for any crimes relating to off-worlders and more importantly, Traders. Trade equals money. Frenzek had the ear of movers and shakers, and he used it to shake me loose from the luxurious prison accommodation I had so recently enjoyed. And avoid the beating, mustn't forget the beating.

We left the prison with Frenzek behind the controls of some sort of land vehicle which, as far as I can tell, ran on wheels. That's the limit of understanding of the technology. I'm okay up to and including a horse, but beyond that, the intricacies of various modes of transportation lie outside my ken. Way, way outside. We have encountered strange stuff since leaving Earth.

Teddy Boy was in the back seat with me, up front next to Frenzek was another copper from this world, one with lots of ribbons on his chest and some impressive scars down his left cheek. Not a desk man, I guessed.

"What's going on, Ted?" I asked.

"No thanks, necessary, Val. Glad to help out."

I sighed, "Gee whiz, guys, thank you so much for rescuing me from the nasty prison. I was having real trouble joining the in-crowd, I think I must have offended the Head Boy."

Scarface turned and looked over the seat to give me the full benefit of his battered looks. "You offed the 'Head Boy', Sergeant Valentine. I understand you used him as a club to kill another prisoner, the meanest and toughest killer in the prison who was also the mob's top enforcer." His voice didn't have any inflexion. Not a note rose above the rumble similar to the sound a ship makes as it hits rocks and sinks with all hands. This guy had the sort of voice that made you think of these things.

I liked him.

"Maybe," I admitted.

"And you put another prisoner into Intensive Care," added Frenzek. "I understand it was a kick to his face while he was lying down?"

"Possibly. Is there a point to all these vague charges?" I started gazing out the window,

"You were also insolent to some of the guards, even attacking one and breaking his nose," this from Frenzek again.

"You were in that prison less than an hour, Val," said Teddy Boy. "Two deaths, a serious injury and an assault on authority. Must be some sort of record, even for you."

"I'm gifted."

Chapter 4

Scarface raised one eyebrow, I suspect he only had the one, before turning back to face front. We drove in silence for the rest of the trip, any further conversation from me could wait until my heart rate returned to normal and my brain started working again. Where were we going? Why was Ted involved? Why was he on the planet at all?

I was tired and confused, functioning without any knowledge of the current situation or any understanding of events. Not an uncommon state of affairs in my life.

The last time I had seen the NightWatch they were in our Trading Ship, orbiting the planet. The vessel we had so recently defended against pirates. And lots of Undead, but that's another story. That little episode had seen me screaming my lungs out in terror as I rode a Sled down to the planet in pursuit of a pirate. A chap I had subsequently killed, which resulted in me being placed in prison.

Pretty normal day for me.

We drove down a small laneway between two tall towers and entered an underground parking area. Lots of concrete pillars, or something similar to concrete, with various vehicles parked around the floor. We drove past a row of Personal Sleds, my favourite means of transportation except for the whole 'riding from space to planet' thing. Ted and I both drooled a little at them, I nudged him and said, "Shiny, eh?"

He gave me a big grin, punched me on the shoulder and said, "You big goose, good to see you again."

"Give us a kiss, sweetheart."

Frenzek came to a halt, turned off the engine and said, "If you two can stop falling into each other's arms we might just get on." He opened the door, we followed and entered one of those little rooms that go up and down instead of using stairs. Lifters, they call them.

I was feeling untidy and grungy in my prison-issue clothes; the various beatings I had both given and taken added to my dishevelled state. Ted took me to a room where I was able to clean up and change into clothes more suitable for an innocent civilian and not a dangerous off-world lout. When I returned to the gang, I wore comfortable clothes including a natty scarf. I felt debonair and on-trend.

Frenzek looked me up and down and said, "You look like a pox doctor's clerk. Come on"

"Where are we going?" I asked.

Ted gave me his best enigmatic smile, irritating me no end, and said nothing. Infuriating man.

The lifter doors opened onto a very swanky corridor, lots of fresh paint and soft floor coverings. We walked past a row of doors, each one had the top half of almost transparent material. It wasn't possible to see through, but it softened the effect of being in an austere passageway.

We stopped at the last door in the corridor, a large double set of doors with lots of fancy writing on them. I recognized it as writing but had no idea what it said, my translator nanobots only work on sounds, not alien script.

Ted knocked, smirked at me again before opening the doors, and stepped to one side. I walked into the lion's den.

Behind a big desk was the Man in Black, Captain Franz, commander of the NightWatch and my boss. Behind him stood Meataxe, Right Honourable and a bunch of other ne'er do wells from the home team.

My face lit up with a smile, I was among friends again. All would be okay.

"You're in a lot of trouble, Sergeant Valentine," said the Man in Black.

Right Honourable snorted agreement, Meataxe gave me a dopey grin and the rest of the lads made various nods in my direction or just shook their heads in disbelief at my continued existence.

Again, all pretty normal.

"Want to bring me up to speed, boss?" I asked.

"Not particularly," he responded. "I have a meeting with the Area Commandant to finalise our paperwork and then we can get back to work." He looked at me and said, "Your hair is growing back nicely, get a hat so we don't have riots in the streets; the beard and moustache need work. The scarf looks ridiculous, And why are you dressed like a civilian and not a proper copper?" I felt this was rhetorical and stayed quiet, nursing the savage judgement on my fashion sense. He went on, "I'll leave Peter to give you a briefing, he's functioning as my aide." He got up and left, accompanied by Frenzek, Right Honourable and a few lads, the rest drifted off leaving me with Meataxe and Teddy Boy plus Scarface.

Meataxe, whose real name is 'Peter', stood beaming at me for a few moments and then sat in the chair recently vacated by the captain. "How good's this, eh, Val?"

"You're the boss's aide?" I may have stuttered.

"Too right, I get to hang around with the good and the great."

"What's an aide do, Meataxe?" I asked.

"Dunno. I just sort of, open doors and answer communicators and stuff."

"You can use communicators?"

"When I hit the right buttons. Some of the time. Anyway, if someone wants to see the boss they can always come and see him personally."

Teddy Boy loafed over to a chair and stretched out, "The Man in Black has all his visitors meet his aide." He indicated Meataxe with a slight nod of the head, "Tends to give the newcomers a moment of pause."

Meataxe gave me his best toothy grin and dribbled into his beard.

"And you're going to give me a briefing?" I asked, "'Peter'."

"Nah, I'll just tell you what's been going on." He thought for a moment, we knew he was thinking because his face screwed up, "Uh, Ted, want to help out a bit?" he asked.

"No worries, mate." Ted stretched his legs out, gazed into space for a moment before speaking, "Magic's taken the ship to a repair yard on another planet; Lydia's gone with him for technical advice. We saved most of the people on board after we got the cure into them. Pirates all dead, except for a couple we managed to stop ourselves from killing. They're in prison here somewhere. Man in Black is setting us up here as coppers, that's where he is now finishing off the deal."

My head spun a little. "Magic's taking the ship to another planet? Magic? In charge of a spaceship? Our Magic?"

"The very same," replied Ted. "The guy who used to be a corporal in the NightWatch is now in command of a ship that sails between planets. Now don't tell me there's no room for advancement in the Watch!"

"And why are we here?" I asked, needing a deep mental breath. This was all a bit much to take in. I sat down and asked again, "Magic's in charge of the ship? Our spaceship?"

"Let it go, Val," replied Teddy Boy. "By the way, Right Honourable is a lieutenant in the Watch, I'm the ensign."

"What about me, do I get to be a lieutenant? Or an ensign? How about a captain?" I asked.

"There's only one Captain for the NightWatch, Val, and it's not you. But we do need our sergeant," he gave me a meaningful look, "That'd be you."

"You guys all outrank me?" I needed this cleared up. "You're going to be giving me orders?"

Meataxe stuttered over his drink which caused more spray to hit the big desk. Ted saved the day, "Yeah, like that's going to happen. No, we'll be doing whatever you tell us, we might have the rank, but you have the scars. You might want to lose the scarf."

At least we had that settled, "Tell me again, what's the plan? And scarves are cool."

"The boss reckons this planet has a few clues on it, clues about the Chief Trader's death, the theft of goods from the Traders and, of course, the attempt to take over the ship by pirates."

"And our job is to...?" I left it hanging.

"Find the answers. We are being granted the status of official investigators or police consultants due to our credentials as coppers back on earth."

"Coppers! We weren't coppers," I laughed. "We were thugs and bullies, just barely keeping society from falling apart."

"Not a bad definition of a policeman," came a rumbling voice.

We all turned to look at the speaker, it was Scarface from the car. I nudged a thumb at him and mouthed to the rest of the room, "Who is this guy?"

"This is Sergeant Thulani, our liaison with the regular police," introduced Meataxe. "He drinks a bit."

"Fits right in," contributed Teddy Boy.

"Does this mean we have to be proper policemen?" I asked, "Do we have to wear funny uniforms, patrol horrible places late at night and all the other regular, yawn-inducing stuff?"

"No," said Thulani. "You are not members of the Planet's Police force. You are receiving accreditation as Independent Contractors. Sometimes known as Private Investigators."

"What does that mean?" I asked.

"It means we get to keep sticking our noses into places they shouldn't be until we find who's behind all the grief we've had come our way." Ted looked happy with the deal.

"Great," I stated, "How do we start?"

Meataxe stood up and walked towards the doors, "We also have to investigate crimes brought to us by the general public. And the authorities pay for it, Val! We actually might get paid! Come on."

"Paid! Dream on, Meataxe," I said. Thulani and I followed him out the door, "Where are we going?"

"Your office!" replied Meataxe. "I kid you not. You have an office! You get a little room with a desk and ... and ... everything!" He opened one of the doors in the corridor near the lifter, I looked in and saw a desk, some chairs, paper, and writing instruments. A communicator and a screen nestled on one side of the working space.

It looked like my own personal hell.

"Can I get some more stuff?" I asked.

Sergeant Thulani chipped in his bit, "We can provide you with most of the normal pieces of police tech. What do you require?"

"A hammer." I took another look at the room. "A big hammer."

Chapter 5

The next day I started work as a Private Investigator. I kept the same clothes as yesterday as, contrary to popular opinion, I think I looked cool. Especially the scarf, I loved the scarf. I sat at my desk and looked at the wall for all of three minutes before boredom set in. The room was empty of other people, not another soul, no one to talk to, torment or pick on. This is the quiet life, I reasoned, this is what people yearn for. I should like it, I should just take it easy and gather my thoughts and think a bit about ...stuff.

This was not working, I am a people person, I need other faces around me to stop my brain from talking to itself. I've listened in a few times and it's not pretty. It was the work of a moment to leave my clean, personal office and lurch into the corridor in search of distraction.

Standing outside my door were two characters from my recent past, Amadi Pickpocket and Babajide Arson. Both looked a bit worried and slightly nervous. I gave them my friendliest smile and they both stepped back.

"Mr. Valentine," said Amadi, "we need to talk to you."

"Let's go for a walk, fellers," I replied. "I need some fresh air. You can tell me all about the old gang from prison as we mooch about. Bring me up to speed on the news, fill me in on how they're all going, tell me the gossip."

"Are you all right, Mr. Valentine?" asked Amadi.

"Just need to stretch my legs, Amadi, I'm not good at sitting around by myself. Prison changes a man."

The lifter door opened and we were confronted by the stern and unwavering visage of Sergeant Thulani, "Going somewhere?" he asked. He was not in uniform; instead, he was wearing some sort of heavy one-piece garment with extra protection on the elbows and kneecaps. Under one arm was a helmet and gloves and tall, black boots came to just below his knees. Boots with shiny bits of metal on the toes. I liked the way this guy dressed.

"Amadi the Pickpocket and Babajide the Arsonist, meet Thulani, or as we call him, 'Mr. Happy'. One of the kindest, gentlest men you could hope to meet. Don't be put off by the scarred face and ugly moosh – he's just a gentle little lamb." My day was improving already.

"How have you lived so long, dipstick?" asked Thulani. I was liking this guy more and more. He beckoned us all to join him in the lifter, "I was on my way up to see you, the downstairs guard said two low and dangerous-looking types had asked for your office." He flicked a glance at Amadi and Babajide, "This'd be them? The dangerous ones?"

"Don't be fooled by their seeming fragility, Thulani," I replied. "These guys stuck by me in the joint. Lifelong friendships are made under adversity over extended periods of shared suffering."

"You were there five minutes, idiot. Any suffering was done by everyone else." He looked at my two companions, "What do you want with Valentine?"

This action seemed a little high-handed for such a new acquaintance, "Surely that's a question I should be asking?" I muttered.

The lifter doors opened and Thulani strode out, we followed in his wake, baby ducks after big momma. Amadi and Babajide were falling over themselves to answer the scarred sergeant's questions. I was just stumbling.

"We were released from prison this morning," said Amadi. "Both of us. I suggested that Babajide might be able to get work with my father's business, so we had the prison transport drop us off in midtown and we made our way to the store."

"Your father has a need for arsonists?" I asked.

Babajide threw a reproachful glance over his shoulder at me, "I have served my time in prison, I am ready to embark on a new life. It is most improper for you to bring up my previous crimes. All debts are paid."

"Crimes?" I asked, "As in more than one? How many fires did you set, Babajide?"

"I was convicted of burning down three warehouses over a period of several months."

"Convicted of three, plus a few others they didn't know about, I bet." I was going to keep this guy away from naked flames.

He seemed to be somewhat exasperated and threw a little steel into his voice. At least, he probably thought it was steel, I only heard soft paper. "I am a certified Rorcha extractor. I am not a criminal."

How many times have I heard some low life claim they weren't one of the criminal crowd? Frequently, and usually from my mates in the NightWatch.

"Shut up, Val," Thulani did put some real steel in his voice. I shut. "Get to the point, Amadi," he commanded, "Why did you want to see Valentine?"

"On the Prison Transport Shuttle, we heard he had been made a consultant to the police. My cousin has been kidnapped."

"You should report it to the regular police," said Thulani. I noted he didn't let on that he was himself a copper.

The big surprise came with Amadi's next words, "It was the regular police who kidnapped her."

Even Thulani slowed a pace at that comment. We had left the building and he was leading us to the side of the pedestrian walkway. A few more steps and we would be on the main thoroughfare and dodging wheeled vehicles. "The police don't kidnap people, especially children," he said. "They arrest those who do."

"Not this time," said Amadi. "My father was working in the back of our shop when he heard my cousin, Emilii, scream. He ran to the front of the store and saw two men attacking Emilii. One had her from behind while the other was hitting her in the stomach."

Even to my hardened senses, this seemed a bit much. "Your coppers do things a bit differently here, Thulani."

"Shut up, Valentine. What happened next, Amadi?" asked the scarred man. His voice had taken on a growl.

"My father tried to stop them, but he was knocked to the ground. One of them showed him a police badge before they bundled Emilii out the door, they put some tape over her mouth to stop the screaming. By the time he got to his feet, they were gone."

"Maybe they were just impersonating policeman," suggested Thulani.

"Then they were doing a good job of it," answered Amadi. "They even had a police vehicle waiting outside. They left with sirens on and lights flashing. My father contacted me, and I came here to find Mr. Valentine."

"A bit quick, aren't you, boys?" I said. "Maybe your father misunderstood the scene, your cousin might have been arrested for some unknown act. She puts up a fight and it all looks a bit grim to your poor old dad. Why don't you just wait until you get the full story from the local police?"

We had stopped on the side of the road beside two Personal Sleds. Thulani put his helmet on and took another from one of the containers on the largest sled, he handed me the helmet and instructed, "Put this on, I'm told you can ride these things?"

"Is the pope a catholic?" I asked, my eyes lighting with joy.

"I have no idea what you just said. Get on the other bloody sled. You two," he turned to Amadi and Babajide, "get on behind Valentine and me. We're going for a little ride."

No second invitations were needed by me. I love Sleds. Just a big engine making lots of noise between your legs, all grunt and roar. Boy heaven. Amadi and Babajide hesitated until Thulani growled again and we pulled some more helmets out of cleverly designed storage boxes. Within minutes I was fanging down the road behind

Thulani. Babajide was clutching my waist in the vain hope it would keep him safe.

There's fun and then there is riding a Sled. Nothing like it. While most of the wheeled vehicles around us were quiet, our sleds were loud. I don't know what powered them, but I preferred our destructive noises to everything else's silent motion. I think I'm a sick man.

After far too short a ride, we passed between two high gates into the parking area of a large, functional building. I say functional because it was just ugly. No attempt at exterior carvings, no colour, no sense of pleasing the surroundings. Bit like Thulani.

I was curious why we were going to so much trouble with Amadi and Babajide. Thulani wasn't dismissing their story the way I would. I mean, there were several explanations for why Amadi's cousin was taken by the police. Perhaps their method was a bit high handed but nothing I hadn't seen back on earth in a crowded tavern brawl.

So why had Thulani brought them along with us? And where were we?

"Where are we?" asked Amadi.

"Police Weapons Range," growled Thulani. "Valentine needs to prove he can be trusted in our society with a weapon. I need to see his skill level, especially his ability to be safe around weapons." I was looking forward to whatever came next; 'safe' and 'weapons' have rarely come together in my vocabulary.

Thulani took us into the ugly building where we stood at a large reception desk in front of a uniformed copper who was taking down details of who we were and what bloody right we had to make his life untidy.

Thulani was having none of his poor attitude. He produced a wallet with some ID and the uniformed copper fell over himself in deference to my ugly acquaintance. I assumed Thulani carried a bit of weight in police circles.

"Yes, sir. Everything is ready for you, sir. Please come this way, sir," gushed the poor uniformed sod.

Why don't people talk to me that way?

Amadi had picked up a few clues and, in a small voice, asked Thulani, "Are you a policeman?"

Thulani stood to one side of the door into the building's interior, a door held open by the uniformed flunky wearing a big, ingratiating smile. I strolled through followed by a nervous Amadi and fidgety Babajide. Thulani entered after us before answering the question, "I am."

The door shut with an audible clunk. I thought my two prison buddies were going to faint dead away from stress so I thought I could help them a little. Keep their spirits up.

"Looks like you're in a bucketload of trouble, boys," I said.

"Shut up, Val," said Thulani. "Follow me." He turned and led us deeper into the building, finally stopping at another heavy door with a keypad entry. He tapped a few mysterious codes and we entered a large, bright room. Off to one side was an observation area that overlooked a series of waist-high benches. Behind some of the benches were members of the NightWatch holding small hand blasters. Teddy Boy was one of them and I watched as he brought the weapon up and fired it down the length of the room at a set of targets. We were in an indoor shooting range. Indoor! How good is that?

"Valentine, you need to demonstrate your proficiency with these weapons before you are permitted to carry one in our society," said Thulani. "Your teammates have shown a remarkable ability to be sloppy, unsafe and dangerous with all manner of ranged weapons." Sounds about right, I thought. He pointed at Teddy Boy, "Except for your Ensign, he is gifted and has already qualified as an expert marksman."

"How about Meataxe?" I asked, indicating the slovenly form of the newly promoted aide. "What are his skills like?" The big guy was slumped in a chair in the waiting room while being harangued by another copper in full uniform, off to one side was a sorry-looking policeman being treated by one of their medics.

Thulani rolled his eyes, "God help us, the man has managed to damage several weapons and wounded the Range Officer. He seems to have no coordination, no spatial awareness and only a passing acquaintance with the concept of weapons safety. Why do you keep him in your Company?"

"He's good with kids," I said.

Chapter 6

The sound of grinding teeth came from Thulani, "Get over there and do the test?"

This didn't sound good, "Test? What test? Last one I had was Latin declination, 'amo, amas, amat...'" I stumbled to a halt, just like the first time. "Nothing written, I hope?"

Another uniformed copper had sauntered over by this time, no doubt drawn to the fine tendrils of smoke coming from Thulani's ears. "Go with this officer and demonstrate you can be trusted with a weapon," my new best friend said to me.

There was a great temptation to state I could not be trusted with anything remotely dangerous. But I resisted, I felt Thulani was close to exploding and while I would normally like to prod that bomb a small part of my brain suggested he was a man it may be wise to befriend rather than antagonize. Even stranger, the rest of me listened. Mature, that's what I am. Dead mature.

"What about us?" asked Amadi.

"Sit over there," the copper growled, pointing at some benches near the wall. "Don't leave the area or you'll be arrested." This piece of news was guaranteed to keep my old prison buddies in one place. Neither of them would be keen on revisiting the penal system.

I followed my guide to a set of tables facing a long open stretch of room. Dotted along the length of the open space were a series of targets, some nondescript, others meant to represent living beings. On the table were a variety of weapons, blasters and other forms of things which would undoubtedly go bang. This could be a bit of fun, I thought.

The next few hours were a combination of boy's own bliss and mind-numbing boredom. The bliss was shooting things, sometimes with a loud bang but more often with a hum or just a flash of light. The boredom was the interminable lectures I had to suffer through as my guide described each weapon in great detail. He spoke of muzzle velocity for the projectile weapons, battery charge for the energy types and something about pellet capacity for a few others. My mind wandered off at these moments while the rest of me did my world-famous impersonation of someone actually listening.

"Sergeant Valentine!" My guide was raising his voice, so I brought my brain back into focus to pick up the threads of his latest spiel. "Sergeant Valentine! Have you been listening to anything I have said?"

"Absolutely," I replied, "Riveted, I am, positively riveted." I picked up the nearest weapon, "This is the end I point at the bad guys and then I press this trigger." I demonstrated and the weapon shot a series of small pellets into the target in front of me. It also sent a few spares into the lanes of the shooters next door. Some loud cries came back as the weaker types took cover.

My instructor snatched the weapon out of my hand, "Step away from the table, please, Sergeant. Unless you can demonstrate sufficient knowledge in the handling of these weapons, I cannot issue you with a permit."

"What permit would that be?" I asked.

"The permit to carry a concealed weapon, something you will need as a Police Consultant or a Private Investigator."

"Why can't I just stick a gun in my pocket?" I asked.

"Because that would be against the law!"

"Still not seeing the problem," I said.

His mouth opened and closed a few times, but no sound came out. There may have been some slight mewling.

He gave me the old look again which historically precedes stage two, usually a huffy walk-off. I decided to put some effort into things. Again, I seem to be growing up.

"What have I got to show you to demonstrate I can be trusted to carry around something that kills people?"

He continued to stare a bit more, the walk-off was on a knife edge but he was a professional. He took a deep breath to show he was suffering and said, "You must show me you can safely fire the weapons without endangering others. You must also be able to place each weapon into a safe or powered-down configuration for transport and storage. Finally, I must observe you loading and unloading each implement."

"What about the other stuff, muzzle velocity, degrees of penetration, quality of materials in each design, all the other info you've been pouring into me? Do I have to know any of it?"

He looked a bit shocked for a moment, "No, not really, but most serious practitioners take a keen interest in everything to do with their weapon." He took a breath, "It's what makes us professionals."

"Fair enough, I'm just a hobbyist. I only need to know which end kills people."

"Surely you know enough about weapons to understand they gain most of their impact as a threat. I have rarely had to discharge my sidearm even though I have been forced to draw it several times. You must have had similar experiences."

"Nah, if I point a weapon at someone, I mean to kill them. Never been big on threats."

He paled a little and muttered, "You're a walking threat...." He shook himself a little, "How about you just show me where the safety switch is on each of these weapons, and I give you the permit?"

"How about we do that," I agreed. I pointed, pushed and tugged at each implement of destruction to show him I had been paying the bare minimum of attention and he made various marks on a piece of paper.

"Give this to Sergeant Thulani, it certifies you as being .... safe with weapons." I think he stumbled over those words, but I take what breaks I can get. I took the chit to where Thulani was chatting to some other uniformed types, passed it over and gave him a wink.

By the time I rolled back to my two buddies on the bench they were looking very down and out, "Hiya, fellas," I gave them the big greeting, "How about you tell me more about your problem while we wait for the next bit of nonsense to come along? Tell me what happened to your cousin and why you think I can do anything about it."

"Can you come and see the shop? Talk to my father and my Bunica?" pleaded Amadi."

"What's a Bunica?" I asked, "And is it contagious?"

Amadi gave me a hurt look; I felt I had kicked a puppy, "A Bunica is our term for grandmother. She helped raise Emili and looked after me when my mother died. She is a kind and gentle woman and deserves respect." I was right, I had kicked a puppy, an emotional puppy.

"Before we talk about that, tell me again why you came to me."

"Like we told you," said Babajide, "we were on the Prison Shuttle with the rest of the released prisoners, just talking to pass the time and...."

Amadi interrupted, "They all wanted to know about you, Mr. Valentine, we were quite the centre of attention because we were cellmates!" He stopped and gave Babajide an embarrassed grin, "Sorry, Babajide, you tell him."

"Well," went on my friendly neighbourhood fire starter, "one of the guards told us you were a member of a security squad from a spaceship. He'd heard how your whole team were on the planet investigating an attempted hijack of their ship. Pirates, they said!" He leaned back in wonder, marvelling at the concept of such evildoers. "Can you believe it? Pirates!"

"I can believe it," I said. They both looked at me, I saw a light going on behind their eyes.

"Ah," slurred Babajide. "Right.....so your team fought the pirates off? And then you came down here looking for those responsible."

He exchanged a look with Amadi, "We hear stories about this sort of thing, but you never expect it to happen...so close."

"But we were told your team had only arrived today. How is it you were already on the planet?" Amadi had those hero-worship eyes in his head, the sort that gets a young man killed. "Were you an advance scout?"

"Not really," I replied, "I fell off the spaceship and crashed landed while chasing one of the pirates. I'm a bit clumsy."

"Did he get away?"

"Nope."

A small pause stretched into a longer one.

"You caught him?"

"Yep."

The silence went on for a few more beats before Amadi came out with the question "What happened?"

I sighed and leaned against the wall, "I asked him a few questions and he died. The police took a dim view of my behaviour. He was technically one of their prisoners at the time. I got arrested and, well, you know the rest."

They both looked at me for a few more moments until Amadi asked, "So, will you help, Mr. Valentine? Help me find my cousin? She's alone and scared, we don't have anyone else to turn to."

Talk about having your buttons pushed. I groaned "Okay. Might as well have something to do while I wait for the judges to work out what to do with me."

Thulani came over and ushered us out of the facility, on the way back to the sleds we agreed to take Amadi back to his father and dig into things a bit more. We rode the sleds through city streets, I was interested in the feel of the place, the ebb and flow of the living creatures who made up the society of this planet. So far, my interactions had been usually of a violent nature with the more unsavoury models of citizenry.

Admittedly, when we first arrived, and I learned how to ride these sleds, I met some quiet, decent people. Since then, it had been just a parade of unpleasant types. My conversations at the prison had not endeared all and sundry to me and I felt sure the feeling was returned by whatever passed for organized crime in the area. The more I thought about it the more I realized there would be some repercussions to my little episode in the slammer. Perhaps Thulani could give me a few clues.

We pulled up in the parking area next to a set of buildings, one of which I assumed belonged to Amadi's family. As we put our helmets away, I decided to bring up the subject of mob retaliation with my granite sergeant. "Say, Thulani, the guys I killed in prison...."

"Calcout and Shaqir?"

"That's them. What are the chances I can just walk away from all that unpleasantness and start a simple farmer's life? Settle down somewhere and put down some roots. Marry a local lass and lead the quiet life."

We walked up to the front door of a small shop, he put his big paw on the handle, turned to me and spoke in his soft growl, "Never going to happen, Valentine. There's probably contracts out on you already." He sighed and fluttered his eyes, "I'm probably risking my own life just standing next to you." He opened the door, smiled at me and said, "But I live for danger."

"You would have to be the ugliest bloke I have ever encountered," I replied. "How have you lived so long?"

"Personal charm."

Chapter 7

Amadi ran past us into the shop where he embraced a skinny, older man. The two made small, gentle sounds to each other, the noises people make who care about each other. Finally, Amadi turned and waved us closer, "Father, these men are here to help us. This is my friend Babajide of whom I have already spoken." Babajide and the old man reached out their right hands and clasped each other's shoulders. They murmured small greetings before Amadi pulled me forward. "And this is Mr. Valentine" I felt like a pony at the show, "He's going to help us get Emilii back!"

The old man did not give me the hand-on-shoulder greeting, instead, he stood with his arms by his side while he gazed at me with pale, watery eyes. I gazed back, searching his face and seeing the grief he wore, grief over the loss of a loved family member. I watched his eyes flick to Amadi and saw his mouth tighten a little. Poor old man, I thought, his son's a criminal and his niece kidnapped – not much of a day he's having.

"How do you do, Mr. Amadi'sDad," I said.

My greeting brought a small smile to his face, "My name is Bako, Mr. Valentine. Thank you for coming but my son is perhaps a trifle premature in seeking help. When I told him of the events from this morning, I did not think he would run off and seek help from ...." He looked at Thulani and me, "people like yourself and this, er, gentleman."

"He's not a gentleman," I replied. "He's a policeman and I am technically his prisoner."

"A policeman!" the old man grimaced and took a small step back, "Why have you come here?" He looked towards his son, "What have you done, my boy?"

Hello, hello, I thought, not quite the words I expected from a grieving uncle.

Thulani stood quietly, looking around the shop, finally coming back to rest on the old man, "Debt, was it?"

Amadi and Babajide exchanged bewildered looks, I wanted to get in on that action too but felt I should try to maintain an air of understanding and competence. Both states were reasonably unfamiliar to me, so it was a stretch. The old man turned away, he rested one hand on the counter bench, rubbing it back and forth along the polished surface while he went away inside his head for a few moments.

"This is a family matter, po-lice-man," he drew out the title slowly, imbuing the word with inherent threat and disgust. "This morning when your.... colleagues...arrived I was not fully aware of the circumstances."

"Dad...," said Amadi, "what do you mean? What's happened to Emili? Where's my Bunica?"

"Your grandmother was very angry with my brother," said Amadi's dad. "She said some words, some unpleasant words to him. He yelled at her and told her to leave."

Another man came through a curtained doorway at the back of the shop, he was a taller, leaner version of Amadi's father. Doing my best to be a quiet observer, I was able to watch the body language of the room's occupants as they adjusted to this new social factor. Amadi took a small step back, Bako had his back to the newcomer but sensed his entrance by his son's reaction. He didn't turn around, but his shoulders dropped a little.

Thulani broke the ice with his steady policeman's courtesy; a politeness borne of years spent negotiating the various social strata of a diverse, multicultural community resulting in an unerring ability to choose culturally appropriate words. "Who the bloody hell are you?" he said.

I liked Thulani more and more.

Bako made the introductions, "This is my brother, Sefu. It was his daughter who was .... taken this morning."

Sefu didn't seem too upset about the loss of his daughter. He wasn't rushing forward asking for help or news, or demanding someone bloody well do something. No, he just stood in front of the curtained doorway and gazed at his brother.

"Tell these men to leave, brother," he said.

Quite the charmer.

"Come on, Valentine, we're not needed here." Thulani put his hand on my arm and gave me a gentle pull towards the door. He spoke over his shoulder as we left the shop, "Better tell these boys what is happening here, Bako. Before they get hurt." We left the shop to the unspoken queries from the two young men, queries drowned in a sea of quiet threat from Emili's father.

I was quite proud of the fact I was able to keep my mouth shut until we reached the sled, "Want to tell me what that was all about?"

Thulani gave me my helmet, strapped on his own and grimaced, "Young people, particularly girls who look sweet and innocent, are in demand by certain business sectors of our society."

I nodded, this was an old story.

"But not for the purposes which might immediately spring to the mind of a person such as yourself. Someone used to swimming with the more unpleasant characters one meets in the typical day of a copper."

"Not sex, then?"

"No, more like delivery systems." We got on the sled, he started the engine and gave a final comment over his shoulder, "They get injected with black market nanobots. All sorts of yucky stuff, custom-made diseases, body upgrades, whatever the market demands. Then they travel to other planets and have their blood harvested. The process usually doesn't kill them but there is always some attrition. New employees welcome, a ground-level opportunity."

We travelled through the town as I digested this new information, at one point we had to wait for other traffic, so I yelled into Thulani's ear, "And parents put their own children into this game?"

"The kids can be kidnapped or even bred for the purpose. We hear stories of farms out in the wilderness where children are raised until they are old enough for the job. And then of course there are the sweethearts like Sefu back there, they just sell their offspring for a profit."

"Nice planet you've got here."

We moved off into traffic again, "Was yours any better?"

He had me there, in my city there was an Archbishop very keen on burning people who didn't share his belief systems. Plus, we had our share of children embroiled in child labour. The mines loved a small kid who could get into the narrow seams for a good dig and delve. It was all slavery. By the time we arrived back at our new base, I had built up a good head of steam, a proper bit of righteous indignation, "So how come we just walked away from that situation back there? Why is Sefu still vertical and holding on to all his teeth?"

We entered the building and made our way up to the floor given over to the NightWatch. "Because," sighed Thulani, "he has done nothing illegal."

I grabbed his shoulder and spun him around to face me, "Listen, sport," I spoke through tense lips and bared teeth. "Anyone who sells his daughter into that sort of slavery is in the wrong. Damn the law. I want to go back and have another chat with Sefu, one that involves getting him to see the error of his ways. Then we go and get his daughter back."

"And do what with her? She's his child, we can't interfere in the workings of a family, especially where a minor is concerned." He led the way into my office and plopped down in the visitor's chair. "Plus, we cannot, as you so colourfully put it, 'damn the law'. We are only assuming he has done this with his daughter. She could be having a sleepover with friends."

"Friends who dress like police and drag her out of her home?" I plopped into the big chair, the one behind the desk. My desk. What the hell was I going to do with a desk? We sat in silence for a few beats before I returned to the attack, "And you must think the daughter's gone that way, otherwise why tell me all about it? And what was that question about debt? You asked Bako like you knew what was going on straight away. Come clean, Thulani, you think she's been taken, don't you?"

He grimaced and wriggled in the chair, "Pretty sure. But we are the law, Valentine, we cannot break the rules when it doesn't suit us."

This was news to me. "But he sold his own child!" I exclaimed.

"We have no proof. And you can be sure none of the family will testify. It is obvious that Seku is the head of the family and that gives him a lot of power. He has massive authority over the entire clan. No one will step out and speak against him, they would be thrown out of the family."

"Big deal."

He leaned forward, "It is a big deal, you moron. On this planet, family is everything. People do not seek advancement for themselves but to better the entire family. Everybody benefits, everyone moves forward together. It's a haven, a refuge and a home. Leave the family and you die alone."

I didn't get it, this family business didn't seem like such a big deal to me. Obviously, Thulani put a lot of store by it. And, by extension, that meant the rest of the planet felt the same way. Maybe it was like those Italian gangs Right Honourable used to tell me about. He came from Venice and was full of stories about families at war with each other. Poisoning, knife fights in the main street, kidnappings and ransom; no one bad mouths a Medici. Venice was a party town. Right Honourable got out when suggestions were made about his life expectancy. Something about cheating at cards.

"We do nothing?" I asked.

"Let me dig around a bit, you stay here and think pure thoughts. I'll send someone up to teach you a bit more about how to be a copper, maybe a bit of criminal theory. You look like a lad who enjoys a good lecture."

He left to some mild abuse, plus I threw something at him. He's a sick man.

Chapter 8

I spent the afternoon in the company of a tedious little man who tried to instruct me in prisoner interrogation, hostage negotiation and so on. Teddy Boy and Santini wandered in and joined the class. Much to my disgust they seemed to enjoy it and insisted on dragging me along with them to other sessions. I may even have learned something.

Teddy Boy walked me back to our barracks, a building only a few blocks away from our headquarters. We passed a few obvious bars, Ted suggested we partake of local hospitality, but I insisted on going home and getting a good night's sleep. This was my petty revenge for his part in the afternoon's suffering. It didn't last, by the time we came up to the third noisy joint I was ready for a drink and a good sit down.

Three guys emerged from a vehicle parked a little way ahead of us, three guys intent on doing us harm.

When Ted and I patrolled the Thieves' Quarter we developed those instincts which keep a guardsman from early retirement due to death. One of those instincts was an ability to recognise a threat, especially from three strange men striding purposefully towards one.

They stopped a few paces in front of us, so we stopped too. It seemed the polite thing to do. The biggest bozo was in the middle, he had short hair, a broken nose and carried himself like he knew a thing or two. His two buddies also possessed an air of threat, their dark clothes and menacing expressions contributing to the sense of bad men on the prowl.

"You Valentine?" asked the leader. He had his hands by his sides, big hands with knuckles like walnuts. His jacket was stretched across broad shoulders, and he rolled his neck to loosen the kinks. Probably thought he was going to whale on me a little.

Ted and I looked at them in silence, neither of us made any threatening moves, no reaching for hidden weapons or posturing. No, we just looked at them.

The two guys on either end flexed their fingers while their fearless leader cracked his knuckles, "Hey, stupid, I'm talking to you. Are you Valentine?"

Some thugs just don't get it, they embarrass the rest of us thugs who try to maintain certain professional standards. They were standing and asking us questions, for goodness' sake! If they didn't know who we were then they should go back and do more research. You do not stand and chat, asking if you got the right victim.

Mr. Bozo raised his eyebrows and flicked an exasperated glance at his two buddies, they smirked back at him.

I stepped forward and kicked the big guy in the groin as hard as I could – which is pretty damn hard. The force of the kick raised him off the ground. His eyes went wide and I suspect he would not be fathering children anymore.

Ted whipped out a blaster and shot the guy in front of him in the leg. His victim fell to the ground, screaming.

I looked at Thug number three, "Yeah, I'm Valentine. Who wants to know?"

This guy was a picture, open mouth, thumb in bum and mind in neutral. I smacked him in the mouth hard enough to knock him on his backside and then stood over him, "You guys are really bad at this."

"You.... you....," he stammered. The guy with the shot leg rolled around some more, still screaming.

I squatted beside my latest victim and punched him in the nose. He yelled for me to stop it. "That's the way, pal," I said. "Let it all out. Don't bottle it up." I grabbed his collar and dragged him to his feet, "Now who are you, why are you looking for me, and who sent you? Answers in any order. Ted, can you make your guy stop screaming, it's getting on my nerves." I kept looking at my guy and only heard the dull whack. The screaming stopped.

"We're just looking to make some extra cash, that's all."

"By looking for people called 'Valentine'. Is it a secret treasure hunt? What does the winner get?"

"Ghost wants you. We heard we could make easy money by putting the grab on you and letting Ghost know. You know, he'd be grateful."

"But why me?"

"Aren't you the Valentine who put the hurt on Lennux in prison? And killed his brother Shaqir? And you smashed the boss's head like an egg. Syndicate wants to see you dead, that's why they called Ghost."

"And Ghost would be....?" I felt I was getting the hang of the interrogation technique as discussed in that afternoon's lectures.

He looked up at me with big puppy dog eyes. I looked deep into them, past the bloodshot and weak vision, beyond the casual violence and inherent cruelty of a bully. All of this was there but I also saw something else, something that looked like sympathy. The little snot was feeling sorry for me. "Ghost is the one who enforces the law on this planet. Forget the police, forget the Council and Senate. Ghost rules."

"Nice guy, is he?"

"Dunno, never laid eyes on him." He rolled onto his side to let the blood from his mouth and nose drip onto the floor. After a small spit, he turned back to me. "No one sees him, he just appears and things happen, people die. That's why they call him Ghost.

"What about 'Cyril'?" I asked, "Maybe his name's 'Cyril'. Or 'Derek'? I knew a Derek once. Total prat." I stood up and brushed my hands off against the legs of my pants. "Looks like I'm a marked man, Ted. Got the mob after me."

"Been nice knowing you, Val" He moved away from his prostrate victim, stepped over the thug on the ground clutching his groin and tucked his blaster into an unseen holster. "I might turn in, been a big day. What are you going to do?"

The guy at my feet rolled his eyes between Ted and me, watching our little bit of dialogue. I moved beside Ted and tucked my hands into my jacket pockets, it was getting a bit nippy as the night settled in. "Good idea," I responded. "Probably a wise move to get some sleep before more of these bozos turn up. But maybe a drink first." I turned back as my recent conversational partner slowly rose to his feet, "What about you, Curly, fancy a beer?"

"Are you insane?" the thug said.

"Probably," said Ted and moved off towards a bar. "Come on if you're coming."

A few steps led down to the entrance to a tavern, Ted and I strolled down them and entered the bar as sets of bright flashing lights appeared in the street behind us signaling the arrival of the local police. No doubt alerted by the sounds of Ted's blaster shot and the resulting screaming. Seemed like a good time for a drink. My last glance back at the scene showed two men on the ground and the third legging it down the street.

"I think our mate has decided against drinking with us," I observed.

"Something we said?" asked Ted.

"No, mate, people love us."

The next morning, I briefed the Man in Black on my current status as a hunted man, plus the small side story about Bako's daughter and potential child abuse. I also told him of the meeting with the three twits the previous night and the mention of 'Ghost'.

"This 'Ghost' character you mention," he said. "He – or she - may be the one behind the recent attempt to take over our ship. Well, done, Val, you're getting results again, in your usual efficient manner."

Meataxe and Right Honourable stood behind our leader while Teddy Boy sat on a nearby couch and cleaned some sort of weapon. Outside the door, Wilks was busy moving pieces of paper from one side of his desk to another. Wilks was a member of the NightWatch, how I do not know. He was a desk man, loved a good rule book and avoided violence. He was, however, a mean hand at paper shuffling and was the go-to guy for a filing system. He'd also saved my life a couple of times – at least one of them was actually from me. While I often considered taking him for a long walk along a short pier, he managed to keep on living.

"Thanks, boss, but you may have missed the bit where Ghost wants to see me for one of his fireside chats. Probably a terminal conversation."

"More than likely," he agreed.

"So," I asked, seeking guidance from my caring superior, "what do I do?"

"Well," he drummed his fingers on his desk, "off the top of my head the only suggestion I can make is try not to die."

Right Honourable sniggered, Meataxe looked blank, his normal state. "Thanks, Sir, big help. I can move on now, secure in the knowledge my betters have it all worked out."

"Are you pouting, Val?" asked the Man in Black, "Right Honourable, is he pouting?"

"Possibly a small sulk, sir," replied my long-term friend. "Val's always had trouble with his emotions. Bit fragile."

"Don't I owe you a good kickin', Right Honourable?" I asked.

"Probably, dear boy, I tend to lose track."

"Look, Val," said my boss, "the best we can do is hope you can stay alive long enough for the rest of us to get a handle on this planet and track down this Ghost character. Maybe you should just stay in your quarters for a few days." I was sure I saw his mouth twitch, was that a smile? "A week or two at most."

"Stay cooped up inside? It'd kill me."

The door opened and Wallace came in. The room was now seriously overcrowded with major thugs and killers. Wallace shut the door and said, "It's definite, Valentine has a price on his head. It's all over the bars and low-life hangouts."

"How much?" I asked. It's good to know your worth.

"Shut up, Val," said the boss. "Tell us about it, Wallace?"

"I spent the night following those leads you gave us, one of the clubs was full of Val's latest discussion on the street. The one which left one man needing major groin surgery and the other with a blaster wound to the leg."

"Ted did some of that," I felt I needed to stand up for myself. "It wasn't all me!"

"No mention of Ted, just the evil bastard Valentine who kills and maims anyone in his way."

"Well, not anyone," I muttered, "just the dropkicks."

"Shut up, Val," put in Right Honourable. He seemed to be enjoying my predicament far too much, "Let the man speak. You can't pay for this sort of stuff."

I ground my teeth and tried to look all put upon, but no one seemed to take any notice. Wallace leaned on the boss's desk and went on, "This character who runs the planet...."

"Ghost?" asked the Man in Black.

Wallace looked a little surprised "That's the one, how'd you know about him?"

The others looked at me in a meaningful fashion, "Oh!" said Wallace, "Might have known." He cracked his knuckles before continuing. "Word is, there's a sizable sum of money going to anyone who brings Valentine before the Syndicate. They want to pass him on to Ghost as a demonstration of their loyalty and efficiency."

"We saw a sample of that efficiency last night," I said.

Wallace rumbled, "Yeah, I heard about that. They were strictly small-time. The one survivor has just been fished out of the river after trying to swim with an anchor strapped to his chest. These guys don't like failures." He leaned back against the door, the frame sagged but held on grimly. "The big-league players are after you now, Val. Been nice knowing you."

"Aww, you guys...."

"Just hang around the main building for a few days, a week at most," instructed my boss. Use the time to learn a thing or two, listen to some more lectures. Wallace, get back out there and find some leads to this 'Ghost' character." He pushed a button on some gizmo and spoke to his desk, "Wilks, send in our newest recruit."

***" Right away, sir!" *** replied the desk. Now we had talking desks.

After Wallace left, the room seemed to enlarge before a small, mousy-looking creature sidled in. The room didn't notice him.

"Watchman Greenash," said the Man in Black. "How are you settling in?"

"Yes, sir. Just lovely, thank you, sir. Ready to start my new duties."

"Good. Right Honourable, take Greenash and visit the NightWatch members who are in hospital. Get our people up and about quickly, I need them. While you are there, start digging; this is a good opportunity to clean house with the rest of the ship's crew. Get a handle on some of the more troublesome people from the ship, ones who have caused us grief in the past. While they are all in the hospital, we have a chance to do some," he paused, "social filtering."

He looked at Right Honourable and something passed between them. Right Honourable nodded. The boss gave his final instruction, "Any known troublemakers or violent criminals can meet with a ... medical episode."

"No worries, boss." Right Honourable didn't bat an eyelid after receiving this instruction to coldly murder the sleeping sick. "Can I just stick a knife in, or should I try and be a bit clever?"

"Better be quiet about it," said our boss. "This society doesn't approve of our more hands-on approach to policing. What about it, Greenash? Can you do anything with their nanobots? Bring on a seizure?"

"Are you asking me to.... commit murder, sir?" I could see Greenash was going to have a longer-than-usual settling-in process if he was to stay with our team.

But the boss has always been good at reading people, "No, Watchman Greenash, I am not asking you to kill them. Perhaps just a slightly longer sleep while Right Honourable furthers his investigations." We all knew what that phrase meant, a pillow over the face should further the investigation quite nicely.

Greenash nodded slowly, he caught my eye and I gave him a big smile and a wink, "Welcome to the gang, Greenash." I had come across Greenash while investigating our recent attack by the Undead, he had proved himself to be useful around nanobots.

The boss hadn't finished, "Teddy Boy, stick with Valentine, throw a net over him if he tries to leave the building. Meataxe, you're with me. Let's go and visit someone important who might take offence at our intrusion. I do like giving offence when I intrude."

You gotta like this guy.

Chapter 9

Everyone started to move about, at which point my mouth took over the running again, "I might be able to help a bit there, sir" I said. When the boss talked about 'someone important' I remembered the name I had dragged out of the pirate. The one I killed. Before he joined the choir indivisible, he had dobbed in someone who may be able to help us with our enquiries.

Captain Franz sank back into his chair, everyone else just stopped in mid-stride. I think I detected a certain resignation to the slumped shoulders of my comrades. A touch of a sigh may have escaped Teddy Boy.

"Don't tell me, Valentine, you have some more information, another clue." The Man in Black was not impressed. "Were you thinking of sharing this with us at some stage?"

"Look, the guy I chased down to the planet and later interrogated," there were a few snorts of derision over my description of the incident in question. In all fairness, the pirate did die. "He gave me a name before he died. 'Elector S'eenyur'. He has men inside the police, seems to be a major player in the attempted takeover of our ship. He may even be this 'Ghost' character. Plus, every mention of a group called 'The Syndicate' causes people to have conniptions."

"Conniptions?... he said 'conniptions,'" murmured Right Honourable. "You can't afford a word like 'conniptions' on a watchman's pay!"

"Shut up, Right Honourable," said the Man in Black. "Everyone just shut up a moment and let me think." He tapped at a device on his desk and read the screen, I gathered he was looking for information.

We quietly waited. Meataxe leaned against a wall and closed his eyes, probably drifting off to sleep. He was able to doze anywhere like any experienced guard. Teddy Boy did fast draws with his blaster,

Right Honourable checked his nails and pulled a few invisible pieces of fluff from his already immaculate uniform. That left Greenash and me standing there, his eyes darted around the room seeking some escape from the madhouse, no doubt. When he looked at me, I practised my stone face on him, he gurgled but didn't fall over.

The Man in Black said, "From what I understand, this 'Elector' is some sort of politician." We groaned. "Should be worth a chat," he went on. "And, Val, you have confirmed some other rumours. This 'Syndicate' seems to be the main criminal organisation on the planet. And now we know the name, or at least the code name, of its leader, 'Ghost'. Right, same plan as before," ordered the boss, "Jobs as instructed, but now Meataxe and I will call on the good Elector and ask him what he knows about this and that. Off you go, lads, try to leave some of the citizenry alive. Val, don't leave the building."

We all shuffled out, I followed Right Honourable and Greenash with Teddy Boy keeping a close partnership on my right shoulder. When we entered the reception area Right Honourable said to Greenash, "We have a driver and a vehicle outside, let's get to the hospital." They moved off and I tagged along.

When I followed them out of the building there was a soft cough behind me, I ignored it. A slightly louder cough followed, also ignored. Before Greenash could shut the door I ducked and entered their vehicle, leaving Teddy Boy standing on the footpath outside. He put one hand on the roof and leaned into the vehicle, "What are you doing, Val?"

"Going to the hospital. Want to see how the lads are doing."

"The Man in Black specifically told you to stay in the building. You're disobeying orders?"

"Well, d'uh, of course I am."

He climbed in with us, "Just so we're clear."

Right Honourable had treated our little conversation with supreme indifference. He'd heard it all before, anyway.

But poor Greenash began to look worried.

We drove to another big building in this city of big buildings. Out the window I saw wide, even footpaths laden down with pedestrians. Small alleys slotted between some of the structures but generally, the front of one building abutted the next to make a continuous street frontage. The small alleys didn't seem to be too inviting; I saw boxes, crates and various bales in most of them. Greenash told me the alleys often linked up with a small service road that ran behind the main buildings. Utility services like garbage collection and so on used this back road so the straight citizenry were not confronted with odious workers smelling up the main thoroughfare.

"How are you settling into the NightWatch, Greenash?" I asked. "And why does a nanobot technician such as yourself want to join a bunch of ill-bred clods like these guys?" I nodded towards Right Honourable and Teddy Boy.

"I am very well-bred, you ignorant buffoon," said Right Honourable, "As you may recall, I was studying for the priesthood before joining the merry band of revellers we now call companions. My parents were quite keen on me becoming a Bishop or perhaps a Cardinal."

"Was this before or after you pushed the Prior out of the tower window?" My question had been asked before, the answer varied depending on Right Honourable's mood and state of inebriation. "Does the word 'defenestration' mean nothing to you, you yob?"

"You are a tiresome little man, Valentine. Of very little worth."

"My mum loves me."

"Only because you are not around. We, on the other hand, must put up with your garish presence day after day."

Greenash was looking worried, no doubt expecting a fight to break out after strong words were exchanged. "Umm, doesn't

Lieutenant Right Honourable, er, outrank you, Sergeant Valentine?" he asked. How sweet, he was trying to be the peacemaker and get me to see the error of arguing with a senior officer.

"Good question, Greenash, and just call me Valentine. You're dead right. Lieutenant Right Honourable," I smirked at the name because it sounded ridiculous, "and Ensign Teddy Boy," more chuckles, "do indeed outrank a mere sergeant."

I smiled at the three of them, Right Honourable gave me one of his patronising smiles, Teddy Boy rolled his eyes and Greenash's mouth dropped open a little. We sat in silence for a few beats before I went on, "The question, however, is do they outrank **me**?"

More silence. Greenash shuffled in his chair, I raised inquiring eyebrows at the other two and nodded towards Greenash. Right Honourable sighed and said, "We have a line of authority in the NightWatch, Greenash. The guy most capable tells the rest of us what to do. The Man in Black is the Boss, Magic is our Captain and Valentine is our Sergeant. So far, they have kept us alive and, as long as you stay behind Valentine, you will be safe. He will generally be the one that gets hit first. We all win."

"Stand a long way behind Valentine," added Teddy Boy.

"But your ranks?" stuttered Greenash. Poor little man was having trouble coping with our organised chaos, "You're both officers...and...."

"Ranks don't mean snot," said Teddy Boy, finalizing the discussion.

"Just settle back and enjoy the ride, Greenash. But back to my question, why are you with us?" I asked.

"I'm a nanobot technician and you all have nanobots running around your bodies." We had all been injected with the damn things as a new communication tool. Most people wore a Translator Bead in their ear. This somehow talked to the wearer's brain so they could understand any language. Our Trading Ship had been volunteered to try the new process which turned out to have some interesting side effects.

The NightWatch proved immune to these side effects and we were able to rectify the situation. Now, all of the gang carried these 'nanobots' inside us. I only had a hazy grasp of what they did but the very thought of tiny beasties crawling around inside me gave me the horrors. Fortunately, strong drink quieted the little bastards down.

"Can we skip any mention of little monsters in my brain," I was feeling ill already.

"Plenty of space up there," said Right Honourable.

Greenash kept on like a good 'un, "Your captain, Charles Althorp, asked me to...."

"No one calls him that," I interrupted. "He answers to 'Magic.'"

"Magic? Why 'Magic'?" asked Greenash.

"Because he can do things," said Right Honourable. "He just...talks to you, and you end up doing whatever he wants."

"Plus, he can get us out of the weirdest shit," commented Teddy Boy with admirable clarity, "Guys a magician."

"Hence, 'Magic'," I finished. "Now you, keep going with your story."

"Uh, yeah. Well, 'Magic' asked me to look after the nanobots inside you and the crew. We managed to turn off the crew's programming, the instructions which turned them into the walking dead. But there could be anything at all still lurking inside them. We left all of yours fully activated, but the NightWatch seems to have different reactions to them. The communicator application works, but who knows what else is in there."

"Right now, I'm feeling good about myself, not anxious at all," I muttered. Self-deception rules.

"What else can you do, Greenash?" asked Right Honourable. "The little beasties are already in us. Bit hard to get to them."

"It's pretty simple. I'll just take samples of your blood, some of the nanobots will be extracted at the same time. With a bit of work, I can analyse their instructions. Especially since I have the journal of the scientist who designed the nanobots."

"That was lucky," said Right Honourable. "How'd you get that?"

"Valentine found it."

Right Honourable leaned over and patted me on the knee, "Such a clever boy. Another one of your 'clues', Val? Did it have a big sign on it saying, 'Read Me!'?"

"Drop dead, mate. Keep going, Greenash. Are you saying you can make sure we don't have any more little surprises living inside us?"

"I think so. The hospital is giving me access to their equipment and I've been able to get some specialised gear from the police. It should be all I need."

"But you joined the NightWatch?" I asked. "Why? When we leave the planet, we might not return. You'll be saying goodbye to your life here."

"Gee, fancy that," he said. "No more days wondering if I'll get a job. Plus, I need to kick a few bad habits. A new start seemed in order."

"Are you talking about your little drug problem, Greenash?" I asked. When we first met, Greenash and I shared adjoining cells, me for violent crime and him coming down from an illegal high. "I have noticed you don't have that offensive odour," I said.

"Way to go, Val," said Right Honourable. "Make the man feel welcome by commenting on his body odour. Which, I might add, is indistinguishable from the normal citizens."

True enough, I thought. Greenash's drug of choice had the side effect of causing an extremely pungent secretion from the user's pores. Reminiscent of dead fish. But today he had a distinct freshness to his bouquet.

"I've been clean for days," said Greenash. "I'm hoping the NightWatch will be the right group to help me give up drugs."

Teddy Boy gurgled at this statement, Right Honourable's face was a picture.

"Boy, did you pick the wrong guys," I muttered.

Chapter 10

We arrived at the hospital, and Greenash departed to parts unknown in search of arcane pieces of technology to help him investigate our nanobots. I nudged Right Honourable, "Do you think Greenash will find ways for our little beasties to do wonderful things to us?"

"Such as?"

"I dunno, give us a superpower or something. Maybe we could all be able to fly or turn invisible. Be cool."

Teddy Boy breathed in my ear, "Here's a superpower for you, Val, the power to stay out of trouble." He pushed through some doors into a long corridor, "Come on, the lads are down this way."

We spent a few hours wandering around the hospice, or Medical Centre or whatever it was called. Most of the NightWatch were fine because we all came from a planet. The particular nastiness in our nanobots only affected people (or aliens, things, whatnots) if they had spent a long time aboard a spaceship. Since our ship was one of the giant Trading Ships, the majority of its personnel spent most of their lives in space. Only touching down on a planet for some recreation or business.

That's how me and the lads came to be with them, one of their Traders had come to Earth looking for a new market and lobbed into the middle of our fair city with his Tharl bodyguard. Unfortunately for him, Tharls are big and muscled with red skin, little horns and poor attitudes. The Church – led by the Inquisition – felt they would both benefit from a touch of fire-and-brimstone style questioning and tossed them into prison. When we came across them in the cells, we also discovered a gaggle of women and children in a very sorry state. The Inquisition had been putting them to the torture with very little opposition. They were from the underclass of gypsies, vagrants and generally the bottom of the pecking order. When we saw them, they were in a very bad way.

The drawback was the Man in Black and the rest of us in the NightWatch. We were also members of the lower classes, except for Captain Franz who is a real, live Lord. None of us thought it was a good idea to hurt women and children. Certainly not with torture added in, the poor little mites. We set them free, killing a few torturers on the way. This pretty much put us out of a job as members of the City Watch, the Church takes a dim view of our simplistic approach to problem-solving.

Faced with an outcome involving death and torture we took the sensible option and ran away. The NightWatch is big on running away. The alien Trader we rescued got us a job on his ship and suddenly we were transferred from smelly alleys and poor personal hygiene to gleaming corridors and shiny bits that go bang. Some of the lads were still struggling with the personal hygiene thing.

"Hey, Val!" called a voice behind me. I turned to see one of the Watch leaning on a stick and covered in lots of bandages. Teddy Boy rejoined me, and we wandered over to our stricken companion.

"Ragnar," I said, "How are you doin', you old Viking?"

He grinned at me and waved an arm ending in a stump, "I'm getting a new hand, Val! I get to pick if it has any special features. Trying to decide between a stabbing knife or drinking cup – what do you think I should get?"

My face must have betrayed my total lack of understanding because he stepped a little closer and waved his maimed paw under my nose. I felt a little sick. "They can attach bits to us, Val. Metal bits! Since I only just lost this hand, they say that most of the necessary ...stuff... in me is still in place. They're saying I can have another hand or even something special. I like the idea of a knife for a hand. How good would that be?"

"How would you scratch your bum, Ragnar?" asked Teddy Boy. "You know you are always doing a bit of digging down there. You might want to have a bit of a scratch when you're half asleep and then where would you be? You'd have an extra bum crack."

He paused, lost in thought, "Oh, you're right. That wouldn't be good."

"What's more," I said, joining the fun, "what if you had to do a little readjustment of, you know, the Ragnar Love Machine? Could end up with some things sliced off. Things you'd rather were still a going concern."

Watching his face imagine the scene gave me a small happiness. Ragnar is head and shoulders above me, his beard is usually unkempt, wild and full of his last meal. I've seen him work himself into a lather before a brawl and then charge into the heaviest fighting. I've never really seen him nervous or anxious but watching him think about losing his precious plumbing gear allowed me to see a Viking examining the depths of nightmare. It was a good look. I was wondering how else I could torment the poor sap when a voice came from behind me. A voice that hinted at layers of steel sandwiched between iron. A voice that could cut through a glacier and bring a wild storm to heel.

"Mr. Ragnar, why are you out of your bed?" the voice asked.

I turned to see a female medical staff member stepping out of a door leading into one of the sick rooms. She moved towards us and I felt Ragnar shrink. He could have picked her up in one hand, he could have towered over her, fed her fears and breathed all the rage and fire of his icy home into her small, soft face.

Instead, he took a step back, bowed his head and muttered, "Sorry, matron. I'll get back into it now."

Interesting. This slip of a girl could cow a Viking, not an easy task. As I debated how to get away from someone who could intimidate Ragnar she was hailed by another girl. "Matron, the Chief Surgeon has just arrived. You wanted to be informed when he enters the children's ward."

Matron's eyes narrowed a little and I noticed a slight compression of the lips before she flicked her gaze from me to turn and walk away. I felt the air flood back into the room, Ragnar muttered in adoration, "Ain't she something?"

He hobbled after her and said, "Come on, guys, this should be worth watching."

We followed the mini hurricane into a large room containing about a dozen beds, each one occupied by a small, limp figure. Oh, great, I thought, kids. We're in a room full of sick kids.

Ragnar grabbed my sleeve and pulled us off to one side where we could watch the unfolding scene without drawing fire. "Matron's been waiting for this guy to turn up for a few days," muttered my Nordic friend. "She's a bit cross over what's been done to these kids."

Looking around the sick room I empathised. Each bed held a small figure, faces drawn by suffering. Suffering no child should ever endure. "What's going on here, Ragnar?" I asked.

"Ah, matron," said an oily voice coming from a tall, thin figure with long and delicate fingers. His eyes did not go with the tone of voice. While he spoke with the measured tones of one who should be given respect his eyes betrayed nervousness. They darted around the room as if seeking an escape. "How encouraging to see you again."

"Surgeon General," said our little firestorm. "Thank you for coming. As you can see, these children need help. This situation needs help. What do you plan to do about it?" This matron person seemed to have the surgeon in a state of quiet terror.

He licked his lips and took a pace towards the door before realising this would take him closer to the matron. He shuffled back a little, "It seems to me you have the affair well in hand. These children are obviously receiving the best possible care." Again, his eyes flicked around the room flashing across us without finding any succor. I've found a lot of people give me that look. I'm not big on the whole succour-giving concept.

Matron took a firm step forward, "But we will see more of these children in here until you in the government address the key issue." Her voice drilled into the surgeon, lances of disgust striking her unctuous victim. "You must stop this disgusting trade in children's lives!"

He bobbed his head and gave a somewhat mealy nod, "My dear lady..." He stopped when he saw the matron giving him ice from the eyes. "We in the government are desperately trying to find a solution to this problem. Our strongest efforts are currently being directed towards erasing this blot on our great land."

She stood beside the bed of one of the little waifs, her hand stroking the child's head. To me, it seemed an unconscious act, just something she did. "These children have been abused and mistreated," she said. Her lips were thin, and her very stillness spoke of caged wrath. "The ones you see before you are but a small fraction of the many still left to this vile practice. They are held captive somewhere, they are traded like animals. You, and the rest of the government, are aware of the location of these 'child farms'. Even I know where some are. Why does the government drag its feet?"

Her voice had a passion, a relentless tone that had me thinking of escape routes.

Ragnar chose this moment to cough, the big lout. The sound made both parties turn towards us where we were trying to hide against the wall. "Mr. Ragnar," said the voice of steel, "you are not obeying my directives. Must I come over there and drag you back to your bed myself?"

I would pay good money to see that, I thought.

The Surgeon General used this break in proceedings to dash past the matron and exit the room. Which left Ragnar, Teddy Boy and me to face this little fireball. We were outnumbered and doomed.

"Val can help you!" babbled Ragnar, pointing to me.

I looked at my compatriot with some surprise and considerable astonishment. "What did you say that for?" I asked, through clenched teeth.

"I also question your wisdom, Mr. Ragnar," said the matron. She turned to me, eyebrows raised in a query.

"Umma...Umma...," I babbled. Giving Ragnar my filthiest look, I gathered myself and said, "I don't know what he's talking about. He's obviously sick and weak in the head." I lowered my voice conspiratorially, "He's never been the same after that incident with the baker's daughter, the miller's wife and the donkey."

"You swore never to mention that!" grinded Ragnar. "My head still pains where they hit me with...." He realized he was off-topic and swung back to the matron. "Val's my sergeant. Our team are like the police." He thought a bit. "But better."

She looked at me with that oh-so-familiar gaze, weighing me up and finding me wanting. "Police, are you?"

I'd had enough of this sideshow and decided to bring it to a close, "Yep. Me and the gang do a Security run on a Trading ship. We've got some downtime owing due to," I pointed at Ragnar's bandages, "some tidying up we had to do with things that wanted to eat us."

I was pleased to see her eyes widen a little, "Oh, you're that group. Well, perhaps you're not totally useless. Not like our own corrupt and blind leaders."

She waved at the room full of damaged children. "You heard what I said to that slime of a Surgeon General. These little tykes are just the few we find each day. Someone needs to do something. "

I didn't like where this was going, especially when she finished with a look at me before saying, "Someone needs to go into one of their farms and rescue these children." She put a strong emphasis on the 'Someone'.

Ragnar and Teddy Boy both gave a small head nod in my direction, raised an eyebrow to matron, turned and gave me a MEANINGFUL LOOK.

Is it really murder if you shoot your mates? Really?

Chapter 11

I was ready to just slope off through the door. I snagged Ragnar by one of his bandages and had a terrific exit line ready to fire off when I felt my other hand being taken by a small grip. We had somehow ended up next to one of the beds, and its occupant had opened her eyes and taken my hand. Her little fingers wrapped around my paw and she looked at me. Big eyes.

Children. What are you gonna do?

I looked at the little girl, hung my head and said to the matron, "I need a name, I need a place."

"Why?"

"I intend to...," This was tricky, honesty can be overrated but there's a first time for everything. "I intend to damage those people, free the kids and generally make anyone who hurts a child feel a lot of pain."

She looked at me, I wondered about the effects of honesty. Our small tableau held for several beats before she said, "Fine by me."

Who says the healing professions are losing their touch?

"Where do I go?" I asked.

"I get to come too."

"No," I said, firmness in every fibre of my voice.

Ted shuffled his feet which equated to a strong personal statement from him.

"Good luck with the rest of your life," she said and left the room.

There are times to stand firm and speak up for your beliefs and then there are times to run after the girl. I pushed the door open and caught up with her in the corridor. "You play hardball, lady."

"I don't play." She stood and gave me the old steel glare, it was way better than mine.

Ted came out of the room after me and said, "I like her, Val." Ice formed around us, he recoiled from me a little and was saved from further sarcasm by the arrival of Greenash. Our newest recruit was walking slow, acting dumb and talking stupid. Just the way I like 'em.

"Hi fellas," he said. "What's up?"

Ragnar said, "Val's going to do a good deed!". Ted was smiling fatherly towards me and Greenash just looked amiable.

I looked from them back to the matron and realised I was in the company of lunatics. "What's your name, nursie?"

"Call me 'Nursie' again and you'll walk with a limp."

Ted chuckled, a rare sound so I took the higher moral ground, "You're the bloody, ensign, Teddy Boy. Be a senior officer and sort her out. Ragnar, get back to your bed and heal up, I may have to hit you later."

An interesting scene transpired after that, Ted talking earnestly to this warrior Amazon while I tried to work out what button she had that needed pushing. Generally, I can pick that in another person, I know when they need to be cajoled or threatened or begged, I'm very good at begging. But this woman was a wall, impossible to read. She seemed to be all hard edges and pointy ends.

Ted turned to me and said, "Sylvia will show us where to find the farm."

"And Sylvia is...?" I asked.

"Get a grip, Valentine," replied my superior officer. "The matron has a name. It is Sylvia. You will treat her with respect. Do I make myself clear?"

Abundantly, I thought. She has you around her little finger and it couldn't happen to a nicer guy. "Welcome to the gang, Syl."

"Sylvia," she replied. "Not Syl, or Sylvie. Get it right." Statues would kill for her visage. "I don't like you," she stated.

Fabulous, another fan.

"Most don't," I agreed, "But don't worry, I'm like mould. I grow on you." My boyish charm was met by her wall of indifference and loathing. Hey-ho, are we off to a good start or what? I looked over at Teddy Boy. "A little help here, mate?"

He sighed and said, "Sylvia will take us to the farm, we go in and rescue the kids. Everyone wins."

I asked Sylvia, "Who owns the farm? Do you know who is behind this little operation?"

"I do," she answered. "The farm and its attendant activities are supervised by the organized crime group on the planet. A nasty, mean and cruel group with links to politicians, the police and the media."

"Are you talking about 'The Syndicate'?" I asked.

She rolled her eyes in disgust, "That sounds like the name they use. Typical of their need for grandeur, makes them sound secretive and shadowy. Good for scaring the weak-minded." Here she gave me a particularly significant look. I took it like a man. "They are a bunch of low-lifes," she snorted, "bullies and thugs. 'The Syndicate', indeed - just a mob of gangsters."

Teddy Boy asked me, "Where will the kids go after we release them?"

I shrugged, how should I know, "Back to their parents, I guess. What do I care, they aren't slaves anymore."

"No, you must find other accommodations." stated Sylvia, "Their parents probably sold them. Giving the children back is like granting them an extra income source. They will just sell them again. Not everyone, of course, some will be thrilled to have their loved ones back. But not all, perhaps not even most. We cannot put those children back into a situation of risk. We have to assume that any child we recover will be carrying black market nanobots of unknown function."

I turned to Teddy Boy, "What would your instructions be...Ensign Sir?" I asked.

There is a perverse enjoyment in watching a hitter and slugger like Teddy Boy grapple with big-picture concepts. He chewed his bottom lip, looked up and to the left (it's the glance people usually give when they are about to tell a lie. I know stuff like that). He finally came out with a decision.

"I dunno."

"Yeah, well done, Ted," I said. "Good stuff, gripping strategy." They both looked at me with the old, big-eyed pleading gaze. "Ah, come on," I said, "Let's go. We'll work something out."

Teddy smiled his imbecilic grin, he assumed I had a plan. Sylvia gave me another jaundiced look. I winked at her with my irrepressible boyish charm. She turned her back on me.

I, of course, had no idea what to do.

But my mouth did, "We'll need someone to handle the kids and their embedded little beasties. That's you, Greenash."

To his credit, he didn't fade away immediately, "No, sir, I don't go out at all. The captain said I was purely back-room support, no going out into the nasty bits."

"Yeah, sure, Greenash, stay with that dream. Now pack what you need and be ready to move in five minutes," I said.

"But I can't," he pleaded. "I don't do that sort of thing..."

His voice trickled away as I looked at him. He turned away to begin packing. "Ted, leave Sylvia alone and go and find some more NightWatch to come along for the ride. Some of the wounded may have recovered enough to hold a blaster. The two of us can do the heavy lifting but I would be happier knowing we have someone else behind us holding a gun. A big gun."

Ted trundled off. While we waited for him to return with some of the lads, I had Sylvia give me a briefing on our target.

"It's a small farmhouse with several outbuildings, some have been converted to dormitories and a food hall. The main house is where the guards are quartered, a tall fence runs behind this farmhouse and around the property, with a second fence inside this perimeter. Guard beasts roam between the two fences, these are killers and trained to attack anyone between the fences, especially children." She had been piling medicines and other paraphernalia into a large bag. When she finished speaking, she thrust it at me, "Here. Do some heavy lifting with this. Come on."

Greenash fell in behind me and we trooped off behind the juggernaut known as Matron Sylvia. As we went through the corridors towards the main reception area other people stood against the walls to let us pass. No one seemed to want to get in her way.

At Reception we were joined by Teddy who had three other team members with him, H'nuth and Lonely were two of them. Both these characters had been infected by the Nanobots, due to their extended shipboard life, and turned into Undead in our recent session of fun and games. H'nuth had locked himself in the cells before he turned and felt the need to chow down on his fellow Tharls. I had left Lonely tied to a hospital bed in Sick Bay, infected and about to turn. Poor bloke just had no luck.

They both looked decidedly peaky. The nanobots fueled their little Undead adventure by burning up flesh. Any flesh would do, the little darlings would consume the host body if there wasn't any nearby victim. This habit led us all into some very sensitive and delicate relationship-building exercises which generally finished up with one of the undead eating their neighbour.

Or the said neighbour could try to kill the undead person. A bit tricky but usually the option I went with.

"Hi, boys," I said. "Anyone still hungry?"

H'nuth ignored me and studied a nearby light fixture. Lonely gave me his best piercing look and said, "Give it a rest, Val. Try not to be a bigger annoyance than usual."

"Since when did you get to be so brash and cocky, young feller-me-lad?" I took a longer look at him, he had certainly travelled an interesting journey since joining our happy band. "What makes you think you can talk to your older, more experienced mentors with such a snippy tone?"

"Since I died and came back as a monster. Since you led the delegation which started the whole nightmare. And, since you ask, because I bloody well feel like it."

I looked at Ted who was beaming at Lonely like a proud father, Sylvia snorted and Greenash tried to disappear into a wall. Personal conflict, what an emotionally charged atmosphere we seemed to inhabit.

"Well done, Lonely, glad you got that off your chest. Hope you're feeling better now. A little cleansed, perhaps," I said.

I turned to the last member of the trio, Max. Max was an interesting character, his real name was not, of course, Max. Like Ragnar, he was from the far northern lands, the country of ice and snow, of big, bearded men in shaggy furs who rowed longships in the dead of winter. Usually, they were mad, bad and dangerous to know; Max was an oddity in his clan, he was certainly dangerous but not quite as mad. Blond, clean-shaven with blue eyes and a permanent air of happiness, he rarely scowled, probably because he wasn't stuck in the wintry climate of his younger days. Trying to pronounce his real name dislocated the jaw, so we just called him Max. No particular reason.

"Has Ted told you what we are going to do?" I asked them.

H'nuth grunted, "Rescue some kidnapped children. I need to get a bit of exercise; a little light pounding is desirable but I'm as weak as a newborn. What's the full story?"

"Follow me, kiddies, Uncle Valentine will tell all." After passing Sylvia's heavy bag off to Max we left the building, my companions following along due to my strong leadership. On the footpath, I stopped and looked around.

"Something wrong, boofhead?" asked Sylvia. She had a knowing smile and was giving me the pitiful look one gives dumb animals.

"How are we going to get there, Sergeant?" asked H'nuth.

"Er...," I began.

Chapter 12

That was the key question. We would need a large vehicle capable of moving all of us, and then we would need something bigger to pick up all the children. The road in front of me was empty, our own vehicle had gone to wherever police cars go when not transporting us hither and thither.

Sylvia walked off to the right and called over her shoulder, "Oh, come on. We'll get something here." She led us to the underground parking bay where several large vehicles were parked. A small door opened onto a waiting area containing various hospital employees sitting around a table, all wearing the same uniform as Sylvia.

"Sergiu!" she called. "Come on, I have a job for you." One of the uniformed types looked up with a bored expression, spotted Sylvia and immediately leapt to his feet, the rest of the room's inhabitants avoided eye contact and began studying interesting room corners and fingernails.

"Yes, Matron, right away." Sergiu grabbed a coat, plucked some keys from a rack and moved over to a big vehicle with a large box-like room behind the driver's space. "Where are we going?" he asked, "Do you have a transport authorisation number?"

"Just get in and drive, Sergiu, and do as you're told. Open the back so these clods can get in."

Sergiu bobbed his head, slipped into the vehicle and popped the rear doors on the box room. The rest of us looked at Sylvia who had begun to climb into the only other seating space beside Sergiu. She looked back and saw us all standing around and barked, "What are you waiting for, a written invitation? Get in!" We got.

We drove for about two hours, long boring hours. I dozed or annoyed the others as best I could. The box part of the vehicle was used to transport the sick and injured, it had two bed-like devices strapped against each wall. H'nuth and I sat on one while Max,

Teddy Boy and Lonely sat across the way. H'nuth and I took up a lot of space, so Greenash was forced to sit on the floor. He didn't object and I didn't care.

"Why are we doing this, Valentine?" asked H'nuth.

"You said it yourself, big guy, we're going to rescue kids. From slavery."

"Sure. And the real reason?"

"What makes you think there's another reason?" I asked.

"You are well known as a thug, not the saviour of mankind."

"Yeah, come on, Val," joined in Teddy Boy. "We're all fine with doing the job but there's more to it than just helping some stray children."

Max had just smiled all through this exchange. Lonely continued to glower and Greenash was, well, Greenash. "Okay, kiddies, here's the deal. This farm is run by the Syndicate, the very same group that has a kill contract out on yours truly. I'm thinking they might find the whole 'Let's kill Valentine' deal a bad idea if it becomes too expensive."

"Which means you want to find someone at the farm who can give you the name and address of the next target," said Teddy Boy. He was always quick on the uptake, "and then keep going. Hit a few more of their operations."

"Rinse and repeat," I agreed.

A small sliding window connected the driving cabin of the vehicle. I slid it open and asked, "How much longer?"

Sylvia glanced over her shoulder at me, "Bit more time."

"How much is a 'bit'?" I asked.

"More than a little. Shut up and plan something, we'll get you there."

She slid the window shut, I turned to face my comrades who were looking at me with high hopes. Poor sods.

"Do you have a plan, Val?" asked H'nuth.

"What sort of vehicle is this, Greenash? What's all this stuff in it?" I was cleverly changing the subject.

"Don't change the subject, Val. Answer the man," said Lonely.

"Still waiting, Greenash," I said.

"Um..." Greenash's head swivelled around, searching for some help in his hour of need. Not a lot of encouragement from us. "It's an Emergency Vehicle."

"What's an Emergency Vehicle?" I asked.

"You know," he replied. "A special vehicle for.... well.... emergencies."

"Not getting this, old chum," I said, trying hard not to choke him.

"You must have had them, transporting sick or injured people...... fighting fires.... all sorts of sudden happenings."

"Like an emergency," said Lonely.

"Exactly!" agreed Greenash. He sat back and beamed at us, confident in his high-level communication skills.

"Let me get this straight," I said. "This vehicle can transport the sick and injured," I patted the bunk. "I get that. But it can also fight fires and do other stuff as required?"

"Of course not. For fires, you would need a Fire Engine."

"An engine for fires? Why would you want an engine for fires?" I was floundering.

Greenash struggled for words, finally coming up with, "Where are you guys from?"

H'nuth chipped in, "They're primitives, Greenash. We found them on a planet still using swords and open sewers. Now how about you tell us your plan to rescue these children, Val?"

"Don't have one. I need to see the place first. Sylvia gave me the overall layout, but a small reconnaissance might be in order."

"Who are you and what have you done with the real Valentine?" asked Lonely.

"Whaddya mean, sport?" I said.

"He means," sighed Teddy Boy, "that you never had a plan in your life. Beyond walking into a dark space and hitting everyone, that is."

"Maybe I'm growing wiser, more mature."

"I may just throw up," said Lonely.

"I'm just saying, that's all, just saying that I'm trying very hard to think ahead. These bozos with the kids might need a bit of careful handling. We need to ask a few questions, see what's what."

"Bloody hell," said Lonely, "the big boofhead is making sense. I don't believe it."

That all looked at me.

"I know, fellers," I said, "I'm scared too."

Through the little front window, I saw the landscape change. We had left the city and entered one of my alien environments, the country. Gradually the quality of the roads deteriorated, eventually we were driving along a narrow, dusty track.

"Okay," I said, "when we get close, I'll have the driver pull over and let us out. We need to sneak around and see what sort of place they are running, how many guards, that sort of thing. Then we'll meet back at the vehicle and work out what to do. Sound all right?"

"Sounds amazing," said Lonely. "Not rushing in headfirst. Be a nice change from your usual methods, Val."

"How about some positive feedback, a little encouragement would be nice," I said.

"You're wonderful, Val," said H'nuth.

"I want to marry you," said Teddy Boy.

"And have your children," said Lonely.

I looked at Max, "Anything from you, sport?"

He beamed at me, "Just happy to be on the team, Val." Max probably wasn't being a smart arse like the rest of my mates. He was genuinely happy most of the time. Once, when I asked him why he was so cheerful he said, "Happiness is a choice. You can't help bad things happening to you, no control over that. But I have control over how I react, I have a choice. I choose to be happy."

Max was always a bit dippy.

The front window slid open as the vehicle pulled off the road onto a grassy verge. "We're getting close," said Sylvia. "What do you want to do?"

"Let us out here and we'll have a look around," I said.

"There's a drop gate near the guardhouse," she said, looking through the front window. "Just around that corner up ahead. How will you get through that?" she asked.

"What's a drop gate?" I asked.

She turned back to face me, "It's a gate that drops, genius." I heard sniggers behind me. "You won't even be able to enter the property until you raise it."

Hmm, could be a problem, I thought.

Two large dark vehicles drove past us and down the road, clouds of dust blossoming from their passage. "Pull out and follow them!" I yelled into the front cabin.

Our driver obediently drove back onto the road and we saw the other vehicles up ahead, "What else is down this road?" I asked Sylvia.

"How would I know?" she yelled back at me.

The two big machines ahead of us turned into a small access road to a large gatehouse. The gatehouse effectively blocked the entire access through the wall with a tunnel-like hole through its base. Any vehicle trying to enter the property had to pass under the gatehouse by going through the tunnel.

And across the tunnel was a thick metal pole. I was guessing this was the drop gate.

"Follow the other vehicles, catch them and tag along behind," I instructed the driver.

The first vehicle had stopped at the drop gate while its driver spoke to a burly guard from inside the gatehouse. As we came up behind the last machine, the drop gate was raised and our little convoy moved through the tunnel and under the gatehouse. The guard stood to one side as we passed, I ducked back and watched Sylvia give him her friendliest glare. To his credit, he didn't cringe too much.

We drove up a small access road until the other vehicles stopped in front of a large, low-set building. "That's the main house," said Sylvia, "the children are kept in barracks behind it."

I sat down on the bunk beside H'nuth and had a good worry. What were we going to do now?

Lonely interrupted my thought path by saying "Great stealth skills, Val. I don't reckon anyone has noticed us as we DROVE UP TO THE FRONT DOOR!"

"Shut up, Lonely," said Teddy Boy, in a quiet voice.

Sylvia was watching the house and other vehicles out the front window of our machine. I was looking through the little panel and saw the doors of the other machines open. Out stepped four guys, three of them moved towards the house. The fourth looked at us quizzically before yelling something at the others, they stopped and looked back at us.

"Keep calm, Sylvia, just sit still and keep looking back at them," I said.

She spoke out of the corner of her mouth. On any other day, I would have called it a snarl, "You are going to get us all killed, numbnuts! Get out there and do something!"

"Not yet, let's see what happens," I said.

The four men spoke back and forth for a while until a decision was reached, the original three turned back to the main house and stepped up onto the porch. The front door opened and they stepped inside.

The fourth guy pulled out a blaster and walked towards us.

Chapter 13

"What do I do now, Genius?" she asked me.

"Tell him......." I stopped, having no idea what she could say. "Umm....say.... something...." I ducked back into the body of our space before the armed thug could see me. Sitting on the bunk with the others I endured their stares and raised eyebrows. I shrugged my shoulders and tried to look pathetic. Not hard, really.

We heard a voice used to eating rocks say, "What's going on, sweet cheeks? What are you doing here?"

Through the metal panels between us and the front seat I could hear Sylvia grind her teeth, "Don't call me 'sweetcheeks', pal, or you can forget about fathering children."

The woman had rare people skills, I looked around for a weapon since we were about to get into it in a big way. Nothing, this vehicle was meant to save lives, instruments of death and destruction were remarkably absent.

After a small pause, we heard a low growl from the thug; it dawned on me he was laughing. "You're all right, babe, I like 'em feisty. Now, answer me; what are you doing here?"

"We got a call from Ghost. Thought you might need some help with the special delivery." Sylvia sounded calm and relaxed, a little mean but no more than her normal state.

"Yeah? How about you open the back so I can give it the once over? Make sure you're not smuggling a van full of heavies in here." He chuckled again; we heard his footsteps in the gravel as he moved down the side of the vehicle.

The rest of the gang all turned their gaze on me, eyebrows were raised and unasked questions hung heavy in the air.

"You guys have any weapons?" I whispered.

Ted pulled out a blaster – no surprise there, H'nuth grinned and showed me his fangs. He had nice fangs, big ones which jutted out of his lower jaw. I had always thought they were some throwback to an earlier, more primitive time in the development of is species. Perhaps they were still trotted out on special occasions and so on.

Max showed me a War knife – I've always liked Max. They looked at me expectantly.

"What?" I asked. "I'm under house arrest, remember. Not allowed around sharp and pointy things." I nodded at Teddy Boy, "It's his fault."

I pulled a heavy metal cylinder off a wall mount. I'd seen these in the medical rooms, they contained some sort of gas which helped people to breathe. Or something.

The rear doors were pulled open by the guy outside. I hit him full in the face with the base of the cylinder, he dropped to the ground and lost consciousness. Plus a lot of teeth.

"Well, we're here," I said to the others, "might as well keep going and get the kids." I picked up the thug's blaster and gave it to Lonely, he was the next best thing to an experienced marksman. Max would have broken it.

We all trundled out of the vehicle, Sylvia getting out of the front cabin, "Stay there," she instructed the driver.

"No problems with that," he said. Greenash said he would also stay in the back of the Emergency vehicle and pretend he was somewhere else. Fair enough, the little guy was doing his best to remain out of danger - not an easy trick with our team.

Sylvia joined us as we walked to the front door, "Is this the standard of deep thought and careful planning I can expect from the NightWatch?"

Ted answered her, "Usually it's worse. Val must be feeling in good form."

She looked at my mate and smiled before ruffling his hair, "You're all right, handsome."

I will never understand women. Or the laws of attraction between people. Or lots of other stuff.

Before we reached the front door, it opened and another thug exited, probably coming out to check on his mate. When he saw us, he turned and yelled a warning over his shoulder before drawing a pistol. Ted shot him in the face. The thug fell and caused the rest of his gang a bit of bother as they tried to leap over his body enroute to us.

And they weren't happy. Lots of big fists, shooty things and stabby things.

When the guy first appeared, H'nuth and I had begun to run forward, closing the distance. Ted's shot zipped over my shoulder causing me to hunch down and run like a man in gastric pain, a run I have done many, many times. By the time the rest of the thugs had started to get out the door, we were on top of them and swinging wildly. I still had the metal cylinder and got in a few good hits.

There seemed to be no end to them, had we stumbled on a Convention of Crooks, the annual Thugs Dinner? I heard a cry behind me, some more shots whistled overhead and then two guys hit me at once causing me to fall like a sack of potatoes. The rest of the fight was a bit of a mystery, I lost track of H'nuth as my two assailants seemed to take me on as a pet project and spent a lot of time kicking the stuffing out of the old body.

Eventually, they stopped, probably through exhaustion. I was dragged to my feet and saw the rest of the team; they didn't look happy.

Sylvia was holding Teddy Boy's head in her lap, he had a nasty groove across his skull - probably a projectile weapon. Max was still grinning, but it seemed a bit more forced than usual, his new broken arm was a clue. H'nuth lay unconscious; Lonely stood looking at me with an accusatory stare, several small darts stuck out of his shoulder and face. He gradually folded to the ground as the chemicals from the darts hit his system. No doubt he would whine about it to me later as if it was all my fault.

Guy can't take a joke.

The chief thug nudged me with his pistol, "Who are you idiots?"

It took a few good spits to clear the blood out of my mouth before I could answer, no-one else seemed to be in a chatty mood. "I hear you've got some kids here."

"You think they're worth dying for? You come in here and expect to walk out again? Hey," he was now looking at Sylvia, "Don't I know you?"

I had wondered how she knew so much about the place, its location and layout. She even used the word 'Ghost' to get us in here. Sylvia knew stuff. For now, she was keeping her head down and stroking Teddy Boy's fevered brow.

Thug number one gestured with his weapon, "No matter, get them inside." He looked at H'nuth's comatose form for a few beats – I was hoping we were not about to see an execution. "I know some people who'll pay good money for a Tharl, good for medical research. Tie him up and leave him outside. We'll keep the rest in the house until the boss arrives – she'll work out what to do." He gave me another poke in the ribs, "More a question of where to bury the bodies." Then he laughed.

I'd gone right off this turkey.

He turned and moved into the house, three other thugs in front of us and another five bringing up the rear. Even on a good day, we couldn't handle all of these guys - what was I thinking? Max supported Lonely and we all trooped off to meet our fate.

The men in front had reached the end of our small entry corridor, we were next in line and I could see some rooms off to either side of the corridor. The last five goons were just entering the house when the vehicle hit them from behind causing arms, legs and bodies to be catapulted along the corridor.

Greenash had watched us all get beaten up but didn't run away, showing remarkably poor judgement. Instead, he had crept into the front seat of the Emergency vehicle, pushed the terrified driver out of the way and waited for a chance to make a break. But rather than save himself he had started the machine and rammed it into the house - right at the front door where our escorts were debating future burial sites.

When the crash came behind me, I grabbed Sylvia and dived into one of the adjoining rooms. Max and Teddy Boy hit another room which left a drugged Lonely to fend off the front of the vehicle by himself; he's always had very poor reaction times. I had a small hope he might still be under the influence from his knockout dart and not feel much pain. Fortunately, the five thugs cushioned most of the blow, but he still received a healthy thunk and probably more bodily damage. He was never going to let me hear the end of this.

All these bodies flew past us as we crouched on the floor of our chosen side rooms, I caught a glimpse of broken bodies hurtling by and into the front crew of our escort. These guys hadn't even realised there was an accident happening behind them, there is a poor standard of staff training in the local underworld. Reaction time is critical, it has to be immediate and instinctive; waiting for instructions from the brain will get you killed. As they all fell together, I decided I would have a close and meaningful discussion with their leader.

I left Sylvia to roll around feeling put upon, moved back into the corridor and started hitting bad guys. A few solid blows put them all out, these fellows just had no tenacity, no resilience. Never make it in the Watch. By the time the rest of my gang turned up, I had a blaster in each hand and a sappy grin on my face.

" Are we having fun yet?" I asked, ever cheerful.

Chapter 14

"Yeah, we're good, Lonely might need a bit of an assist," said Max. You had to admire his fortitude, holding his own broken arm and trying to get help for someone else. As I was doing this spot of admiring, he keeled over and lay unconscious at my feet.

Sylvia started tending to the hurt and maimed, Teddy Boy came over and took one of the guns. His skull looked quite nasty, but we breed them tough on Earth, he said he'd go and check on H'nuth. Lonely lay with his back against a wall while Sylvia strapped him up, he was barely conscious and spent the time giving me nasty looks.

"Every time, Valentine....," he said, "every time I hang around with you, I get into trouble. And usually hurt." He sucked in a few deep breaths, "Why is that, Val?"

"You'll be right, sport," I replied. "One day, we'll look back on this and laugh."

Ted returned with a slowly walking H'nuth behind him; the big guy did not look well but you can never tell with Tharls. I do know from first-hand experience they are very hard to kill. Not impossible, just very, very hard.

"I better check the rest of the house," said Ted. Sylvia said she wanted to get the children and H'nuth decided to go with her - I left them to find their own amusement.

"Good idea," I replied, "I'm just going to stay here and groan." I spat out more blood and gave one of the unconscious thugs another decent whack with my pistol. Seemed to be called for.

Greenash struggled through the remains of the front doors and flopped down beside me. He told me what he'd done, and I patted him on the head. I asked him why, why take the risk of driving a large vehicle into a house in the faint hope it might help us.

"Seemed like a NightWatch sort of thing to do," he said.

"You'll fit right in, lad," I said.

"What about the guards in the gatehouse?" he asked.

"What about them?"

"Won't they have heard the commotion?"

"Probably, but I think we can hold them off, even beat up and damaged as we are. It'll take them a long time to drive into town to get any sort of reinforcements. Pretty dopey set-up, if you ask me - putting a facility like this a long way out of town with no hope of immediate support in case of an attack. An attack like us. They should have carrier pigeons or something for when they need help."

He looked at me with that look, "Why wouldn't they just use their communicators?"

A sinking feeling developed in my gut; I sensed modern technology was about to kick me in the teeth again. "Communicators?"

"You know, Val," he was struggling for a sensible description "...communicators! Like on your spaceship."

"But we're not on a spaceship! Do you mean to say these devices are on the planet's surface? What possible good are they? Why would you always want to be able to communicate with someone else?"

He waved a hand towards the devastation around us. Oh.

I pushed myself against the wall and struggled to my feet, "Get the Emergency Vehicle driver in here. The two of you load up our wounded and then the kids when Sylvia brings them out. How long do you think we have before more nasty men arrive at the gatehouse demanding our blood?"

He shrugged, it was an unfair question - the bad guys could come anytime. I needed a plan.

My standard plan involved running away - a good option right now.

When Sylvia and H'nuth returned they had about twenty children of various ages from 8 to 13. H'nuth had three on his shoulders and they were tugging his hair and teeth in between laughter. He growled a lot but seemed to be enjoying himself. I noticed the children gave one of the bodies on the floor some more than normal terrified looks. The thug leader was not well-liked; one of the older girls bent down to check his consciousness level, saw he was no threat and proceeded to administer a vigorous but ineffectual kicking. She was only young, after all.

Other kids came over and hit or spat on him. They all jumped back when he started to regain consciousness, so I went and stood on his hands; I weigh a bit, there were some crunching sounds from bones breaking and more whimpering. But not from the children, one of them, showing a complete lack of social distancing, even hugged me.

"What's the story here, Sylvia?" I nodded at the struggling man at my feet.

"He rapes and beats them," said an incensed Sylvia. H'nuth growled and stepped forward, I held up my hand to stop the big guy and was mildly surprised when he ground to a halt.

"Does he now?" A plan was forming in some dark and ill-used part of my brain. "I reckon I might be able to do something about that. Get everyone in those vehicles outside, use all of them. I want you out of here in two minutes."

Greenash and the driver had returned and heard me, "How do we get past the gatehouse and its guards?"

"I have a cunning plan." I pulled a sullen Mr Nasty to his feet, stuck a blaster in his ear and said "Let's go for a short walk, sunshine. See if we can put a smile on that face."

Lots of activity was happening around me, children crying and cluttering up my personal space, hanging onto my knee and generally getting underfoot. The thugs hit by Greenash as he drove the Emergency vehicle through the front door were all damaged in various serious ways. Their groans added to the atmosphere of mayhem.

Sylvia was herding kids, Max, with a broken arm in a sling, stood alone and isolated, an island in the sea of people. I soon found myself in a near-empty corridor, my only companions the thug beside me and a bunch of comatose bodies on the floor. Max looked at me and asked the question.

"Just drag the living ones outside, Max," I said. "No killing. Then you can use the house to show us all how you warm up the cold winter nights back home in your godforsaken frozen country." He still had one good arm. And he was Max.

He brightened at that and began hauling anyone twitching outside, he clipped them together using our little security Guard ties - so useful - while I dragged my sullen thug out towards the guardroom. It's amazing how dexterous he is with only one functioning arm; everyone should have a Max on their team. A shout stopped me a few steps away from the house, I saw Teddy Boy emerge with another prisoner, something about the new man looked horribly familiar.

"Don'elk? Is that you?" The target of my remarks was a very bad imitation of a crook. God knows, he tried but he couldn't quite pull it off. I think it all lies in the swagger. Don'elk couldn't swagger.

When he saw me, he groaned and hid his face in his hands. I told my thug to be good - jabbing my pistol into his nose at the same time emphasized the seriousness of my request. He stood very still as I waved for Don'elk to approach.

"Do my tired old eyes deceive me? Is that you, Donny? Still hanging around with the wrong crowd?" Donny and I had history, he once tried to frame me for murder and, in return, I had hit him a lot. A good deal from my end.

"What are you doing here, Donny? Child abduction and abuse are a long way from plain and simple lying and stealing. Looking for a new career path?" I asked.

He held up his hand, the one with damaged fingers - I had done the damaging. "Look what you did to me! Look at it!" He thrust it into my face, so I swatted him with an open hand slap, nothing serious. A tap. He barely shuddered.

"Leave him alone!"

I turned to see Sylvia in full sail about to engage with unfriendlies - me.

"Sorry?" I asked.

"Get away from him, you bully.... you.... thug!"

She had me there, while I agree with the 'Thug' appellation I did not concur with 'Bully'. But now was not the time for a philosophical discussion with Matron. A cross Matron. I looked around at the others and my mates had their 'watching street theatre' faces firmly in place. Lonely was smiling as he swayed.

"You didn't object when we knocked seven bells of pain out of everyone else," I pointed out. "But a little slap on Donny here and you think I'm going overboard?"

She thrust her way to stand between Donny and me, I stepped back a pace. Sylvia cradled his face in her hands and rubbed some dirt off his cheek. There may have been some soft crooning, hard to tell with Sylvia.

"Are you all right, Don'elk?" she asked.

Donny's face was a picture, a combination of surprise and embarrassment fought with studied insouciance and a desire for a good cry. The guy was severely mixed up. "I'm fine," he snuffled, "I'm fine, Syl."

Oho, I thought, here it comes. Sylvia's going to drop the hammer because she doesn't like to be called anything but her full name.

"Poor baby," she crooned, "come on, let's get you out of here." She started to guide Donny to the waiting vehicles.

"Err..." I said, masterful as ever. "He's, like, one of the bad guys."

She ignored me, they kept walking. I could feel my control of the situation disappearing - who am I kidding, I never had control of the situation.

Teddy Boy moved over to intercept the duo, "Do you know this character, Sylvia?"

They stopped walking. "He's my brother," she said.

Chapter 15

We had one of those moments, you know the ones I mean. That moment when you hear something spoken in a completely matter-of-fact voice that reveals a deep, dark secret. Stuff like "I know what you did last summer", "I enjoy cross-dressing", "I've been sleeping with your mother", "I'm a vegetarian."

Ted coughed, Max smiled inanely, it was up to me to make the appropriate response, "He's your brother!"

"Are we leaving here or not?" asked Sylvia, dragging a grumbling Don'elk with her to one of the vehicles.

"What's the plan, Val?" asked Ted. Which pleased me no end until he finished with, "I can't believe I just said that."

"Max, ride with Sylvia, keep an eye on Donny - get her to drive. H'nuth, get in the back and look after the kids. Greenash, you drive the other big vehicle, the other guy - what was his name? - can drive his Emergency Vehicle. Lonely goes with him to make sure he stays honest. Get the kids to the Man in Black."

Greenash stated the obvious question, "We can't leave while the drop gate is down, Val. And the rest of their gang should be here real soon."

"Ted and I will take care of the gate. You'll be on your way in a few moments." Lots more activity as everyone got organised, I had a quiet chat with Greenash involving communicators and their possible uses. I even issued him some instructions that might help us all get out of this mess. When I had finished, it was just Teddy Boy and me standing in the parking lot with a belligerent thug and three very full vehicles carrying lots of nervous and damaged people. Max had been enjoying himself, the house behind us was blazing merrily. He danced around waving a burning brand before throwing it away and getting into a vehicle. He looked happy in his work and it's good to give the kids a treat now and then.

"Come on, Sunshine," I said this last to our local child molester as I dragged him with me towards the gatehouse.

The three of us approached the robust building with some care. I kept our prisoner in front as a shield just in case one of the guards tried a play. Ted just hung around.

"You in there!" I called. "You've got 10 seconds to get into your vehicle and leave. After that, I'll come in and kill you!"

"You're bluffing!" came the shouted reply. "We can wait here all day. But you ain't got all day. Say your prayers, you moron. We ain't scared of you!"

"You might want to re-think that stance," I said and put the pistol against the head of the raper of children. He looked nervous and I didn't care.

I loudly counted down from ten. When I reached zero, I pulled the trigger which shot a bolt into the rapist's skull. His head vanished in a spray of superheated gas, the headless body stood for a moment before slowly sinking to its knees and collapsing.

"Let's go, Ted," I said and began walking to the gatehouse. Ted had to step smartly to catch me.

"Val," he said. I ignored him. "Val," he tried again. "You've got that look on your face, the one which scares us shitless." I continued to ignore him and focused my whole being on reaching the gatehouse to clean it out. "Oh, bugger...," he said, running to keep up.

We heard the sound of slamming doors, running feet and an engine starting up. By the time we reached the gatehouse the guards had left, we raised the drop gate and let the vehicles out. Sylvia avoided looking at me, but a few kids had faces at the windows and they were all smiling at me, giving me happy waves and generally making me feel good.

As the last vehicle left, I dropped the gate back down and said to Ted, "Now it's just a matter of waiting for the bad guys to show up."

I felt my emotional temperature dropping, a few more breaths and I would be, once again, my calm and placid self.

"And then they kill us?"

I smiled, "Maybe not, because..." I smiled at my pal. I hoped it was an evil smile.

He groaned, "Don't say it."

"...I have a plan," I said, Ted just rolled his eyes. The man has no poetry.

Silence descended after the vehicles left; we spent a bit of time looking out the windows to the dusty road. The front of the guardhouse had this small, reinforced door with a mesh-covered sliding window beside it. A little bench seat was outside in a pleasant garden; no doubt so any callers asked to wait could do so in comfort. How pleasant, how civilized. Anyone approaching the building could be screened by looking and talking through this window. Nice idea.

I got bored after a few minutes when no one turned up to kill us, bits of my body began to play up, and my pain centres felt it was a good time to bring in the status reports. That sort of thing. I knew if I sat around too much I would either fall unconscious or simply fall. Not a lot of fuel left in the old Valentine tank after the morning I had been through. I lurched to my feet and exited the building by the back door, a few steps brought me to my goal which I picked up and carried out to the front of the guardhouse. Soon I was arranging an artful package on the bench seat for all the world to see.

When I re-joined Ted, he indicated the package I had left, gave me a soulful look and said, "Pretty crass, man, even for you."

"Why don't you go and get our prisoners," I instructed Ted, "the ones we left tied together up near the main building; hopefully Max didn't burn them. Bring them down here and sit them in front of the drop gate. Be another suggestion of restraint for any unwanted guests who may come barging in. Human speed bumps."

He looked out at the bench seat, "Fair bit of restraint right there." He trundled off and I was soon alone with my thoughts and various bodily aches and pains. Ted poked and prodded our guests down the road before coming back into the guardhouse where he found me rummaging in various cupboards and drawers looking for painkillers.

"What are you doing?" he asked.

"Got a slight headache, thought there might be something here."

"How would you know if you found it? You can't read their script?"

He was right, I paused and considered his remark plus tried to think of a clever rejoinder. Not a thing.

A cloud of dust signalled the arrival of several large vehicles, one of which had a distinct look of luxury. The other vehicles were definitely troop carriers, I knew because a small army of humans and Tharls emerged from them. One particularly large Tharl - and we are talking continent size here - moved to the front passenger door of the luxury vehicle and deferentially opened the door. Ted and I watched as a human female got out, a very lovely human female. Very lovely indeed. She wore a figure-hugging full-length red dress made of a shiny yet sinuous material. Looking at her made you think of the word 'sinuous'.

I gurgled, Ted sighed.

She walked regally up the small path towards the gatehouse, all alone and - judging by the snug fit of her garb – unarmed. Her long dress was slit down one side revealing a highly attractive leg each time she took a step. I suggested Ted stop stepping on his tongue.

She paused at my little tableau on the waiting bench, studying the headless corpse of our recent child molester as it sat haughtily surveying the front drive. I had placed a small bouquet of flowers in one dead hand while the other arm stretched out casually along the back of the seat; I thought it added a homey touch. Her face never changed expression.

She began walking towards us again, slow and stately. I was getting a bit edgy, she seemed too self-possessed and confident for someone to be approaching a guardhouse full of murderous thugs. That'd be Ted and me. My nerve broke, "Stop right there!" I yelled, most of which came out in a squeak.

"Way to go, Val, that's the voice to terrify armies," muttered Ted.

I ignored him, "Stay where you are, honey, and no one gets hurt!" This time I sounded a bit more manly and gruff. Certainly enough to scare some slip of a girl.

"How sweet," she chuckled, "you're thinking no one will get hurt." She nodded towards my last victim, "Bit late, isn't it?" She stopped walking, put one hand on an outthrust hip and took up a stance to drive mortal men wild. "And who might you be, Mr Growly?"

"I'm the guy with a gun on you, sweetheart. Now just stand still and tell us what you're doing here." That should do it, real tough guy talk.

She mimicked me, "'I'm the guy with a gun on you, sweetheart', oh, that's priceless! Genuine brawler lingo. You could give performances, have your own act." We all went quiet for a few beats before she continued, "Is there someone else up there I can talk to? Someone with a brain?" Before I could riposte back some witty repartee she said, "Never mind, let me in and you can try to explain your way out of this mess. I don't give you much chance but so far you're a real hoot, I need a laugh after the day I've had."

She resumed walking up to the door while Ted and I exchanged furious looks and raging silences. His eyebrows wiggled questions, I pulled faces. And that's where we were when she knocked on the door. "Open up, boys, momma's home."

It seemed rude to leave her out there so I opened the door and let her in. She entered the room in sections, each piece worth long and serious study. Ted and I decided to remain standing for a bit longer until things settled down.

"Why, boys," she said, "I do believe you're pleased to see me." She flowed into the main room and perched on the arm of a large, soft chair. One bare leg swung gently to and fro, she took off a small jacket to let us see her upper body works and leaned back a little. Various bits of her anatomy thrust out.

I was a dead man.

"Care to tell me why you decided to break into my establishment, steal my property and then burn down a perfectly good building. Then, of course, there is the loss of my highly trained staff." She wore just enough make-up to make a man understand how beautiful a woman can be. My brain had wandered off along this line of thought until Ted poked me in the ribs.

"Yeah, about that," I said.

"He speaks!" she exclaimed.

I ignored the jibe, "Headless out there was sexually abusing the children. Did you know about that?"

She looked through the wall at where the recently deceased would be sitting, "Yes, I'd read the reports." She went still for a moment, "Probably about time he was retired, too much damage to the business."

"The business be damned!" I said. "You put a child molester in charge of children! And all you're concerned about is the loss of business."

"It's all business, darling. Is that why you came in here all guns blazing? To avenge the little ones and set them free from his brutal treatment? Are you just a do-gooder with a hero complex?" She studied Ted and me for a few moments, "Or is there something more behind it all? Are you deeper than you look?"

"Nah," said Ted, "Pretty much what you see is what you get."

"How disappointing," she said. "Still, let's move things along, shall we?" She stood and stretched, again placing Ted and me in danger of stepping on tongues. "Any particular reason I shouldn't just have you killed on the spot?"

Ted always did have good reflexes, he pulled his blaster out and pointed it at the girl. I took that as a hint. "You'd be first," I said. The knowledge that this woman was just another thug helped me to get my libido under control. I took a breath and entered the fray.

"We have the house, we have the children, and we have prisoners. Now is the time for talking deal." I said.

"Possibly not," she said. "Why don't I just have several dozen of my men come in and take it back?"

This conversation was making no sense, "Then why are you in here anyway? You knew something was wrong but you walked in here alone and unarmed. We could be any sort of killers, what do you know that keeps you safe?" This was the key question, I didn't think we were dealing with an incompetent, so why did she walk into the lion's den?

"What? You think I'm helpless? Oh, dear, don't you boys know who I am?"

This sounded bad. "No," I squeaked.

"I'm Ghost," she said.

Chapter 16

Talk about a conversation stopper. This rather beautiful woman was the head of criminal enterprises on this planet. Maybe. Then again, maybe not. My mouth took over, "I don't think you are Ghost. I think you are merely a flunky. A great looking flunky, but just one of the boys."

She thrust her chest out a little at this, "One of the boys! Are you serious?" she said.

"Poor choice of words, but you know what I mean."

"What makes you think I'm an also-ran?"

"You got out of the front passenger seat of the vehicle; it looks like the sort of carriage that has large and luxurious accommodation in the back - that's where the big wheels sit. The assistants sit up front." This was wing and a prayer stuff, I was just making it up as I went along. Fortunately, a part of my brain was thinking ahead and sent messages to my hands. I gripped a nearby chair with a thought to the future.

"Very clever, maybe there is a brain cell in there somewhere. Oh, well. I guess I better do my job since you've sucked all the fun out of the meeting." She stood up and stretched her arms up to the ceiling which set bits of her anatomy to jiggle. Ted's gun wavered a little and I started to lift the chair off the floor.

I'm pretty sure she had used this technique many times before. Many, many times. All her stretching and lounging was designed to cause nearby males to be awash in desire; a great trick and one which would have normally had me panting with the best of them. But something wasn't quite right, she was a bit off, a bit too extreme in her poses and sexual display. Plus, me being a naturally suspicious lad, I couldn't help wondering why a total doll like this was playing footsie with a couple of ne'er do well guardsmen.

She turned her stretch into a slow spin and then kicked out with one foot to sweep Ted's gun out of his hand. I enjoyed the fleeting look of surprise on his face. I would remind him of it later over and over again, because I'm a mate and mates are supposed to keep other mates humble. I'm very big on humble.

Her right hand pulled out a small blaster from somewhere and her other hand grasped a small knife which leapt towards Ted's throat. Things were about to get very red and messy.

I threw the chair at her, it was heavy and I'm strong. It hit her leg and hip, causing her to bounce into the wall so I followed it up with another heavy chair and all the sting went out of her. She lay in a tangle of arms and legs - very attractive legs - with her head doing a slow loll. I recognized that loll, it's the one you get when some bozo clocks you on the head; the second chair had caught her a healthy thwack across the forehead. No blood or broken bones, thank goodness, that would have been a real waste.

Ted picked up his blaster, pointed it at the girl and gave me an embarrassed look.

"I should bloody well think so, sport," I said to him. "What were you thinking?"

"Sorry," he muttered.

The woman started to get to her feet but I convinced her to stay down by another chair - I seemed to be big on chairs for some reason - I put another one over her body thus pinning her to the ground. Then I sat in the chair. "How you doin'?" I asked.

"Get off me, you clod! You hurt me!"

"Hey, you're the one who attacked us," I replied. "Be fair." I wriggled the chair, "Now, I've got a proposition for you." She stopped moving and fixed me with a cool stare, I could see the wheels turning. Ted was also giving me a questioning look because he had no idea what I was doing.

I smiled at him, "I have a plan."

"Does it involve you dying?" she said. "Because I am totally on board with that plan", she groaned as she tried again to get to her feet.

"Stay where you are, princess," I said. "On the floor, on your back, hands over your head." This woman was far too dangerous to be allowed on her feet, better to keep her off balance.

"On my back and at your feet! What are you, some sicko? Is this your fantasy position? Come near me with your pants down, buddy, and you will lose the will to live!"

We all paused for breath, I moved off the chair and she assumed the required position, Ted and I had guns out and pointing.

"How about you just shut up and listen? That way your boss can hear what I have to say" I said.

"What boss?" asked Ted, looking around.

"I'm betting she has a communicator; I also think the reason we are not knee-deep in the forty thieves out there is because she has not sent them a distress call. Yet." I gestured for her to stand up.

"You just hit her with a chair," said Ted. "That's not going to cause distress?"

"Two chairs," I corrected. "She's a tough chick, aren't you, princess? Got a name? You can get up. Slowly."

She groaned again, "There will be a bit of blood and pain after this, Tall, Dark and Gruesome. All of it yours." She slowly stood up, popping a few kinks out of her elbows and knees. I didn't shoot her because I was hoping we had reached another level of the negotiations. Ted followed my lead but he did step back a pace out of swinging foot range.

"We took out your kiddie daycare centre so you would come here and we could meet," I said. "I was looking for a meeting with The Syndicate and Ghost."

"Mission accomplished, Bozo," she said. My well-known charm was having its usual effect. "Get to the point."

"How would you like to be given a complete Trading Ship, full of lovely items and Trade Goods?" I asked.

"Hello, darling, my name's Louise. Keep talking."

Ted shifted his feet and muttered growly noises.

"Shut up, Ted, mum and I need to talk," I said.

I smiled at her, "How you doin', Louise?"

"Are you saying you planned this whole raid just to have a sit down with me?" she asked.

"I was thinking of seeing Ghost, trying to cut out the middleman. No offence," I said.

"I've told you, I am Ghost. Talk to me."

"Want to pull back your hair a little, let us see your beautiful ears?" I suggested.

She smiled and raised her left hand to pull back the golden locks, nestled in her ear was a small object; it had a certain familiarity about it.

"She's wearing a Translator Bead!" said Ted.

"Yeah, well......no," I said. "That's a little communicator isn't it, Louise? Probably out to the vehicle, the comfy back seat. Who's there? Ghost?"

Louise picked up her jacket, Ted twitched and heroically refrained from shooting her. She raised her eyebrows at him but restricted her movements to the non-threatening variety. "Can't a girl get dressed around you guys?"

"Dressed, yes. Armed - no" I said. "Where did you hide the weapons, anyway?" I asked. Her dress was marvellously snug, quite wonderful really. She opened the flap of her little jacket to reveal two small, fitted holsters, just the thing for her miniature blaster and tiny knife.

"Tell me about the Trading Ship," she instructed. "You might get to live another day."

"Can Ghost hear me?"

"Forget Ghost," she said, "talk to me."

"I dunno, Louise, your negotiation skills are a bit limited. Got anything else besides sexual teasing and random violence?"

"I do a mean salad. Now talk."

"We're on the security team of that Trading Ship which was almost hijacked by your dumbass pirates." This caused her to mutter under her breath, I guessed she was having a quick consultation with a higher authority.

"Do you know someone called Valentine?" she asked.

Small pause. "Maybe," I replied. "Why?"

"We have reports that it was him who caused us to lose the ship. Not happy with him."

Ted is not just a pretty face, he chimed in by saying, "He can be a dick."

"Let's stick to the point, do you want the ship or not?" I said.

"Let me get this straight," she said. "You are saying you can take over the ship and hand it to us."

"We already have control of it."

"What about Valentine?" she asked.

"Won't be a problem," I said.

More muttering. She finally looked up and said, "We can do business. What do you want?"

"Can we meet the boss?"

"No. Next question?"

"Why not?"

"Ghost doesn't meet just anybody. You can deal with me".

I turned around and walked towards the front door. "Let's go, Ted." We made it out the door and a few steps down the path before she caught up with us, it must be hard to run in high heels.

She grabbed my arm, "Wait!" I kept walking, she was little and I'm not; she was pulled along a few feet. "Stop!" she said, "Where are you going?"

"Out to your vehicle. Thought I'd check out the back seat."

A group of Tharls strode between us and the vehicle, all had empty hands and nasty eyes. Little, brutish eyes full of malevolence and a predisposition to violence - pretty standard for a Tharl, they could have been thinking about dinner and a show yet still look like they wanted to murder someone's mother.

The three of us stopped, I could tell Ted was considering using the old equalizer so I placed a conciliatory hand on his arm. A rather flustered Louise pushed in front of me, pushed a wayward lock of hair out of her eye and jabbed me in the chest. "Do you have a death wish? The only thing keeping you alive and undamaged is the barest possibility that you could help us get that Trading Ship. And I have to say I am just about willing to give it up to dance on your spleen."

She seemed upset, time for me to use my well-known people skills. I gave her a little push, just a shove, hardly anything in it; she fell onto her rump with a surprised "Oof!" I got the impression she wasn't used to having men treat her in such a cavalier fashion - the old Valentine charm still has a place in the world. Also, I had noticed something in the sky approaching our little conclave.

"Shoot this clod!" she shrieked and out came a lot of shooty things, all aimed at me.

We were interrupted by an amplified voice, "DROP YOUR WEAPONS!" Up in the sky was a flying machine, all whirly bits and flashing lights; funny badges adorned the sides, badges I recognized as belonging to the local police force.

Hanging out of a side door was my old pal, Sergeant Thulani. He had his own big shooty thing pointed at all and sundry but his had a little red dot on it. The dot was sitting squarely over Louise's head.

The machine landed and a variety of armed coppers stormed out to discuss gun safety with anyone interested. The Tharls quickly returned their weapons to various hidden pockets until we all stood around like old chums, each of us with bulging bits in our clothes.

"Allo, Allo, What's all this, then?" asked Sergeant Thulani, in a wonderful rendition of Policeman Plod.

Louise had struggled to her feet, "Go away, little man. We are having a private conversation."

The sergeant turned to me, "Got your message, Val. Need a ride home?"

"You betcha," I replied. Ted and I waved goodbye to the assembled throng and climbed aboard the flying machine. "See you around, Louise. Tell Ghost the deal's off."

She was spluttering, turning a shade of red to match her dress, "You're Valentine!!" I gave her a wink and blew her a kiss before settling into a seat next to Ted. He was looking at me with quiet awe.

"Told you I had a plan," I said.

"You're amazing, Val," he said.

Ain't that the truth, I thought.

Chapter 17

When we arrived back in the city I was unloaded into a small, quiet room to await further questioning. I was used to this process, given the number of times I upset the rules it seemed only reasonable for the powers that be to hold me accountable. It was all very understandable and I had developed a useful routine for these debriefs. At its heart, I was always trying to see if I could make my questioner's head explode.

Sergeants Thulani and Frenzek entered the room, followed by The Man in Black; I could see I was going to have to bring my A-game to this discussion. The trio arranged themselves according to some invisible protocol. The Man in Black sat on the only chair, Thulani stood beside the door, crossed his arms and leaned back against the wall. Frenzek stood next to The Man in Black and leaned on the table, taking all his weight on both arms. I recognised the pose, aggressive and in your face – Intimidation Level 1.

A good start, I countered with Innocent Victim Stance. I stood up, hands correctly clasped behind my back in approved military fashion with my posture indicating a soldier willing and eager to serve. My eyes were fixed on a spot on the opposite wall, just above Thulani's head. I did not, of course, start the conversation. Less is more in these situations.

"Ah," said the Man in Black, "we're playing that game, are we, Sergeant Valentine?"

I remained silent. He sighed and clasped his hands together on the tabletop, "Let's review, shall we? A quick look back over your recent history."

This was not going to end well.

"There were a few fatalities around you back in the City, before we embarked upon the Trading Ship." The Man in Black leaned forward a little before continuing, "I even witnessed you performing your duty in a very admirable fashion with a few torturers. A few now deceased torturers. If I haven't said it before, allow me to congratulate you on your efficiency in the performance of your duties."

"Thank you, sir. Happy to be in the service!" I said. Definitely not going to end well. Anytime your bosses say you are doing a good job you know you are doomed.

"And once we joined the ship you managed to upset some powerful people by killing that young female thief. Decapitation, as I recall. Then you were down on the planet and struggled to confine yourself to just a few deaths. The most significant, of course, being Captain Chayla the Tharl and some psychotic priest. Have I missed anyone, Sergeant?"

"Couldn't say, sir, too busy running away," I replied. Frenzek grunted, Thulani continued his impression of a statue.

"Well, you managed to thin out the shipboard population a little during the recent ... unpleasantness; before riding a sled down onto this planet's surface and destroying a small fishing cabin as well as injuring an escaping pirate. Whom I believe you subsequently killed."

"Just a misunderstanding, sir. Could have happened to anyone," I replied. Silence wandered about.

There was a small pause in this litany before my boss went on, "The bodies form large piles, Sergeant. And if you're not actually doing the killing you seem to be enmeshed in situations where people just die. People like Captain Boaths. What is this skill, you have, Sergeant?"

"Couldn't say, sir. Too busy trying to stay alive," I replied. The numbers do seem to add up when you lay them all out.

"Prisoners in jail, mob bosses, enforcers, stand over merchants and assorted killers. Child kidnappers and abusers. All grist to the Valentine mill. You seem to have a knack for violence and mayhem."

"I'm an equal opportunity thug, sir," I said, eyes fixed on the opposite wall, back straight, thumbs running down the side of my pants. I believe I may have quivered in my determination to be Sergeant Perfect.

Frenzek sighed, "I had no idea you were such a walking health risk. Have you always been this way?"

"I don't understand the question, Sergeant." When in doubt, confuse the issue.

The Man in Black leaned back in his chair, "Val, I can't afford to leave you alone. With Magic off-planet, you don't seem to have anyone who can ... navigate ... your life choices." He looked up at Frenzek, "Would you be willing to help out here?"

Frenzek grimaced, turned and sat on the desk and said, "Not a chance, sir. Valentine is a useful man on those rare occasions when mindless action is called for. That's not a big part of my day." He looked at me over his shoulder and then glanced back at Thulani, "What about you?"

Thulani snorted.

I remained as still as possible, part of my brain trying to cope with what I was hearing. First of all, Frenzek called the Man in Black 'sir'. This, while quite normal for us knuckle draggers, seemed to be a significant statement from someone like Frenzek who was, I am sure, far more than a mere sergeant. He seemed to have a lot of political pull, but he still called my boss "sir".

The second, and far more salient point, was their seeming dilemma in dealing with me. This reiteration of some of the more colourful episodes in my life didn't make any sense to me. Unless, and here I could see the devious hand of the Man in Black, unless they had a cunning plan in mind and wanted me on board.

I cleared my throat.

"Something to say, Sergeant?" asked the Man in Black. I felt all three turn eyes of significance on me.

"I was wondering if I could possibly volunteer for some hazardous duty, sir?" I asked.

Thulani grunted again, Frenzek said to the Man in Black, "Damn, you were right, sir. He is a devious bastard."

"Come for a walk, Sergeant," instructed the Man in Black. He got up and moved towards the door which Thulani opened for him. I noticed this display of deference from the big, scarred sergeant and tucked it away in my mental room, the place in my head where I keep all the junk stuff. It was getting full.

I coughed a gentle, questioning sort of cough, "Something on your mind, Val?" asked the Man in Black.

"Just wondering what happened to the kids from the farm, sir," I said. "And also, Don'elk. He may be worth occasional serious questioning. I'd be happy to participate, he seems to like me, I think we have a bond."

"A bond, you say?" said my boss.

"Old shipmates, we are, sir. I'm sure he'd appreciate a little one-on-one time with me. Especially if I could have a hammer."

"Not going to happen, sergeant," he said. "He has, of course, filed a complaint of brutality against you. I believe Meataxe is supervising the paperwork."

I snuck a look at him, "Meataxe, sir?" I asked. "Handling actual paperwork?"

The Man in Black nodded, "Of course," he said. "He is my aide. I'm sure he will process the appropriate forms with his usual efficiency and competence." We had to stop while the boss turned and faced the wall, he waved me back but I'm sure I saw his shoulders heaving, there may have been chuckles escaping. He pulled himself together and we resumed our stroll.

"We've released Don'elk, he does us more good on the loose," he said. "His plans usually go awry and he ends up in trouble. Remind you of anyone, Val?"

"Is that a veiled reference to my own work, sir?" I asked.

"I do apologise, sergeant, it was not meant to be veiled in any way," said the boss. He clapped me on the shoulder and went on, "But the children – well done there. You won't go far wrong looking after the weak and helpless. Once they are released from the hospital, we will find a place to put them. In the interim, we will place them under the supervision of Wallace and H'nuth. They both asked to look after the children and the little ones seemed to like them."

"Ye gods, sir," I said. "You're putting vulnerable children under the care of those two? Children are easily influenced, or so I'm told. Is that wise, sir?"

"Are you working under the assumption this is a negotiation, sergeant?" he asked. A slight chill of steel wafted in his breath.

I shut up.

We trundled down a few floors and eventually came to a small set of rooms with access to street level. Two points of access, actually – one, quite obviously, led to an office reception area; useful for welcoming some sort of clientele. The other was the door through which we entered - a nondescript opening tucked behind some potted plants and decorative furniture. They could have been chairs but I was willing to bet no one would ever sit in them.

"Welcome to your new home, sergeant", said the Man in Black, gesturing to the reception area. A small reception desk stood guard over another doorway leading to the deeper bowels of the complex.

"Does it come in blue, sir?" I asked.

We walked behind the reception desk, through the door behind it and came into a large, open office area. Desks were scattered about in what may have been a highly efficient layout but, since I hate desk work, I really didn't care. In the centre of the room was a larger table where many important meetings could be held. No doubt it had seen much action already because I spotted nicks and gouges across the surface, stains showed where cups and plates had been placed on its once fine surface. The chairs were a mixed bunch, no two alike. I was sure I was looking at a lot of rejected office supplies.

"Let's all sit down, shall we," instructed the boss. We sat. I picked a chair that looked like it might last the day.

He leaned forward and clasped hands on the tabletop, Thulani leaned back in his chair with little regard for personal safety and stretched out his arms before placing them behind his head and looking bored. Frenzek just sat and gave me his best non-committal copper face. It's a good look and I've used it myself many times – so I knew bad things were coming.

"Not feeling the love, sir," I said.

The Man in Black stretched his fingers, "Sergeant Frenzek and I have been investigating a growing list of crimes, all of which seem to be based on this planet. Piracy, murder, extortion, kidnapping, the list gets bigger every day."

He paused and I took the opportunity to do nothing.

"I have been tasked by the Trader's Council to work with the government of the planet in investigating the root cause of all of this. We suspect it may go quite high, Sergeant Frenzek – incidentally he is not a sergeant, he is the confidential aide for their planet's president."

"Bit like Meataxe, then, sir," I said. "He's your confidential aide. I bet the two of them have a lot in common." I looked at Frenzek and winked, he rolled his eyes. "Do you two swap tips and tricks? You know, Aide stuff?" I asked.

"Let it go, Val" replied Frenzek. "Listen to Lord Franz", he nodded towards the Man in Black. "This will help us find the killer of Captain Boaths."

I quieted down, I liked the old captain. Someone had blown his head off while he was negotiating with a supposedly friendly group. Someone who wanted him silent. And I wanted that someone dead.

"Back in the City," said the Man in Black, "you were a rank-and-file guardsman, a member of the NightWatch which was a lovely collection of the lost, the forlorn, the angry and the mad. I understand the squad led by Magic seemed to be the final gathering place of those found incapable of getting along with even the rest of the NightWatch. Your squad not only survived but you were a part of this team for some years. Years, Valentine, when most Watchman in that position lasted months."

I could feel all the eyes on me, never a good thing.

"And then," he continued, "we all became swept up in this mayhem. You were promoted to squad leader and then to sergeant. You find in yourself qualities of leadership, qualities which the other men - and women - of the Watch have come to recognise. And, hence, you are widely regarded as the one, true sergeant of the NightWatch. It doesn't matter that others outrank you, all seem to defer to you and they will follow you willingly. That is quite a skill set you have, Sergeant Valentine."

"Mad, sir," I said.

"I beg your pardon," he asked.

"Put me down in the 'mad' category, sir. And a fair dose of 'angry,'" I replied.

He hemmed a little before continuing, "Yes, I can see that. In a crisis, you are usually angry and certainly mad. You also have the ability to find a way out."

"Generally, by hitting something, sir" Thulani contributed. Didn't want to feel left out of the conversation.

"Or someone," put in Frenzek.

"Still not feeling the love, sir," I added.

"We're in a bit of a tight spot, Sergeant. I have been commissioned to investigate, with Sergeant Frenzek, and we have found out much. But we are stymied in the next step in our path.

Neither of us are allowed to ...do certain things in the course of our investigation."

I could see the boulder coming at me now, a big rock rolling downhill. I was being set up here.

Chapter 18

"Plenty of handy lads in the Watch, sir, I suggested. "Lots of the chaps enjoy a good, vigorous investigation. Especially one involving some property destruction. I could probably organise volunteers by the end of the day. Happy to serve, sir."

"Yes," he mused, "no doubt. Unfortunately, we cannot involve the NightWatch in their usual shenanigans. Sergeant Frenzek and I are engaged in a delicate dance. We have to, as it were, subcontract out a few tasks."

"Don't see how I can help then, sir. I do know a few likely lads from the prison but none are what you would call heavy hitters." I could see his problem. But since I was also in the NightWatch then .... oh, dear. A strange and uncomfortable thought came to me.

"You say you can't use anyone in the Watch, sir?"

He nodded. Frenzek started to fiddle.

"And these are my new rooms?" I asked, looking around the awful place with new eyes.

"Yes, I'm kicking you out of the Watch, Sergeant. Crimes against society, bad influence on others, no self-control, a very poor representative of the high standards to which we aspire in our role to protect and serve."

Thulani snickered, "Protect and serve! Val's more of the Hit and Run type."

"Glad you feel that way, Sergeant Thulani," said Frenzek, "because you will be joining Valentine in his new endeavour. You, too, are being expelled from the police and must fall back on a career in private law enforcement and security consultancy."

There are those moments in life one treasures, the wedding to a loved one, the birth of a child, winning a large bet and then there was today - watching Thulani's face.

I do believe there was an actual splutter before he started speaking, "What? No!" He pulled himself together before continuing, "But..." You can't pay for this stuff, I thought.

"Settle down, Sergeant Thulani," said the Man in Black. We all took a breath. He gazed around at each of us. "You are now two of the primary investigators in a security consultancy firm. As such, you may be hired by anyone, including government agencies, to conduct a variety of tasks."

"I don't understand," muttered Thulani. "Just get me to do the investigation, I'm already in the police force. You don't need an outside agency." He looked at me and must have been put off by my grin. "What?" he asked.

"I suspect we are to be the naughty boys in this recipe." I turned to the boss, "I'm guessing there is a small investigation that may require the application of NightWatch subtlety."

Thulani looked blank, the Man in Black grimaced and Frenzek sighed deeply. "Subtlety and Valentine are complete strangers," he said.

The Man in Black stood up, and so did Frenzek. I stayed where I was and when Thulani began to rise he was gestured back into his seat by Frenzek. "Stay here, Thulani. I need you to keep an eye on this character and make sure he doesn't step too far out of the bounds of decency. You will also report to me your progress each day."

"Our progress?" Thulani mumbled. He was taking this hard, poor lamb.

"Just the two of us, sir?" I asked. "We're good, but I'm not sure if we're that good."

"No," my boss replied, "you're not. Take two more, you can't have Teddy Boy or Right Honourable - I need them to run things. Not sure if anyone else has the required set of skills." He mused a bit, before musing "I don't suppose Meataxe....?"

He stopped; my face must have given it away. "No, possibly not. Any thoughts?"

I sat for a moment, "How about I take Wallace and H'Nuth? Both strong hitters, both capable of thinking on the spot. I think they'd fit right into this team." This might also get them out of looking after a bunch of smelly, noisy children; I'm sure they would thank me later.

They moved to the door, "And neither have a long history with the NightWatch, plenty of deniability there," said the Man in Black. "They are all yours." He looked around the large room and said, "I think the children will like this place. And take Greenash for the technical stuff."

"Children? Technical stuff, sir?" I asked. My brain had split in two, both sections raising alarm flags. "We're going to be knee-deep in rug rats and I have to know technical things!"

He sighed again. Seemed to be a lot of that about recently, "Yes, you may need some help in finding buttons, blinking lights and on/off switches. Things that require a knowledge of the arcane world of technology." He ruffled my hair, surely a breach of Lord/commoner protocol, and said, "You're just a big kid yourself, Val. The children will feel right at home with you, they already talk of you as their hero. Something about a man's head."

The door shut on our two overlords, leaving me with a stunned Thulani. I looked around the room, wondering where I could hide from children. What else would we need? Perhaps we could get some of the clever devices which allowed one to have hot drinks any time. And a food preparation area wouldn't hurt, either. A list was forming in my mind, a list of things to make life more comfortable.

Perhaps Greenash could be of some use after all. But I was staying well away from any children.

Chapter 19

It was only after he left that I realised The Man in Black had not referred to my predicament. After my last little adventure, I was pretty sure the criminal underworld – especially those following this 'Ghost' character – would be after my head. My erstwhile commander-in-chief had not given any hints on how I was to carry out whatever tasks he had for me while staying alive on the streets.

It's nice to know that people have faith in your abilities but a little sympathy and some reassuring words would not have gone astray.

I got up and poked around the room for a bit, opening cupboards and generally just filling in the time while Thulani calmed down. After a few minutes, he sighed and said, "I really hate you, Valentine."

There didn't seem to be anything I could say to this comment, I could see his point of view. So, against all my previous history, I kept quiet. I needed to get out, to wander about the area and find a few dark alleys in which I could hide. I needed to get the lay of the land and, hopefully, find a hole I could crawl into before various street gangs danced on my spine. "I'm going out," I said.

Thulani grunted and stood up, "I better come with you. I wouldn't want to miss the next act in this sorry drama."

As I passed him, I clapped him on the shoulder and said, "That's the spirit, Thul, always look for the bright side".

He shouldered past me and out the door, grunting, "Don't call me 'Thul'". I smiled and followed my new best friend out into the jungles of the city.

We spent the rest of the day mooching about. We explored crowded streets, roamed down lonely, dark spaces between structures, climbed to the viewing platforms of buildings and generally tried to stay invisible while surrounding ourselves with lots of innocent bystanders. We stayed out of low taverns, seedy clubs and anything resembling a gathering place of lowlifes; it was only the clean and the decent locations for us - I felt well out of my depth.

Thulani booked us into a small boarding house which did not require identification. When he told me it was a place for those plying the sex trade, I couldn't help myself - as we started up the stairs, I gave his bum a squeeze in full view of the lounging desk clerk.

"I hate you, Valentine," he whispered.

The room was fine and we negotiated rules for sharing the only bed. Thulani's rules consisted of him stating he would pound me if he was touched in any way. Seemed fair. We chatted like two lovers before drifting off to sleep, I vocalised the issues as I saw them, "My original plan was to cause a bit of havoc for this 'Ghost' character and his organisation. Then see what would happen, shake things up a bit. I wanted to do this because he had tried to cause me harm a few times and I am a vengeful soul."

"Let me get this straight," he said. "This organisation was out to get you because you had interfered with their takeover of a Trading vessel. You had also contributed to a grand investigation being conducted on this planet into their affairs. You wrecked their ventures, killed their personnel, and brought the entire organisation to the attention of the authorities. You created havoc and cost them huge sums of money. When they retaliated, you took offence. Your solution was to cause them even more harm by breaking up one of their farm operations?"

"Correct," I agreed.

"And the cherry on top was your humiliation of Ghost's number two, the woman. You made her a public laughingstock by fooling her and besting her in combat."

"Again, correct. You're getting good at this whole line of argument thing, Thul."

"Don't call me Thul. And in your head, by escalating the damage, by causing even more mayhem, you hoped they might...what? Forgive you? Forget about it all? Realise you are just a heck of a nice guy? Maybe send you some flowers?"

"When you put it like that it sounds so ... ordinary," I said. "Surely you see the romance of the whole package." If I kept up this banter there was a chance I would see his head explode, he was already getting redder. Is that a word?

"And now you have lost the protection of being a member of the NightWatch. You have no resources; you are hunted by every villain in the city and yet your commander – your ex-commander – intends to give you another hazardous task."

He paused for a moment; I lay there with my eyes shut trying to think of a way out of this mess. "You're bringing me down, man," I said. I mentally reviewed all he had said and could spot a few flaws in my chain of logic. As I began regretting my hasty ways another thought popped into my head, "And on top of it all," I said, "I also needed to consider 'The Case of the Stolen Child.'"

"Sounds like a bad detective story," he said. "What are you talking about?"

"Remember Amadi and his cousin, Emilii," I said. "We ran across that ratbag father of hers."

"What," he asked, "do you intend to do about any of this?"

I gave a snore and pretended to be asleep, mainly because I had no answer but also because I thought it might annoy him some more. I'm very shallow. The fatigue of the day, both physical and emotional, was catching up and I did feel myself descending into the calming arms of slumber.

As I drifted off, I heard Thulani mutter, "I hate you, Valentine."

Seemed fair.

Chapter 20

The next day we snuck into the new office and found Greenash sitting in the reception room behind the fancy desk. It had a set of screens and lots of wires and switchy things so I assumed the Man in Black had given him instructions. No children, so far.

"Morning, Greenash," I said with a twinkle in my eye. He looked at me with a face devoid of cheer. His mouth formed a large arc dragging his cheeks into his boots. Bleary eyes looked out of a face drawn and haggard, his hair was dishevelled and I saw hands twitching and turning. All the signs of a diligent labourer who has been toiling away the entire night.

Leaning on the raised front edge of the counter I asked, "What have you been up to, my old son?" I noticed a cup on his desk with a small wisp of steam rising from its obviously hot contents. "What's in the cup? And is there any more?" I queried.

He sighed, stood up and picked up his cup before giving me a resigned look. "This way," he said.

We went into the back room with the large centre table. Along one wall was a long bench atop which sat a variety of new machines and devices. I followed my teammate as he walked to one of the machines and opened a cupboard to extract another cup which he put under a small nozzle. He pushed levers, pulled handles and twisted nobs until the machine gurgled and a stream of something hot came out of the nozzle into the cup.

When the machine stopped gurgling, Greenash handed me the cup and raised his own in a small toast. I looked at the contents of my cup, the liquid was dark, villainous-looking and strongly smelling of a dark flavour. A dark, rich flavour. I took a sip.

My day improved considerably.

"This is amazing, Greenash!" I said. Thulani made himself a cup of the liquid and took himself off to a side bench covered in shiny things. He seemed to brighten a little, I assumed they were weapons.

Greenash smiled at me and waved around the room. "I've installed a range of devices, stuff we will need. I'm working on a method for communication, hubs to let me talk directly to our nanobots. Been at it all night, no progress at all. I need to do more research and go over Slynkor's notes again."

"Uh, huh," I grunted, having no idea what he was talking about. I sipped and thought about what he had just said. "So, these hub things can let me, what, talk to these bugs running around inside my body. Why would I want to talk to my little beasties?" I asked.

"Not you. The hub lets us communicate. Or it will, once I work out the protocols Slynkor put in. Then we will be able to talk to each other," he replied.

"You can talk to me now, Greenash. In fact, we are talking. Now," I said. I moved to one of the chairs around the side of the room and sat down.

He sighed again before placing a small, flat object in front of me, "I was asked to give you this," he said.

I looked at the technical piece of equipment. About the shape of a small book, it had a screen embedded across most of its top surface. Great, I thought, more stuff. "What's it do, Greenash?"

"You must have seen these before?" he asked. I looked at him and he looked at me. Finally, he muttered, "I had heard the stories about you; it seems they are true." He reached a thin finger towards the device to press a small button on its side. The screen lit up and a small box appeared in the centre of the screen. "This is a data pad. The commander asked me to give it to you."

"Because I've been a good boy?" I asked.

Another groan, "I may need another drink," he said. "This probably contains information he wants you to have without anyone else knowing about it. Place your finger on the screen in the box, it will only respond to you."

"What happens if someone else puts their finger in the box?" I asked as I extended my hand towards the screen.

He swallowed before replying, "The finger would be severed, acid would also be sprayed into the user's face."

I pulled my hand back quickly, "Really?!"

"No," he smiled, "I just wanted to see your face. Anyone else trying to access the data would result in the contents being erased. Essentially, the data would just disappear."

I looked at the small device and tried to understand how it could not only contain information but also have some way of destroying it for the wrong person. I put the thought into the "stuff I don't know and don't care about" file – another big section in my brain.

After I pushed my finger onto the screen another face appeared, a face I knew - the Man in Black.

"Well done, Val," he said, "still prepared to put your finger in strange places, eh?" he chuckled. I opened my mouth to say something disrespectful but he cut me off, "Don't bother replying, this is just a recording." I shut my mouth. "Right, since you are no longer a member of the NightWatch you can undertake a few jobs which might be viewed with some misgivings by the coppers of this planet. There are some documents on this tablet you will need to read – I know, stop whining – but they won't take you long. Basically, I need you to go to a certain address and obtain some evidence. We can't do it because this planet has some quaint notions about privacy and rights of the individual. Can't fathom it."

He looked off-screen and spoke to someone I couldn't see, "Yes, tell them I'm coming." He looked back to me and went on "Be careful, Val, we understand you now have a significant contract on your head. To sum up, I need you to go somewhere very dangerous, do something incredibly stupid and avoid being shot, stabbed or otherwise maimed by large numbers of the local citizenry. When you've finished reading the attached document, place your finger on the red dot at the bottom of the screen."

His face disappeared and was replaced by what looked like a sheet of paper, I touched it and the thing expanded to fill the screen allowing me to read a lot of words, at least they were in English. I groaned and settled in, reaching for my cup and thinking fondly of alcohol. Time passed, Greenash wandered about and Thulani played with things that, presumably, went bang. I gave him a hurt look and went back to the document; the last line was an address that I committed to memory. Coming from a planet without a lot of recording mechanisms is useful because we, in the NightWatch, are good at memorisation. When you cannot write stuff down you have to be able to lock it away in the old skull. Even Meataxe can generally remember his own name. On a good day. With the wind behind him.

At the bottom of the screen was the red dot. After thinking about what I had read I placed my finger on it and was not surprised when the screen blanked. I placed it back on the table and Greenash picked it up, "Are you all done with it?" he asked.

I nodded and he took it to a large metal cupboard. He placed the tablet in the cupboard, shut the door and pushed some buttons. There was a loud "thunk" noise. He removed the tablet and tossed it into a junk pile. "Have you done something destructive, Greenash?" I asked.

"Just wiped the tablet, pretty much destroyed it. I hope you can remember what was on there because it has gone forever. I'll melt the whole thing down later," he said. He sat across from me and went on "So, what now?"

"Good question," I replied. "I have been given a task by the Man in Black, a task for which I am well suited. A little bit of burglary, possibly some light violence and more than likely a touch of mayhem. My only problem was I had no idea where to find this place."

"Do you have an address?" asked Thulani. I told him. Both he and Greenash did things with small screens while I stared into space. "I've got it," said Thulani. "A small club, a known haunt of our local villains. You'll never get in."

"What'll you do?" asked Greenash.

"Not to worry, my small, wizened friend. For I am a changed man, no more running headlong into situations. I leave behind me the practice of unthinking destruction".

I heard Thulani gurgling behind me as I finished up my eloquent little speech, "For now, I..." small, significant pause, "... have a plan."

"I hate you, Valentine," said Thulani.

The problem was the address. I could find the location but rushing over there without some thought might prove detrimental to my health. Mainly, I did not know what sort of place it was. Even casually wandering past it might set off some sort of alarm – criminal masterminds usually do not have a lot of foot traffic outside their secret headquarters. Thulani had no more information about the club and, since we were no longer coppers, we couldn't just bash our way in. Well, we could, but I suspected my boss wanted me to be clever. Poor man, living in dreamland.

My experience with nasty people in power consisted of various ecclesiastical members of the church. The ones who were ecclesiastical and corrupt. As such, they surrounded themselves with layers of protection including thuggish brutes, cunning planners and hordes of suspicious sods ready to view my normal lumbering approach with homicidal intent.

Given that background, plus the fact I was not backed up by a sizable cohort of my own thugs like the boys and girls in the NightWatch, I felt the need to be sneaky. Not my strong suit. I needed someone who could tell me about the building, someone who knew the area. Someone who may have a slightly criminal bent to their life. Thulani had already ruled himself out and we didn't want to raise suspicions by using his contacts.

My two recent cell mates, Amadi the pickpocket and Babajide the arsonist, came to mind. Further investigation of these two may be useful, plus I could find out more about Emilii. I cheered myself with the thought that I was acting like a real copper. I set out to see how they were doing at the shop, Thulani tagged along - most likely hoping to pick up a few tips about detecting.

At the shop I paused, realising I had no cover story for being here again. I doubt if either of my erstwhile cellmates would be delighted to assist me if I told them the truth so perhaps some positive spin was needed for my mission. Pushing open the door, I strolled in and called out, "Hi kids, I'm home!"

The shop was empty but I hoped someone would emerge from the back rooms. We waited. Thulani leaned against the counter, I riffled through some odds and ends on the bench – no one appeared.

"Not big on customer service," grunted Thulani. I moved around the counter and into the back room. Amadi's father, Bako, was lying in a small heap in the corner.

The heap wasn't moving.

Chapter 21

Thulani crossed and squatted beside the old man, he grunted, "He's alive, but badly beaten. I'll get help." He pulled a communicator out and spoke into it for a few moments. Thulani told me to stay with the old man while he went outside and waited for the Emergency Vehicle. I sat on the floor and stoked the old man's forehead. It seemed a quiet act of consolation was called for.

The old man groaned, I whispered some reassuring sounds and continued to stroke his forehead. His eyes flickered open and he raised his head, briefly catching my eye before his eyes closed again and he slumped back down. After a few more moments he murmured something. I shifted position so I was closer to his mouth.

"Find my son, Mr Valentine," he whispered. "He went looking for those responsible for all this pain, he is just a boy, not used to violence. He will be killed by the Syndicate. His grandmother, his Bunica, is already looking for him."

Another mention of the Syndicate. "Where did they go?" I asked.

He was quiet and still for so long that I thought he may have fallen unconscious; his hand moved to a pocket to pull out a small round coin. As he succumbed to the pain, he opened his hand, and the coin clattered to the floor. I picked it up, pocketing the item just as Thulani re-entered the room with some Emergency workers.

They treated the old man, told us his injuries would be painful but not life-threatening and took him out to their vehicle - they would take the old man to the hospital for a more intensive check.

Thulani and I watched the vehicle drive off as I told him what the old man had said. "He said the grandmother is already looking for Amadi," I said. "That would be this Bunica person."

"Bunica is not her name, it's an affectionate term for grandmother. Makes sense, even if it is dangerous for an old lady to swim in these waters," said Thulani. "Amadi and Babadji would be known as associates of yours; any slight infringement they made would have served as an excuse to inflict a severe response - when you killed Calcout you placed anyone close to you in danger. It would be known that Amadi and Babadji visited you so it would only have been a matter of time before the family's shop became a target. I assume the gang came here with demands for an increase in payments – which wasn't possible – so they beat the old man."

"But it wasn't just any gang, the old man said it was the Syndicate," I said.

Thulani looked at me, paused and asked, "Anything else?"

His gaze never wavered from me. He knew there was more to come, I tried a comment for deflection, "That's a world-class stone face you have there, Thulani." The silence stretched on. "Oh, heck, if you can't trust an ex-copper who shoots rioting prisoners, who can you trust?" I asked, opening my hand to show him the disc. "Any idea what this is?"

"Looks like a coin or something," he said. "Gangs use these as passcodes to get into restricted back rooms in clubs. You shouldn't show this to just anyone, never know who they might be reporting to." He took the disc and turned it over, "This might help you in your task for Lord Franz."

"Great," I said, "let's go." I moved to the door.

When I opened the door, I realised he hadn't moved, "All good, Thulani?" I asked.

He moved to stand beside me and settled his scary face on my delicate visage again, "Sometimes I just want to punch you in the face, Valentine," he said.

I smiled, "Aw, shucks, I get that a lot, no worries."

He growled out "And then you trust me with this ... thing...," he held up the disc.

"I'm a heck of a guy," I smiled.

"No," he grumbled, "you're an idiot. I could be one of the untrustworthy police, someone in the pay of this Syndicate. I could be tasked with watching what you do and maybe taking you out."

"You want to go out with me?" I asked.

"No, you worm. We have only just been teamed up, and you are a sought-after target in the criminal circles of this city. If Ghost wants you dead, you need to be less trusting. Especially of people with whom you have no history of trust."

"I shouldn't trust you?" I asked.

"Of course, you can trust me! God, you are infuriating!" He visibly breathed in control. "Valentine, start looking around, get a grip on your surroundings. You seem to have no sense of the danger you are in. People, bad people, LOTS of bad people are out to get you. This is the city, the big city. You seem to be the sort of guy who is out of his element. Have you ever been in danger, real danger before?"

This caused me to stop suddenly, my action meant he continued walking for a few more steps before realising I was not with him. He looked back at me, a question on his face. I walked on with my hands in pockets and we trudged together for a while. How do I explain to him that I was a teenager in the city of Ostend during the Spanish siege, how to talk about living every day, for years on end, with a constant and never-ending threat of violent death; living through bombardments and unrelenting attacks from an enemy who just wanted us all to die?

But I didn't die. I was one of the few thousand left alive when we finally surrendered. I arrived there when I was young and lived through 3 years of siege. I grew up learning how to live when all the world wanted me dead. I remembered the redoubt we defended until our swords broke and our hands bled from using bricks, stones and rubble as weapons.

Have I ever been in danger, he had asked me.

"You feeling okay?" he asked.

"Yeah," I grunted, "Maybe you're right. I need to be more on my guard."

He clapped me on the back, "That's my man! Be more with it, more in tune with your surroundings. And stop being such a smart alec."

"That, too," I agreed as we exited the shop.

We mooched around for a few hours waiting for evening, we tossed ideas back and forth but I kept returning to just rolling up to the club and talking my way in. Or hitting someone. We sat on benches at an open-air food shop, I was eating something strange while the big guy drank quietly, he finally sighed and leaned towards me to say, "Val, ..."

I stopped slurping my meal and blinked at him, "Thulani! You called me Val! Does this mean we're friends again?"

He sighed, "What do you intend to do now?"

I shrugged, "I dunno, probably go to this club and see what's what?"

"How have you lived so long, Valentine?" he asked.

"What do you mean?"

"I mean," you boofhead, that you cannot seriously consider strolling into this place, showing the disc and then asking loudly for anyone to come forward with information? Are you telling me this is the extent of your plan?" He leaned back and folded his arms, giving me a very familiar look. The look which conveyed a low opinion of my skills.

I bristled a little, "Well, ... maybe." I took a breath. "Look, how about I just go in and look around, leaving out the loud asking of questions. You could come in with me and sort of keep an eye on things."

"So we both get killed?" he asked.

"Well, what about you, smarty pants, what would you do?" I demanded. I'm vicious in the repartee.

"I'd raid the place with two squads of troopers, lock it all down and then start questioning everyone. Very vigorous questioning. Lots of it," he answered, "perhaps with blunt instruments."

"Can we get two squads of mean troopers?" I asked.

"Of course not," he scoffed. "They only allow real policemen to have those toys. Not," he spluttered, "an off-world adventurer and a disgraced former sergeant."

We both fell quiet.

"Just to be clear," I asked after some deep-thinking time, "I'm the off-world adventurer, right? Cool."

He stood up, "Come on, it's late enough. We can probably try your sorry excuse for a plan now." We drove around for a while until he showed me the club entrance, he parked in a dark alley - my favourite type. He pointed to the end where the alley entered a brightly lit street and said, "Turn right at the corner and you'll see the main entrance. Good luck. The front part of the club is open to members, the restricted area would be deeper inside. I don't know how that coin is used but it is the key to getting back to those restricted areas."

With an unexpected, explosive burst of speed, Thulani opened his door and leapt to the footpath, intercepting a hooded figure. What followed may only be called a tussle if one is generous. It was a beautifully executed snatch on the poor, lonesome figure slouching down the street. Thulani grabbed the man's shoulder, spun him around and threw him into the vehicle. A very surprised face blinked back at me as the brain told him he was no longer walking under his own control.

"Hiya, Amadi," I said. "How you doin'?"

"Wha ...What ...," stammered our new guest. He swallowed and said, "Let me out! I need to go into the club and get a few answers!"

"Yeah, sure," said Thulani, regaining his place in the vehicle. He turned to Amadi and said, "You would just get yourself killed. Leave the moronic acts to the professionals like Valentine."

"But I need to sort this out," said Amadi. "Otherwise, they will take it out on my father. I don't care if they beat me or kill me. I have to set things right."

"You can start," said Thulani, "by going to the hospital and visiting your dad. The Syndicate got to him today."

The boy's face dropped, "Is he ..." he asked.

"He'll recover," said Thulani. "I'll take you there now while Val goes and does what he does best." The big, scared man looked at me, "Nick of time, Val. Off you go."

"You're sure you don't want to come in with me?" I asked.

"Are you crazy?" he said.

I huffed a bit and then left him to his thoughts. His treacherous, friend-denying, self-preservation thoughts. Damn, he was probably right and this was going to end badly for me. Wouldn't be the first time. Still, at least we had stopped Amadi from doing something stupid.

Because doing something stupid was my thing.

Chapter 22

I turned into the main street and walked towards the front entrance of my imminent demise. An elderly lady walking with a cane approached the same door from the opposite direction, she had that tenacious, determined gait signalling trouble to the youth of today. I slowed my steps a little and edged to the side of the walkway because I did not want to intrude into her line of sight. She looked like she had no time for lollygaggers like me.

As she came up to the club entrance the doorman slid a glance over her, ascertaining her threat level. He must have thought it was low because he shunted his attention to me. I recognised the look, having used it myself many times. His eyes crinkled and narrowed; I believe I had registered as a person of interest. I do try to look small and meek but body language is a bitch. I plastered my best sappy grin on the old dial and tried to think of a clever way to say hello. Clever enough for him to let me skip by into the club.

We were therefore both surprised when the little old lady hauled off and hit him with her cane. She swung a few good hits while loudly insisting he was a lower life form.

It was worth watching, quite a thing of joy. The old lady continued to thump the doorman while he struggled with the appropriate level of response. I am sure he would have normally just punched anyone who pulled such a stunt, but this was a little old lady. What sort of thug drops the hammer on someone's grandmother?

He managed to grab the cane while remonstrating, "Lady! Will you stop hitting me!" They stood glaring at each other, "What is your problem, old girl?" he demanded.

This may have been a tactical mistake on his part. You do not, ever, call an elderly female 'old girl'. Not if you want to keep your teeth or other exposed body parts.

She wrenched the cane away from him and collected herself with some effort, "Does your mother know what you do for a living? Would she approve of you calling me 'old girl'?" She leaned on her cane and continued to flay him verbally, "You accost innocent citizens in the street, demanding money and making threats. Your family must be so ashamed of you. Ashamed!"

For an instant his head dropped, I must admit I shuffled my feet a bit and I wasn't even in her line of fire. The bouncer was made of stern stuff, he came back like a good 'un. "Look, lady, I'm sorry I called you ...what I said. But why did you hit me? I'm just a doorman, I'm not doing anything wrong. This is a private club, I'm just here to keep the riffraff out."

He sensed he had made yet another error. "Not that you are 'riffraff'," he said, "but the club is for members only and you can't come in." A stray brain cell must have sparked because he then asked, "Uh, you aren't a member, are you?"

"I want to see the manager," she said, with quiet authority. "I have questions about missing people."

"No, lady," he said, "you can't come in. Unless you are a member or in the company of a member, you don't get to go inside."

She bristled, "I will stand here all night until I see someone in charge. My family deserves answers!"

A quiet pause broke out between the combatants, there was a sense of reserve troops being mustered. Time for some of the old Valentine charm.

"Auntie May!" I exclaimed, "I finally made it! Come on, let's go in."

The bouncer sized up the situation anew, I tried to look unassuming and not at all scary. "Who are you, buddy?" he asked, a sneer loitering around the lips.

I could see he was a heartbeat away from calling for backup. Time for a cunning plan. I held up the coin and said, "We're going in, pal."

He took the coin and closely examined it before handing it back and opening the door. "Go right on in sir, ma'am. Have a good evening."

I took the old lady's elbow and gently guided her through the door, "After you, Auntie May," I said, with just a hint of smirk. She would probably need some careful handling in case she became flustered with my smooth moves.

She brushed past me with a firm step, "Come along, Lenny," she said, "Try to keep up." She pushed ahead under full sail.

Chapter 23

The door opened into a large room with tables and booths accommodating a range of characters. I edged around the side wall, looking for a quiet spot from where I could look around. The old lady reached out and grabbed my elbow in a firm grip but allowed me to lead her into wherever the heck we were.

It looked to me just like any tavern or drinking hole, albeit not as grubby or dingy as those places I would frequent. This one was all shiny surfaces with quiet wait staff gliding around tables and chairs; chairs which looked amazingly comfortable. Lots of leather and polished wood. The lighting was subdued and hinted at quiet conversations and low mutterings regarding matters of great import.

But the underlying bones of the place reeked of ne'er do wells and the exclusion of outsiders. If you entered here, you better have a good reason.

We slid into a booth and I finally looked at my companion, I gave her a smile while keeping my eyes roving and said, "Hello, lady, my name's Valentine. Can you look after yourself now if I leave you here?"

I started to get up when she grabbed my arm with the grip known only to ferocious aunts and said, "Sit down, Mr Valentine."

I sat.

"Thank you for getting me in here, young man," she said. "Would you please show me that coin?"

"What coin would that be?" I asked, going for the 'play dumb' scenario. Verbal jousting is not my strong point.

"Don't be dim, Mr Valentine. I want to see what you have, whatever it was that allowed us to enter this pit of abomination," she said.

There was steel in the old girl. Anyone who used words like 'pit of abomination' deserved to be heard, even if the words came through a translation device. I pulled the coin out and laid it on the table between us, she quickly placed a hand over it so it could not be seen by all and sundry. The room was about half full of patrons, they sat around small tables chatting and drinking, a bar ran along one wall behind which stood two well-dressed young men dispensing drinks to a discreet gaggle of wait staff.

The old lady opened her fingers and studied the coin while I did my room inspection. She flicked a glance at me from time to time before finally leaning back in her seat.

"Who are you, Mr Valentine?" she asked. She sat before me, dressed in old but clean clothes, her hands were strong and her movements sure. I liked her, she reminded me of female relatives I would never have.

"I'm just a guy," I said.

"Nonsense," she said. "I recognise this coin. It's a passkey, I have a rather disgraceful family relative who has one. It is used by bad people to show they are in the tribe. Are you in the tribe, Mr Valentine?"

"I am a bad person," I replied and then leaned in, "But perhaps you could not use my name so forcefully around here. Some folks have taken an unreasoning dislike to me."

She grinned. "Not in the tribe, then. Nor, for that matter, am I." She looked at me for a beat. "Tell me, Mr NoName, why did you help me get into this place? I might be one of those 'folk' who have taken a dislike to you."

I had not thought of this, but she was right. She might be the manager's mother for all I knew. Perhaps I had just done yet another stupid thing.

"Ahh...," I said.

She patted my hand, "It's all right, dear boy. You don't look smart enough to be dangerous. No, I'm not after you. I wanted to get in here to find out some news of my grandson, Amadi."

"Amadi?" I asked. "Guy with a liberal interpretation of property rights? Recently in the slammer? Friend of Babajide?" the phrases just dribbled out of my mouth.

You would think, after all I have been through, my brain would have some sort of filter on my mouth but no, here we were again spilling everything I knew at the first hint of some news. "He's okay," I said. "A friend of mine is taking him to the hospital now to see his dad. We found him outside and stopped him from coming in and getting hurt."

Her eyes softened a little. At least, I think they softened, it may have been just poor eyesight from an elderly citizen. A figure loomed up to the table. 'Looming' is a required skill in the Watch. You get a lot from someone if you just hover over them with a potentially life-threatening attitude. I enjoy looming and I could see this character had the requisite skills. It undoubtedly worked with most citizens and the bottom-of-the-food-chain thugs, but I was able to resist the social pressure quite manfully.

"Can I help you, sir?" he asked. "I understand you showed our doorman an entry coin?" His eyes flicked to my elderly companion but I sensed he dismissed her as a threat. More fool he, I thought.

As I opened my mouth to speak, my newfound aunt interjected, "Are you the manager?" her voice had a certain quality, it penetrated the brains of all males and sent them back to a childhood where they had been found tramping mud through the house. "Come along, sonny, speak up," she demanded.

Ahh, street theatre, you can't beat it.

Chapter 24

I sat back to watch the show, a small part of my dwindling intelligence registering I was not remaining inconspicuous but I did manage to ignore any trend towards common sense. Let's just go with the flow, I thought.

"Madam," he began, turning to my companion.

"Don't 'madam' me! I'm old enough to be your grandmother. Now get me the manager. Come on, jump to it!" She emphasised her words by swatting him across the legs with her cane. I could quite get to like this old girl.

She spotted my smile and said, "And you can stop smirking! Sit up properly, back straight, don't slouch."

Our loomer waved a hand, attracting reinforcements. A waitress approached and he said, "Get these people anything they want. Guests of the house!" He sort of bled away, making for a nondescript doorway in the back wall.

Oho, thinks I, does that door lead somewhere special? This could be a clue.

As I watched the doorway to see who else might use it, I could feel the old lady watching me. We all seemed to be watching each other these days. Thus it was, I missed the arrival of a pair of heavy hitters at our table. My first intimation of something being amiss was a large hand being placed on my shoulder. It was accompanied by a voice unused to speaking in tender tones.

"You need to come with us, pal," gargled the voice. "The boss wants a word with you over that coin."

I could see this was not going to end well, especially if I was dragged off to parts unknown by these low types. My brain began sorting through various plans but my body had its own ideas. I suspect the years trapped in Ostend had developed a whole new set of communication processes intended to keep me alive. And then the following years bouncing around various mercenary groups contributed to my thinking being driven by physical reactions rather than thinking first. Seeing as how I was still alive, there did not seem to be a lot to complain about; but I was, after all, trying to think before I hit. A plan doomed to failure.

My hand grabbed the old lady's cane and I swung it in a brutal arc into the face of the chap with his hand on my shoulder. He lost interest in any further discussions as his body endeavoured to deal with his newly broken nose and various grazes and contusions. I added a few more grazes and contusions before the cane broke after several more collisions with his face.

This left me with a jagged stump and one remaining thug. A very surprised thug. He was no doubt unused to clients of the club engaging in high levels of physical violence, the place reeked of sensible decorum. Sure, they may all have been involved with some level of crime but this room was not a place of open violence. Until I rolled in.

A voice near the bar shouted, "That's VALENTINE!!!"

I looked up to see my old pal Don'elk pointing at me. His face was torn between glee at seeing me and his inbuilt survival sense – again, at seeing me. I looked down at Amadi's grandmother and said, "You better leave now. And quickly. I'll be okay but things are about to get out of control." She gazed back at me and I felt she was going to volunteer to stay by my side, so I went on, "Amadi needs his Bunica. Tell him I think he's a good and brave man." She smiled, got up and left. Now the party could really start.

The tone and mood of the place changed, this seemed to me to be a good time to leg it so I king hit the bloke holding his broken nose and he fell down like a sack of potatoes. Unfortunately, this gave his companion time to pull out a weapon, some sort of pistol. He started to wave it about but he wasn't being serious. What is the point, I ask myself, of having a weapon and then not using the damned thing. He would have gotten around to pointing it at me in a few seconds but those beginning seconds make all the difference.

He had a gun but I had a sharp stick. I reached over and plunged it into his mouth, causing him to fall over and lose interest in his professional obligations and, quite possibly, his life. I picked up his pistol and decided it was time for the ever-popular Valentine disappearing trick.

A quick look around showed that many patrons were about to engage their other, more animal brains and I was going to be in real trouble. Where to go? Don'elk was still standing and pointing at me so I headed for him while waving the pistol in the air. I pulled the trigger a few times but nothing happened, not even a dry click. There must have been some sort of safety switch I needed to activate before using the damned thing – I reconsidered my stance towards those earlier firearm lessons. Still, bit late now, I threw the stupid thing at a nearby face. Good nose contact.

Don'elk was a good 'un. He saw me running at him and did what I hoped he might do – he ran to find somewhere safe. You and me both, pal, I thought. He hot footed it towards that mysterious door at the back of the club with me raving after him. A few customers had risen to their feet between me and the door now closing behind Don'elk but these were as wheat before my thunderous passing. I knocked over men and women amidst screams and curses, tossed at least one table aside and just barrelled through the door. It shut with a click behind me. Was I safe?

I was in a short, bright hallway, almost a room, containing a large desk and a larger man seated behind it. He was leaning forward trying to make sense of the gabble coming from Don'elk who was pointing back at the door we had both just used. "Get out there!" he was saying. "It's Valentine! Get out there and grab him!"

At this point, he turned and saw me as I leaned back against the door trying to catch my breath. I gave him a smile, "How are you

doin', Donny?" I asked. I also wanted to ask more about his role in
The Syndicate.

He gave a little shriek and headed off to the only other door in
the room. His new pal was made of sterner stuff and stood up, taking
another pistol out of a concealed pocket. This was not going well; I
may have spoiled the element of surprise and forfeited any claim for
stealth. Sneaky is not my strength.

As Donny disappeared through the door, I put one foot on the
front of the desk and pushed. Pushed very hard. It shoved into the
thighs of the guard, causing him to stumble backwards and drop
his weapon which decided to hide under the desk, conveniently out
of reach. He staggered back into balance as I moved toward him
intending to push past after Don'elk.

I changed my mind about this strategy when he clipped me on
the side of the head with a fist, possibly made of rock.

We separated and stood for a couple of beats as we sized each
other up. He was easily as big as me; we each adopted a fighting pose
and I could see this guy might know a thing or two about fisticuffs.
His nose had been broken several times and his ears had that scraped
look they acquire after a career of bare-knuckle fighting.

I could be in a bit of trouble here.

I do get into a lot of fights but I never, never, seek a one-on-one
with anyone who knows what they are doing. I'm not into strutting
around as the toughest guy in the room. Generally, I'm not the
toughest. There will always be someone tougher, smarter and faster
than you. Pride and ego have killed a lot of good men. Good, but
stupid.

My dance partner shuffled his feet and held his hands at odd
angles, everything about him screamed danger.

Bugger.

I stepped back to put some more room between us and did a quick once-over of the room. Nothing useful. The desk and chair were the only pieces of furniture and the desk was bare of any accoutrements. Same with the wall. It would be nice to have a few decorative crossed swords about the place but no, they went in for a very minimalist look.

He noticed my gaze drifting to the desk as I contemplated diving for the pistol but his evil grin put me off. I'd gone right off this bloke. Nothing for it, I decided, but to put him down before his pals arrived behind me.

I stepped in to throw a lazy left cross which he blocked easily before I took his return blow on my forearm. We stepped back and I panted heavily – this club was wearing me down. He took a turn at me and pivoted off his left foot to aim a hefty right boot in my midriff. A foot to the gut can make you lose all interest in a fight, especially a slow-moving, panting guardsman who has been eating too many rich foods.

But I spun around as soon as I saw him start the move, recognising his stance from my training with the mad monk. Countering a blow by turning your back on an aggressor goes against every survival instinct but it does allow one to pivot away from any flying foot. It also surprises your opponent. I knew this because when I again faced my partner his face had that little "oh" look to it.

I continued the force of my spin into a left kick to his testicles. It was a thing of beauty, my balance was perfect, the leg extension spot on and the final delivery was with a rigid foot encased in my heavy combat boot. I could tell he was impressed by the way his face turned red and he made a small "meow" sound before sinking to the floor.

He may have been tougher, smarter and faster than me but good looks and dirty fighting will win every time.

I snagged his gun from under the desk and hot-footed down the corridor to the exit door. As I pulled the handle, I heard the door behind me burst open followed by howls of rage from the newcomers. I looked over my shoulder and gave them a merry wave before stepping into the new space. I was looking for a way to lock it when a voice in the new room wheezed, "That's him."

My reflexes pulled my head close to my shoulders and I stepped to the left before spinning around with the pistol aimed at whatever new danger loomed.

The danger did not so much loom as gaggle. I think "gaggle' is the group term for a room full of thugs all pointing pistols at you. In the front rank – there we so many they were lined up about three deep – stood Don'elk.

Smiling.

Chapter 25

"Hey, Donny, long time no see," I said, in my best conversational voice.

"Drop the pistol, moron," he said. I let the weapon fall to the floor.

"Shall I raise my hands or are you going to shoot me right here?" I asked.

"Shut up, Valentine," said Don'elk. "If it was up to me, I would drop you where you stand. How did you know I was here?"

"It's not always about you, Donny," I said. "You need to think about other people in all you say and do. Share the love."

He took a step forward, an angry step, "I said SHUT UP! Now, what are you doing here?" he asked. His voice rose a few octaves.

Donny doesn't handle stress well. Yet he chose a profession requiring him to deal with people like me. I looked at him in silence and eventually gave him a wink.

"ANSWER ME!" he demanded.

One of his associates said, "Mr Don'elk, you told him to shut up."

My erstwhile interlocutor opened and closed his mouth a few times. Watching Donny work was a joy, like playtime at school. He gathered himself and took a few deep breaths. "Ghost wants to see him. Tie him up and get him ready for transport."

I would like to say I allowed myself to be manhandled but they did not seek my permission. Several rough types stepped forward and tied my hands securely behind my back while another opened the door behind me to greet the reinforcements from the other room. Much whispering took place which led to a few grunts of surprise. My recent dance partner was not among these arrivals so I assumed he was considering career choices elsewhere.

A voice next to my ear growled, "We saw what you did to Laslo back there. He's on his way to get medical treatment – he's in a lot of pain."

I said, "When he wakes up, tell him his old pal Valentine said 'Hi';"

There was a brief pause as I heard a collective intake of breath, and then the beating began. I rolled into a ball to protect delicate bits before eventually blacking out under a barrage of feet and fists. These guys were amateurs because I blacked out very quickly; hello, darkness, my old friend.

Coming back to consciousness was not pleasant, it never is after a good beating. This one had been administered by angry thugs which means they got in each other's way and generally missed a lot of blows out of exasperation. So, it was not a good beating - lucky old me. A good beating should be administered by cold-blooded bastards who systematically work the body, inflicting lots of pain without allowing the recipient to drift into unconsciousness. The NightWatch is full of cold-blooded bastards.

My face was smooshed on the floor allowing drool to fall out of my mouth before making a small puddle under my cheek. My hands were tied, my body ached but my heart was pure; voices muttered over my supine form.

"You have to stop hitting him. Now!" This sounded like Don'elk. My hero. "He's no good to Ghost if he's dead."

"You should see what he did to Laslo, he's probably ruined for life," said a sullen voice.

"Look at my hand!" said Don'elk. "Look at it! I know what this guy can do, I am very aware of the hurt he lays on people and no one wants to see him in pain more than me. BUT Ghost wants to talk to him and that is what we will do. Transport him, alive and unharmed to Ghost. Unless you want to tell the boss you felt differently about the whole deal. Do you think you would enjoy that conversation?"

There was more muttering but it dropped away until Don'elk spoke again. "Right, now pick him up and put him in the speeder. Put him in the cargo bay and throw something over him so we don't get pulled over by nosey coppers. Something smelly and unpleasant."

With a lot of grunting – because I am a large lad – I was heaved off the floor and carried about. I could follow my progress if I squinted and easily saw a shiny vehicle parked on a side street. The lads opened a cargo bay and dumped me inside.

"What about something to cover him?" asked a voice.

"I'll get something out of the garbage in the alley," volunteered another. Sure enough, I was soon rejoicing under damp, rotten and foul-smelling food refuse and assorted sticky discards. My day just kept getting better. The door to the cargo bay shut and I was left to enjoy my splendidly odiferous environment.

Still, I wasn't dead. And I was on my way to see the Ghost!

My cunning plan was working.

Eventually, I felt the vehicle begin to move and managed to doze off from time to time. The aches and pains never went away, plus the ropes on my wrist were incredibly tight. A last parting gift from a grateful crew. Since I couldn't do much about it, I settled down to persevere, it's what you do when you cannot do anything about whatever dilemma has erupted around you. Some people declaim about the unfairness of life or want SOMETHING DONE ABOUT IT! Sure, like God is ready to attend your every beck and call.

Toughen up, buttercup.

I toughened up and thought uplifting thoughts until the vehicle came to a halt and the cargo bay was opened.

Rough men stood around me. Rough men and Don'elk. They pulled me out of the stinking mess under which I lay and dragged me to a waiting aircraft. Don'elk was not happy and sounded off about the mess I'd left in his vehicle. No one paid him any attention, least of all me.

When they dumped me on the floor of the aircraft I grunted and must have said a few choice words because one of my porters spoke up. "I think he's conscious, Mr Don'elk."

Donny grabbed my face and peered into my slitted eyes, "Are you with us, Valentine?"

"Sure thing, Mr Don'elk," I said. "Yes sir, ready to go. Say, you wouldn't have a breath mint, would you?" I paused, "Your breath could kill a brown dog, Donny. Terrible stink in here."

"How have you lived so long, Valentine," he said. "All you do is aggravate people".

He climbed in and sat on a very comfortable-looking chair. A few of his buddies also joined us for the ride. A few drinks and we'd have a party.

More time passed as we travelled to who knows where. Eventually, we landed and the doors opened to my new location. During the ride, I had managed to pull myself into a sitting potion so I was able to enjoy the sunshine and beautiful views as the doors slid open. We were facing a beach upon which gentle waves broke and receded. Several trees framed the view which included more of the thuggish crowd. This lot looked very serious and extremely competent.

One of them leaned in, sniffed and said, "You are not taking this man anywhere until he is cleaned up." He looked at Don'elk and continued, "You might need a wash yourself, Don'elk. Ghost does not approve of poor hygiene." I noted the absence of the 'Mr' before Don'elk's name, I assumed this meant he was not a Big Deal around here. The chief thug pulled his head out of the vehicle and gave instructions.

In short order I was placed in a wheeled chair, strapped in and pushed up a lovely path that took us away from the beach and the landing pad. Ahead was a clear delineation between beach and land marked by a low stone wall and a large expanse of manicured grass. I'd seen this sort of lawn before in England. When I asked the snotty gardener of that estate how he managed to have such beautiful grass he just sniffed and said, "A flock of sheep and six hundred years." Put me firmly in my place.

I asked, "Where are we?" No answer.

"Does Ghost live here?" No answer.

"Is he at home?" No answer.

"What time is it?" No answer.

"Does he have any pets?" No answer.

"I like dogs. Does he have a dog? I bet he has a dog!"

A firm blow landed on the back of my head. "Shut up," said a voice. A voice used to command, a feminine voice I had heard before.

"How are you doing, Louise?" I asked. I was out of my depth already.

"Can I go home now?" I asked.

"Shut up, Valentine. Gag and bag him," said Louise. "We haven't time for a proper wash, just brush some of that muck off him." Something was stuffed into my mouth and another something was placed over my head. Hands brushed me down. Ungentle, mean hands.

The last time I saw Louise she was looking daggers at me as I was whisked away from her clutches by the local constabulary. Back then she had failed to be swayed by my boyish charm and I suspect she was still gamely resisting the pull of my charisma.

After a short interlude, my head was freed from the smelly sack but my gag remained firmly in place. I gargled an objection but no one took any notice. We were in a formal reception room; my wheelchair was on quite a sumptuous carpet and facing two chairs.

I say "chairs" but they were not for the run-of-the-mill backside; they were all gilt and soft padding, intricately carved arms and ostentatious headrests. If they were intended to impress the lower classes, they had done their job with me.

The chairs were separated by a set of screens forming a box, behind which it would have been possible for a third person to sit and observe the room while maintaining their secret identity. Louise moved from behind me to take one of the chairs and a side door opened to allow a well-dressed man to enter. He took the remaining chair and they both looked at me.

"Hggh," I said.

"Take the gag out," commanded Louise. The obstruction was removed and we all looked at each other.

My plan, such as it was, had worked, I had made it closer to finding Ghost. Now I was beginning to see some flaws in this plan, the most prominent factor being my survivability. I had envisaged myself creeping stealthily through the night before springing into the villain's den like an avenging angel. Instead, I was sitting trussed up as a pig for the slaughter in a room filled with people who wished to do me harm.

This planning lark is harder than it looks.

Chapter 26

"Just be aware, Valentine," said Louise, "I am restraining myself from doing you serious bodily damage by a supreme act of will. Feel free to act up but I cannot answer for the consequences."

I swallowed. She had set out the ground rules. I had to use my self-discipline and show great personal control while avoiding snarky comments.

I was doomed.

"Why am I here?" I asked.

The man answered, "Because we wish it, Mr. Valentine. Because you have information we seek." He smiled before leaning back into the chair and crossing one well-tailored leg over another. "And because we can."

There was a pause and Louise leaned into the screen. Was she listening to someone tucked away? Could this be Ghost? And they wanted some information from me? What information did I have?

"Where is the ship, Valentine?" asked Louise.

"What ship would that be?" I asked.

The man steepled his fingers together and peered at me with his best master villain gaze, "The Trading Ship you stole from us," he said.

"Still not with you, champ," I said. "The only Trading Ship I know is the one we were hired on as security guards."

"That is our ship, Mr Valentine," the man said. "We bought it fair and square. And we would like to take delivery."

"Well, you're speaking to the wrong man," I said. "I'm just a knuckle dragger in the Watch, the security section of the ship. Who owns it and stuff like that is above my pay grade. Have you asked anyone in authority? Like a Trader?"

Louise stood and stretched, mainly for my benefit, I thought. And I certainly appreciated it. She sat on the arm of her chair and dangled one well-shaped foot in space. Her deep red dress was still slit up the side so I also saw a lot of leg. A lot of really good leg. "Where is the ship now, Valentine? Who is in control of it?" she asked.

"Sorry, what?" I asked. "I lost concentration there for a moment." She smiled at me before nodding to someone behind me. This was followed by a severe blow to my head.

"Where is the ship?" she repeated.

"I don't know!" I yelled. "The last time I saw it, I was fighting hordes of the undead before riding a sled down to the planet. The furthest thing on my mind was where we parked the damned thing!"

Louise leaned into the screen again, and listened for a few moments before continuing, "Who is in command of the ship now?"

"Magic," I replied.

This time the man stood up with fists clenching and a face turning a tad red. He seemed tense. He took a step towards me before regaining self-control. "Don't play games, Valentine! Our patience is running out! You have already cost us a lot of time, money and energy with your behaviour. Several of our men are either dead or incapacitated, plus you interfered with one of our farms which will slow our production down for this quarter."

"So, not happy then?" I asked.

Another blow hit the back of my head.

Louise asked, "What do you mean by saying 'Magic' is in charge of the ship? Are you asking us to believe supernatural elements are at play?"

"No, "I said, "and please stop hitting me. 'Magic' is the name of our captain, the Captain of the NightWatch."

"And where is Captain Magic," asked the man.

That sounded silly, "Don't call him 'Captain Magic," I said, "you're just embarrassing yourself." I took a breath to give myself some space, "It's just 'Magic'. And I have no idea where he is. I believe the ship needed some repairs after the undead tried to eat everyone."

"You can use your Communicator Bead to contact him. By now you should have realised this island has shields preventing you from using it to contact the outside unless we wish it," said the man. "We could boost your signal and only allow closely monitored communication."

I followed about every second word of what he said, but one point needed to be cleared up. "I don't have a Bead," I said.

Louise harrumphed, "Obviously you do. Otherwise, you wouldn't be able to talk to us."

I turned my head sideways so she could see my ear, "Look for yourself," I said. "No Bead."

Louise told the uglies behind me to check and a pair of rough hands grabbed my head while another set of fingers poked about my skull. "No bead," said a voice, probably belonging to the owners of the fingers.

"How are you talking to us, Valentine?" asked Louise. "And how are you able to understand what we are saying? The beads are the only way we have of communicating with every sentient species in the universe."

I told them about the wee beasties in my body, not a comfortable topic for me as I envisioned tiny demons wandering around my inner bits.

Another voice behind me spoke up, my old pal, Don'elk, "He's telling the truth, most of the ship's complement were injected with the nanobots - they needed a controlled environment for the experiment and we thought a spaceship would be the answer. That was the cause of the undead, I told you all about this. I avoided the injections while Valentine and the NightWatch seemed to be immune. I told you all this!" There was a hint of petulance in his voice.

"Don't take that tone with us, Don'elk. Now be quiet," said Louise. I heard the sound of feet shuffling behind me. Embarrassed feet shuffling. She looked across at her companion, "We will need to discuss this further. Talk to our technicians, find out if we can harvest these nanobots from Valentine and use them ourselves. We will need volunteers."

Both Louise and the well-dressed guy leaned into the screen and I caught some low mutterings but nothing I could understand. When they pulled back the two boss types looked very serious. Louise was panting and her eyes sparkled, this could not be a good sign for me.

"But you can serve another purpose, Valentine," she said. Several people entered the room and assembled equipment in front of me, my eye was drawn to a flashing light on a small box pointed at me and held steady on a tripod. "While we consider how to move ahead with your nanobots you can serve as a useful object lesson to others who may wish to cross The Syndicate." You could feel the capital letters as she announced the organisation, here was a girl devoted to the cause.

She nodded and a new face stepped into view. It was a masked man, a very big, masked man, dressed in black, even up to his hooded face. He was putting on black, close-fitting gloves.

Then he began to hit me. He worked the face with some big, meaty blows which got the blood flowing. He didn't touch the eyes or the top of my head and he avoided loosening any teeth. He had quite the skill set. He stepped back to allow Louise a good look at his handiwork. She bent down and I could see her gaze studying my face with some professional judgement.

Finally, she waved to another technician who set up a screen within my sight lines, "Here you are, Valentine. A screen to watch what happens to you," she said. "We are sending this out for others to watch, for all to learn what happens to those who cross us." My face filled the screen, my poor bloodied and beaten face.

"You have the unfortunate role of being our object lesson," she said. 'We will beat you a little more each day, we will apply pain in the most grotesque ways, we will let the world see every piece of your suffering. Each day, we will take you down the road of pain a little further."

She turned back to me, "Today was Day 1, Valentine." On the screen some writing appeared, I recognised the digit representing the number 1. "But that's enough for today. I think we will build up a following as word of this little exercise gets around." She cupped my face in her hands, hands I now saw on the screen. She was careful to only show her hands, complete with manicured, blood-red fingernails. "You only have yourself to blame, Mr NightWatchman. You have made yourself a visible obstacle to all we do. And so, we must make your destruction a memorable spectacle. You have only yourself to blame."

She signalled to the heavies behind me who again bagged my head but left my mouth ungagged. I felt my bonds loosen but any thought of making a daring escape was lost in my now groggy brain. My wrists were tied again and stronger hands grabbed me under each arm, pulling me to my feet.

I didn't feel too horrible, the beating was more to produce a physical reaction on my face, a visible marking which included lots of blood. It looked bad and I suppose it was bad to anyone who had led a sheltered life. But as beatings go it was tame. I've probably hurt myself more when I shaved.

I felt other hands and arms twisting me about before a voice spoke softly in my ear "We're all going on a small walk, Mr Valentine. You can choose to use your own two feet and be guided by us or we will drag you. Either way is no problem for us. Just be aware there are some stairs and other obstacles that may make the drag option not so tempting. For you, I mean; makes no difference to us."

I tried to speak but only coughed up some blood. I spat it into my hood which, in retrospect, was not a good idea. Through the slimy mess, I managed to say, "I'll walk."

"I see you've made a mess of your hood," said the soft voice. "We will be sure to use it again. Without cleaning."

It seemed I was to be a prisoner, and I did not like the sound of that 'harvest my nanobots' comment from Louise. It had undertones of other bad things happening to me. Daily beatings for the amusement of the general populace coupled with a side job as a lab experiment. Further evidence that my cunning plan needed work.

The journey was far from pleasant. I staggered a lot, tripped over things that could have been chairs, fell up a few steps and tried to breathe through my befouled headgear. Eventually, they pulled me to a stop and the voice came back. "We're about to go down some stairs. Don't make a fuss or we will just let you go and you will fall a considerable distance to the bottom. Step gently now."

Down the stairs we went. They were made of a hard substance, possibly marble or concrete, there was no give as in wood steps. I stepped very carefully and gave them no trouble.

At the bottom, we again resumed our walk until I was pulled to a stop and I heard a door open. The room we entered had a cold and dank feel, the floor was covered in bits that crunched under my feet – probably bits of grime. I assumed the cleaners rarely popped by. The hood was pulled from my head.

My wrists were tied to a ring firmly planted in the wall, facing me was a man in a hood. When he spoke, I recognised the soft voice who had spoken to me earlier. "Welcome to your new home, Mr Valentine," he said. Behind him three similarly attired goons took up most of the available floor space; they even had matching hoods.

"Are you guys brothers or something?" I asked. "Does your mum know what you do for a living?"

Chapter 27

A fist punched me in the stomach. It was one of those punches which takes all the air out of the lungs and sends the brain on holiday for a short time. Previous experiences in these situations stood me in good stead and I had clenched my muscles in expectation of such a blow. Even so, it hurt a lot and I doubled over while playing up my response. I even moaned a little. Guys like these usually like a few moans from their victims.

"We're going to leave you now, Mr Valentine, but we will be back for the next session," said my softly spoken tormentor. "I have been asked to make you last as long as possible and I hope to exceed my current record of 10 days. Imagine that, Mr Valentine, you can look forward to pain for at least the next 10 days. I hope to double that figure with some new techniques I have devised. Such fun we will have."

He turned and waved his colleagues towards the door, "But we leave you with some companionship." He stepped back to reveal a small, thin man dressed in rags, a fellow prisoner. His face watched mine with a combination of innocence and curiosity.

"Thanks," I said to my happy torturer, "Do you have a name? I may need to find you one dark night after I get out of here."

"My name?" he repeated. "Certainly. My name, Mr Valentine, is Cezar. But you may call me Pain." He pressed a finger into my neck, just a finger and some pressure. Nothing else. But fire flared down my spine and I truly gasped in agony.

"Anything else you wish to say?" he asked. I wisely stayed quiet while I waited for the wave of fire to leave my body.

"No?" he said, "Then I leave you to the gentle care of Silent." He indicated the small, raggedy man. "Silent has been with us for some time. How long has it been, Silent?" he asked my fellow captive.

There was no reply.

"And that is why we call him 'Silent'. Hasn't spoken to us in years." With these parting words, my escort left the cell and shut a very serious door. I was left facing Silent, a man who did not seem to be shackled in any way.

"How are you doin'?" I asked. I slid down a wall and tried to relax, time for another cunning plan.

Silent tilted his head and looked at me before coming over and poking my face. "Ow," I said, but I didn't really mean it. He peered into my eyes, closely examined my various cuts and bruises, even leaning in to sniff me. Personal space meant nothing to the little guy. He finally ceased his inspection and went to sit against the opposite wall.

We spent some time sitting facing each other without speaking. I spat out some more blood and pulled faces at him until it got boring. From time to time, he would stand up and walk around the cell, casting quick glances at me. I think I heard some low muttering but couldn't be too sure.

Eventually, he took a small step towards me, rubbing his hands together nervously. "Do you...", he said, "Do you want me to untie you"? His voice had a high quaver and he combined the hand rubbing with some back-and-forth foot shuffling.

Colour me surprised. This guy had not talked in years and here he was gabbing away.

"If you would be so kind," I replied. My bonds had been tied by professionals, I had already looked them over and realised there was very little he could do. But, hey, let him have a go.

He moved to my wrists and pecked away at the ropes for some time. "These are well tied," he said.

"I appreciate your help," I said. Trying to strike up a relationship. "My name's Valentine"

He grunted at this and kept working on my bonds, "Extremely well-tied," he muttered.

"And you are...?" I prompted.

"What?" he said, moving back to my front and resuming the hand rubbing and foot shuffling.

I took a breath, "My name is Valentine. What's yours?" I asked. Softness and gentleness oozing out of me.

"Oh, yes," he said, mid-shuffle. "Er, my name is, er..." He stopped very still and looked up at the far wall for a few beats before giving his hands a vigorous rub. "Mykle," he said. "My name is Mykle. Bishop Mykle."

Great, a bishop. A man of the cloth. He stood looking at me, saying nothing. His eyes wandered around the room and he watched the ceiling for a time, his lips moving softly.

"Mykle," I said, but got no response. "Bishop Mykle," I said with some severity, "That nasty guy said you hadn't talked in years. They even call you 'Silent.'"

He shook his head, "I don't talk to those bad people. And they are all bad here," he said.

"So why are you talking to me?" I asked.

"Because they have put you here and treated you harshly. Sometimes they put someone in my cell and hope I will tell them all my secrets. I do not talk then. But they have never put someone in here after beating them. And because you are not a bad man, Mr Valentine."

I grunted, "Don't be so sure." He seemed like a harmless little man, probably lost a piece of his mind after being a prisoner for so long. Still, I liked him. No reason why. I guess he was such a change of pace from my recent run of compatriots.

"You were untying me?" I reminded him. It was a forlorn hope but it gave us something to do together. Bonding, I'm all about the bonding.

He focused on me as a new apparition. "Was I?" he asked. More hand rubbing, "Of course. Yes. Untying you. So I was." He continued to stand still, eyes gazing at my face. At least his foot shuffling stopped.

I pulled, testing the bonds but they remained immune to my efforts. Bit like Louise, I thought. "Do you think you could try again?" I asked.

"Of course, of course, dear boy," he said, moving around me. "Now let me see." He tugged at the ropes before asking, "Do you have a knife?" he moved to my front and leaned down to peer meaningfully into my face, "I could cut them with a knife. They're awfully well tied."

Self-control is, I am told, a wonderful thing. Mine was fast leaving home. "No, I don't have a ..." A thought struck me, had I been searched while the lads tiptoed over my comatose body back at the club? "Um, wait a minute. Have a look in my right boot."

He stuck a skeletal hand down beside my leg and rummaged about before coming out with one of my backup knives.

"You do!" he crowed in triumph. "You do have a knife! How wonderful!"

His face was very close to mine since he was still leaning down, and I became very conscious I had just handed a dangerous weapon to this man. A bloke who may have only a passing acquaintance with reality. And I was tied up and helpless.

Way to go, Valentine, I thought. You sure can pick 'em.

He moved around me and I was pleasantly surprised to feel my bonds loosen. Another win for positive thinking and clean living. I quickly stood up and reclaimed my knife before the good Bishop reconsidered his stance on human sacrifice.

"Thanks, Bishop," I said, replacing the knife in my boot. I now had a chance to study the little man from a more relaxed position. Being tied up while a man with a sharp knife stands nearby is not the posture for calm thoughts.

"Just 'Mykle'. I no longer have the right to my title." He slid down a wall to a seated position before continuing, "It has been some time since I performed any pastoral work for my God. A long, long time."

I stretched various bits of my body and checked for any long-term damage. While I had a lot of new bumps, cuts and bruises, no serious injury seemed to be present. The bleeding on my face had ceased, all my teeth were present and correct although my jaw ached. Don'elk must have stopped the original beating before things got too serious. I may owe the little guy for saving me from harm. Unbelievable.

And the work done by the jerk calling himself 'Pain' was aimed at producing a visible reaction to a beating. Hence, he had cut my face, bloodied my lips and gums and generally made it appear worse than it really was. "How long have you been a prisoner?" I asked,

"Me?" answered Mykle, "A prisoner? Oh, no, I'm not a prisoner."

I surveyed our room. Or rather, our cell. No furniture, no bed, just lots of straw-like material. The only door looked strong, I stood up and gave it some healthy shoves but it was sturdy and obviously a door to a cell. There was a small window high up on one wall and that was it. The walls were unclean, just like Bishop Mykle.

His gaunt body spoke of deprivation and privation. I've seen a few holy men who had the same appearance, acquired from years of fasting and prayers. I've also seen the same look on the super fit, on those who have a good diet and excellent health care - I was guessing this would not be Mykle. It appeared that my friendly neighbourhood Bishop had suffered long-term imprisonment, ongoing beatings and starvation. Poor bloke needed some sympathy.

"You're a ... guest?" I asked.

"Certainly, my son," he replied. "I have chosen to seek God's peace through quiet tranquillity and silence." He shook slightly before continuing in a stronger voice, "Until today! Until you came in!" he stood up, shaking or trembling. "You have interrupted my silence!"

He stopped and gazed at me, eyes flicking over my body and back to my face. At this point, I was glad I was no longer tied to my chair. And very pleased I had reclaimed my knife.

"Are you a demon, sent to test me?" he asked. He had returned to rubbing hands and shuffling feet.

"No, Bishop, I'm just a man. A man you helped," I said.

"Then why are you here?" he asked.

"It's a long story," I said.

His eyes widened, "A story! I love stories!" he sat down again, his whole demeanour changing, sparkling with anticipation. He patted the floor beside him, "Tell me a story, please."

Chapter 28

The little guy had mood swings. Sometimes it seemed I was talking to a completely different person. Now he was my buddy and wanted some companionship. I had nothing better to do so we sat and chatted. I told him of the Watch and what we did, leaving out the nasty bits.

Surprisingly, when you extract the gratuitous violence from the job, it sounds almost boring.

"Do you mean to say," he asked me, "that you spent your time wandering the streets at night in the company of other armed men? You just walked around?"

"Well, when you say it like that it sounds rather pointless," I defended my position. Any further reasoning, or lack of it on my part, was interrupted by the opening of the door so my old buddies could storm in.

They grabbed me, threw me against the wall and proceeded to whale on my ribs for a time. They had these big, wide clubs which hurt like hell. When I fell to the ground, they continued to thump me over the head, arms and legs. Even the soles of my feet got some attention so I knew they were pros. I was wearing boots but even so, I could feel the heavy blows. When you started working the feet, things got serious.

I tucked myself into a ball and saw one of the goons grab Bishop Mykle and drag him out of the room. As soon as he exited the beating mercifully stopped while my bonds were retied before l was left alone. Alone and in pain.

The little window gave some light, the day came to an end and night set in fully. No food or water was brought in, no other visitors, no more Bishop Mykle. Had they heard us talking? I was sure there was some sort of technology that allowed them to hear us. Perhaps they could even see us.

If so, they would be cranky with Mykle. He doesn't speak to them for years but yarns away with me like long-lost friends! Although, as I recalled our conversation, it was mainly me talking. He had told me his name and then drifted off into silliness.

I dozed during the night before coming fully awake around dawn when Mykle reappeared, now looking beaten up. The poor little guy had bruises and cuts, he walked in with a limp; he was whimpering and collapsed on his side of the cell. Before I could check on him the guards grabbed me, bagged my head in the foul-smelling hood and dragged me out of the door.

The hood was removed with a flourish and my eyes met a blinding light. I couldn't see anything except for the light but I could sense others in the room. Off to one side of the light, a smaller red light blinked slowly. This must be their device for transmitting pictures, I assumed I was being watched by many others. I was getting to know this technology stuff, Greenash would be impressed.

This all added up to a session to which I was not looking forward, more beatings and other, sundry torments. O, Joy.

A woman chuckled, a voice I recognised, "Hello, Louise," I said.

"Good morning, Valentine," she said. "Say hello to all your fans. We understand word is getting out about our little show and watchers are joining us in large numbers. You will notice we have you tied to a wall, all ready for today's session. Let's begin, shall we?"

I was indeed tied to a wall. My arms and legs were spreadeagled but my feet were on the floor. At least I could stand. Into the light stepped a hooded man, either Cezar or one of his buddies. He grabbed my clothes and cut them away, he even took my boots. I did have some small measure of achievement as they discovered the knife in my boot, plus the other selection of sharp things I carried about my person.

You can never have too many knives.

Louise clucked a little at the growing pile of hardware building at my feet. "Was this man ever searched?" she asked.

No answer was the stern reply. I suspected some underlings were going to have a vigorous performance appraisal review.

I now stood naked before them, exposed in the glaring light. As a technique for making the recipient feel, well, naked, this method has its uses. But it also has drawbacks for it relies on the victim having a sense of embarrassment when being shown bare-arsed to strangers. It works well on merchants, bankers and city people with money. I was none of these.

I do know it works on women but it is not a technique I ever used in this fashion. Mum and Dad gave me a strong sense of my role in the world; look after the weak and helpless, defend women and children. Some of it stuck; Mum had *views* while dad just lived it. I miss them.

Being naked is highly ineffective if the focus of public humiliation doesn't give a stuff. People like common soldiers, manual labourers, woodsmen and gutter thugs. Pick which one was me.

I smiled at the blinking light and blew it a kiss.

Hooded man hit me in the stomach, hard enough to make me try to double up and retch. This guy knew his trade. He stepped back and Louise spoke again, "We welcome the viewers to today's session of the Valentine Show." I could hear the capital letters.

"Today is Day 2," she continued. "We show this so all may be aware of how the Syndicate deals with those who cross us, cause offence, or hinder our operations in any way. We particularly call out to that security service called the NightWatch. Here is one of your men, he has caused some minor inconveniences to our operations and has come into our hands. We will destroy this man before your very eyes, day by day. We will cause him further and further pain and suffering. We do not want anything from anyone, this is not a ransom situation, we do not seek to negotiate. What you will see here in the coming days is the slow and painful death of Valentine. Take note, all of you, and be wise around the Syndicate."

All through this little speech, I watched the blinking light. I kept my face still, even when she spoke of what was to happen to me. To be honest, I wasn't looking forward to the coming sessions but I also did not want to break down too early.

And I would break down, I would be begging for mercy, pleading for a cessation of the torment. Torture injures the body and the mind, it flays away all our ideals, our hopes and our very self. We can talk about never giving in, of being strong until the end but I have seen a lot of awful deaths. I have seen strong men broken after having unspeakable actions performed on their body. Not by me or any of the NightWatch, but I have seen awful things. There is nothing like a true believer - who sees their way as the right way, as the only way - for inflicting pain on those who think differently.

I've caused a bit of pain over the years and will probably do more if I survive my current adventure. But never pain for the sake of pain. Never cruelty as a means of power over another. Not just for the joy of hurting someone. I may be a thug, but I have standards.

Hooded man stepped up to me again and I caught his eye, I held my gaze steady as he approached. My exterior may have been seen as brave and steadfast but internally I was a quivering mass of expectancy. Let the good times roll. He studied my naked torso, running a gloved hand over my various scars, lingering a while longer on my stomach. It still looked a little different to the rest of me due to some nutcase scraping away many layers of skin. By God, it had hurt. The healers had repaired a lot of the damage but the skin of my stomach still had a different pallor.

He leaned in and whispered to me, too soft to be heard by others, "You've had a full life, Valentine. Lots of wounds to this tired old body. It will be my pleasure to get rid of some of these scars for you.

No thanks are necessary. Then again, perhaps I shall just add some new scars. Decisions, decisions. Life can be so complex sometimes, don't you think?" I recognised the voice of Cezar, a man who enjoyed his work.

"What do you mean 'old body'," I said. "' Lived in' perhaps but 'old' is just being mean."

"Time to start," said Louise.

And away we went.

This session was all about hot irons and burning. Cezar had a small stick that somehow remained red hot; in my day they had to keep putting it back into a brazier but technology keeps moving along. Ah, progress. It was about the size of a small dagger and hurt like hell when he pressed it into my arm. I may have said a bad word or two.

After burning small holes in both arms, he then used this neat little tool to run lightly over my chest. He stepped back and let the viewers see my steaming carcass before returning to his job. I believe he whistled a few times, happy in his work. Cezar made the little stick dance across my poor old stomach in little curves, each sweep getting lower and lower on my abdomen as he edged towards the family jewels.

My genitals were trying to claw their way back into my body cavity. Couldn't blame them. He teased his movements, lifting the stick off before running it gently over my now sizzling pubic hairs. He wasn't hurting me physically but my eyes were bugging out as he approached my manhood. Manhood I hoped to keep.

Then he stopped and re-entered the darkness beside the camera, leaving me hanging and sobbing in my bonds. I could smell the flesh of my arms where he had burned deep and I could see the faint burn lines he had left on my torso, lines which all pointed down to my nether regions.

"And that ends today's session, viewers," said Louise. The little red blinking life was extinguished and I could hear a few breaths being exhaled from the darkness. My little show gave some of the guards and observers a few uncomfortable moments. "Take him back to his cell," instructed Louise.

As I was dragged off, she called out to me, "See you tomorrow, sweetheart."

Chapter 29

On the way back to my new home, I pulled myself together. Pain is pain, you either whinge and moan or put up with it and get on with things. Easier said than done but I had a pretty tough mental outlook on life. What cannot be cured must be endured. I think Mum told me that, bless her. Bet she wasn't thinking of her little boy being used up by the torturers.

Soon enough I was thrown back into the cell where I lay groaning while Mykle clucked over me. "Sit up, Mr Valentine, he said. "If you lie there in the filth your wounds will become infected, and you don't want that. You might die."

Yes, indeedy, must be careful of infection, I thought. Must keep myself pure for the boyz in the hood. I sat up and rested against my wall before fully leaning back and falling asleep. Or blacking out, it's all one to me.

I had a strange set of visitors when I awoke, some sort of medical people. They examined my wounds, swabbed and cleaned them all and applied various creams and unguents. Considering they were part of the team engaged in beating seven types of hell out of me I asked them what was going on.

Mykle sat huddled in the corner during this little episode, his eyes watching all their movements. I caught a couple of them flicking glances at him from time to time but otherwise, he was ignored. I repeated my enquiry, "What's with the tender care, fellas? I'm not objecting, just curious."

They maintained their silence and left after applying bandages, the last one shone a light in my eye and peered into the back of my skull. Still no comment. Then they left.

I turned to Mykle, "What was all that about?" I asked. "I thought the whole point of the game was for me to be tortured while their audience watched everything. Now they're fixing me up. Change of heart, do you think?"

The little guy just shrugged before coming over and looking at my wounds. He poked one with a finger and I yelped. He watched my face for a few beats and then leaned in again to smell the burns; finally, he sat back on his haunches and gave me a big grin.

"You really are a prisoner," he stated.

"Well, duh!" I said.

He went back to his wall and sat down again, looking at me for some time before speaking again. "They put people in here with me in an attempt to get me talking. They want me to reveal the location of my treasure."

Part of my brain went to full attention, the part always looking for the end of the rainbow. "Treasure?" I murmured, trying to look only politely attentive, not grasping at all. I may have leaned forward with eyes a-flashing but I hoped I came off as just another working slob.

"Don't look so avaricious, my young companion," he said. "Someone in authority has formed the impression I have secreted a large fortune away in some remote cave, probably on a tiny island off the coast." He leaned his head back against the wall and closed his eyes, "They are in error. I have no treasure. At least not an earthly one."

"Why would they think you have lots of the good stuff stashed away?" I asked. "Were you absolutely rolling in it before they put the arm on you?"

I knew a lot of priests, many were good and decent, poor as poor could be. They gave away everything to help others, they lived their faith by helping their community.

I also knew the lazy and sanctimonious, the ones who paid lip service to their God and lived an easy life while others toiled for them. They usually could be found wearing gaudy vestments and seeking a placement in the larger cathedrals, hunting for that bishopric. Harmless if you slipped them a few coins or loomed at them from the shadows. I enjoyed a good loom.

And then there were the absolute bad 'uns. These gathered wealth and power, they fought their way up the promotion ladder and wallowed in their hypocrisy.

I could stand the company of the ordinary priests, at least for a short time. I could even put up with the odd Bishop, as long as I could hit something occasionally. But those higher echelons, the cardinals, the archbishops and so on, were, in my opinion, just bad news. To be fair, I only really knew one in any detail but he was a complete nutter; cruel, selfish, mean, cold-hearted...I pulled myself up. Going down that memory lane is a waste of time.

He must have seen my face reflect some of these thoughts, I'm rubbish at any gambling game. "Fear not, lad," he said, "I am as you see me. Rich in spirit, beloved of my God. But not a penny do I have to my name."

He looked innocent and believable, so much so that I immediately distrusted his answer. I looked at him for a few beats and said "Yeah, right." The king of verbal duelling, that's me.

He smiled, rolled over and went to sleep. The room was now quiet, I had time to consider my options; they did not look good. The gangsters seemed keen on knowing the location of our Trading Vessel but I was no help there. All I knew was that Magic was in charge of it; that fact alone meant it could end up embedded in any handy rock or planet. Magic is comfortable walking. That's it, just walking on his own two feet. Any other form of transportation he instinctively distrusts and does his best to leave. He may well be sauntering around a massive crash site at this very moment.

No good thinking about the ship, that ruled out option 1 – reveal the location of the Trading vessel.

Option 2 - slowly torture me to death for an unseen audience to have a laugh. This option did not thrill me.

I went straight to option 3. I did not have an option 3. Right, back to option 2 – torture me to death.

I rolled over and went to sleep.

Chapter 30

The next day's session began with the arrival of the guards pushing a trolley. I was on my feet when they entered, there were three of them - Cezar and two flunkies. Cezar did not wear his hood; I think he liked me knowing it was him behind all the tormenting. Guy was a sweetheart. Even though I was chained to the wall I wanted to try and hit one of them a solid blow. When they entered, they saw me in a fighting stance and stopped.

They laughed.

"Really, Valentine? Really?" chuckled Cezar. "You think you are going to hit us?"

"Crossed my mind," I said. "Want to come over here and say hello?"

The two goons took out small rods which they flicked to one side. The rods extended into long batons. Neat trick, I thought. Okay, three-to-one odds were always going to be hard. Three-to-one with me chained ramped up the difficulty scale even more. Three to one, me chained and them with batons or clubs made the whole plan look very ridiculous. Still, I might get one good hit in, especially if I could grab one of the batons.

"You look ridiculous, Valentine," said Cezar. He pulled a short, fat staff from his belt and activated a control. The staff had two small prongs on the end, not enough to really hurt me, I thought. The prongs had a slight glow about them.

The two goons spread out so one was coming at me from each side. They stayed out of my grabbing range and teased me with the batons. If I lunged towards one the other would give me a good wallop. I've seen bear baiting and now I know how the bear felt. Seriously ticked off.

After one of my lunges, Cezar stepped in and jabbed his little club at me. I ignored it because the prongs were too small and the entire weapon was pretty stupid in a brawl. Honestly, poking someone with a little stick was not going to do any damage.

Fire erupted in my chest where he touched me with the little staff. I fell over and reconsidered my plans for the day before blacking out. When I came around, I was secured on the trolley. It had two wheels at its base and a metal frame running up the back. I was strapped on so I was vertical, one of the goons tipped it up onto the wheels and pushed me out the door. I was erect, facing front and terrified.

We exited the cell and moved along the corridor to one of the rising rooms. Cezar chuckled all the way, "You are just a treasure, Valentine, letting me hit you with a shock rod," he said. "Ridiculous and stupid. You are the gift that keeps on giving." Then he laughed some more.

The day consisted of the home team beating the life out of me with these big paddles. They could grip the handles and thump me with the large leather pads. Like being hit with a saddle. Hurt like hell.

I recognised the technique, inflict lots of pain with little damage to the surface area. I'd used it myself from time to time when I was seeking answers to my steadfast enquiries. I would have been happy to tell them anything and I may have offered up my life story at some point but all to no avail.

I would black out from the pain, and they would let me hang until I came around. When I recovered, they would beat me again. This was repeated over and over, the pain was incredible. I blubbed, I whimpered, I told them anything I could think of until I blacked out.

Then they beat me some more.

When the session ended, I was incoherent, covered in snot and dribble yet not a mark on my body except for some reddening of the skin. Normally I may have admired their skill but today my mind seemed to be elsewhere. Silently screaming. They strapped me to the trolley and took me back to my cell.

And so, the days passed, a parade of daily torture.

On one occasion, I had wires attached to my delicate bits and then a switch was turned. I screamed a lot. Mykle was very attentive when I returned from this particular interlude. He stretched over to me and fussed. Some deep and very unkind part of my brain considered he was paying too much attention to my nether regions but perhaps I was just being judgemental.

He was, after all, a priest.

Chapter 31

Each session started when the guards entered my cell and strapped me to the trolley. I had stopped giving them trouble because I felt they were hoping for more reasons to use the shock rod. Cezar had all the tools for the up-and-coming torturer - a shock rod, a baton on his belt and a knife. Where were the pliers, I wondered. And the hammer? You can do a lot of damage with a hammer. I decided not to ask these questions, they seemed to have enough tools and I'm only borderline stupid.

Each day was a different experience. After each session, the medics would come in and check on me, bandage and salve where necessary. Sometimes I even got painkillers. When I asked Cezar why I was getting the good treatment he just laughed, "To extend your usefulness, you poor dumb slob. We're already getting viewers placing bets on how long you will last. Others are offering suggestions for further treatments – you, my good sir, are a star on the World Web."

"What's the World Web?" I asked.

"That's the platform for communications across the planet," he said. "We are showing you across a range of platforms, the betting apps seem to be particularly interested. Louise is, of course, thrilled."

We were having this discussion in my cell one afternoon after the day's activities, "I misheard you there. Did you say betting app? What's an app?"

"Nothing for you to worry about. I must say," he said, bouncing on his toes and grinning at me, "I am so enjoying my work."

He was a sick bastard, "Happy for you," I muttered.

We had water day. I was strapped into a chair and dunked in a large tub repeatedly. They kept me under for varying amounts of time to increase the tension. I was already tense.

Mykel wasn't in the cell when I returned but was shoved in shortly after me. While I lay croaking and gasping, the door opened and he was thrust back in, smacking against the opposite wall. He seemed a bit more beaten up than normal, a few kind words seemed called for.

"Bad session?" I asked.

He slouched down, covering his face with his hands before looking up at me. "I feel I may have come to the end of their patience," he said.

I gazed at him for a while, "You seem to have collected a few more bruises, especially about the face," I said.

He touched his forehead gingerly, "Yes, they take a quiet pleasure in merely hitting me," he said. "Nothing to what you are receiving, I am sure. But still painful."

Let's have a look at them," I said, I beckoned him over. "Come on, mate. My turn to look after you."

He was hesitant but eventually shuffled over to me. I took his head in my hands and turned it about to see the damage. "It looks like it's just surface stuff, the skin hasn't been broken," I said. The eye is the worst, you must have copped a big one."

He covered up and moved back to his side of the cell. "I'm sure I will not have to worry too much longer," he said. "I will have to pray for a quick end, not a lingering trial such as you are suffering. They know I have nothing to tell them, what about you? Do you still hold some secrets?"

I sat looking at him, rubbing my fingers together to wipe off the bits of his bruised skin from the tips. They had a slightly greasy smell. "No, I'm all out of secrets."

Our eyes met in the silence. "But I reckon you might have one more," I said.

His eyes widened before his face resumed a passive demeanour. He stared at me for a few moments before rolling over and facing the wall. I had to think about this; he definitely had bruising accompanied by assorted cuts and nicks. But when I closely looked into his eyes, I did not see the depth of misery I expected. I didn't see a lost soul, there was a gleam inside them. But what did that gleam indicate?

A variation on water day was drowning day; it had them pouring water into my face while a cloth covered my mouth. This was bad. Really bad, I felt I was drowning each time they did the pour. Again, I wanted to tell them anything they asked. I would have answered any question, anything at all. But they never asked me a single question.

Mykle was not in the cell when I returned.

I had a day off at some point. They just left me in the cell and sent in the medics and lots of food and water. Mykle was back in with me but we had lost our previous closeness. I caught him looking at me with lowered eyes now and then. Cezar stopped by and thanked me for the show. Said he was proud of my first week and he was looking forward to phase 2.

"What's phase 2?" I asked.

He chuckled, "You'll love phase 2. We start to work the body. Up until now, we have not inflicted any visible damage."

I pointed at the burns on my arms.

"Yeah, we weren't supposed to do that," he said. "Sorry."

Unbelievable. I may have given him a scathing look. Scathing looks were all I had.

"We'll do some light work on the fingers and toes and then move on to some real damage. Nothing life-threatening, you'll survive it all for days." He murmured slightly, "Weeks, even."

Mykle spoke up after Cezar left, "Valentine, why are they doing this to you?"

"I think I upset them," I replied.

"Is there anything I can do for you?" he asked.

"Do you have a secret tunnel nearby, something I could use to escape? Any disguises tucked away so I could impersonate a guard." My voice was rising as I spoke, I may have been losing it over my situation, "How about I pretend I'm dead and then dig my way out of the grave? Can I pull the bars from the window and scale the wall to freedom!"

I cackled some more, despair and pain taking control of my mind. I cried, sobbed and even prayed. I did a lot of praying during these days. And a lot of crying.

Night came and I fell into a restless sleep. Tomorrow, the good stuff begins.

Sometime the next day the team came by and gathered me up. I had finished my PLOM phase. PLOM stands for Poor Little Old Me. One of my tutors used it to describe my temper tantrums when I objected to learning Latin rather than running wild in the woods. He let me moan and whinge for a while and then asked If I had finished moaning and could we please get back to work. Having a PLOM is okay, but, at some point, you have to get back to work.

I had to get out of here.

This session saw the team pull out some of my finger and toenails. They took their time, holding up each digit and securely attaching a mechanical device to the nail. Louise came to observe this one. I watched them hold my hand up to my face and then pull the nail out slowly. Really slowly. I could feel grins behind their hoods. These guys loved their work. Hurt like hell.

The lights flickered, accompanied by a loud thunder roll. The storm outside would match the one in my breast. The dimming was only for a moment, nobody seemed worried. At the end of the session, they held up my bloodied extremities so everyone could get a good look at the damage. I was still securely tied to the vertical bed and could do nothing to resist. In fact, I slumped in the bonds and whimpered.

Someone untied me, probably Cezar. I fell into his arms and he cuffed me erect. "We've decided to make you walk today, Valentine," he said. "No reason, we just thought it would be fun to see you manage on those toes. Off you go now." The pain in my fingers and toes was intense, I could barely walk when he shoved me towards the exit door. They shackled my hands behind my back as usual, obviously fearing I would make a wild and acrobatic lunge for freedom. There was no chance of me being able to accomplish any type of wild lunge, given my physical state. And I was only going to get worse as each day wore on.

They did not shackle my feet, they liked the suffering groan I emitted with each step I took on my poor, tormented tootsies. I did a lot of groaning and a lot of painful shuffling.

Cezar laughed and nudged me forward, "I'll take him back, no need for anyone else; he might be persuaded to do a little dance for me. You others make sure that lightning strike didn't cause any damage." He pushed me through the door out of the torture room. I had a feeling he intended to have a private session with me in my damaged state. Our journey took us through a few rooms and eventually to a corridor where we turned left towards the cells.

I looked to my right and saw the corridor continue and eventually finish at a wall - an outside wall, complete with an inviting window. Cezar saw me look, laughed, and punched me. "Thinking of escape, Valentine?" he chuckled. "Ha, bloody, Ha. Take a good look at that window, it leads to freedom. Let's have a look." He guided me to the window and opened it up. I could see the distant forest, the dark, ominous clouds overhead and the gathering dark.

"You're in an old castle, I think the thunder and lightning add to the whole 'house of horror' feel we've got going. Don't you agree?" He nudged me just as a bright flash lit the sky and we could see forked lightning hit a tall tree in the nearby forest. It was accompanied by a devastating bang as the tree exploded, followed by a deep and sharp crack of thunder. "I feel like giving an evil laugh." He proceeded to make 'MWYA HA HA'! sounds while slapping my back like we were old friends.

"Of course," he said, "after tomorrow you might not be as mobile and limber as you are now. Not so light on your feet. We find that breaking a leg does wonders for slowing clever chaps like yourself. Go on, look at the window, dream of it, see how close it is. Who knows, you might be able to find a secret door and a hidden passage to freedom. After all, an old castle must have secrets. Tell you what, when we get to the cells, you can dance for me on those bloodied feet of yours, should be quite the laugh."

We moved along the corridor until we came to a strong metal door, Cezar unlocked it and gave me a shove. "Almost home, matey," he said, shutting the door which locked us away from civilised realms. No sound escaped this area, no unseemly cries were allowed to break out, and even sobs were prisoners. He made me stop and look him in the eyes, somewhere behind his face lurked a psychotic torturer, he slowly stepped on my bleeding toes and paused to watch the grimace on my face. His voice had a smile as he said, "Tomorrow's leg day."

He laughed, "You don't want to skip leg day."

Chapter 32

We were standing at the top of a flight of stairs leading to the cells. My brain had turned off some time ago, recoiling from the situation, cowering in gibbering fear in some dark corner of my mind. No help there.

The lights flickered again. "You might be sitting in the dark tonight, pal," he said. "We get a few lightning strikes and the power goes out. But don't worry, we have backup power, just not enough for everything. Let me see now, what parts of the castle don't need power? I know! The cells! Who cares if you spend the night in a dark, dark room." He laughed again. Dickhead.

The main lights flickered again and died. Emergency lighting came on, small red squares of illumination glowing in the darkness. He swore, started forward and then turned to drag me along. With my hands tied behind my back and my feet in pain, I did not have a lot of options for resistance. I weaved and tottered, he reached to steady me.

A spark went off in my brain. I pushed into him. I shoved him down the stairs with my shoulder, lunging my entire body and causing him to fall down the metal stairs with me floundering after him. We both landed together in the darkened gloom with me on top of his semi-conscious body.

He groaned and began to come around. He was going to be berserk with anger but what was he going to do, torture me?

I had no weapons and my hands were tied behind my back. I lay across his body; he had cushioned my fall. My head was pressing against his neck, we lay like lovers in a morning cuddle. I heard him begin to mutter, "You stupid, stupid oaf..." I raised my head, saw his eyes begin to open and realised my time was up. It was now or never.

I bit his throat out.

My teeth tore into his life, I spat bits of skin, blood and gristle onto the floor and then went back for more. He kicked and screamed, thrashed under my body trying to escape. I had too much leverage on him and my attack was so sudden and so terrifying to his mind that was unable to comprehend what was happening to him. Blood gushed over my face, some trickling down my throat, and more splashed my eyes.

He kicked, his heels hammering the floor in a staccato of death and despair. I kept biting and spitting until he was still.

Then I lay there in the wreck I had made of his life.

I rolled off his body, panted and worked myself to a sitting position. I did not have the luxury of time, time to be horrified at what I had just done. If I did not move, I was doomed.

So, I moved.

I shut doors in my head, I isolated any semblance of unease because I needed to crawl back to his body and loot the corpse. With my hands still tied behind my back, I was clumsy and uncoordinated. I sat in his blood and fluids while my hands searched pockets. The mind can bring intensity to any action, I focussed on the movements of my bleeding fingers as they roamed over his body, seeking his knife. When I found it, I cut my bonds and sat up, my body screaming.

I was a mess.

The rest of his pockets gave up his shock rod, keys and one of the extendable batons. Nothing else. Since I was naked, I also took his shoes and soiled clothes and made a bundle of them all before hobbling back up the stairs.

I felt the extra time taken in stripping Cezar of his worldly goods was worth the risk. But really, I just didn't want to be embarrassed by being found running around bare-arsed naked. Picture me, if you will; torn and bleeding feet and toes, a naked and bruised body clutching a bundle of clothes dripping bodily fluids from the recently deceased. Heroic stories never have this scene. Oh, the humanity!

At the top of the stairs, I opened the metal door and peeked through, no one in sight. The emergency lights cast faint illumination, I saw no torches or random groups of wandering thugs. There was still no rain or storm, just the occasional flash of lightning. Perhaps the blackout would cover my exit. I hobbled down the corridor towards the window, pushed it open and leaned out. Below me was water, either a moat or a lake; the question was, how deep? Beyond the water was forest, perfect for hiding rugged bandits, sun-browned men of the forest. And perhaps the odd escaped prisoner.

I looked back down the corridor and saw my bloody footsteps; the traitorous imprints would show precisely where I had gone. The corridor was normally well-lit with large chandelier-like things hanging down at various points, all chains and family crests. In the gloom, I could see the chains and the bottom part of each wall. Up above my head, I could make out a ledge, high up towards the top of the wall The upper sections of the walls were cloaked in darkness, I could see old paintings and non-functioning light sconces which may be concealing secret doors. They would, of course, remain secret because I could feel my time running out.

What to do? I wish I could sit down and have a good think. I wish I had a blaster and about twenty mates, I wish I was in a warm bed with Lydia. Whoops! Focus, Valentine, focus.

I sat on the window opening, cut the sleeves out of Cezar's shirt and wrapped my hands and feet. The rest of the clothes and equipment I tied together and hung them around my neck. I stood on the windowsill, facing the moat and getting blood everywhere.

Then I took a mighty leap into space.

Chapter 33

I did not leap into the moat but rather jumped back into the building, intending to swing off the ceiling chains. These chains, holding the light fixtures, were hopefully strong enough to take my weight. They were, lucky me. My hand coverings would soak up any blood or fluid leakage, I didn't want anyone to see bits of me hanging from the light fixtures; it would give away my clever plan.

Yes, I did have a plan. I was in no shape to swim the moat and then run off into the forest, I was not the sort of lad who grew up huntin' and fishin' in the wild wood. No craggy gamekeeper or crafty poacher had taught me to hide in trees, light a fire with two sticks or even trap bunny rabbits. No, being the wild man was not for me, I needed a place to hide and heal, a warm and cosy hole.

By dint of swinging and swearing - plus sticking the tongue out at the right angle – I was able to climb the chain until I was close to the ledge, a ledge which should have a reason for its existence. By the time I made it this far, I was tiring, not much life left in the old body. But I am a stubborn bastard, I tend to bull ahead. While this characteristic is not great for coldly weighing up choices and calculating the odds, it is ideal for getting from point A to point B. I will always push ahead; I will always keep going.

My vision had narrowed, all I could see was the ledge as I swung my legs back and forth building up a decent swing. Doing it in poor light just made the exercise that much more enjoyable. I groaned. Eyes on the ledge, swing, eyes on the ledge, swing, eyes on the ledge, let go and grapple for a hold. At this point I could not see anything, my eyes refused to function and the rest of my body was also asking to shut up shop for the day. I felt my arms hit the ledge and hung on, sweat pouring from my forehead and fire raging along my muscles.

I may have blacked out, at least my mind may have gone away but my body just kept on going. I regained some semblance of consciousness lying along the top of the ledge, in a lot of pain. Lotsa pain.

When my vision cleared, I could see why the ledge existed - It concealed a vent, large enough to take me if I could manage to get the cover off. After all this effort, I was not going to be stopped by a bloody vent cover. Before I attacked the damn thing in my usual smash and grab method I decide to look. Just look, take a breath and think. There was a small handle on one side and, when turned, allowed the cover to swing open like a little door; I crawled in. The vent was large, I could feel the air circulating around my body. I was able to contort myself and turn back to face the vent opening; I crawled back and poked my head out into my recently vacated corridor.

My plan depended upon them seeing the story I wanted them to see. An escaped prisoner, half-mad in pain, runs down the corridor and leaps through the window to freedom. I was banking on the water being deep enough to absorb a dive from this height – but that was out of my control.

It was important that no blood trail came to this vent, thus my swing from the chains trick. And I had wrapped my hands to keep any blood residue off the chains; just in case some clever lad looked around. I wiped the ledge of the few spots of blood and sweat and then wriggled back deeper into the vent while pulling the swing door back into its closed position. The holes in the vent door were big enough for my fingers and I pulled it shut until I heard a satisfying click – it was closed again. I lay down and waited. If they found me in here it would all be over, I was spent.

On this happy thought, I lost consciousness.

Chapter 34

The siren woke me. Light bled into my little space, light from the chandeliers; power was restored. My grogginess cleared enough for me to watch the running about of guards, flunkies and other assorted members of the criminal element. Eventually, Louise herself entered the corridor in the company of two masked torturers. She stalked into my line of sight; her companions grovelling around her flaming temper.

"How did this happen?" she raged. "How can anyone function after what he has been through?" she stalked back and forth while the minions went into full cringing mode.

"He came down this corridor and jumped into the river through that window," said one of the torturers. "We have searchers in the forest and people examining the banks of the river."

"I am sure he will be found, mistress," said the other. "He cannot have gotten far in his condition."

"What sort of creature bites out another's neck?" said the first torturer. "He is nothing better than an animal."

"We will put him down like the raving dog he is," added the first flunky.

"Oh, grow up. Just find him and kill him, lose the poetic metaphors" said Louise, as they moved off.

When I was quite sure they had gone and no one else was in the corridor, I turned myself around and crawled deeper into the duct. The damn thing had to go somewhere. It would be safe to say I do not have familiarity with the architecture of great houses or castles; in my experience, any building with more than two floors is just extravagance. The question was – how many floors were in this place and where should I go? Yes, I know, that's two questions. I said I wasn't up to any sort of deep thinking.

All the good stuff would be down on the lower floors, the kitchens, stables, water sources and so on. Next would be living and eating quarters and after that...well, I don't know. After you eat, sleep and sit around, what other uses are there for a dwelling? Whatever. I decided I needed to go up; each time I came to a junction of vents I took any which sloped up. There were not many of these but I did come to another little vent door. This one was in the ceiling of the vent and demanded I lie down and look at it while I had a think. I, of course, dozed off.

I started awake, surprising myself with the vehemence of my distress and fear. I needed to find a place to hide. Lying on the cold metal floor of the vent was not going to work, my body was beginning to stiffen up. I pushed open the ceiling vent and crawled out into some sort of storeroom or playroom. I don't know which because toy soldiers were lying around as well as buckets and mops. A suit of armour stood imperiously in one corner next to racks of colourful clothes. They appeared to be dress-up costumes for children – I tried a few with absolutely no success, far too small. Still, they would make a bed if I could find somewhere to place them. Somewhere safe and out of everyone's sight. Definitely not a storeroom, these places tend to be used at odd times by people storing stuff or amorous couples seeking a bit of hanky panky. I know about this sort of thing. Right Honourable tells me stuff.

The storeroom door opened easily and quietly, another danger sign. Seldom-used doors tend to squeak while those in constant use get a touch of oil to keep the damn things quiet. I slunk into the corridor and spotted some stairs going up. How terrific it would be to say that I covered the distance in one bound and it was the work of but an instant before I reached the next floor. If I get out of this alive, that is exactly how I shall tell it; I will not describe my arthritic and nervous hobble with frequent scares and jumps at every stray sound. Us heroes don't walk around wide-eyed with fear.

Isn't it interesting how our minds can be working out what we will say for future descriptions even while we are in the middle of the adventure? Oh well, keeps the brain occupied and unable to dwell on our imminent danger.

I kept this movement up for one more floor, each new set of stairs becoming less and less aesthetic and more functional. No more carpet or pretty carvings, just plain wood and probably splinters. The last stairs were very rough, almost a ladder. They were tucked away at the end of a short corridor, looking like they were an embarrassing afterthought and would people please stop staring. I climbed them to a small door, I opened it and gazed upon my place of succour.

The door opened into the ceiling space, overhead was the sloped roof; piles of junk were gathering dust in various puddles on the floor. The piles included old, broken furniture, a large cupboard, a truly huge rocking horse, dust cloths, rags and assorted bric-a-brac. I found a darkish corner, spread out my improved bedding and settled in. To be even safer, I threw some of the dusty clothes and rags over me before dropping off to a soundless sleep. I was warm and dry. Later when, and if, I awoke, the plan would be to search for food and water and think about my next moves. For now, I was safe.

Time passed, a noise woke me. I opened my eyes to find an alien girl sitting on the floor near me, she sat with her legs pulled up and her arms around her knees, she was very young but I didn't have the experience to judge her age. She had another large dustsheet bundled up on the floor next to her.

"Hello," she said. "Are you hiding?"

My nap had not refreshed me. It probably wasn't even a nap, more like a lapse into unconsciousness. I shifted around in my pile of dress-up costumes and rags but stayed supine. I didn't want to scare her into running away screaming. Was she a threat? I kept quiet.

"My name's Layla," she said, "It means I was born at night. What's your name?" The wee thing wore a long garment covering her from neck to feet with bare toes poking from beneath the hem. She had big eyes, eyes currently fixed on me. Her fingers twirled together, just fidgeting. The face was longer than human, I had seen its like before but could not think where.

She stopped speaking and leaned her head forward to gaze fixedly at me, "Can you talk?"

"Hello, Layla", I grunted. She remained motionless, like a bird about to fly. How had she found me? Was she a danger? My hand crept around until I found the clasp knife. I kept it hidden but opened the blade. Oh, dear lord, was I going to kill a child?

She leaned back, unclasping her hands, "You don't look well. Should I get you some help? I'm staying with my auntie Louise and she has lots of people working for her, I'm sure one of them is a doctor."

Auntie Louise. Who says God doesn't have a sense of humour. "No, I'll be right, just need a rest. Best not to tell your aunt." Best if the child never left the room, I thought. "Tell me about yourself, Layla," I asked.

She smoothed her robe over her knees and began picking at random pieces of thread as she spoke, "Well, my daddy's very important," her eyes strayed around the room, taking it all in. "He's a doctor. Well, a scientist, really. But he had a big job to do and asked me to come and stay with Auntie Louise while he worked. At least I have some company, I'm sharing a room with my sister, Nashwa – her name means 'happiness'. She's not really my sister but she was already here when I arrived. Auntie Louise isn't really my auntie, obviously. After all, she's human like you." She raised herself proudly erect and announced, "I'm an Anipe woman!" She deflated and went on, "At least, I will be when my next birthday happens, until then no one takes any notice of me. I'm just a girl."

She leaned in towards me again, "Are you sure you are well? You don't look well. You're right about leaving Auntie Louise out of it; she can be very bossy. Can I tell you a secret? I don't like Auntie Louise very much. But my daddy had a big argument with the rest of our family and now they're not speaking. Can you imagine that? Not speaking to your real family and having to come and live with yukky Auntie Louise? But Nashwa is lovely, her daddy's very important, something in the government. You haven't told me your name, yet. What's your name? Is it a secret? Are you a supervillain come to spy on Auntie Louise? Or maybe a stylish and charming thief searching for the jewels? Do you want to know where they are? I can show you. You don't speak a lot, do you?" She sighed, "People say I talk too much."

I lay back, relaxing my grip on the knife. "Not a bit of it, Layla," I said. "I like hearing you talk. What's an Anipe?"

"You're funny," she giggled. "I'm an Anipe, it's what we call our people. You're a human, I'm an Anipe, Nashwa is an Anipe woman because she is a year older than me. Then you have the Tharls, the Glitchens and, oh, lots of different beings. You can tell if someone is an adult Anipe by the way they dress and look. We are very tall and traditionally wear colourful robes with bright threads and lots and lots of glitter. I'm looking forward to getting my grown-up abal – that's what we call the robe. I want mine to be bright blue, like the sky, and I'll have little speckles of dark purple jewels sewn on so they look like the stars. Don't you think that would be beautiful?"

"I think I've met some Anipe. Tall, skinny people, gave me some injections," I said. We remained quiet for at least two heartbeats before Layla started to look bored. She was definitely young, not able to sit still for more than a few minutes. Time for some of the old Valentine cleverness, engage her with clever banter, that sort of thing. I opened my mouth, she looked at me expectantly, not a sound came out. Finally, I got to say, "Uhm. So... how did you find me?" Sparkling, I was.

"Oh," she said, extending her legs and examining her toes, "I get bored staying in my room; Auntie Louise wants me there but it's so dull. We normally spend the day in a big room with books and games but when the power went out some men came and took us back to our bedroom. There was some big commotion today, lots of people running around and our door was left unlocked. Nashwa stayed in the room – I don't think she's as brave as me – but I decided to explore. And they don't let me have my communicator so I can't call any of my friends."

She looked at her fingers, bit a nail, checked it again and said, "I sneak out when I can and explore. You left a trail of footsteps through dust and I wanted to see what it was. I found the room where you came through the air-conditioning vent – why did you do that? And I could see you had walked around the storeroom – knocking things over, I might add. Are you always clumsy?"

I detected a hint of the censorious in her tone. Heck, my work was being appraised by an alien youngster; I was not scoring well. Time for some distraction, "Ummm...," I said.

"Are you hiding from Auntie Louise?" she asked.

And there it was, we had reached the point of decision. What was I going to do with her?

Chapter 35

"But don't worry," she said, "I used this to conceal your tracks." She nudged the dusty sheet beside her. "I made it look like I was dragging it around. If they ask, I'll say I was playing dress-ups as the Empress."

"Thank you," I said. "But why did you do that? Why would you help me?"

Before she could respond, we both heard footsteps coming up the stairs outside. I tensed up again and grabbed my knife. Those stairs only opened into this room – we were about to have visitors; several sets of visitors, all wearing big boots. I began to struggle out of my little cocoon, the various costumes and rags had become entangled in my legs but I did not intend to be found by these mongrels all wrapped up in a princess dress.

Layla leapt to her feet, grabbed her large dust sheet and threw it over me. As it settled on my head, I wondered if I had been betrayed by this slip of a girl. Then she spoke in an urgent whisper.

"Lie down, be very still. Here, give me that dress." She yanked some yellow concoction from under my arm, pushed me back down and plumped up all the clothing and rags around me. The door opened and she softly said, "Trust me."

I don't mind a fight; I don't even mind running away when the occasion suits. And hiding in dark alleys? Colour me there, brother. I've even, on one memorable occasion, hid in a cupboard while an angry boyfriend spoke to his girlfriend. His ex-girlfriend, he just didn't know he was ex- until that moment.

But lying prone under a dusty sheet was new. Especially lying prone while the bad guys entered the room. I was on my left side, facing the doorway; one hand gripping the knife. A weight settled against my stomach; it was Layla, sitting in front of me and leaning back into my body. I could see a piece of the room through a gap in the rags. My ability to leap into instant action was close to zero.

Encumbered by the sheet, the costumes and Layla's weight meant a heroic joining of battle was out of the question. I could still stab Layla, close as she was. It wouldn't help, just be an act of vengeance.

A loud, commanding voice exclaimed, "Who is there? Identify yourself!"

Kill a child? Yeah...nah. I held myself still, breathed softly and waited for the party to start.

Layla's voice sounded very regal as she replied, "I am the Empress and Queen, Layla the Magnificent, seated upon the eternal chair of majesty! You may approach the throne and perform obeisance." This was some kid. I debated holding my breath to see how it all played out but decided against it. Shallow breathing is called for, not a big gulp when I ran out of air. I admit to a certain tenseness in the situation.

"Is that you, Miss Layla?" asked a voice. It had lost its aggressive tone and descended into mildly exploratory. "What are you doing here, child?" I could see the action through a small gap between my covering sheet and Layla's left hip. Into my vision stepped a uniformed flunky, behind him a few more dribbled in.

"Oh, hello, Mr Bogdan," said Layla. "I was just playing. See what I found in a storeroom, lots of dress-up clothes. Do you think this will fit me?" I saw a flash of the yellow dress being waved about before she put it down. Naturally, she put it down over my eye gap. Now I was watching the scene through a gauzy film of yellow mesh. "I don't think it will," she went on. "It's made for a human, not an Anipe. And besides, it's too drab. Why do we have dress-up clothes in a storeroom, Mr Bogdan? Does Auntie Louise play dress-ups?"

I wished I could see Bogdan's face at this question. I caught a blurry glimpse as he contemplated Louise doing any sort of playing. He stumbled over a response, "Dress-ups? No, I don't think so ...." He caught himself and drifted back on track, "We've had a report of a strange man, possibly a thief, in the building. We followed your tracks, why were you in the storeroom? Have you seen anyone?"

Layla leaned forward and I stifled the urge to make an 'oof' sound. "A thief!" she exclaimed. "How exciting! Is he dashing and debonair? Dressed in sophisticated evening clothes and a silk mask? What would he be after? Does Auntie Louise have lots and lots of jewels and precious things in a secret vault?"

Some of the blurry bodies moved through the room, I guessed they were poking into cupboards and the like while looking for this mysterious masked man. Hang on, that's me. Bogdan had stepped closer to Layla; I had a better view of him through my gauze. He was dressed in black with a hood hanging over his shoulders. If that hood was in place, he would resemble one of the goons who tortured me. Either Louise had all her riff-raff dress like these bastards or I was looking at one of my tormentors. I was going to remember Mr Bogdan.

He growled, "You had better go back to your room, Miss Layla, and stay with Miss Nashwa. One of my men will accompany you."

Layla stood up, picking up the yellow costume. The clothing and sheets around me moved slightly and she turned back to the pile to re-arrange them. She made sure I was still covered. "Very well, Mr Bogdan. But please, leave these things as they are. It has taken me all morning to find and place them just so. I want to come back and keep playing my Empress game." Her voice changed as she clapped her hands, "Perhaps you could come with me? You could be my trusted bodyguard and I could issue orders. Could we do that? Please? Do you want to play dress-ups? I'm sure there is a costume in her for you!" She sounded positively giddy with excitement.

"No, miss," answered a scared Bogdan. "I have my duties; we are still searching for the thief. Please go back to your room and remain there."

I heard Layla's voice prattling away as she left the room. A guard approached Bogdan to say, "Nothing here. I don't see how anyone could hide in this room with that little chit bouncing around." Their boots filled my vision, good workmanlike boots. Boots made for kicking the weak and helpless. My sort of boots. "Is it true what he did to Cezar?" asked the voice.

They began moving towards the door, "Yes," replied Bogdan. "Tore his throat out, the animal. He's obviously unhinged."

The other man asked, "Do we keep looking for him inside? I thought he jumped through the window?"

"I'm sure he did but we lost all the cameras during the blackout. Don't know if they're back up yet, damn things are very fussy. Come on, let's go make our report. And be prepared to go into the woods, he can't get far. Hell's bells, I'm surprised he can even walk," said Bogdan.

As they exited, I caught the last few words of the conversation, "What's his name again? Val ...something? Valerie?" The door shut on any further discussion.

'Valerie', how humiliating. And what was a camera?

As soon as they left, I crawled out of my cocoon and rearranged the pile to some semblance of its previous appearance. I wasn't keen on staying under all the clothing, just felt too helpless. I don't like to feel helpless. The room had some large pieces of furniture, including a cupboard big enough for me. And the rocking horse. I walked over to it and stroked the huge shape. Closer inspection revealed it was not a horse, it had six legs and three eyes. It sat on a large platform with two legs rearing up, the eyes shone reflected light and I walked around the beautiful thing.

The door opened, and one of the guards entered.

I dropped to the floor, hiding behind the rocking horse-thing platform. My position was quite exposed, I probably wasn't visible from the door but a casual wander around the room would reveal my battered body. The guard extended one of those batons they all seemed to like, walked over to my recent hiding place and poked the clothes. He flipped some pieces up and generally spread all the costumes and dust clothes around.

I pressed closer to the floor and peeked between the horse thing's legs, hoping my skull resembled a piece of the structure; something like a rock. I thought rock thoughts.

Bogdan appeared in the doorway, "Anything?" he asked. "Can we get on now?"

The guard stood over the strewn remnants of Layla's throne and said, "No, nothing here. I just had to check."

"Come on, Doru," said Bogdan, "Precious Miss Slynkor is going to be upset with you, messing up her playthings like that."

"Like I care," came the reply. "She'll forget all about it after Louise reveals her father's dead."

"Yeah, I'm guessing Louise will put her with the brats, get some use out of her," said Bogdan. "Control wants us to move both the Anipe girls in with the other ankle biters, we can do that after we finish here. That madman escaping has thrown Louise off her stride, I don't envy her telling Ghost about it. Let's you and me keep a low profile for the next hour or two, I'll tell Control we're doing a deep sweep after we transfer the girls. Being 'conscientious' and searching the building, they love that sort of initiative. We can hole up and play cards. That should give us a few hours away from the centre of the storm."

They laughed and left the room, I stretched out, exhaled and had a think. Layla had saved me; she didn't like Louise. Her father was recently dead. She was an Anipe. I now knew who she was, I had seen her father's dead body. It sounded like Layla and her friend, Nashwa, were here as...what? Hostages?

How did all these jigsaw pieces fit together?

I opened the door and peeked, all was clear. Now for some creeping about. I wanted to find Layla's room and have a chat with her and Nashwa. I also could do with some food, water and bandages. My feet were still wrapped in cloth making my steps noiseless. And very uncomfortable. Now the trick was finding the one locked door in the facility behind which two Anipe girls would be cowering. I had no idea how I was going to identify the right door, opening every one of them seemed risky.

Bogdan and his mate were headed there now, maybe I could follow them. I could silently creep up on them while gliding through the rooms like an assassin; I could be the invisible nemesis, a scourge to all evildoers. Fortunately, sanity prevailed before I tripped over my own feet; the two thugs were still chatting ahead of me so I just followed their voices and kept well back.

I followed them to another corridor with several doors along each wall. When I turned the corner, the corridor was empty, where were the two guards? Had they stopped talking and were still ahead of me? Or had they entered one of the rooms here and, if so, which one? In front of one door was a yellow, gauzy dress. Could be a clue, I thought.

The door was unlocked, I listened but couldn't hear a thing. This modern architecture has taken all the frivolity out of construction – doors fitted properly, windows did not have gaps for icy winds to explore, walls were no longer thin which meant a casual punch hurt the hand without leaving a hole. No romance anywhere.

When in doubt, charge ahead. Probably a good headstone for my grave. I slammed the door open, stepped in and punched the first neck I saw. Luckily, it was one of the guards; could have been very embarrassing if I'd just cold-cocked the cook. He slid to the floor without any fuss, getting a full-bodied punch to the back of the neck can make the body all loose and limber. Often permanently.

Bogdan was on my left, the collapsed guard was falling at my feet and I was facing the two girls. They were standing on their beds holding implements of destruction. Layla had a bedside lamp and the other girl, whom I assumed was Nashwa, was swinging a soft toy in meaningful arcs. Both were glowering at Bogdan. Each time they moved, their mattress wobbled and they did a little balance dance. These two young chits were taking on the two thugs, giving it all they had.

All these events took less than a second – my entrance, the thump to the guard and my taking in the scene before me. Bogdan still had a supercilious smile on his face as he mocked the girls and their tiny resistance. I saw his face start to change as I followed up my initial blow to his mate with a knife-hand to Bogdan's throat. He went from gloating evil doer, straight past perplexed thug and settled on 'man losing the ability to breathe'. As he considered his other options, I gave him a right cross to his ear which sent his head crashing into the wall. His eyes widened before closing for the duration. I discovered it is possible to leave a hole in these walls if you hit them hard enough.

"Hiya, Layla," I said, "How are you doin'?" Bogdan's body hit the floor.

Chapter 36

Layla jumped off the bed and hugged me. "Mr Valentine!" she said, "Mr Bogdan told us we were to be taken to the cells! What did he mean? What cells? We haven't done anything wrong!"

There we stood, Layla hugging me as I stood in torn and bloodied clothes with my hands and feet wrapped in rags. My mouth probably still displayed blood and gore from Cezar. Nashwa lowered the soft toy and blinked at us, her mouth opened and closed, her shoulders slumped and she sat on the bed.

"I...I," she said, "You look very scary..." Stress will do that to you, it makes the brain go blank. Stress and immediate, catastrophic danger will cause most people to shut down, to freeze. I've always found that this moment, those precious few seconds when all around me are taking a mental breath, is the best time to punch someone in the face. Not good manners but terrific for getting answers.

"I'm not scary," I said to her. "My name is Valentine and I'm a friend of Layla." I got an extra squeeze in the hug when I said that. "We need to get you girls somewhere safe."

Layla released me and sat on the bed, "Why? What's happened?" Nashwa came and sat beside her, the girls held hands and leaned together for support. Was this the time for me to tell them her father was dead? At least, I think it was her father. Better check before I rock their world.

"What's your full name, Layla?" I asked.

"Layla Slynkor. Why?"

"You said your dad was a scientist. Do you know what he was working on, what was the big job?"

"Oh, yes," she said, "he was so excited. He had worked out that nanobots could be used to translate languages. We could get rid of those stupid Translator Beads," she pulled back the hair on Nashwa's head to display a bead. "Why do you want to know?"

I looked at their faces, both staring at me in that after-danger flush as the body slowly resets. They were just children, for goodness' sake, how do I tell them that one has a dead father and the other has...something else? Two things happened before I got to a decision, the body of the thug I had first struck groaned and Layla asked me "Why haven't you got a Translator Bead, Mr Valentine?"

She was right, "I've got your dad's nanobots in me," I said. "Just like you." She blushed and touched her ear, her empty ear. I had noticed her lack of a bead in our earlier meeting.

"Daddy gave me some after he worked out they were safe," she said. "All our family have them, it's just so cool." She started to look worried as the thug groaned some more, "What are we going to do, Mr Valentine?"

I rolled the thug over and dragged him to a sitting position before slapping his face until he regained consciousness.

"Owww!" he said. "Stop it!" I searched him and found another knife and other odds and ends which I tossed onto a bed.

"What's your name, pal?" I asked as I squatted back on my heels to look directly into his eyes. The girls huddled together some more; this guy had scared them badly. I peeled off the cloths from my hands, the blood around my fingernails had dried and the wrappings came off with a wet slurp and considerable pain. And more blood.

"Eww!" said Layla, "That's so gross!"

I put my hands on either side of his face and leaned into him, "I'm waiting, sport. Name?"

"Doru!" he said, "My name's Doru!"

"Where were you taking these girls?"

"Umm, I don't know. I was just following orders. Bogdan's in charge, ask him."

I took my hands from his face and held them so he could see the fingernails. My missing fingernails. "Bogdan's in charge, you say?" I asked. He nodded furiously. I indicated where Bogdan lay against the wall, "That's Bogdan?" I asked. I knew the answer, I just wanted him giving me responses. Get them talking or responding, that's the trick.

He nodded some more. I held one finger up to him and said, "Stay there. Do not move." More nodding. I shuffled over to where Bogdan lay and checked his neck for a pulse. There might have been one, hard to say through the throbbing of my fingers. I took his head between my hands and gave it a quick twist. We all heard the sharp crack. I shuffled back to a sweating Doru and settled myself before him again.

"Mr Bogdan's retired," I said. "You've just been promoted." I glanced at the two girls, they were both frozen in a huddle, each with arms around the other. Big eyes on me, open mouths and that stillness that comes when you want the bad man to go away. Valentine, king of the kids.

"I heard you talking about Slynkor. Tell these girls what happened to him," I said.

He gulped and thought about lying, looked at my face and reconsidered. His eyes shifted to Bogdan and he whispered, "Slynkor's dead."

Layla came off the bed, "What? What did he say about my daddy?" She was leaning over me, one small hand resting on my shoulder.

"Louise ordered us to get you girls," said Doru, "and take you to the cells with the rest of them. She said since your father was dead, we had no need to keep you safe, you could be used like the others."

"What do you mean by saying my father's dead?" croaked Layla. "He's Auntie Louise's friend! He's not dead! He's not!"

I pulled out my clasp knife and held the point towards Doru's eye, "Tell it all," I instructed, "and tell Nashwa about her father, and what he does for the Syndicate."

"No, I can't," he muttered, "they'd kill me." He shook his head from side to side, the point of the knife not bothering him at all. Time for some more intensive interrogation.

I turned the knife in and held it point down, then slammed it into his hand where it lay on the floor, splayed out against the carpet. It went through the flesh, the bones and stuck into the ground; yet another hand I had destroyed; maybe I had a fetish. I leaned in and let him see the bits of flesh and blood still adhering to my lips and gums from where I had torn out Cezar's throat.

"What do you think I'd do to you?" I asked. My face was very close to his, he had a good look into my eyes and started talking. It was more a gabble than a talk but he certainly spilled his guts.

"Slynkor's dead," said Doru, "The Syndicate had him killed because the police were onto him. He wouldn't hold out under questioning, Ghost decided to cut our losses."

"The girls?" I prompted with a head nod to them. Layla was still leaning over me while Nashwa had moved to sit on the bed close to our little tableau.

"Louise said there was no point in holding them anymore," he said, "She wanted them dead but Ghost decided to use them as mules. Get some value out of them."

Ghost was a sweetheart. "Why take Nashwa to the cells? She was still good as a hostage," I asked.

Both girls looked at me, "Hostage?" asked Nashwa. "We're not hostages. We weren't kidnapped or anything. We're guests of Auntie Louise."

Oh, boy. "No, you're not guests," I said. "Both your fathers were useful to the Syndicate. They probably got paid but Ghost wanted more security, more than just a promise. He would have threatened to kill your entire family if hostages were not given. You girls served as a good behaviour bond for your fathers' continued cooperation with Ghost and the Syndicate." I touched Layla on the shoulder as gently as I could, "When your father was killed, there was no use for you anymore." I turned to look at Nashwa, "Your father is Elector S'eenyur, isn't he?"

Nashwa gazed at me and nodded slowly before moving over to cuddle Layla, their arms going around each other as they grew up all at once. "Is my father dead, too?" she asked in a small voice.

We all looked at Doru, he had slumped back in defeat, "No, he's alive. Ghost wanted to send a message about his continued silence. He figured to use you as a mule one time only, let your father see what happened and then threaten more of the same if he got a conscience."

"What's a mule?" asked Nashwa.

I could answer that. "It's a name given to someone carrying a load of nanobots, usually an illegal load. The Syndicate uses children to transport nanobots through customs. These are dodgy nanobots, not cued to the host's body."

"But that's dangerous!" said Layla. "Nanobots have to be linked to each person, the code going into them has to be specific. Otherwise, they risk seizures or death as the nanobots act like an invading disease. People don't do that, it's horrible!"

"The chances are reduced if the host body is pre-pubescent," I said. The girls looked at me. "If the mule is a child." I took a breath, "Like you."

Time passed as this information settled in. The girls continued to hug each other, I went on feeling grubby, dishevelled and filthy. Doru probably didn't feel too crash hot either but I wasn't worried about his wellbeing. I needed a wash, and definitely a mouth rinse. I pulled the knife out of the floor, Doru gave a small gasp as it came out of his hand but wisely refrained from any other attention-getting statements. I sank back on the floor and stretched out my tired legs. This gave me the opportunity to examine my feet and bloodied toes. God, I was a mess.

"How do you communicate with Control?" I asked Doru. He blinked at me and pointed at one of the things I had taken out of his pockets, a small box with buttons. Good, while I had it we didn't have to worry about squads of goons running in.

The silence stretched on. Layla took a deep breath and asked, "What do we do now, Mr Valentine?" She was sitting straighter, I noticed she was doing more giving of comfort than receiving. Tough kid.

"Good question," I answered. "We've got a bit of time before these two idiots are noticed as missing." I ignored Doru and continued to let my mouth do the planning, "I need to clean myself up, get some bandages and better clothing. We need a place to hide, we need food, water and shelter. If we leave this facility, we have to find a place in the woods or seek a town or city. I'm not a creature of the wild; I can't hunt or live off the land unless I have to - maybe there's a town nearby?" This ranked as first-rate planning, lots of questions with no answers. How does the Man in Black do all this stuff?

"We've got a washroom," said Layla. She pointed at another door in their room. "You could use it," she finished.

I stood up and opened the door. Sure enough, it contained all I would need to wash the accumulated sweat, blood and smell from the body. I recognised the little nozzles which sprayed warm water in a shower and I decided to use it as soon as possible. It would hurt like hell when the water hit my wounds but I had to get clean, I had to wash the stench of my captivity down the drain. I had to reinvent myself, change from trapped and hunted fugitive and back into the sergeant of the NightWatch.

But Doru was a problem, he was sitting still and nursing his wounded hand while I moved about. I didn't trust him to remain this way if I disappeared into the shower, this needed some thought.

I said, in a conversational and thoughtful tone, "I may have to kill you, Doru."

Chapter 37

Doru's eyes widened. He cuddled his hand some more and adopted the pose of 'helpless victim'. Like that was going to work. The girls were another matter, Nashwa yelped, "No! You can't just kill him. That would be murder!" Neither of these arguments carried any weight with me.

Layla was another story. She looked at my face, I saw her eyes narrow and her lips took on that tight quality some people get when they think. It seemed the Anipe race had similar facial mannerisms to human beings; maybe they had just hung around each other too much. Still, she didn't make the standard 'Don't hurt the helpless man' response I had expected. She was, after all, just a child; I waited for her to plead for mercy and compassion. And Nashwa had already broken ground by stating her feelings about murder and so on.

Layla said, "We might need him." I could feel the ice coming from her as she rebuilt herself. The Syndicate may have made a big mistake in killing her father, they may have made this little girl into an enemy to be feared.

"I can help!" pleaded Doru. "I can help you to get out of the building, I can show you food and supplies. There's a storeroom on this corridor for uniforms and clothing, the kitchens are nearby. Please don't eat me!" He was going off. He thought I was going to eat him; inspiring fear in another is a wonderful thing. You just need to tear someone's throat out with your teeth to get a big rep.

Nashwa looked up at me with big eyes, "Do you eat people, Mr Valentine?' she asked.

I moved over to Doru and tied him to a bed. "Only on the weekends," I said. I stuffed some clothes into his mouth and gagged him securely. When I pinched his nose, he went red until I released my fingers – a good sign. You don't want your helpless and trapped victim to be able to breathe through their mouth, they might loosen the gag and yell. More tips for the new player.

"Layla," I said, "watch him. I'm going to get cleaned up. If he moves, hit him with something."

"Can I have one of your knives?" she asked. I swallowed at this; she was beginning to scare me.

"Not just yet," I said. I knew Bogdan would have a knife so I quickly frisked him to find the weapon. "Search them both again and tell me what all the items are for. There should be a communicator on Bogdan. I'm going to have a wash."

I bent down to Doru, "Be good, be very still and cause me no grief," I said, "or I'll give this little girl a sharp knife." He paled, nodded to me, and shrank into himself.

I have outstanding communication skills.

The shower stung. My fingernails and toenails - or rather, the spaces where they had been -invoked massive pain. I slumped against the cubicle wall as I let the hot water steam onto my damaged extremities. The other injuries, the burns and various cuts and bruises, all contributed to the fun. I shaved as a means of showing my body who was boss. The clasp knife did the trick, the blade was much sharper than any I had seen before, probably a factor of some strange and mysterious alien metal. Or someone just likes a sharp knife. Whatever the reason, it served the purpose, I scraped my cheeks and neck but decided to keep a rakish beard and moustache. My Viking pals would be dead impressed.

I came out gleaming, fresh blood trickling from various parts of my anatomy to accompany my severely diminished viewpoint on mercy to my fellow man. I was also naked and stepping into a room containing children. Somewhere, my mother was having a fainting attack over her boy's insensitivity. I argued that they were aliens and so didn't count – her voice in my head indicated she did not agree. I have frequently disappointed my mum.

Everyone in the room ignored me. Probably because Layla was crouched in front of a wide-eyed Doru and holding one of the batons. She had extended it to full length and was allowing the thin tip to wander over his face, very slowly. She seemed to hesitate near his eye and perhaps smidged the tip a trifle closer to that delicate organ. Sweat spotted his forehead, he kept his head very still while swivelling pleading eyes towards me. Nashwa was poking through the belongings that had been taken from the guards and generally ignoring everyone else. Very wise of her, I thought.

My body needed clothes, my hands and feet needed bandages and I desperately wanted a strong drink. "Hi gang," I said, "is everybody happy?"

"Gross," said Nashwa, "we can see your yukky bits. Would you at least put on a towel?" this seemed a reasonable request so I stepped back into the washroom, wrapped myself in a large towel and returned to the party.

Layla had used the time to stand up and was now lightly tapping Doru's head with the baton. She didn't speak. Doru, on the other hand, gave me a pleading look. "Say, Doru," I said, just passing the time, "you said there was room nearby with clothes and stuff? Where would that be?"

"Two doors down on the right," he quickly answered. "Would you like me to show you? Please?"

"No, I'll be right." I opened the door and peeked out, no one was in sight. "Layla," I said, "take this." I gave her a knife. Her eyes gleamed as she took the blade from my hand, she turned her head to look at a very nervous Doru. I clasped her shoulder and said, "I'm leaving this weapon in case I get caught or otherwise don't make it back. I'm going out there bare-arsed naked, in no condition to put up much of a fight." I shook her gently until she looked back at me,

"Do not use it unless they come in through this door. We need Doru alive, we need to find out how to get to Ghost and Louise. Ghost and Louise, Layla, Ghost and Louise are the ones who betrayed you and killed your father. We need to get out of here and get help, then we come back and get them. Make them pay."

"We find them," she said. "We kill them."

Holy shit.

"Keep Doru alive until I get back," I said, slipping out the door. I know I was taking a risk, I understand Layla was not stable and I had just given her the opportunity to further damage her mental health. Not to mention Doru's physical health. The voices in my hand were united in criticising my handling of this child. But the voices in my head were not walking around a criminal gang's headquarters holding a wet towel over the family jewels. Nakedness disarms in more ways than one.

The storeroom was as described, unlocked and available. I popped inside to find shelves of clothing as well as boots, belts, bags and all the gear necessary for the well-dressed henchman. But no weapons. No knives, batons, blasters, or useful bundles of explosives. This was only matched by the distinct lack of maps, communication equipment or anything vaguely useful for those in need of a quick getaway. It was room for clothes. Terrific.

I dressed myself in appropriate evil henchman attire, even finding boots the correct size. My feet were not thrilled about being so ill-used but I wanted to be able to kick the stuffing out of anyone – just as an option. I took some extra belts, socks and other gear, stuffed them into several bags I decided I really needed and left the room. I did a quick check before leaving, ensuring I had not left evidence of my visit. I'm sure a careful stocktake would reveal my heinous crime but a cursory search should not hint at my presence. I hoped.

I exited the room dressed to kill. I loved the jacket and pants, all dark and ominous looking. Around my neck was another scarf, very woolly and soft. But my prize was a cloth cap, a wee thing with a tiny brim of no use whatsoever. With my sexy beard, moustache and scarf, I believed I looked dashing and romantic. Look out ladies, I thought.

Layla had not killed anyone by the time I returned. When I opened the door, she was positioned behind the tied-up Doru with the blade of the knife against his neck. She had her eyes on the door and relaxed when she saw it was me, the knife rock remained steady in her little hand. Doru was having a bad day.

Nashwa had used her time to pack a bag of clothes and other girlie stuff. Probably make-up and things that smell nice. She had put a bag for Layla on the bed, a bag which remained resolutely empty. She looked at me, and gave my attire an obvious up and down before judging, "The clothes are fine, not sure about the scarf but lose the silly cap."

"Caps are cool," I replied, looking to Layla for moral support. She had given herself other duties but did glance at my headgear with an unnecessary withering roll of the eyes. Kids, eh?

"Okay," I whispered, "time to go."

"Where are we going?" asked Nashwa.

I stopped. Good question. "Umm," I replied. Be good to have a plan, I thought.

Nashwa said, "We can go to our homeroom." I must have looked mystified because she went on, "We don't stay in this room all day. At least, not normally. We have a place we go to each day, where we read or study, it has a small kitchen attached and leads to a walled garden. We can go to a small dock and swim or sail a small boat." She grimaced, "It has been a delightful retreat but now I see it has always been a prison."

"We need to find the other children," said Layla. She had turned to face us, just being a part of our discussion. I did notice, however, that she kept her knife poking Doru's neck. He continued to be very still and sent me pleading looks. Nothing I haven't seen before. Given a few in my time, too. Layla used her free hand to brush a strand of hair away from her face. "We cannot leave them here." She seemed very conversational.

Okay, this rescue mission was officially out of control. "Layla," I said, "we can't do that. We don't know where they are, how many or what condition they are in. And if we find them, how do we get away? I'm not in my peak form at the moment."

Surprisingly, Nashwa joined Layla. She sat on the bed and put a hand on the other girl's shoulder. Layla's knife remained at Doru's throat. "Layla is right, Mr Valentine. Now that we know what was intended for us, how can we walk away knowing other children are at risk."

I groaned. "Fine," I said, dropping my extra gear on the floor. "Just one question, where are they?" I asked the girls. There we go, I thought, a bit of harsh reality for them. Let's get to the nuts and bolts of the situation and forget about wild flights of fancy. "We don't have enough information on these children, they could be anywhere. And I'm hungry and thirsty." I felt a touch of selfishness was called for.

Layla sat up straight, closed the knife and put it into a pocket. She stepped over to her empty bag and began putting clothes into it. "We find them. We save them." This girl was strong-willed, painful, arrogant, and a bloody nuisance.

And she was right. "Yeah," I said, "Righto."

Bugger.

Chapter 38

We left the room and crept along the corridors, I clutched a knife in one hand and my bag in the other. Doru was secured by belts linking him to me, he also rejoiced in a gag stuffed into his mouth and several of the large bags hung from his shoulders. His hands were secured behind his back, he wasn't going to run off or cry out. The girls carried their bags as well as anything I thought we could use. Nashwa carried a soft toy under one arm, I could see she was struggling emotionally, she became more and more fearful with every step, waiting for the monster to leap out of the cupboard.

Layla just gripped her knife. The girls had their priorities.

We found their homeroom without any trouble; it was all you could wish for in a recreation space. Large, clear windows showed off the outside world, a world of tall trees, blue sky and white clouds. Immediately outside the windows was a cleared, grassy space that developed into the far woods. I hoped the nutcases searching for me were all tramping through the bush and scrub accompanied by small insects, lots of sweating and possibly scratches from unfriendly flora. Please, God, I thought, let there be snakes.

Our large room was comfortable. Several big, well-padded chairs were scattered around the place; low tables held boxes of puzzles and probably games. Bookshelves stood hopefully against the walls, keen to involve you in a little reading. These weren't the bookcases from libraries, the ones that sneer at you, daring the passerby to decipher some arcane text. No, these bookshelves were colourful and positively smiled in welcome. I didn't like them. I'd want my bookcases to sneer. If I had bookcases. If I had books.

Off to one side was a smaller area with a hard floor surface. It held cupboards and tables, plus taps and strange machines for doing cooking-related tasks. A ladder was bolted to one wall, it flowed upwards to a ceiling trapdoor for no purpose I could fathom. I moved towards the taps and sink, desperate for a drink. The girls seemed to know what was needed; while I stuck my face under a tap and turned it on, they opened cupboards and pulled out food. Nashwa passed me a cup and told me not to be disgusting. We packed our bags with non-perishable food, Layla opened a cupboard containing chilled food but we decided we should leave it. Anything that needed to be kept cold would become a liability.

Or rather, it would be a liability IF we had a plan. We certainly could not stay here, comfortable as it was. We needed to get out and away. And not into the woods, we needed a town or city, we needed transport. We needed rescuing. I needed help.

"How do you get to that garden and the sailing boats?" I asked. Visions of stealing aboard a small craft and sailing to freedom flitted across my mind. I can't sail and I know nothing of small boat handling. Yes, this was going to be a fun escape.

Nashwa pointed to a door, "Through there," she said. "That door opens to a sun deck with steps down to a walled garden. The garden has a big patch of lawn where we sometimes play. There's a gate in the wall leading to the docks. The gate is locked but someone always came with us to open up."

I walked across to the door; it was locked. I could break it down. Maybe. Especially if I had something big and nasty. But no. all I had was a knife and a sissy little baton. I had also taken the shock rod from Cezar but it was useless as a weapon of mass destruction. If I had a hammer, I'd hammer in the morning, I'd hammer in the evening, all over this land...

Behind a leather couch was a set of steps going down, a decorative rail and a wall kept the unemployed from falling into the hole. The entire structure fitted into the tone of the room; tasteful, calm and serene. And lotsa money.

"Where do these go?" I asked, pointing to the descending staircase.

The girls shrugged, "We don't know," replied Layla. "No one ever used them, at least, not when we were in the room. We never thought to ask."

"Let's ask now," I said, moving over to Doru. I had placed him on a comfy chair – I'm all about the care and welfare of prisoners – and pulled the gag out of his mouth. "Whaddya say, sport? Where do these stairs go?"

"Downstairs," he blurted.

"No kidding?" I said. "These stairs, obviously going down, go ...down?" I sat on the arm of the chair and placed a caring hand on top of his head. "Anything else you might want to add to that colourful description, Doru?" I asked.

He gulped and said, "They go to the cells."

"Would these be the same cells holding the children? Were you taking Layla and Nashwa to these cells?" I asked. Layla had moved across and joined our little tête-à-tête. I noticed she had also taken out her knife, perhaps I should have taken it away from her. Or not.

"Let's find out," I said. "Layla, stay here and guard Doru," I ignored his pleading eyes. "Try not to kill him. Unless, of course, he cries out, or attempts to escape. Or moves." Or breathes, I thought. "Nashwa, come for a walk." The older Anipe girl crossed to me and we both descended the stairs. They finished at a locked door, another very solid and serious looking locked door. She came hesitantly, but she did come. Brave girl.

"How do we open it?" asked Nashwa. She looked at the door and then retreated up the stairs where she sat down and talked to me. Her courage was running out, poor lamb. "I'm scared, Mr Valentine. I don't want to stay here anymore, I'm coming apart. Can we break the door and just run away. Please?"

"Doubt it," I said.

Nashwa said, "But we have keys. We took some off Bogdan, they're in one of the bags. We could go through the room and escape.

We have to escape! I'll get the keys." She scampered off and I followed. Nashwa seemed to have changed her mind about any rescue, she wanted to be gone, a sentiment with which I heartily agreed.

If this door opened on to a bunch of imprisoned children I would be in a spot of bother. Layla would wish to free them but Nashwa and I were determined to keep moving. I didn't want to waste time freeing child prisoners. How was I going to convince Layla we must pass them by? How was I going to convince myself? Life can get complicated in the world of the modern thug.

When I reached the top of the stairs, I still had no convincing argument to give to Layla. Maybe she would just accept my authority. And pigs might fly.

Doru was still alive when I crossed to him, that was a plus. "Show me the key for the door to the cells," I said to him. "And tell me what the other keys are for." By this time, Nashwa had found the keys and passed them to me. She ran back and prepared our bags for departure; she was keen to be gone. I held the keys, one by one, and Doru identified each one. Layla's knife against his neck was probably his greatest motivator. Or maybe he just warmed to my charisma. Hard to say.

We gathered up our bags containing the supplies and moved back down the stairs. We made Doru sit on a stair with Layla standing over him, the bags we piled on another stair and then I looked at the girls. "Ready?" I asked. They nodded. I unlocked the door and stepped through, knife in one hand, shock rod in the other and vengeance in my heart.

The door opened into a large room, big enough for the entire NightWatch to hold an assembly. Large metal bars came down from the ceiling to the floor, dividing the space into separate spaces. We stood at a sort of clear walkway between two of these large spaces, the corridor led to another door in the far wall. That was the door to which I wanted to go, out of this room. Out of this noisy, sad room.

Because inside each of the larger areas on either side of our walkway were children. Bunk beds, carpets and lounge chairs filled each space, making it both a sleeping and a living area. Some bundles of rags may have been other children, dead or resting. Those on their feet stood and looked at us. No sound came from them except a low background noise of weeping. Children softly crying. Not the loud wails for attention designed to get a parent to run and cuddle. Not the determined tantrum screams of a child demanding its own way.

No, these soft noises were the results of utter sadness, of a child having no real hope of succour and merely descending into bottomless grief.

And I was going to walk by all of them to get to freedom.

Nashwa ran forward to the far door, her shoulder jostling me in her haste. "Come on," she said, over her shoulder.

Layla pushed Doru next, brushing past me apologetically, bags hanging off his shoulders. Layla had seconded Doru as a pack animal; seemed fair. She wasn't demanding I release the children; I think her emotional bank had also emptied, her mind had fled, leaving the body to just get on with it.

"Mr Valentine!" said Nashwa, "You will have to pick up the rest of the bags. I have the keys to the outside door. Please hurry." I noticed she resolutely refused to look at the other children. I could see the torment on her face, the need to flee this place. Against this need was the knowledge of those children she would abandon; she was far too young to have that burden on her young shoulders. Sometimes, life's a bitch.

I stood there. Beside me, in each cage, the captive children had become quiet and still. They were not ragged and ill-treated but nor were they acting like children. They were mute, their faces did not light up with curiosity, no one came forward to chatter to us. They stood or sat in their prisons, awaiting the next demand on their young bodies.

"Mr Valentine!" Nashwa cried, a plaintive loss had crept into her voice, her face screwed up in pain. "Come on.....!" I looked at her as she stood next to the door, one hand on a bag, the other touching the door handle. Layla was still holding a knife to Doru, both of them next to Nashwa. But Layla's face was on me, her look combined fear, anguish and a begging request to save her. And everyone. And make it all better. Only a few steps separated me from my bizarre trio, I could cross over and we could all leave this building. Nothing to stop me.

Nashwa started to cry, her face screwed up and I could see the tears even from where I stood, "Please, Mr Valentine. Please help us get out of here ..."

I walked slowly to her and held out my hand, she gazed up at me with a face awash in tears; her nose ran and her shoulders shook. Her sobs wracked her tiny body, she snuffled and put the keys into my hand. "I'll help you, Nashwa," I said, "but you don't really want to leave these children here, do you? You're just scared." I took her hand and gave it a gentle squeeze, then brushed back some hair that had fallen across her face. She dropped her head and the crying slowly died away.

"My daddy," she said, "my daddy might be dead." She flicked a glance to her companion, "I'm sorry about your daddy, Layla. I don't know what to do. I just want to be safe."

"We are going to free these children, Nashwa," I said. "I will keep you safe. I will keep you all safe." What a ridiculous thing to say. How could I possibly keep that promise? I was in no position to guarantee my own safety, let alone that of any alien children.

All I could do was try. Thanks a lot, mum.

Chapter 39

I took the keys and unlocked the cells, none of the children moved. "Nashwa," I said, "come and help me. Layla, stay with Doru." Nashwa dropped her bags and moved into the girl's cell, she walked stiffly at first but then with purpose, she even managed a smile. Just a little one. Good girl, she was trying. I went into the group of boys. "Come on, fellas," I said, as gently as I could. "Let's see if we can get you home."

We herded our charges back to Layla and Doru. Interestingly, Layla had not allowed the knife to leave his throat during this entire period. I had noticed this when I first went up to ask for the keys. Even though Nashwa was a blubbering mess, even though Layla probably wanted to have a good howl herself, the hand that held the pointy bit against Doru's throat never moved. Her tiny arm was an immovable bar, Doru was almost - but not quite - on tiptoes as he tried to avoid any sudden movement.

Layla may have been having an emotional moment but somewhere, deep inside this young girl, was something strong. And, I suspected, bloody fierce.

Our time was disappearing, we had to leave. I unlocked the exterior door and asked Doru, "What are we stepping into, sport? What's beyond this door?"

"The walled garden," he quickly said. "There's an exit gate in the north wall, shouldn't be any guards."

"And through the gate?" I asked.

"Choices," he said. "Lots of pathways, one goes to the docks and the boathouse, another takes you around to the front of the building, others go into the woods or down to the river for swimming. It's possible to swim to the other bank from here." He was desperately trying to be helpful. "You could leave me there?" He was dreaming if he thought I was going to let him go.

Once the bad guys started searching, they would find Bogdan's body back in the girl's room. I had smashed their communicators after the girls told me they may be used to track us. Why is life so complicated? Louise would do another sweep of the building and eventually discover all the children gone. They would know it was me, the two Anipe girls would not be able to overpower Bogdan and Doru. When they found we still had our new best friend with us we could expect lots of running and shouting as they did what all guards do when the prisoners escape – try to find someone else to blame.

"Let's go," I said, opening the door. I went through first, full of hope and ill will. The garden was empty and I signalled for the others to come through. The newer children were dazed, just following directions like those in a trance. I didn't think they were drugged but could not be sure. Hopefully, it was just shock keeping them quiet and gently mobile.

"Nashwa," I said, "Look after the girls, keep them together, keep them quiet and keep them moving. I look after the boys. Layla, can you stay with Doru and push him along?" This was a risky use of both girls. I hoped the need to watch over a bunch of scared girls would keep Nashwa from thinking too much. Layla's knife stayed on or near Doru's throat the entire time and never wavered. He was terrified of this small girl. To tell the truth, I was a bit fearful of her, too.

We made our way to the gate and exited the garden and building complex. Next question, where to go? The front of the house was not wise, pursuers would be behind us anytime and would be moving fast. We needed a vehicle.

Or a boat?

"Mr Valentine," said Layla, "What about the cameras?"

I poked this sentence about, endeavouring to work out what she meant. Cameras? My thinking face may have scared Doru because he blurted out, "They're offline!" Terrific, big help.

Layla leaned into her knife causing a spot of blood to appear on our captive's neck, "Explain," she instructed.

"It was the lightning," blurted Doru. "Whenever we get an electrical storm, it knocks out the power. Everything goes down." This I understood, having experienced the recent blackout and the little red emergency lights.

"But the power's fixed," I said. "The lights are back on." Okay, I understood a bit of this. Power makes the lights work. Terrific. Now what is a camera and what does 'offline' mean?

"The power has been restored, yes. But the damned cameras always malfunction after a blackout. Someone must go around and restart each of the nodes." I saw Layla nodding so I did some head dipping myself. Doru indicated a box outside the gate, a box with a little glass eye. A box resembling the things they had used to broadcast my torture sessions; I realised these were 'cameras'. The new words kept accumulating in one of the many spare rooms in my brain. "The external cameras won't work until the reset is done," said Doru, keen to help.

I had seen these little boxes around the castle, high up on each wall. I asked, "Are there cameras inside the castle, in rooms and corridors?"

He waved his head in a combined yes and no response, "In the corridors and major rooms, yes. In the cells, of course. But not in bedrooms, storerooms and bathrooms. Just the public or more secure spots." If they had been working, my escape would have been visible to any watcher. I gulped.

"No one can see us yet?" I asked.

"No. That's why you're not surrounded by guards. Look, you've got some time to get away, no one can see you, you'll have a good start. The cameras probably won't come back online for a few more minutes. This is your chance, leave me and get away."

I sat Doru down against the outside wall, a desperate, ridiculous plan forming inside my sleep-deprived brain. "What are you doing?" he asked. "I won't say anything! Look, I'll shut my eyes so I don't see where you go. No need to kill me." He was pleading, his entire demeanour had surrendered under the unspoken threat of Layla's implied savagery. He screwed his eyes shut and held his hands up to be tied.

I obliged him by trussing up arms, legs and torso. As I did, I gave instructions to the children, "Okay, this is what we will do. When we leave here, we split up. Some go to the boat shed, you might find something you can row or a little sailboat, and others can swim across the river. I'll take Nashwa and Layla into the forest. Plus anyone else who wants to come. There must be lots of trails in there, we can get ourselves well and truly lost."

I finished tying Doru and began wrapping a blindfold over his eyes. The children looked back at me blankly, they showed no emotion, merely a desultory lethargy. I added to the padding around Doru's head, he looked like a newborn infant in swaddling clothes. "Any questions?" I asked.

No response, no reaction, except for one girl, "I'm going to swim the river!" she said. Who wants to come with me?" She seemed more animated than the others, more alert and lively.

I leaned down to Doru, "Can you hear me, sport?" I asked. He shifted slightly and gave me a small nod. "Right," I said, "We're off. They should find you soon, just stay still and quiet, give us time to get away." He nodded again, agreement oozing from every pore.

With the clasp knife closed and firmly in my clenched fist, I gave him an almighty whack on the side of the head. He slid sideways, unconscious.

Layla and Nashwa stood ready to move off down the path, the swim girl was bristling with energy and showed signs of regaining her youthful vim and vigour. Perhaps she had not had too much ill-treatment. Yet.

"This way," I instructed, waving everyone to follow me. The girls looked surprised and remained motionless, the captured children began shuffling towards me. Layla and Nashwa exchanged a questioning glance and pointed at the paths. I shook my head, put a finger to my lips and motioned for them to be very silent as they tip-toed past Doru towards me. He might be out of it but I certainly didn't want to give him any clues as to our direction.

We took the path back into the house.

Layla, Nashwa and Swim Girl brought up the rear as I hustled everyone back to the door into the building. Each time I caught their eyes they mouthed questions at me. Each time I responded by placing my fingers to my lips. I saw a lot of teenage eye rolling.

I entered the house first. From here, I expected to be met by a search party, a gang of ne'er-do-wells engaged in finding their missing children. As such, I went back into my normal fighting state; this involved a mild panic, starting at shadows, copious sweat on my brow and whatever prayers I could think of. It's not a nice place to be.

The children's rooms, the cells and so on, were still empty. I pushed our luck, opened the door to the stairs and quietly - o, so quietly – moved up until I could see into the big room.

Still no-one. "Right, grab all the bedding you can - blankets, extra clothing, pillows, stuff like that." When they returned with arms full of soft furnishings, I waved towards the stairs, "Follow me," I whispered. "Quickly and quietly, come on." I took them to the ladder, the one bolted to the wall in the kitchen, the one leading to a trap door in the ceiling. A trapdoor, I hoped, which might take us somewhere we could hide.

I had the children gather at the foot of the ladder while I climbed up, each rung hurting my hands, the length of the climb draining my fast-diminishing energy reserves. "Swim Girl," I said, "get ready to come up after me. Wait until I get the trap door open before you start climbing. I don't trust this ladder to hold my weight as well as a bunch of children." She nodded, waited until I climbed up some distance and then grasped the sides of the ladder, ready for her journey. This one was impressing me.

The trap door was not locked, I heaved it open and climbed up. The space I entered was not huge but would cater for all of us, the roof above sloped down, dust hung from rafters and rough boards made a serviceable floor to the space. The short side walls all contained several of the large vents. Boxes and other debris lay scattered about, the attic had no discernible purpose other than a gap between the roof and the floor below.

My inspection was cut short by a small hand pushing my backside as Swim Girl said, "Get out of the way, you great lump!" She climbed in, turned back to the trapdoor hole and motioned for the others to come up. Soon a stream of children joined me in the space, the larger ones carrying bags. Last to climb up were Nashwa and Layla. I had watched them all climb the ladder with one eye on the door into this room. If it opened, we would be spotted.

Again, Layla showed her courage and intelligence. As Nashwa followed the last of the captured children up the ladder, I saw Layla pause, look around and then swiftly run around the room. She toppled chairs and small tables as if someone had run through the room and left by going down the stairs. When she returned to the foot of that ladder, she straightened things up in the kitchen so our passage would not be noticeable.

She was the last to climb the ladder, I held my breath during her ascent, talk about your tension. Would that door open? Would Layla slip? Would she make it up unobserved? I felt sick.

She climbed in and I shut the trapdoor. If the cameras were back online, we would have been spotted. Someone would have had a lovely view of me leading a band of bedraggled children back into the castle and up into our little hidey-hole. In that case, we were doomed for recapture.

But, if we were lucky, the stupid things were still without power and we had a chance to be invisible while they ran about outside the castle looking for us.

We just needed a little luck. We could stay here, rest up and eventually think about a way to escape. We would have to avoid the cameras, find a vehicle or similar, call for help, and possibly perform small miracles. But for now, we were safe. Safe and quiet, I sat down and leaned back against a wall, any moment now I would drop off to sleep.

Someone was tugging my sleeve. I looked down at Swim Girl. Behind her was a smaller boy with a screwed-up face who was twisting his legs together. "Hey mister," she pointed a thumb at the small squirming boy, "Jeremy here needs to go to the toilet."

Chapter 40

Other voices joined this request. I was faced with a bunch of young faces looking for respite. I just wanted to lie down and go to sleep.

"Pick a corner," I said, "any corner, that'll be our toilet. This is an old castle, search for secret passages and hidden doors." I didn't think there would be any secret passageways, they only exist in stories but I was feeling low and mean. "Knock yourselves out, I'm going to sleep." I sat down in preparation for collapsing. I was looking forward to it.

Swim Girl poked me on the shoulder, "That's disgusting, we can't do our business in this room. Beyond the pale. Gross." She folded her arms, raised one eyebrow and jutted out her small chin. "We are not urinating in a corner," she declared. Behind her, the boys tittered. "And we are not performing any major bowel movements in this room." The children gaped in amazement; she had, with astute use of advanced vocabulary, just made herself their queen.

I got down to one elbow, that floor was looking softer and softer, "Well," I said, "then you have a problem. Get your head out of your arse and solve it. That's the rule." I rolled over and went unconscious. Some would call it sleep.

Sometime later, the soft and cosy floor had left, and in its place was a hard, unyielding surface. As much as I crunched my eyes shut and demanded more sleep, certain parts of my anatomy were telling me it was time to rise and shine. My bladder was particularly insistent and the damn thing wasn't going to shut up. I groaned, opened my eyes and wondered which corner was the dedicated restroom. A tentative sniff did not reveal any pungent odours. When I sat up, a blanket fell off me; someone had been thoughtful.

Around me was a quiet and ordered scene. The bedding, blankets and so on had all been arranged alongside one wall; the extra bags had been emptied of their supplies and a small pile of food and drink placed in a corner while all the remaining gear, including the bags, were sitting tidily against another wall. One of the wall side vents was open with a child cautiously emerging. Beside the opening stood Swim Girl who nodded at the emerging youngster and then waved another child forward. This little one climbed into the vent and disappeared. Swim Girl's eyes swept the room, she saw me, raised the eyebrow again and walked over.

"Good morning, sunshine," I said, all cheerful and friendly, "you've been busy." I indicated the set-up around me, "This looks very well organised."

She stood in front of me with folded arms, one finger tapping an elbow. This girl was all business. "We explored these vents while you snoozed, they go to other rooms and areas. No secret passageways." I think she was serious about the passageways. She pointed at a girl squatting beside the trapdoor, "We've got the trapdoor opened up enough to see through. Justine is over there now, we all take turns. If someone comes into the room below, we all remain still and quiet until they leave." I waved at Justine who unfathomably ignored me. Perhaps she was too far away for the Valentine charm to be effective.

"Nashwa is over by the food supplies," she said. "She will give you your ration when you need it. Don't ask for more." She stopped tapping her finger and regarded me steadily as I rose to my feet, "Any questions?" she asked. I resisted the urge to salute, but only just.

"No, you've done a good job," I said. An amazing job, but one shouldn't shower praise too early, it leaves you nowhere to go. "Which corner is the bathroom?" I asked, a certain desperation had crept into my stance.

"Corner? Don't be gross. One of the vents leads to a set of restrooms, you can crawl through, open the vent cover and climb down. We've got a ladder to help you climb up and down."

"A ladder?"

"Yes, we explored the room fully and found it in a corner, I felt we needed to have things organised for when you awoke. Was that right?" she said.

"Yeah.... Good. You have to look after your mates," I muttered. Is everyone I meet an overachiever? I crawled through the vent after being asked – no, make that TOLD – to be quiet by a child who came up to my knee. I returned feeling relaxed and ready for some food and further orders from a wide range of young and dominant females.

When I crawled out of the vent, a pair of children crawled in after me, returning shortly afterwards with the ladder. I was signalled by Swim Girl to join a gathering of the clans. All the children were seated, cross-legged, in a circle, knee to knee; the only exception was Justine who was still on trapdoor duty. Swim Girl seemed to be the conductor of the orchestra, the spaces next to her were taken by Nashwa and Layla. A vacant space sat quietly next to Layla, a large vacant space. A space I suspected was for me.

I strolled across, sat down and looked around the crew. I again wondered why God does this to me. Does He want me to stuff up more than my normal modus operandi? I just want to look after myself. I certainly do not want the responsibility of a mob of children. Surprisingly quiet children. Unnervingly subdued children.

Except for Swim Girl, she kicked us off by saying, "Let's review. Nashwa - food and supplies?"

"We have enough food and water for about three days," said Nashwa. "We have bedding, including blankets and pillows for all of us if some of the smaller children can share. This needs to happen so that Layla, Mr Valentine and I have a place to sleep." She paused and waited for Swim Girl to make the call. Swim Girl looked around the room, catching everyone's eye – I had seen this technique before used by the Man in Black. Not the sort of leadership strategy one finds in the playground of 12-year-old girls.

But everyone listened to her, everyone followed her words with calm deliberation and acceptance. She rattled off some pairings, told them all who would share and who would give stuff up. None of them objected, no one sneered, no one challenged. Who was this kid?

"Other supplies?" she asked Nashwa.

"Layla and I tore a sheet into bandages, we found some medical supplies in the cupboards downstairs. We need to look at Mr Valentine's wounds after this meeting. We have several bags and extra clothing. We can stay here for a few days and then we need to move." Nashwa finished her recital and sat back, calmly confident in her role.

"Thank you, Nashwa. Layla, what weapons do we have?" asked Swim Girl, turning slightly to acknowledge the next contributor. Layla sat beside me rolling a knife from hand to hand and said, "We have four knives, four batons and a shock rod. I am keeping one knife and I assume Mr Valentine will want another. That leaves two available. We have a set of keys."

"Thank you. Layla. Jeremy, what have the scouts found?" asked Swim Girl. Scouts, I thought with some surprise. We have scouts?

Jeremy was the small boy with a weak bladder whom I vaguely remember from those moments before I sank into oblivion. He spoke up in an even voice, no hint of quaver unless you count his age. He was a human child about 9 or 10 years old with a high, tiny voice and didn't seem to be bothered by using it in front of others. "We found several sleeping rooms, the restrooms and the ladder, also another room like this with more vents. We have found a kitchen and other storerooms but have not been into any of them. We will need the ladder to gain entry."

Justine snapped her fingers and everyone froze, eyes turned to Swim Girl. "Just sit still," she said. "Breath normally, Mr Valentine and I will investigate." She stood up and motioned for me to creep across the floor. Layla joined us at the trapdoor and we bent to see what had caused Justine's reaction. She held the trapdoor open enough for me to see a sliver of the room below. We were over the kitchen area and I could see two men had entered the room downstairs. They were dressed in a grey uniform, their words floated up to us effortlessly.

"Oh, god," said Grey1.

"Yeah," agreed Grey2.

"That was awful," said Grey1.

"Worst Assembly ever," said Grey2. We heard the clink of objects being moved around.

"Ahh," said Grey1, "I needed that."

"Pour me another," said Grey2, "I need more. Did you see his throat? What sort of human being does that to another human being?"

"I've heard Cezar ... did ...things ... to people. Bad stuff," said Grey1.

"But that's their job. That's them! We're technical support!" said Grey2. "We don't need to see people after Louise and the rest have... you know...finished with a prisoner."

"She wanted to give us an object lesson, I reckon," said Grey1. "Stiffen our resolve." I heard liquid being poured. "Let's have another."

Silence descended, broken only by the soft clink of glasses.

"In two days....," said Grey1, his voice trailing off.

"Yeah," said Grey2. "Poor Doru."

"But why do we have to watch?" asked Grey1.

"I didn't feel like asking Louise," said Grey2. "She seemed particularly......cross."

"She's going to do him right in front of us," said Grey1. "Motivate us not to be captured."

"I," said Grey2, "am fully motivated. Besides, I do not intend leaving the Control Room, I'm on the roster for the next three days, thank goodness. Anyway, how far could he get dragging a herd of kids? He probably wants them along for food, he can eat one a day to keep going."

"Oh, thanks for that. Thanks a lot. That's a visual I do not need in my head. Eating children!" said Grey1. "Besides, you **will** be there in two days, watching like the rest of us."

"But the Control Room...," pleaded Grey2. "It can't be left unattended."

"Bring an Alert Module. Bring two, one for me as a backup. Set them to send alerts and any video if movement is picked up. Because," went on Grey1, "if your absence is noticed ... well, let's just say that I wouldn't be sticking my head above the parapets any time soon."

"Oh god, oh, god, oh, god," muttered Grey2. "I don't think I can stand to see what she's going to do to Doru. Not without some sustenance."

"Me neither," said Grey1. "Tell you what. Let's meet here just before the Noon Assembly and we'll have a few drinks. Maybe more than a few."

"Good idea," said Grey2. "Come on, put that bottle away and let's get back to our posts. I intend to be invisible for the next month."

They left the room. Justine leaned in and asked, "Are you going to eat us, Mr Valentine?"

Yep, that was her takeaway from that little meeting. I eat kids. I wiggled my eyebrows and grinned at her, showing my pearly whites.

I am a dick.

Chapter 41

Swim Girl calmed Justine down, gave me a slightly puzzled look and suggested we sit and talk. "Please don't do that anymore," she said after we settled down.

"Do what?" I asked.

"Tease the children," she said. Swim Girl had the ability to sit absolutely still, look into a person's eyes and give the impression she was weighing your worth. Terrific stuff, I couldn't do it, of course, but I'd seen others play this card.

"You've almost got it," I said. "The look is good, and you go straight for the eyes - well done. Perhaps try a slight lean forward, it conveys intensity."

She squeezed her eyes shut, took a breath and spoke again, "Why are you helping us?"

"Long story," I said. "I started all this mess trying to help a mate. His cousin was taken by The Syndicate and I went looking for her."

Swim Girl asked, "Did you find her?"

"Uh, no," I answered. "The, er, the Syndicate captured me." This was not going well, I was conscious the children might start to lose faith in my ability to get them out of here.

"We're doomed," said Layla. Swim Girl said nothing, which was worse.

Hey," I said, "Be fair. We can do this, I just need to think out a plan." I couldn't believe what I was hearing.

Swim Girl stood up, dusted herself off, straightened her clothes and prepared to walk off to the troops. "I'll look after the children." She swept her gaze across Layla and me, "Make it a good plan." Sure, why not? Planning is my forte.

Excellent, I thought. No wriggle room there.

Layla and I were still sitting on the floor. She unfolded her knife and practised flipping it into the air and catching it. She swapped hands, threw it higher and then started to repeat the performance but this time with her eyes shut. I caught the knife out of the air, she opened her eyes when she realised the knife was not where it should be. I closed the knife, gave it back to her and said, "Try not to kill anyone, including yourself. I'm going to get something to eat."

As I stood up, she said, "Get us out of here, Mr Valentine. I have things to do. People to see."

I fed and watered and considered the situation. Physically I was in reasonable shape, my torn finger and toenails were just pain and I can overcome pain. Anyone nearby may hear some swearing and general moaning but I was good to go. What else? I had contributed to the psychological abuse of a minor by allowing Layla to have sharp things and use them against other human beings. If Doru could be rated as human. I was now responsible for the care and well-being of a bunch of children, all of whom had been ill-treated. And there was probably a rumour running around that I might eat some of them. We were trapped in a castle, unable to move around or leave without being spotted by cameras.

It's good to know where you stand. No, ma'am, I'm not waving, I'm drowning.

Okay, enough of the pity party. Nashwa found me with bandages and some first aid articles, she insisted I unwrap my damaged bits while she dressed the wounds. The children wandered over as I revealed my fingers, then the toes, the burns, the bruises and so on. They were very quiet. More quiet than normal for this lot. One of them asked me, in a very small voice, "Do they all hurt?"

"Sure, but they take it in turns. Today it's the burns, tomorrow will be fingers," I said.

The same voice said, "You're funny."

Swim Girl was with them, her eyes had been just as large as the rest but now she gathered herself and asked, "What do you want us to do, Mr Valentine?"

"We've got a day or so to get ready to leave," I said. "Make sure everyone is packed and ready. When that big Assembly happens, we will sneak out. Remember, think ahead and when things go bad, suck it up and keep going." I thought I should remember this little speech, the lads would get a right old laugh out of it. Think ahead – oh, dear me.

"The cameras?" she asked.

"I have a plan," I said. And surprisingly, I did.

The next day we had another group meeting, I had told Swim Girl to gather the gang together so we could all hear any updates or problems. This was a technique I had learned from Magic – tell everyone everything. Then hope someone has a solution. Usually worked, even if some of our solutions were ridiculous. At the end of the meeting, Swim Girl asked if I had anything to add. We had heard from Justine who seemed to be coordinating the list of visitors to the room below us; we also heard from Jeremy and his scouting efforts as well as Nashwa reporting on food and logistics.

I scratched my head and said, "Can't think of anything, you guys have it under control. Well done." Swim Girl gave me a tight smile before I went on, "Just remember, we will be going into harm's way. Look after your mates, solve the problems, and keep going. Just keep going. You can give up when you're dead." Stirring stuff, just the sort of inspirational message needed by a bunch of young children as they prepare to go into danger. Should I have told them lies, that everything would be all right? Should I have just kept them in the dark because they are children, and therefore useless? I don't know, I just treated them like people with brains, they'd had enough lies. They all had that entranced look as they gazed at my face. They were either soaking in every word or were thinking about another trip to the restrooms.

On the day our two Grey men returned for their pre-torture show drinks, we were ready. The children were dressed, they each had a bag packed with our remaining supplies and clothes and sat near the trap door. Justine was back on duty. She was ready to pull the door back on my signal.

I watched the two men gather below us, they opened a cupboard and began to knock back the big ones.

"You good?" asked Grey1.

"Yeah," said Grey2. He held up a small box, "I've got this, it's the Alert Module. It will vibrate if any of the motion sensors are triggered from the main Control centre. Or if the cameras pick up something not in their database." While I didn't understand all these words, I got the gist. Alert module = bad news. Grey2 held up a second box, "Here's yours. If we both have one, we shouldn't miss anything. They'll also record whatever the cameras see for the next couple of hours."

Grey1 took his Alert Module, "Will it record Louise's session with Doru?" he asked.

"Sure," said Grey2. "Louise will probably want to see it, may want to look for improvements in her methodology."

They drank silently before Grey2 spoke again, just a soft tone as he looked into his glass, "I, uh, I'm going to see if I can transfer to another facility." He swirled his glass, we heard ice cubes tinkling.

Grey1 looked at him and said, "Yeah." He drank some more. "Me, too. I'm not an aggressive man. I don't mind some theft and general larceny but these guys all seem to be hardcore violent. Yeah, I need to get out before something bad happens here. With my luck, I'd be the one to get it in the neck."

They poured out another drink each and moved to more relaxed poses. "Any sign of Val whatshisname?" asked Grey2.

"Not a thing. His name's Valerie, pretty girlie name for such an animal. No sign of any kids either" said Grey1.

"One more drink and then we'd better join the Assembly," said Grey2. "I plan to be in the back rows when Louise gets going. Doru's already a mess. Or so I've been told."

I nodded to Justine who quietly raised the trapdoor, I stood up and moved to the very lip of the opening. If they had looked up, they would have seen me but they were both focused on refilling their glasses. I dropped down, boots first.

Any hero in a tale would be able to land a disabling boot on each character and rebound to an elegant standing position over two comatose victims. It would be beautiful and may even include a resounding "Hah!" I did briefly consider doing this stunt until my brain submitted the mental image of me doing the splits as I tried to connect with each player. It meant I would need to concentrate on placing each boot in a separate face or head, which means my testicles may well be the only thing between me and the ground. Give that one a miss, I thought.

Instead, I made sure both of my big feet hit the one man, the guy closest to the bottom of the ladder. I hit him with knees slightly bent and, after smashing his head and shoulder, I used his body as a starting position for a dive into his very surprised friend. My knife caught him in the throat before I hurtled into his collapsing corpse. At this point, I had hoped to be able to leap to my feet and easily subdue the first guy. It was a good plan, a solid plan. And it didn't work. When I hit the falling body of the guy I stabbed, I got all tangled up in arms, legs and blood. My nose mashed into his chest with enough force to make my eyes water. Where is the elegance? Where is the grace? Where is the first guy?

By the time I had unpeeled from the mess I had created, retrieved the knife and spun around in what I hoped was a deadly combat pose, it was all over. Layla had scrambled down behind me and had taken up her favourite position. This was 'Sharp instrument digging into bad man's throat'.

We may call this the Layla special.

Chapter 42

"Don't kill him!" I said, with some force. She looked at me, nodded and returned to giving our prisoner a gentle probe with a sharp knife. His eyes were open, albeit with a glazed look but he understood he was in deep trouble. Deep, deep trouble. I squatted in front of him, ruffled his hair and asked, "How are you doin'?"

The rest of the children came down as planned, Nashwa and Swim Girl herding them together. Justine ran to one door while Jeremy ran to another as lookouts. Swim Girl had improved on my original plan and worked on the details. My plan was, 'I'm going to knock one out and capture the other'. That was the sum total of my plan. Swim Girl heard me say this in the group meeting we held that morning, she gave me a stone stare, thought a moment and then expanded on the plan, fleshing out roles and responsibilities. This included timings and all that messy stuff. I suspect I was losing my hero's status in her eyes. Ah, well, the kid's got to grow up sometime.

I grabbed the Alert Modules from the floor where my knife victim had dropped it. Giving it to Nashwa, I said, "Keep an eye on this. Let me know if it sends any alerts." The guy on the floor was almost back to full consciousness, I grabbed him by the collar and hauled him to his feet. "You're taking us out of here," I said.

He gabbled at that, mentioned Louise, said he was just a support person, he only worked in technology, talked about his inability to carry out my instructions and so on. I gave him a hard, open-hand slap to the cheek. The sound cracked across the room, the children started and looked at me with the ever-reliable fearful expression I had seen so often.

"Think this through, pal," I said. "If we leave you here, alive, you get to be the next act after Doru. I'm leaving you alive, no matter what. That means Louise is going to be having one of her intense conversations with you. And let me tell you, from experience,

Louise's chats are bloody painful. Let's go." I shoved him to the door and we all trooped out. Me first, then our dazed and fearful captive, next was Nashwa followed by a bunch of quietly terrified children shepherded by Swim Girl and finally, Layla, my broken and hurting little girl. Make a great song.

I frisked my prisoner some more as we walked, he didn't object to the more invasive searches – people do hide nasty things in amongst their, well, nasty bits. No knife, no shock rod, no weapons at all. A toolkit, another Alert Module and bits and pieces that I farmed back to Nashwa. I had Justine duck ahead at each corner for a peek; so far, we were in the clear.

Nashwa said, "I'm getting lots of alerts. It's vibrating almost constantly as we walk along."

I stopped us all, swung Grey Man hard against the wall and breathed into his ear, "What do those alerts mean, sport?"

He spoke with some difficulty, given his mouth and teeth were smooshing the wall. "It's you!" he said. "It's us, the alerts are picking us up as we move through the corridors."

Seemed fair. Since we had stopped, I asked, "Where is this Assembly? How long will it be?"

I released his face enough for him to say, "The next wing over, you can get there from here but it would take a few minutes."

"How far to an outside exit door?" I asked. "I want one with vehicles." He had begun to recover and find his mental stability; I wasn't sure if this was a good thing or not.

He wiped his snotty nose on a sleeve and replied, "We keep going along here, a few twists and turns and then we get to the main gate. It will be shut and locked during the Assembly."

As an afterthought, he said, "Or you could use the secret passage."

Swim Girl poked me in the ribs and gave me a victorious smile. Jeremy fist-pumped the air and said, "See! Told you there'd be a Secret Passage!" I groaned.

"Where is it?" I asked. I looked around for hidden doors but didn't see any because they were, well, hidden. "Do we push a button or press a special place?"

Grey man waved at a nearby door, "No, it's through there." This had all the set-up of a trap. Flunky takes unwitting fools down a pre-prepared area where they are recaptured amidst much laughter.

"Layla," I said, "I'm going to tie this guy up and look through that door. Get your knife out and keep an eye on him." She came over, unclasped her knife, tested the blade and then pressed the tip into Grey Man's throat. He went up on tiptoes to avoid losing a larynx and stood very still while I tied his arms and gagged his mouth. I tied his ankles loosely, he would be able to hobble but not run. His eyes remained fixed on Layla who returned his gaze with a certain implacability.

The door he indicated appeared normal, with no lock or obvious trap. I waved Jeremy over and asked him what he thought, given he was a child of this world and time. Yes, I am taking operational advice from a 9-year-old. He wasn't perturbed by my request, took it in stride as our normal way of doing things; I sure can corrupt the youth of today. After bending down and peering at the door he gave me a thumbs up, one man to another.

Very slowly, I opened the door. It opened into a comfortable lounge area, all wood panels, leather chairs and sideboards holding things in expensive crystal bottles. The chairs faced each other in conversational poses while a richly decorated carpet took up the centre space. It looked like a room in which The Man in Black would be right at home; I felt awkward and clumsy. So, situation normal. Again, I couldn't spot any obvious trap; I even pulled Jeremy in and waggled my eyebrows at him for his opinion. He poked about, pulled a few books from shelves, picked up some of the drink bottles but put them down again after I gave him a meaningful cough. If anyone was going to be inspecting those contents it would be me.

He sauntered back and said, "Seems clear. Shall I get the others in here?" We had to follow Grey Man somewhere. This room could be a trap but so could any place he took us. And I didn't see him as the deep-thinking, nefarious villain who would join us in a trap room. He was more office worker than evil henchman. I hoped. I told Jeremy to get people in. Once inside, Swim Girl pushed some small side tables to one side and cleared an open space. She stood on the centre carpet and said, "Clump up."

Yes, that was her command, 'Clump Up'. What did that mean? The children knew, they all moved to the carpet and sat in front of Swim Girl, they sat cross-legged on the floor with the neighbour's knees touching. They were a clump. Justine went to the entry door and stood guard; Jeremy wandered about poking things. Nashwa took up a position behind Swim Girl, much the same as I had seen people do for the Man in Black. She didn't stand in a military pose but she certainly gave the impression of a competent officer. Layla pushed Grey Man into a chair and stood behind him, her knife hovering within his field of view.

Everybody had a role and they all knew it. Swim Girl motioned everyone to silence, turned to me and asked, "What now, Mr Valentine?"

Good question, terrific question, yes indeed. What now? I stood open-mouthed in wonder at this crew. They had more self-discipline than my comrades in the NightWatch, although to be fair, that wasn't hard. Puppies had more self-discipline than my mates. I turned to the seated Grey Man and asked, "Where is this secret door?"

I realised he couldn't speak because he was gagged. His eyes bulged in a frantic attempt to talk, encouraged strongly by Layla stroking the tip of the knife down his cheek, I was going to have to have a long talk with her one day. I removed his gag, he gulped and said, "The far bookcase, second candlestick from the left. Pull it forward and the door opens."

Jermey looked to me for permission, I nodded and joined him in front of the bookcase. He put one hand on the candlestick, I took a good grip on my knife and the shock baton and prepared to meet our fate. At my signal, he pulled the candlestick forward until we heard a click and part of the bookcase swung open. I looked around the room, searching for hidden ports to open and spew forth blasters and other awful things, I waited for the heavens to open and loud voices to clamour for our subjugation.

Not a sausage. The secret door opened onto a well-maintained and carpeted corridor, complete with subdued wall lights. It was completely bare of evil henchmen. Totally empty. I went back to Grey Man, kneeled in front of him and asked, "What's the go here, pal? How come this secret door exists and you know about it? Where does it go and who uses it? Who else knows about it?" I had a few thousand other questions but these might get the ball rolling.

"This is Louise's Ready Room," he said. "She comes in for some peace and quiet. I think she meets Ghost here sometimes." He nodded at the new doorway, "It's not really a 'Secret' secret door, we all know about it. It's just a shortcut to an exit, Louise had the original door dressed up to look like a bookcase because she liked the idea."

"She liked the idea of a secret entrance?" I asked.

"In a castle," he replied. "Yeah, I get it, she's a weird one."

I stood up and realised all eyes were on me. Except for Justine who was diligently focusing on the entry door. "Well, I suppose we better see where it takes us," I said.

"It leads to an undercover garage," said Grey Man. "You should be able to find one of our vans there, big enough for everyone." He squirmed, not too much because Layla's knife had not moved. "Take me with you," he pleaded. "Please!" He sounded committed to the idea.

"Why?" I asked. I think I knew but needed him to say it.

"Because Louise will do to me what she is now doing to Doru," said Grey Man. "What she had done to you. She is both angry and ice-cold. Doru told us how you killed Bogdan. He showed us his punctured hand and told us how you forced him to lead you out of the castle. We had no doubt you had terrified him into obedience."

I took this litany of allegations stoically, some of the children's eyes turned to me but most seemed to accept these words as normal behaviour in the Valentine world. Not sure how I felt about that, shouldn't children be isolated from this level of violence and dangerous talk? Oh, right, we're trapped in a castle by torturers and kidnappers keen on doing awful things to every one of us. The 'keep children in the dark about bad things' ship had well and truly sailed.

Grey Man was pitching a strong case. "If you leave me here, even if you rough me up or cut bits off, she will use me as another object lesson to others. I don't want to be that lesson."

"How about I just kill you? Would that help?" I asked.

Chapter 43

I thought it was a reasonable question, it was a logical choice for all concerned. But Grey Man was not fully on board, "I don't want to die!" he exclaimed, with some force and emotion. "Take me with you, I can help!"

Layla looked a question at me, she had her arm tensed ready to plunge the knife into Grey Man's neck. It wasn't mercy that stayed my hand, it was the realisation that this wee girl was willing to kill a man. At my nod, she would have stabbed the knife into his throat, ending his life and sending her own future on a dark pathway. She was the little girl who played dress-ups, the child who talked too much, the one who had saved me.

Now it was my turn to save her. "No, Layla," I said, "We let him live. Put the knife away." Without hesitation, she closed the knife, put it back into a pocket and joined Nashwa in the stance behind Swim Girl. Go, team.

To Grey Man, I said, "We won't kill you, pal. At least, not until you upset me. And I'm easily upset."

Jeremy had been looking into drawers and cupboards, his search turned up a thick wad of notes; he waved them at us with a victorious smile and said, "We're rich!" Swim Girl said, "Take the money, Jeremy. We'll use it for food and things when we get to a town." I took one of the notes from Jeremy, I wanted to see what money looked like on this world. It was a tough material, harder than paper but very flexible; lots of squiggly lines and strange symbols on each side. "Is it a lot?" I whispered to Jeremy.

"You betcha, Mr Valentine," he whispered back. My buddy. I guessed we had stumbled over Louise's emergency money; well, we had an emergency. "I'll see what else we could use." I watched for a moment or two as he grabbed a bag and began stuffing items away. Louise was going to be royally pissed when she found we had pinched all her neat stuff.

We got ourselves organised and moved down the corridor. When I say 'we organised' I mean Swim Girl, my presence was more decorative than useful. Jeremy worked out how to shut the bookcase door; there were no other doors in this corridor, and we snuck along waiting for bad things to pop up. Nothing happened. The exit door looked disappointingly mundane, although it did have an eyehole for checking out the garage. A small video screen was on one wall, it showed a larger view of the parking area. I looked at the screen, peered through the eyehole and could see nothing untoward. Without realising I was doing it, I was looking at Jeremy for his confirmation. He gave me a thumbs-up. What has become of my professional thug standards, I wondered.

"Layla," I said, "Watch him." I indicated Grey Man who again found himself accompanied by my knife-wielding girl. I asked our prisoner, "How do I open the door?"

He had regained that pleading look but carried on manfully, "Anyone can open it from this side, just push that bar across the door. You can't get back in from the other side unless you punch in the code. And I don't know the code, only Louise and Ghost know it. I should imagine it changes regularly."

Shouldn't be a problem, I thought, I didn't intend returning. I could see at least one large van in the garage, it should be able to carry all of us. "Everyone ready?" I asked. I got nods, took a breath and opened the door.

Nashwa said, "We've got an alarm!" She was holding the Alert Module and even I could see the red lights flashing as it vibrated in her hand.

I turned to look at Grey Man, he was endeavouring to be one with the wall as he leaned away from Layla's knife at his throat. "It's all right!" he exclaimed. "Opening this door registers an alarm in the Control Room. I had all the alarms transferred to the handheld there. There's no other alarm in the castle, Louise didn't want any distractions for the Assembly and told me to turn them all off. No alarms, no flashing lights, except on that handheld." He was talking for his life and knew it.

We had to believe him. I pointed at a large van, we all ran to it, opened the back doors and climbed in, shutting the van doors behind us. Jeremy, clever lad that he is, had also shut the door leading back into the castle. We sat for a few beats, all huddled together on the floor of the van. Our panic breathing slowed; we had made it.

Swim girl asked, "If we're all back here, who's going to drive this thing?

Well, this was embarrassing. I could drive a sled, even a large one, but would those skills transfer to a van? I climbed up to the front seat, took in the controls and thought, we're all doomed. Nothing made any sense to me. This machine had dials and pedals as well as a big steering wheel or yoke. I wouldn't even know how to turn it on.

"Nashwa?" I asked. She was the oldest of our little crew and perhaps had been given driving lessons by Daddy. She shook her head in the negative. Yep, we were doomed.

A voice said, 'I can drive." It was Grey Man.

Great, trapped in an underground garage with our only hope being the guy I had been ill-treating and even considered murdering. He was to be our rescuer. Seemed fair.

"Climb on up, pal," I said. "Layla, cut him loose but sit behind him, just in case." A certain amount of shuffling took place before we were good to go. Layla took her duties seriously, she placed a small hand on Grey Man's shoulder, leaned in and whispered something to him. He went white, gulped, and nodded.

"Ready?" he asked. I looked back into the body of the van and caught the eyes of the children, the wide, apprehensive gazes of my little ones. Oh, dear God, I thought, why do you put me in these situations?

"Wait!" said Jeremy. I saw him sitting towards the rear of the van, next to Justine who had taken up her usual role as door guard. "We need to disable the Tracking Beacon." I had no idea what he meant.

But Grey Man did. "Done," he said. He reached under the steering wheel and pulled at something, I heard a breaking sound and his hand emerged holding another black box. "Here it is."

I passed it back to Jeremy and said, "What do you think? Is that the Tracking thingie?" He nodded. We seemed to be good to go. Oh, dear, I hoped we were good to go.

"Get us out of here, sport," I told Grey Man.

The van moved off, up some ramps and into the bright sunshine. A few turns and we were on some sort of main road, fanging our way to freedom.

We settled into a driving routine, I even noticed Layla lean back a little although her hand never left Grey Man's shoulder. She gave it a squeeze every time we hit a large bump or another vehicle came too close. Grey Man sat studiously erect, the picture of the loyal and diligent driver. I asked Nashwa to come sit up front and I climbed back into the body of the van. Time for some more talking with this old gang of mine.

"Where do you kids want to go?" I asked. They looked back at me. No answer. "Umm, how about we take you to the police?"

"No!" was the universal response. Lots of clamouring, lots of raised voices. This was the most animated I had seen them. Several were talking at once, voices were raised, a couple got to their knees to express their objection to this course of action. Finally, Swim Girl settled them down and turned to me.

"The police will only return us to those who sold us into captivity." She scanned the group, some were crying, the rest soon joined in. I was now in a van surrounded by crying and wailing children. Nothing I could do seemed to calm them down, even Swim Girl let out a huge wracking sob. A child's body contains a god-almighty amount of snot. Their dam of grief had finally broken, now that we had a chance at freedom.

Eventually, the noise level receded and died away until we only had a few holdouts giving muffled sobs. Jeremy tugged my sleeve but I ignored him, I certainly did not want to hear about his trials and troubles. The tugging continued, by the time peace came back to the van he was doing his best to dislocate my shoulder.

"WHAT?" I roared at him. I had tuned my head to face him and gave him the full Valentine sick-of-it-all voice, The other children shrank back into themselves and I suspected another crying jag would descend. I gentled myself as much as I could and spoke in a soft and mellow tone, "Sorry, Jeremy, what is it?" I may have snarled.

"I need to go to the bathroom, Mr Valentine," he said.

"Really?" I said. "Now, Jeremy? Now you need to go to the bathroom? We just escaped the castle! Didn't you go before we left?" A hint of exasperation may have crept into my tone. Possibly some censure.

The little guy nodded. I didn't want us to stop, "You'll have to hold on, Jeremy," I said, ever full of compassion. "Tie a knot in it." His face screwed up, he clutched his groin and squeezed his eyes shut.

Oh, God, take me now.

Chapter 44

"Hey, Grey Man!" I called. "Can we find a place for Jeremy to get out and have a wee? Pull over near some bushes so we don't scare oncoming traffic." See, I was thinking of his mental well-being.

"NOOO!" exclaimed my urine filled buddy. "I can't go on the side of the road! PLEASE! I need a proper restroom."

Grey Man spoke over his shoulder, "I can pull into a Service Stop, there's one up ahead. We need to charge up, too."

I left Jeremy to his inner pain and slid over next to Swim Girl, "What's a Service Stop and why do we need to charge up?" I asked.

"You're not serious?" she said. I looked at her, she looked at me. "You are serious!" she stated. "A Service Stop is a place for people to recharge vehicles, buy food and stuff. And use the restrooms." She leaned towards me, "How come you don't know that? Where are you from?"

Okay, that made sense, still not too sure why we needed to recharge a vehicle but I would let that slide. "I'm from another planet, we didn't have this level of technology," I said. I turned back to the driver and said, "Okay, find a Service Stop and we will get organised. Try to park out of sight, Louise must be sending search parties out soon. They're sure to come down the road looking for their missing van."

"Okay," he called back. "I'll charge the van at a concealed station, shouldn't be hard. There's a Stop just up ahead, won't be long." I looked over at Jeremy, he was squeezing parts of his anatomy. Good lad.

We pulled off the road into a facility consisting of several buildings and odd hoses, pumps and cables placed on small islands. Our van pulled up next to one of them, Grey Man stopped the engine and turned back to me. "How do you want to do this?" he asked.

Since I didn't know how it all worked, I was at a loss. "I'll stay with you," I said. "Just in case." We all climbed out of the van, I gathered the troops and gave them dire warnings about talking to strangers. Strangers like me. "Any questions?" I asked, already turning away.

Nashwa piped up, "Can we buy a communicator here? I want to call my daddy." A few other children joined in this request but I noticed most did not. No one to contact, no one who would care for them. Poor little mites. Still, a communicator seemed a good idea, pity I didn't know how we did this little task. Maybe I could just call the boss and go home a hero.

"No," said Grey Man in a voice combining firmness and terror. Quite the trick.

"Care to explain?" I asked.

He kept his head moving, scanning the area. "The Syndicate monitors communications, especially from sensitive locations. We are just outside one of their key sites, I am sure all communication nodes from here are watched carefully. The same goes for victims, their families and other parties of interest." He gave me appointed look, "Like the police and your NightWatch."

Nashwa's eyes grew large, "But," she said, "my daddy. Can't I call him and tell him I'm safe?"

I gently took her hand, Layla moved up beside her and Swim Girl joined our comforting huddle. "If you call him, if any of us call the people we care about, we are placing them in great danger. I don't know how this 'monitoring' stuff works, but I know the idea. Your father is in danger, his safety lies in you **not** contacting him. Until we get you back to him and organise protection." I raised my head, gathering all the children with my eyes, "no communicators." They nodded, Nashwa grimaced and leaned into Swim Girl for support before finally muttering an agreement.

By the time we finished this discussion, Jeremy was coming close to his expiration. He bolted for the restrooms which caused the rest of the children to decide they also needed a restroom. Every one of them, including Layla and Nashwa, streamed off towards some unknown destination. With luck, I would never see them again. Before she left, Swim Girl passed me the wad of notes we had taken from Louise.

Grey Man grabbed one of the cables or hoses and plugged it into a side port on the van. He hit a button and a series of slowly flashing lights appeared on the cable. He stood back, surveyed his work, and said to me, "Won't take long. These newer stations only take a few minutes to get to full charge. Want to grab a drink inside while we wait? We can pay at the same time." I liked the idea of a drink but the concept of payment brought up a problem.

"Can we use this stuff?" I said, holding up the notes from Swim Girl.

He answered while looking around, surveying the area, "Sure," he said and took a bunch from me. "I'll also buy a few other useful odds and ends. Consider it a token of my trustworthiness. Drink?" He moved off towards an illuminated building, not even looking back to see if I was coming. Surely this is not how a prisoner/captor relationship functions, shouldn't he still be at least a little in awe of my presence?

"I've got my eye on you, sport," I said. A thought struck me and I surged to walk beside him and asked, "What's your name?"

He smiled at me, "How about I keep my real identity to myself and you just call me ... Mr Grey." We entered the main building; I had a hand on the knife in my pocket as insurance but no slavering hordes greeted us. Not quite true, there were slavering hordes, but they were the other customers buying food and drink from a range of enterprising vendors, and others milled about examining racks of brightly packaged items. I saw lots of stuff I didn't need but probably desperately wanted.

We approached the counter, waited while another customer was served and then stood before a lumpy, unshaven human who appeared to be in need of sleep, a shave and a change of clothes. This guy defined the word 'rumpled'. "Number?" he asked.

What did that mean, a secret code? Mr Grey replied with "Thirty-seven." I spotted Jeremy emerging from a door on the far wall and gave him a wave. When he saw us, his face broke out into a lovely smile and, for some reason, it made me feel good. While Mr Grey exchanged notes with the rumpled man, Jeremy walked over to me and took my hand in the most natural way possible.

Rumpled Guy said, "There you go." He handed a piece of paper to Mr Grey and saw Jeremy who gave him a big smile. Reflexively, the old fart smiled back, "You've got a good boy there, sir. Your son?"

I was confident the local culture would take a dim view of a grown man holding hands with a small boy if that boy was not a relative. Before I could articulate any sort of reply, Jeremy smiled up at me and said, "YES! He's, my daddy. He's the best dad in the world." Way to go, Jeremy, I thought and gave our questioner a sappy grin. Mr Grey was biting his lip trying to hold a smile. The rest of the children dribbled over to us until the whole gang stood with me.

"They're not all mine," I said, a certain weakness had gained traction in my speech.

Chapter 45

No other customer was seeking service, Rumpled Guy had no demands on his time and appeared happy to chat with us. "Nashwa, take them back to the van," I said. For some reason, Jeremy stayed with us; perhaps I could use the protective camouflage his presence provided.

"Would you be going to the School Tournament?" he asked. "My boy's going. Now where is the lazy bastard." Great parenting skills here, I thought, must watch and learn. The old guy turned and yelled into an open door leading into the depths of the building, "Stefan, get out here, boy! Your ride will be here any minute!"

A lumpy teenager slouched through the door carrying a large bag over his shoulders. In his hands, he held a small device which he tapped with fingers and thumbs. The loving father gave him a clip around the head and said, "Put that thing down, you'll go blind."

The boy rebounded well and kept his eyes on the device, "Almost at the next level, Dad. Just one more .... YES!" He looked up at us, eyes shining and face beaming in pleasure, "Paladin class! Now I can ..." He saw us and stuttered to a stop, "Who are these guys?"

Father of the Year waved a hand towards us and said, "They're going to the Tournament, too! Come and say hello, make some new friends, for goodness' sake. Get yourself out of that screen." Rumpled Guy turned to serve a customer, leaving his son to make conversation with us, his new best friends.

"Hello," said Jeremy, "Is your name Stefan?" Obviously, it was since we had heard Superdad calling his name. Still, I recognised subtlety in Jeremy's approach, break the ice with easy questions and soft topics. Asking this slob his name should qualify as a simple question.

"None of your business, pus face," said Stefan, endearing us all with his winning ways. "You going to the Tournament? More losers," he said. He had already dropped his head down to his device and was working thumbs at a championship level.

Dad came back at this point, clipped his son's ear again and said, "For God's sake, Jeremy. At least TRY to have a human conversation. Look, I can see your bus outside, now give me a hug and off you go!"

Jeremy gave his father a token hug while his eyes never left his device. He picked up his bag and pushed past us, making a determined effort to drop the shoulder into Jeremy. An effort that was not wildly successful because Jeremy had leaned into him, obviously expecting such an action. Jeremy looks like a soft pre-teen and certainly no match for a young slime several years older. But he braced himself and pushed back quite smoothly. Stefan grumbled, shuffled a step around us and headed for the exit. Jeremy's my boy.

"We better get going, too," I said. "Thanks for your time, come on guys, the big tournament awaits!" We walked back to the van, Stefan had found his way to a large bus-style vehicle, full of excited children. Looked like hell on wheels. At the door leading into the bus was a man with his own device, he seemed to be checking names before letting his new passengers get on board. The bus had multi-coloured balloons hanging from windows and several banners draped along each side.

"What do those banners say, Jeremy?" I asked.

He looked up at me, "They're all about the tournament. The usual sort of rah-rah stuff. 'Go team' and 'We are the Champions.'" We walked past the rear of the bus, Jeremy pointed at two smaller signs there, "These are more informational, more about the tournament and how everyone should come and watch their team."

I noticed these rear signs were not tied on with cable or such like, "How are they attached to the bus?" I asked my young friend.

"They're magnetic, peel right off," said Jeremy. Magnetic, right. I had heard about this property. Teddy Boy told me it was like a lodestone while Right Honourable explained that some guy called

William Gilbert thought magnets had souls. My brain retains the weirdest bits of information.

"Jeremy," I said, "When no one is watching, peel off those two magnetic signs and put them on the sides of our van." He looked up at me, smiled and nodded. "Be sneaky," I said. His smile widened.

"No worries, boss," said my young apprentice. He sidled across to the bus and hung around with ill intent. Love his work.

"Mr Grey," I said, "Go back to that guy and buy some balloons and something to fix them to our van." I indicated the decorations on the bus, "Make it look like that." He strode off, a man with a mission. When he moved off, I signalled for Justine to come over, "Follow him," I pointed to Mr Grey. "Watch what he does. Let me know if he does anything suspicious." Talk about your vague orders, how would Justine know if he did anything suspicious? Still, she nodded acquiescence and moved off in full observation mode. These kids were growing on me.

I watched the man at the large bus accept new passengers, double-check attendance, walk around looking for lost souls and yell at a latecomer. By the time they were ready to move off, we were also good to go. Tournament signs on the side of our van, balloons and colourful streamers hanging from windows and other handy places. We looked like refugees from a circus, loud, garish, and impossible to miss.

Mr Grey started the vehicle and asked, "Where to?"

"Follow that bus," I replied, pointing at the now departing large vehicle. "Stay close."

Swim Girl stuck her head in from the back compartment, "What's going on? Aren't we trying to hide?"

I smiled, "What's the best place to hide a tree?"

Mr Grey furrowed his brow, Swim Girl looked blank but Nashwa called out, "In a forest!"

"Correct," I said. "We are going to be just another vehicle full of loathsome children attending the Tournament. Once we get there, we will see if we can work out what to do next."

"You just make it up as you go along, don't you?" said Swim Girl.

"Pretty much," I replied.

Chapter 46

We followed the big bus until we reached a city. Was it my city, the one hosting the NightWatch and my revolting office? "Where are we? Is this the capital city?" I asked all and sundry.

"This is Vaslui, it's the administrative centre of this District," said Mr Gray. "Not the capital." We continued to follow the bus through various streets and thoroughfares until we arrived at a large building festooned with more decorations and banners. "Do you want me to pull in behind their bus?" asked Mr Grey.

"Yes," I said. "Drop us off then take the van and lose it. Strip off the signs and decorations. I think we've pushed our luck as far as we can with this vehicle. Meet us back here, we should be inside that building." I turned to the children, "Let's get inside with the rest of the tournament attendees and we'll see if we can stay lost. Swim Girl, you're in charge of the children. Nashwa, help her. Layla and Jeremy, stay with me."

We disembarked and entered the tournament building; the children were orderly and subdued. Swim Girl had them gather once we were inside and gave instructions. I hovered nearby, interested in what she was going to say. Layla and Jeremy stayed close to me.

"Listen up," she said. All eyes were on Swim Girl, the children focused on every word. "What are the rules?" she asked. This was new, I had not realised these apprentice mobsters had rules. Hands shot up and Swim Girl took answers. Each rule was volunteered by a small, innocent child whom I may have taught some bad words. Whoops.

"Rule one, Head out of arse!"

"Rule two, Think ahead, dimwit!"

"Rule three, Look after your mates, dickhead!"

"Rule four, Suck it up, buttercup!"

"Rule five, Listen to Mr Valentine!"

These words rang a chord with me, I must have said them at some point over the last few days. They certainly sounded like something I would say. Except for rule five, I would never recommend rule five.

"Good," said Swim Girl. "We are going to go over to that corner," she indicated a clear space near a grand staircase, "and wait. While there, eat and drink. Justine, find the restrooms. Any questions?" They all nodded soberly. "Right," said my mini boss, "Make it Happen!"

I took Jeremy and Layla over towards a big central desk behind which a small army of helpers tried to cope with the chaos. Each group of children had one or more adults with them, these seemed to be their minders. Children and adults were in front of the desk, all engaged in conversations with the helpers behind the desk. From time to time, a group would leave the desk, clutching several bags and papers; they would gather up the rest of their charges and wander off into the depths of the building. As soon as a gap appeared at the central desk it was filled by another adult and several children.

"Any idea what's going on?" I asked my companions; these two were my team. I had a brief sense of the strangeness of my situation; my team consisted of a young boy with bladder issues and a pre-pubescent Anipe girl who had developed a fondness for sharp objects.

Jeremy wandered over, spoke to some children, and returned. "They're registering for the tournament," he said. "Each team logs in, gets a bag containing competition items and the adult ends up with a lot of paperwork. How do you feel about paperwork, Mr Valentine?"

"Bite your bum, Jeremy," I said. "Come on, let's get over there and see what we can scrounge. Be good to have some protective colouration."

We stood in line, listening for clues from all the noise around us. I paid close attention to the adults; they all had a cord around their necks with a tag and their photo. Closer to the desk, I heard an exchange where an adult told the helper their group name and other details. The helper looked at a datapad, made a mark and then handed over some bags and a wad of papers. When it was our turn, I stepped up to the counter manfully, looked into the eyes of the helper and opened my mouth to speak. Nothing came out, I had no idea what to say.

"Group name?" prompted the helper. She was a young adult female, her hair done in blue streaks, purple eyeshadow surrounded her eyes and she had some sort of metallic object stuck through her nose. She was an Anipe; her tall, thin body was covered in a gown of something that looked like leather, her earrings resembled skulls and she had tattoos across each finger, just below her jet-black fingernails. Her eyes were on her datapad, waiting for me to get to the point.

She raised her eyes to mine, a small sigh escaping her lips. "I need a name, sir. Who are you and what have you registered for?" She was the picture of youth faced with aged idiot. Swim Girl had come over to see what the problem was.

I opened and closed my mouth a few times. I wondered if I should hit her. No, probably not. My normal problem-solving technique may not be the best course of action here. Rescue came from Layla, "We're the Vaslui Team," she said. "This is our driver, he's a bit slow. I just love your tatts, did you get them around here? I so want to get some!"

Goth girl looked at her datapad and said, "Most of the Vaslui schools are already in, just two to go. Are you Vaslui High or Vaslui Secondary? Oh, wait, Vaslui High has just registered, that makes you Vaslui Secondary. Is that right?" I nodded while the girl kept talking, "I got my ink near here, I'm thinking about getting the Tournament Shield on my arm. Want to come with me when I go?"

"That'd be great, when are you going? asked Layla. Goth girl reached under the counter and pulled out some bags. She passed them to us and then handed me a library worth of papers. Layla continued to gush while Jeremy and I gathered up all the bits and pieces.

"I finish her in another hour, I'll meet you in front of the stairs over there," said Goth girl. She indicated the stairs where our group had gathered, Swim Girl saw us looking and gave a wave. "Wow, that team is focused," said Goth girl. "They look pretty young for high school."

"Yeah," said Swim Girl, "We're the accelerated class, all high intelligence types."

"Cool," said Goth girl. "I gotta keep going, see you in an hour." We trundled back to the group, I just tagged along behind trying not to step on my tongue.

"Layla," I said, "That was amazing! How did you know to use the name Vaslui?"

"Oh," she said, "That was easy. This is Vaslui City, I guessed there had to be some teams from here."

We rejoined our gang just as Mr Grey came into the building and found us. We opened the bags. Inside were a bunch of compressed jackets, when pulled out of their individual containers, the jackets expanded. It appeared they were the one-size-fits-all type of jacket. Looking around, I saw other teams putting their jackets on. They were all the same colour, emblazoned with the logo of the tournament. They all looked the same.

"Everyone," said Swim Girl, "Put on a jacket. We'll blend right in." She waited for her instruction to be followed and then said, "Okay, follow me." She headed up the staircase, followed by Mr Grey and all the children including Nashwa, Layla and Jeremy. They stopped at a small landing halfway up and looked back at me, I hadn't moved. Mainly because I had no idea what was happening, I was feeling lost and out of control.

In a loud, clear voice, Swim Girl called down to me, "Do hurry up, Valerie."

Rule five was looking shaky.

I followed the team upstairs and into a large theatre space where we found seats overlooking the stage. The seats were all ramped ensuring every person had a clear view. Lush drapes, luxurious wallpaper and loads of gilt combined to give an air of opulence bordering on the tacky. The seats around us were all filled with other children, everyone dressed in the Tournament jackets. The adults sat next to their charges like islands of adultness in a sea of noisy, high-pitched babble. Right Honourable had spoken of the seven circles of hell, this felt to be about circle two.

A well-dressed man and woman came onto the stage and spoke, every word being picked up somehow and broadcast to the entire room. "Welcome, teams, to the Finals of the 31st Annual Tournament of Minds, the ultimate test of teamwork, intelligence and inventiveness of the brightest students in the country! That's YOU!" The crowd erupted into applause and cheers. The woman took over the speech and droned on about the rules of the Tournament, none of which I heard because I was signalling for Swim Girl to come and sit next to me. She shuffled down the seats, swapping places with a child on one side of me. Layla also moved, taking up position on my other side. I needed to be on my best behaviour.

Swim Girl leaned in and said, "We can stay here for a while, blend in with the crowd. I've sent a couple of the others off to chat with the other teams and get the lay of the land. At least we get a chance to rest for a couple of hours. Mr Grey has gone off to find food for us, and Justine is watching the doors. Have I missed anything?"

"No," I said, "Sounds good." In truth, I hadn't thought of doing any of those things. "Can we trust Mr Grey? What if he contacts Louise or some other villain?"

"Jeremy is following him," said Swim Girl.

How did I end up mixed up with this capable bunch of junior mobsters? They had transformed from an amorphous gaggle of frightened children into a frighteningly effective team. "Gotta go," said Swim Girl, "Some reports are coming in." She moved to where two children stood in the aisle. They huddled together and conducted a brief conversation in whispers. Swim Girl looked back at me and said something to one of the children who began to move to my seat. Swim Girl walked down the aisle towards the front of the theatre and moved into a small access door leading, I presumed, to a backstage area.

The child she had sent to me stopped and said, "The boss has found a lead, she's going to make a deal."

The boss? Wasn't that me? And Swim Girl was making deals. Who was this girl? As I mulled these questions and wondered how things had yet again blossomed out of my control, I felt a small hand grasp my shoulder.

"Don't turn around," said Justine's voice.

Chapter 47

I turned around. Justine gave an exasperated sigh, grasped my head and twisted it back to face front as Layla plopped a bag on my lap and proceeded to pull out various items as if searching for something. She hung random clothes on my head and generally covered me in junk. I spied the second Alert Module in the bag, grabbed it and settled it in a pocket next to its twin. I had earlier taken one back from Nashwa so now I had both devices. And the glimmerings of a plan.

"They're here, Mr Valentine," said Justine. She had squatted down behind me effectively eliminating her from any sight lines. "I saw some big men coming up the stairs, they don't look like anyone who would work with children, they also had bulges in jackets. I recognised one of them as the guard who used to deliver food to us."

At last, a crisis I could deal with. "How many?" I asked.

"Only two," answered Justine.

I whispered back, "Hunker down where you are, watch what they do. Tell me if they move in our direction." She squeezed my shoulder in acknowledgment. I slid down further into my seat.

Justine kept up a running commentary, "They're just standing at the entrance, they seem to be looking around. I don't think they are seriously looking. They're chatting, one is laughing at something the other said." A few moments of silence followed, and then she said, "They're leaving. I'll go back to the door." Layla repacked the bag while I considered what this surveillance meant. If Mr Grey had betrayed us, we would be knee-deep in thugs by now. I was hoping these two were just ticking the boxes of a search, probably found the van nearby and spread out to check everywhere. Layla nudged me and pointed at another entrance about halfway down the theatre, it was Mr Grey rejoining us. When he reached our row, he moved to sit next to me; he was moving fast and low. I also saw Jeremy enter by the same door, he looked up at me, caught my eye and gave a thumbs-up. Bloody hell, Jeremy, I thought, you are way too cool for someone who is barely into double figures for age.

"We've got company," said Mr Grey as he slid into the seat.

"I know, we've just been visited," I said. Swim Girl emerged from the stage door and made her way up to us. She moved along the row of seats and stood in front of Mr Grey, "Please move," she told him. Without any argument, Mr Grey got up and moved to another seat; I think I heard him mutter, "Yes, boss." Swim Girl plopped in the now empty seat, turned to me and said, "I've got us a ride."

When all those around you are engaged in focused activity and you alone do not know what is going on, take a tip from me, and keep your mouth shut. Say nothing, keep a neutral face, perhaps give a wise nod from time to time but do not open your big mouth and confirm you are hopelessly confused. Adopting this strategy, I looked at Swim Girl with my all-knowing face and gave her a small nod. She took this as a sign to explain all.

"We've been talking to all the different groups, she said. "One of them came from the capital in a big bus. I went and spoke to their adult team leader and explained how our idiot driver had broken our transport and we were stranded here." She smiled at me; I realised I was the idiot driver.

"They're returning tonight, straight after the Tournament and driving all night to get back home. If our Adult team leader, Mr Grey, goes and talks to him I am sure we can arrange to go back with them. We'll all fit in their bus."

I was still getting over the 'idiot driver' thing. "Go and talk to Mr Grey, sort it out," I said. I stood up, "Louise and her gang are nearby, I'll give them something to think about so you get clear." I pulled one of the Alert Modules from my pocket and passed it to Swim Girl. "When you get back to the city, find a group called the NightWatch. Give this to them, say it's for The Man in Black or a man called Magic. You can also talk to a Sergeant Thulani from the police, although he's not officially a policeman anymore. The module contains a recording of Louise torturing Doru to death, it should be enough."

I moved down to the aisle and headed for the door; Justine saw me coming. She had a puzzled look, Swim Girl followed me, as did Layla. "Wait," said Swim Girl, "What are you going to do?"

"Have a chat with Louise," I said. "Don't worry, I'll be safe." They all looked worried, as if I couldn't be trusted to go out by myself. "And do not follow me, I don't want to look up and see Jeremy smiling back at me. Get them on that bus, girls. Get them home." I left them there and exited the theatre. The other Alert Module still in my pocket.

I walked around the block until I found a bar, it looked rough and hopefully catered for the wrong crowd. Upon entering the bar, I stepped to one side and let my eyes adjust to the dimness. When I could see again, I went to the bar, signalled the bartender, and said, "I've got a message for Louise."

"No Louise works here, pal," said the barman. "Do you want a drink?"

"Listen carefully," I said. "I'm the guy she's looking for. I'm the guy who got away. Tell her Valentine will meet her tonight after the Tournament finishes. On the street outside the theatre."

"Like I said, buddy," said the barman, "There ain't no Louise here. I never heard of no Louise. Now, if you don't want a drink, how about you just scram."

"I'm leaving, but I'm also going to several other bars with the same story. How do you think Louise will feel when she finds out I was here first but you ignored my message." I left him and the bar. If he contacted Louise, which was vaguely possible, she would come here to check it out. Probably accompanied by large numbers of cronies. I needed to be well away when this happened. Off I slunk, immersing myself in the throngs of the city. I figured I could fit in one or two more bars with the same message, just in case this first one was ignored. I was calling down the lightning.

It was beginning to get dark by the time I started back to the theatre. I'd found two more bars and gave the same message; any more dithering would be pushing my luck. I stopped on the corner across from the theatre, keeping in the gloom of a recessed shop doorway. From this vantage point, I could see the front of the theatre and down one side as it sat majestically in its superior position. Towards the rear of the theatre was a large bus, with children beginning to file on board. I crossed the road and skulked down the sidewalk, skulking being a core skill for all Watchmen. Circling the bus, I approached the open door, ensuring I was well hidden by any observers down the street.

Justine came over and said, "I've been watching for you." Of course, she had. "Wait here, please, but stay out of sight," she said, "I'll get the boss." Now everyone was giving me instructions, whatever happened to rule 5?

I huddled in a dark corner until Swim Girl darted out, closely followed by Mr Grey and an orderly line of the gang. Nashwa brought up the rear, ensuring no straggling took place. Layla just sort of glided up and down the flanks like a sheepdog. Jeremy gave me a cheerful wave from the middle of the line. "Hsst!" said Swim Girl.

"Did you just say 'Hsst'?" I asked. "No-one says 'Hsst'!"

"We're boarding now," she said, ignoring my comment. "Mr Grey is doing a great job as Responsible Adult, he's chatted up some of the mothers from the other team and we are well in there." She pressed me back further into the gloom, "Stay out of sight! Now, have you got enough money to get home? When will we expect you?"

"Gee, I don't know, mum," I said. "I want to meet up with some of the guys after school." Any minute now, she would ask if I had a clean handkerchief.

She bit her bottom lip and looked back at the last few children boarding the bus in time to see Layla approaching our little hidey-hole. "Layla!" she hissed, "get on the bus!"

"I'm not going," said Layla, this was news to me. "I'm staying with Mr Valentine, he needs me. I'm his bodyguard."

She was as tall as my chest; Swim Girl was even shorter. Both girls fussed together in a small argument, all done in vehement whispers. "If I could say something?" I asked.

They both turned to me to say, "No!" I ignored this statement and went on, "Swim Girl, I need you to get on that bus and keep everyone safe. Layla, I don't have time for this, you can't stay with me. Shortly, I will be meeting with Louise at the front of the theatre. It will be very dangerous for you to be anywhere near there, I will have to do some fast talking and show some fancy footwork. I cannot be worrying about you if things go bad." There would be no 'if', only a 'when'.

Layla looked me up and down, an appraising study which I may have failed, "You will do some 'fast talking', you say?" I nodded while simultaneously giving my best threatening loom over them. "Accompanied by 'fancy footwork'?" Again, I nodded, putting a bit more oomph into my loom.

Swim Girl looked at Layla, rolled her eyes and said, "Maybe we should all stay, he can't be trusted out by himself. Probably doesn't even have a clean handkerchief." Then she sighed, "But he's right, Layla. Come on, let's go." She took Layla's hand and the two of them moved over to the bus, joining a knot of late borders at the doorway. I lost sight of them for a moment before I caught a fleeting glimpse of Swim Girl's head through the darkened bus windows.

I stayed where I was until the bus pulled out, the last few windows held the faces of my gang, the children I had come to like and admire a great deal. Some saw me and gave a little wave; I think they all looked sad. I was going with sad, I felt sad. When it disappeared down the road I turned, making my way to a potentially lethal meeting with Louise.

Standing on the sidewalk was one of the children, bag in one hand, the other stuck in a pocket and undoubtedly clutching a knife. I sighed.

It was Layla, my bodyguard.

Chapter 48

I waved her over and gave her such a look, which she ignored. "Where to?" she asked.

"Come on," I said, "try not to kill anyone."

"No promises," she said as we trundled up the street to the main thoroughfare. "What's the plan?" she asked.

"Do you even know me at all?" I asked.

I asked if she had any weapons; she looked at me as if this was a stupid question. We reached the main street and I headed towards a sidewalk café. It had tables and chairs next to the street, flower beds enticed one into the theatre facility while a pedestrian crosswalk allowed easy access to buildings on the other side of the road. It was one of these buildings which I hoped would keep me safe.

We sat down, a server came over and I ordered appropriate beverages for each of us. Something hot and stimulating for me, something sugary and sticky for Layla; I made sure it had umbrellas and sliced fruit. She beamed her approval when it arrived. "We just sit here?" she slurped. "In this highly visible spot?" More slurping accompanied by a wandering gaze at all and sundry; she spoke around a straw, the drink never leaving her grasp, "Should I just stab you now?"

"You're a bundle of laughs," I said. "We have to give the bus enough time to get away from this area. We must make sure Louise does not associate the Tournament with us or the rest of the kids."

"And that's why we're sitting in a café right outside the Tournament venue?" she asked. "Yes, I see that. Our plan relies on Louise, the master criminal, being a complete idiot. Louise, the one who runs a major organisation on this planet. Sure, she'll never make that association."

"You are such a teenager," I said. "Heads up, we have company." A large, black limousine had pulled into the curb, the back door opened and a man the size of a small planet emerged. He was dressed in the gangster uniform; black suit, sunglasses, bulges near armpits, buzz cut hair, sour look on his ugly mug. He scanned the area, spotted us, looked behind us carefully and then wandered over to our table. He loomed. I believe the sun dimmed for a moment; he was an expert Loomer.

He nodded and said, "Valentine," by way of the big hello. Turning to Layla his voice softened the merest fraction, "Miss Layla."

We held our little tableau for a few beats. Eventually, I said, "How you doin'?"

His eyes swivelled back to me, "Why is she here?" he asked, nodding towards Layla.

"My bodyguard," I said. He took it well but I caught the hint of a mouth twitch. "Where's Louise?" I asked.

"You'll see her if I think it is safe," he said. "Please empty your pockets onto the table, then place your hands under your thighs and remain seated. Miss Layla, please pass me that bag." We did as instructed, my knife dominating the various bits and pieces from my pockets. Layla didn't empty her pockets but did pass over the bag, the bag that held our weapons. I hoped it held our weapons. Mr Giant-among-men took out a small scanner and waved it over me with no alarm registering. It did beep, however, when he waved it over the items on the table. He honed on to the Alert Module I had taken from the dead guard. Swim Girl had one and I had the other.

"What's this?" he growled. "A transmitter?" he turned the device over in his hands and looked at the small screen on one surface before putting it in his pocket. My knife and other pocket debris went into Layla's bag.

"That, my good man, is what I wish to show Louise. Feel free to carry it across to her, invite the good lady to turn it to channel 3 and watch the recorded video where she can, as they say in the classics, learn something to her advantage." I pointed at the building directly across the street from our café, "I draw your attention to that structure. You will notice it is a bank, a financial institution which I am sure maintains a plethora of cameras. Some must be pointed at us and will track any deeds of ill intent. Play on, sir."

"Did you say 'plethora'?" he asked.

"I did," I said, "and I apologise. I've been hanging around with a loose crowd recently."

He picked up the bag and said, "Stay here, do not move. Remain sitting on your hands. We have marksmen stationed on rooftops with instructions to shoot if you move." He walked back to the car, opened the door, and leaned down to talk to whoever was inside. He passed over the Alert Module, shut the door and leaned back against the vehicle where he remained. He kept his gaze fixed upon me, using the intimidation-through-stare technique. This technique has never worked on me, I tend to poke faces and blow kisses whenever it is tried. Usually gets a few laughs. Usually. Sometimes a smack in the mouth.

The rear window lowered slightly and the human planet bent over to receive instructions. He straightened up, adjusted his clothes to the appropriate grooming level for a high-level thug, and came back to our table. "Let's go," he said, jabbing a thumb towards the car. "Louise will see you now. You and I get in the back." He looked at Layla and smirked, "Bodyguards in front next to the driver."

When we got to the vehicle, he expertly frisked me before opening the back door and motioning me inside. Before I could move, Layla threw her arms around me for a big hug. "Be safe," she said. "I'll just be upfront if you need me." We disentangled and I entered the lion's den.

The interior of the limousine was large with leather seats and darkened windows. It reeked of money and good taste, not quite my social milieu. Louise sat on the back seat while the bodyguard took up a small drop-down seat to her left. He pulled a similar seat out for me, this one jutting from the bulkhead between this passenger compartment and the driver's area so I was facing Louise; above this bulkhead was an opaque screen effectively sealing us off from those up front.

I was worried about Layla until this screen lowered and we could see into the driver's area. Layla's face beamed at me as she knelt on the front seat and leaned on the bulkhead. She had a huge smile and looked like a kid in a candy store. "Oh, Hi, Auntie Louise," she said, "How lovely to see you again. I've been having such adventures with Mr Valentine but it's good to be back with you again. Do you want to hear about them?"

She positively bubbled and launched into a long monologue, "Well, first, I found Mr Valentine when I was playing Empress of the Universe. That's a great game, you'd like it. I had made a special throne and was getting started when Mr Bogden came in and I asked if he wanted to play. He said no, but I think he wanted to. Anyway, he took me back to my room – he's a nice man, Mr Bogdan, I hope he's all right. He fell over and ...,"

At this point, Louise pushed a button on her armrest and the screen slid back into place. Again, we were cut off from the front of the vehicle. "How do you put up with her constant babbling, Valentine?" she asked. "I'm surprised you haven't cut her throat by now. Oh, that's right, you prefer to rip them out with your teeth, don't you?" She gave me a charming smile, much like the one a snake might give a bird before it eats the eggs.

I settled back into my seat, the bodyguard leaned back into his chair to my right and I stretched my legs out in a casual pose. "Are you all right, Valentine, you are moving a little stiffly?" asked Louise. "Carrying an old injury, perhaps?"

"As if you care," I muttered.

"Well, of course, I don't. I don't care about you or that brat upfront or any of those loathsome children. What I do care about is this tablet and the video you suggested I watch. I'm just glad I was alone when I viewed the awful thing. How did you get it?"

"The guys who ran your Control Room left the machines on record when they left. I assume this was a standard protocol so you could go over the videos later if needed. They set the main console to track any new motion while they were out of the room and send the video to their hand-held Alert Module. The one you have in your hand. The problem is, one of the cameras was in the Assembly area. I had a look at it, you seemed to enjoy your work."

"I see," she said. "This would be a problem if the video was transmitted anywhere off-site. But since it is only on this Alert Module – the one I have in my hand – I don't see any problem. I am, however, wondering why you took the lame brain step of giving it to me. I know you didn't have time to make copies, even if you had the expertise – which is seriously in doubt." She draped one gorgeous arm across the back of the seat, crossed her legs and gestured to her bodyguard, "Mr Flaviu has disarmed you, I assume?" The bodyguard nodded his agreement.

"Well," she went on, "it has been wonderful having this chat, I would normally take you back to the castle and continue our sessions but time is money. And you have cost me a great deal of money. Fortunately, Ghost is off on one of his secret errands and is unaware of your shenanigans. He may be somewhat cross when he discovers your escape and the loss of children but I can sooth it over if I offer him your head. Or other body part."

The bodyguard, Flaviu, spoke up, "What video are we talking about, Miss Louise? Perhaps I should see it."

I crossed my arms, sliding one hand into an internal pocket of my jacket. "Damn fine idea," I said. "But, Louise," I went on, "you are mistaken in thinking there is only one recording. I took that one off the bloke I killed. But he had a mate, they both had Alert Modules; these guys love their backup systems." She blanched, so I drove the point home, "Yes, we have you recorded, recorded as you slowly and painfully tortured Doru to death. It should play well with the planetary law enforcement community."

"And where is this other module?" asked Louise, a calmness had settled upon her. All the mockery had gone out of her tone and posture.

"Miss Louise," said Flaviu, "I think I better see this video. Ghost needs to know. I must insist." He had swivelled in his chair, just enough to give his full attention and imposing body threat towards Louise.

"Yes, yes, of course, Mr Flaviu," said Louise. "You must see the video. It will mean, of course, that Ghost will be displeased with me, especially if it gets out to the wider community." She looked at me, "I am assuming it will get out?"

I nodded.

"Hmm," said Louise. "I may have to rethink my future career path."

Flaviu held his hand out and said, "Give me the video, Louise. If what you say is true, consider yourself replaced. I will assume your duties until we hear from Ghost."

He turned back to me and said, "I see no reason to keep you alive, Valentine."

Chapter 49

He started to draw a blaster; I could see his hand on the grip of the weapon as he pulled it from its comfortable bulge. He was bigger than me, taller, wider, and heavier. And I am sure he was very conversant with hand-to-hand fighting and all manner of mayhem techniques one is required to know as the bodyguard of high-ranking baddies. Plus, he had disarmed me and knew I had no way of fighting back against a blaster.

But I had a secret weapon, a bodyguard of my own. I pulled my hand out of my jacket, making a fist around the closed clasp knife Layla had slipped to me as we hugged. Since I did not have time to open the blade, I grasped the thing in my fist and allowed one end to protrude from my closed grip. The body of the knife was metal, I now had an effective weapon.

I hit him in the ear, I swung my closed fist sideways into his head with the metal body of the knife jutting out. I swung it in a short, powerful arc and released the grunting sound I had learned from psychopathic killers. The metal tip impacted his ear and pushed into his head, he staggered and opened his mouth as his mind and body became dazed for a few precious moments. I used those moments to pull the knife back, flick out the blade and drive it into his eye.

It was all over, Flaviu slumped back in his seat, the knife protruding from his eye socket. Louise looked at it, smiled approvingly and said, "Impressive. Shall we continue with our negotiations?" She had already pulled out a blaster, pointing it at my mid-section.

I slumped back. Was I becoming a monster? How could I so casually kill a man? And in such a brutal way? A few deep breaths helped, I hoped I wasn't becoming inured to casual killing like the woman across from me. Yes, I am comfortable around violence, but I've never seen myself as a truly awful man. My mates had given me hints about my behaviour when in a tight spot, perhaps I needed to rethink my aggressive ways.

"Keep talking," I said. She was too far away for me to risk a lunge before she shot me. I had to keep talking and find a way out of this mess.

"It seems to me," said Louise, "that you are either telling the truth or telling lies about this video. Is this the only one or is there another? If it is the only one, then I shoot you now and go home. Ghost need never know of any of this, my position is secure." She thumbed a button on her armrest and said "Lucian, drive us someplace where we can dispose of a body. Possibly a large dumpster in a back street. I'll leave it to you."

The vehicle started and smoothly moved off. My breathing had slowed and I seemed to be back in control of myself; attacks of conscience are not desirable in the middle of tense altercations. I took another breath. I also had a responsibility to Layla; I had said, in my moment of supreme foolishness, that I would keep her safe. "Please, don't harm Layla," I asked. "She's just a child."

"Yes," she said, "mmm ... a child." She indicated the knife sticking out of our recently deceased companion's eye. "Did she slip you the knife during the hug? Flaviu would not have missed it in his search, you must have acquired it in those moments between being searched and entering this vehicle. So, Layla may not be the quiet, shrinking flower you purport her to be" She dangled the blaster over one knee and went on, "No matter. Once he knew of the existence of the video he was destined for early retirement. He may have been my bodyguard but his primary loyalty was always to Ghost. Ahh, the video," she held the little Alert Module in her other hand, looked at it and then back to me. "I can shoot you here and now, as well as the girl IF this is the only copy. In that case, I am free and clear. But if I am wrong and you do have another copy destined for the police, then I am in, shall we say, a ticklish position."

"The copy exists, "I said. "It will be with the police in a few hours."

"So, they do not have it yet?" she said. "Interesting." I bit my lip, stupid, stupid man. Louise was studying me closely, I never wanted to gamble with this woman. "I can read you like a book, Valentine," she said, "and a boring book it is."

The car turned and travelled as Lucian sought a quiet resting place for Flaviu. "Let's consider the negative impacts of each possible decision. Scenario 1," said Louise, "I stay with Ghost and the video emerges. Result, my life will be terminated, no chance to escape since I would be surrounded by quite a lot of dreadful men like Flaviu. Scenario 2: I surrender to you, give evidence against Ghost and seek Witness Protection as part of the deal. In Scenario 1, I die, in Scenario 2, I live but lose my position in the gang. But let's not dismiss that upside, I would be alive."

The silence stretched on; the car came to a halt. "I choose door number 2, with some modifications," she said. She kept the blaster on me, pressed a button and said, "Lucian, come back here and help with the body." I heard a car door open and shut, then the rear door opened and a rough head poked in. A very surprised rough head since I would assume he thought he was about to bury me, not Flaviu. Still, he was professional, he swallowed and looked to the blaster-wielding Louise for instructions.

"Valentine tried a little stunt," said Louise. "Caught Flaviu by surprise. Drag the body out of the car, Lucian. Valentine will help, after all, he killed him." Lucian took a moment to absorb this news but seemed to be encouraged by the fact that Louise was holding a blaster on me.

"Yes, Ma'am," he replied and reached in to grab an arm. With a gesture of her blaster, Louise suggested I help. Together, Lucian and I dragged the huge body out of the vehicle while Louise kept me covered all the time. We managed to get the body across and down

to some large, industrial dumpsters. Lucian raised a lid which fell
back with a clang. I looked around nervously but he had chosen his
spot well, we were at the end of an access road between two large
warehouses. The road was not in great repair, tufts of grass and weeds
thrust through the surface making the environment not attractive to
the random passer-by. I suspected no one ever came here unless they
wanted to discard rubbish. Or a body.

Louise had exited the vehicle and moved to the open door of the
driver's space. Keeping the blaster on me, she sat back in the driver's
seat and watched us in our house cleaning chores. Flaviu was a big
man, it took a lot of grunting and heaving from Lucian and me to
work his body into the dumpster. At one point, I had all the weight
while an arm flopped over my head. Lucian eventually climbed into
the dumpster and dragged the corpse to its resting place.

Much to my surprise - and certainly that of Lucian - Louise
started the limousine and began to drive off. Lucian yelled "Hey!"
from his position in the dumpster while I turned to watch her move
the vehicle. She had a window down and yelled, "I'll be in touch,
Valentine, we can discuss the conditions of my surrender. Don't
worry about Layla, I'll keep an eye on her, just remember I have
your little friend. Oh," she continued, "I've also called the police.
Told them I saw two ne'er-do-wells dumping a body. Sorting that out
should give me a head start. Toodles!"

Lucian and I looked at each other in consternation. While he
was working out his next career move, I took off after the limousine.

Chapter 50

I had no chance of running it down on foot but I had to try. Not for Louise, but for Layla. I had to get her out of that car, I just had to, even if it meant running on my damaged feet. I ran. I was up to full speed as the vehicle turned the corner and disappeared. But I didn't stop, I kept going and rounded the corner with the vehicle picking up speed and a long way ahead. It hurt, it hurt a lot. My pursuit was a vain effort.

Nonetheless, I was well placed to watch it veer off the road and hit a nearby tree. It wasn't travelling at killer speeds but would certainly have shaken up all those inside. Was Layla all right? What had happened?

I reached the passenger door and pulled it open to find Layla sitting erect, held safely in place by seat belts. She was half turned to Louise who had collapsed across the steering wheel, she lay with her mouth open, twitching.

I could not understand what had happened but the main thing was Layla's safety. I unbuckled her and reached to lift her out. That was when I saw the shock rod in her hand; she smiled at me, leaned over to Louise, and jolted her again. Louise's body gave a small spasm as her eyes rolled up, not her most attractive look. Then Layla turned to me, put her arms around my neck and allowed me to lift her out of the car.

"Did you...?" I asked. "Are you...?" I put her down, very gently. "Just wait there," I said. I ran around to the driver's door, pulled it open and took the blaster from Louise; on the floor beside her was the Alert Module so I grabbed it. I then extracted the gang boss from the crashed vehicle and laid her down on the grass under another nearby tree. Layla came around the car and joined us, she still held the shock rod. Louise started to regain consciousness but still presented a delightful picture of 'dishevelled street rat', complete with vacant stare and obligatory drool.

I crouched down in front of her and said, "How are you doin', Louise? I think you've met my bodyguard."

Louise was cross. Absolutely incandescent. "What did you do?" she stuttered. Catching sight of a smiling Layla behind me, she asked, "You, girl, what did you do?" Layla held up the shock rod and smiled.

I sat down beside Louise and said, "Shall we continue our negotiations?"

Louise groaned, lay back and waved a hand in acquiescence. "Do your worst," she said. "Have your way with me."

Layla looked a question at me, "It's a grown-up thing," I said. "Louise wants me to ravish her."

Layla rolled her eyes and made a face, "But she's like old and yukky. So old." I did like the way she emphasised the 'old'.

I turned back to Louise, "Sit up, sport, let's talk about you leaving the dark side and coming across to the forces of goodness and light." I poked her in the ribs, my thumb getting petty revenge for the loss of the fingernail.

She sat up, leaned against the tree, and said, "Okay, let's deal. What have you got to trade?"

Unbelievable. This woman was negotiating shortly after receiving several belts from a shock rod plus various dings from a car crash. Tough chick. On the downside, she tortured the innocent and preyed on children so, not a good person. "I'll prove there is another copy of your favourite video." I held up the Alert Module, allowed her to get a good look at it and then snapped it in half. Remembering what Greenash did to my information tablet from the boss, I borrowed the shock rod from Layla and gave the remaining pieces a few jolts. "There you are, I have destroyed this copy. Would

I have done that if I didn't have another? Your turn," I said, "make it something good."

Louise looked at the smoking bits of the Alert Module, it was never going to rise again. "Well, you certainly know how to give a girl a good time. Of course, this could be a double bluff. You might have destroyed the only copy ... but no, you're not that subtle." She thought a moment, looked at my face and smiled, "I know the very thing. You've already met 'Ghost', you are one of the few people who have seen his face and lived." She sat forward and gave a small laugh. "No other clues, you big dumb oaf."

I looked, mulling over her statement. If I had already met Ghost, it had to be someone in the castle, Louise would not know who I had met before I arrived there. She had stood beside another mover and shaker during my first interview, but they had both deferred to someone hidden behind a screen. Could that have been a ruse, was the other guy the leader? Was he Ghost and they just pretended someone was behind the screen to keep the legend alive? Hmm, some thinking was required. My head hurt.

"By the way, sweetie," said Louise, "I did call the local police, they should be here any minute. I, of course, am the survivor of a terrible car crash and know nothing of what goes on around me. While you, on the other hand, are obviously a thug."

This was a hurtful remark; surely, I presented a more approachable demeanour to the world. Back to the problem at hand, who was Ghost? I ran over the various citizens I had met during my stay at Chez Louise and said, "Silent. He's 'Ghost'." Her eyes widened a fraction. "I thought his bruises and injuries were unusual, plus he had a smell about him, one I am familiar with from my days of hanging around stage doors and chatting up loose living actresses. Make-up. He was wearing make-up."

"Well done, copper," she snarled. She calmed herself, "Ghost loves to dress up, to play with disguises. Occasionally, he would pretend to be a prisoner, he thought he could get other prisoners to reveal secrets if they shared a cell. He particularly loved his crazy 'Bishop Mykle' role. I just think he was a frustrated actor." I could see her change mental gears. "What else you got? Where's the other copies?"

"Your turn to go first this time, you tell me something," I said.

"Okay, let me see if I can answer my own question. You escaped from the castle with two Alert Modules. You have one and one of the children has the other. I discount the man who helped you escape, he's either dead at your hand or he will be by mine when he is found. You would not have trusted him with such evidence. No, a child. And where is this child?"

In the distance, we heard sirens, several sirens. Louise gazed into space and muttered, thinking aloud, "They were all young. You wouldn't abandon any of them. Mr Bloody Valentine, the recent saint, would not turn a single or group of very young bed-wetters loose. So, they must still be together. But they are travelling. Again, not alone because they would need an adult with them. Again, forget my recent employee. How would a group of children travel without attracting attention?"

She thought silently and then smiled at me. "By bus, of course. They're on a bus back to the capital! Oh, how delightful." Her gaze flicked from Layla to me and back again, "I can see it on your faces, I'm right! Oh, this is almost fun. Now, which bus? We found you outside that ridiculous Tournament event, it was finishing and busloads of horrible children were driving away." She gloated in triumph, "They're on a bus from the Tournament back to the capital city. If they drive all night, they will arrive early tomorrow morning. I'm right, aren't I?"

Layla's eyes widened, "I'm sorry, Mr Valentine, I didn't mean to give it away. I just couldn't control my face." She looked the picture of grief in the face of Louise's glowering pride, I wanted to cheer her up so I hit Louise with the shock rod again, causing her to fall back unconscious.

It was a little thing but I hope it helped.

Chapter 51

The police arrived; one car stopped near us followed by one of their emergency vehicles. Another police car sped past and turned into the alley containing a dead body in a dumpster. They seemed excited by this event, perhaps dead bodies on refuse piles were not as common as in my world. Ah, the City, such a magical place; so glad I left.

Layla and I were trundled into the police vehicles while Louise was cared for by the crew of the emergency vehicle. She had started to come around by the time she was loaded into the back of their machine, we caught each other's eyes and I gave her a little wave. Mr Friendly. Shortly thereafter we arrived at a police building where Layla and I were separated, I was placed in a small room containing a desk and some extra chairs. I recognised this from my previous incarcerations; this was the room in which I would be questioned about this and that. A uniformed and bored policeman took my name and initial details, not that I had a lot of details. I gave them the name of the Man in Black which cut no ice. Peasants. However, things changed when I suggested they contact Frenzek or Thulani in the capital. Those names brought wide eyes to my fresh-faced interrogator.

He stood up and advised me that more senior officials would be coming in to ask me some hard questions. He leaned on the phrase 'hard questions'; I suspect he was trying to intimidate me, poor lamb. No big deal, their idea of strenuous questioning stopped at raised voices and verbal threats. Like that was going to work on me.

Time was becoming a dominant factor. I was sure Louise had influence over the police here. Possibly not a lot, but an evil villain's lair in the neighbourhood would suggest that someone had been got at. It would only be common sense to have some of the police from surrounding towns and cities on the payroll of Ghost. Probably not a lot of them, but enough so that Louise may well receive special treatment. If she got out before me then she would go after the children on their bus. What to do? I looked around my room, the door was of that family of doors that laugh at unwanted attempts to open. A broken foot would be suggested from any attempt to escape. I had no options. Only one thing to do then, I dozed off.

Some time later I was awoken by the door opening and a different thug strolled in. "Why aren't you dead yet, Valentine?" asked my old mate, Thulani. Behind him came Right Honourable, Max and Ragnar. The room was seriously crowded with horrible men, I loved it.

I filled Thulani in very briefly, emphasising we needed to get to the children's bus before Louise was released. He questioned some of the local police and discovered that Louise had already left.

We also picked up Layla, Thulani showed the supervising officer at the station a datapad giving him authorisation to do whatever he damned well pleased, this included taking children from police custody. "Where'd you get that from?" I asked.

"Frenzek," he replied. "Come on, we've got transport outside." Layla grabbed my arm and hung on for grim death, she was not letting go for an instant. Thulani noticed the attachment and asked, "Why are we dragging a child with us, Valentine?"

"She's my bodyguard," I said. Thulani had the good grace to lose stride, almost tripping over his own feet before regaining a stately walk. I could feel the questions coming off the big, scarred copper. He needed to relax more.

Layla hugged my arm tighter, she looked up at the large men around her but kept quiet, just staying with the group. And my arm was certainly clutched, that grip never lessened. Right Honourable cruised up alongside us and asked, "Did you say this child was your 'bodyguard', Valentine? You feel you need a bodyguard? You, the man of mayhem?"

"Bit of respect, pal," I said. "This is Layla the Magnificent." Layla squeezed my arm some more, I smiled at her.

"You're unbelievable, Val," he said.

Chapter 52

I was bundled out of the police station into one of the flying machines, inside waited two policemen plus a couple more NightWatch. I asked Thulani why he brought so many, just to pick me up. He gave me a pitying look and said, "You are known to be a walking disaster and a trouble magnet. These guys were in the room with me when I heard you were here. For some reason, members of the NightWatch have been visiting every day, checking for any news of your sorry carcass."

"What about the blokes in police uniform?" I asked.

"Crew of this transport, poor sods," he answered. "How unlucky are they?" We lifted off and sped into the darkness. "Now shut up and let me work, I need to find that bus."

I sat back into the main passenger section, which consisted of drop-down seats along the walls of the vehicle, several occupied by the lads. They all gave me a big hello and I said, "Have you guys been checking up on me? Worried bout my plight? That is so sweet."

"Not worried at all, knucklehead," said Right Honourable. "Thulani has this incredible machine which makes a hot drink unlike anything we have tasted. That's why we visit. And to see Greenash, he has been doing some tinkering with our nanobots."

Our craft roared through the darkness, we had low lights in our cabin, enough to see each other and talk in low tones. "I do not want to hear about any tinkering with the wee beasties," I said. The very thought made me feel ill. To take my mind off current events, I looked at who was on board with me from the NightWatch. Right Honourable, Max, Ragnar and two girls, Maggie and Tabitha. When I say 'girls' I do not mean frail, wilting flowers. Maggie, Tabitha and a handful of others joined us in our big march across Gamma 3; they fought off bandits, Tharls and other assorted villainy. Magic had put them in a squad under Meataxe to toughen them up; toughen up or go insane. Meataxe, guardsman extraordinaire. What time he could spare from drinking he devoted to the neglect of personal hygiene; Meataxe, an uncouth, ill-bred wastrel. This was the man told to care for a band of females. He taught them to be mean, vicious, and dirty fighters and wouldn't hear a word against his girls. For some unfathomable reason, they all liked him. They did, however, have nice smiles.

Thulani came back and sat with us, "Okay, here's the situation. Louise and a handful of men, some of them police, are in two police cars, following the highway. We've discovered the bus carrying your children, it took a detour to drop off another group to a small country town. It will be rejoining the highway soon and then continue to the capital. Louise would be aware of this detour and may intend to intercept the bus before or soon after it rejoins the highway. I suspect they plan to get in front of the bus, set up a roadblock and stop it." He peered through one of the side windows down towards the darkened land.

"Can we shoot at them from the air?" I asked.

"No," he said. "This vehicle is not a gunship; it's only a passenger transport. Their cars could carry, in total, about 12-16 people, all armed. We are outgunned." We sat and thought for a while.

Right Honourable spoke up, "Why can't we just contact the bus driver? Surely, he has some form of communicator. If not him, then some of the children. Mothers do worry so."

One of the policemen answered, "No reception out here. No civilian communicators cut through."

Great, I thought. Do these people live in the Dark Ages or something?

Thulani touched his ear, listening. "Our pilot has reached the point where the side road rejoins the highway. He can see a set of lights across the road up ahead. It appears to be a police checkpoint."

He pulled out a hand device, punched some buttons and said, "We don't have a roadblock here. It must be them."

One of the crewmen said, "There's a bus moving on that side road down there. It's heading for the roadblock."

"Can we land in front of the bus, before it gets to the highway?" I asked. "Or fly over them and use that loudhailer thing to yell at them to stop?"

"No," said Thulani. "We're entering a heavily forested area. The side road goes through the forest, under several tower structures and other nasty obstructions."

Decision time. "Land behind the roadblock," I said to Thulani. "We have to get them before Louise gets on that bus. If she destroys the last Alert Module it won't matter if we catch her, we won't have any leverage."

"She cannot be allowed on that bus," I snarled.

Chapter 53

Thulani gathered us with his eyes, scanning the entire compartment. "We have the pilot plus two other crew on this vehicle. And me. That means we have three sidearms." He asked Right Honourable, "Do any of your NightWatch have weapons?"

Right Honourable raised a cultured eyebrow and turned to the gang, "Anyone have a weapon?" he drawled. Thulani gulped at the assortment of knives, bludgeons, knuckle dusters and so on the guys and gals had in their pockets. Layla joined in by showing her shock rod which caused Maggie and Tabitha to move and sit with her; they looked quite protective. Good Lord, I thought, she's now got her own backup.

"Weren't you lot issued with a blaster or something?" asked Thulani.

Right Honourable looked embarrassed; well, almost embarrassed, "I, uh, misplaced them."

I gave them all a hard look, one of my specialities, "Did you give your weapons to this damn fool? A known gambler? Again?" I was pointing at Right Honourable. He tugged his collar, coughed softly and dropped his eyes. Silence reigned, "Oh, God, you idiots," I said. None of them could meet my eyes, "What were you thinking?"

They all muttered apologies, complete with foot shuffling and low voices. "No," I said, "I don't want to hear it! You better hope you get injured in this little foray, because if any of you are uninjured, I will be having a meaningful conversation with you. Very meaningful." I crossed my arms and leaned back against the wall, "Unbe-bloody-lievable!"

"Still only three blasters," said Thulani. He looked at his team, "They will be expecting us, I'm sure. We may even be fired upon before we land although I'm confident this old bird can handle some small arms fire. We hit the ground," he said to his men, "And we come out shooting."

"We'll be easy meat, sir," said one of the crewmen. "Be lucky to make five steps."

"Obviously," said Thulani. The crewman looked sheepish. "Therefore, let's **not** leave by the door facing the bad guys," said Thulani. "We exit and put the vehicle between us and them." He turned to me, "Since none of you have any ranged weapons, you better stay under cover, you're no use to anyone making a desperate charge and being shot down. After we exit the vehicle, we make it up as we go along."

"You've been hanging around Val too long," said Right Honourable. He was always quick to recover, absolutely no moral compass at all. You couldn't help but like him.

The pilot turned on all our flashing lights and announced us as the police, the real police. His instruction for the ground-based thugs to lay down their weapons and be generally good boys was answered with several blaster shots. None came close, the pilot had done this before; no point in staying in one space while someone lines up a good shot at you. We danced around the sky, each of us hitting a wall or another body as we desperately tried to hang on. As I was considering throwing up, we landed.

Our offside door slid open and out we went. Thulani and the crew found cover and started firing off shots at the bad guys. I pulled the NightWatch to me and gave instructions. Everyone leaned in to discuss our next actions, anyone could contribute to a plan, especially if someone spotted a really stupid idea. I tend to specialise in stupid ideas. "Right Honourable, move back out of the light then circle around this mess, take Max, Ragnar, Maggie and Tabitha with you. I'll go for the bus. Thulani has no hope of shooting them, we are way too outnumbered. All Louise has to do is hold us off until she gets on the bus and destroys the Alert Module. After that, she'll probably just surrender. I don't have any confidence she will receive justice, too much corruption on the planet. Ghost will probably grease a few palms and she'll be released."

"Okay," said Right Honourable. No one else said anything, never a good sign; it indicated there was only one, dangerous way to go. Right Honourable continued, "Right, we circle, come up behind them and then, what? Just the usual?" I nodded. He looked at his team, "You should keep Ragnar, I don't trust that hand thing he's got, we'd never hear the end of it if he got any more damage."

"Fair enough," I said. "Come on Ragnar. Layla, stay with me." We all moved off into the darkness. Once in the gloom, our two teams separated, I took my two on a wide sweep before moving back to the highway. I wanted to get to that bus before Louise knew it was on the scene. Layla tugged my arm, I leaned down to hear her whisper, "What's 'the usual' that the other team will do?"

Growing up can be a bitch. I wasn't going to lie to this child, this girl who had saved my life and held it all together after hearing of her father's murder. "It means they kill them all. We're outnumbered, with no hope of imminent rescue, we are outgunned. We are on our own. The NightWatch is always on its own. That means we must make everyone else scared shitless when they see us coming. It means we want everyone to know that engaging with the NightWatch is always a bad idea. We don't fight pretty, we fight mean. If we can't kill then we maim, cripple and blind."

She looked at Ragnar, creeping along with us. The huge Viking smiled at her, just pleased with life. He spoke up, "That's right, little miss. Bad bastards, the lot of us."

"Language, Ragnar," I said.

"Sorry, sergeant," he answered. He raised his head over some gorse, turned back and said, "I can see the bus, it's already stopped. Doors opening now, someone just slipped inside."

I was up and running before my brain processed Ragnar's message. An open door followed by someone getting on board could be innocent but pigs might also fly. It had to be Louise; she was ahead of me. As I put one foot on the first step into the bus a man rose from a squatting position at the front of the bus and plunged a knife into my left shoulder. She had left guards. Ragnar hit him square on the side of the head with his metal hand protection, the bad guy's head deformed. When he collapsed, Ragnar jumped on his head some more. Lots of squishing noises.

"Keep going, Val," he said. A blaster shot passed by, narrowly missing his head. He never changed his tone or demeanour. Still smiling, he said, "I've got this." He picked up the guard's blaster and settled in.

Sometimes I worry about Ragnar. But not today.

I stood there with a knife sticking out of my shoulder. It wasn't a big knife; the blade was about as long as my hand and wasn't in my shoulder too far. Slowly, very slowly, its weight dragged it down and the blasted thing fell to the ground. It really hurt! I've got outstanding reflexes for those times when things tend to get stuck into my body; when the nutjob rose to his feet I must have noticed the knife and pulled away. Hence, his knife was not plunged into the hilt, more like two finger widths. Still, it hurt like crazy. I bent down picked up the fallen knife and moved into the bus, bleeding. And, I suspect, swearing.

I launched myself up the few steps into the bus to be met by a frantic bunch of children, all those in the front were wailing, crying and sobbing. The bus driver was unconscious, or dead. I couldn't see any visible wounds but who knows with Louise? I walked past the crying children and headed to the back of the bus, there were several rows of unoccupied seats separating the front group of wailers from the children in the rear. The rear group were all silent, not cowed, not panicked and certainly not calling for their mothers. This lot were my guys, my children.

Mr Grey was on the floor, blood pooling around his body. He may have been dead; I didn't have time to check. Standing in the aisle was Louise. She held Nashwa in front of her while aiming a blaster at me. It was a small blaster, I seemed to recognise it from our original meeting way back when. A small blaster, my recent training informed me that this particular weapon did not fire bursts of hellish energy. Rather, this one shot the little darts. Usually, darts coated with something to instantly incapacitate or kill. The things you learn, eh? I wondered how small a dart gun could be before it didn't kill someone. Someone like me. I was willing to bet that Louise would not carry a weapon that did not kill those at whom it was aimed. As I thought these thoughts, I wondered at my use of the word 'whom'; perhaps those years of education were finally paying off.

"Hiya, Louise," I said, very conversationally. "What's new?"

"Which one of the vermin has the Alert Module, Valentine?" she snarled.

"You know, Louise, when you snarl, your face screws up in a most unattractive manner," I said. Ever the calm negotiator.

She raised the gun to Nashwa's head, "I'll kill her, you maggot," she said. I reached back and pulled Layla into one of the spare seats, now there was no one behind me.

"Louise," I said, deciding to go for broke in the diplomacy stakes, "you are an unattractive, mean-spirited piece of human garbage. You dress as if all should lust after you, but you end up looking like a bitch in heat." I could see her rage building, this might just work, I might be able to get that dart gun pointed at me rather than Nashwa. One more push, "You're an ugly slut and ..."

At this point, she shot me. Perhaps I had gone too far by calling her a 'slut', please don't tell my mum I used that word.

I had seen her hand begin to swing the blaster from Nashwa's head towards me and went for it. I jinked to one side in a motion of sheer poetry. I was hoping the darts would whistle past my head as I effortlessly stepped forward and knocked the dart gun out of her hand. It would have looked incredibly beautiful.

Yeah ... nah. She twitched her hand enough for the shot to partially hit my side. Several darts hit my arm, the same arm which had recently gained extra ventilation from a knife. I took a small step and fell down, slowly rolling onto my back. Things were getting dark.

Louise stepped over my body as I fought to retain consciousness. She kneeled on my chest and said, "I really hate you, Valentine." Her red lips parted in what may once have been a lovely smile but recent events had combined to give her the mask of a deranged nutcase. Crazy cat lady. These thoughts crossed my mind as she leaned in, placed the tip of the blaster against my throat and said, "I am so going to enjoy this."

Time to die, I thought. As I sank further into unconsciousness, I saw a blur flash over my body, a Layla shaped blur.

This is how you keep children safe, I thought; show me the funny pages now, please.

Chapter 54

I awoke, which I took to be a good sign. Furthermore, I awoke in a bed with clean sheets, another excellent sign. When I opened my eyes and groaned, a voice called, "He's awake!" I recognised Right Honourable's voice. At least he wasn't dead. Nor me. This day was looking up.

I gained some more consciousness and blinked at my room, "Is that you, mother?" I simpered.

"And he's okay!" yelled the same voice. A face leaned into my field of view, "How are you, dickhead?" asked Right Honourable.

The room filled up before I could reply. It was mainly filled by Layla who had been sitting on the other side of my bed, head down and sound asleep. At right Honourable's words, she flung herself onto my bed and delivered a ferocious cuddle. Some ribs may have bent. I could see a nurse attempting to peel the girl off me with limited success.

"Gerroff," I snorted into her hair. "Lemme breathe!" Reluctantly, Layla released her death grip and sank back into her chair. A chair, I noted, surrounded by food containers and various drink receptacles. All scattered about the place. Made me feel right at home.

The Man in Black entered the room, "Why aren't you dead yet, Sergeant?"

"Sorry, sir," I said. "Poor work ethic. Always had trouble finishing. How badly am I hurt this time."

"Smashed lips, three teeth knocked out," my boss said. "Two cracked ribs, concussion, various bruises. The thumb and three fingers of the right hand are broken. Quite a bit of pain, I'm told."

I did a small check of my various bits and pieces, including teeth. They all seemed to be there. I could also flex all the fingers of my right hand. How long had I been out? "What happened? Did I get all these injuries after I blacked out?" I asked.

"Oh, those aren't your injuries, Sergeant," said the Man in Black. "What I have just described was inflicted upon Louise. She's still unconscious in a medically induced coma."

"But," I said, "I never touched her. Honest."

"That may be so," he said, "but your bodyguard certainly did." He looked over at the small figure of Layla, slumped in her chair with guilt rolling off her in waves.

She raised her head, I caught a moist eye looking at me through her hair, "It wasn't all me," she said in the softest of soft voices. That's my girl, I thought, spread the blame; confuse the issue. When in doubt, lie. I felt like a proud dad.

"Indeed," said the boss. "Quite frankly, it's almost impossible to ascertain who did what to Louise." He caught my questioning glance. "It seems," he continued, "that when Louise shot you - and then prepared to deliver the fatal blow – she was initially forestalled by Layla lunging over your potential corpse and grabbing the dart gun. And a considerable amount of Louise's hair, I have been told. She has several bald patches now, I might add." He looked at some device and said, "I have to go now, Right Honourable can fill you in on the rest of the details." He left.

"Okay," I said. "Layla saved me, I get that." I turned my head to face the girl, "Thank you, sweetheart. You do tend to keep saving me." I rolled back, "What about the other injuries, enough to keep her in a coma?"

Right Honourable jumped in at this point, "Yes, well, it seems the other children rose up in your defence. When they saw you fall, and witnessed Layla's heroic charge, they all attacked Louise. Every one of them. Hence the lost teeth, broken fingers and so on. I daresay her body still bears the imprints of little fists as they pummelled her into oblivion. They only stopped when I got on the bus and pulled them off her trampled body. My god, Valentine, what did you do to those children?"

"Are they, are they all right?" I asked.

"Every one of them is fit and well," he said. "Somewhat undernourished but all clamouring for news of you and your sorry carcass."

"And the lads? And lasses? Any dead?" I asked.

"Hmm," he answered. "Ragnar broke his new hand. When he hit that guy who stabbed you – by the way, we're thinking of calling you 'Pincushion' – he broke the protective covering and proceeded to take his disappointment out on the bloke's head. That gentleman is now deceased and Ragnar has yet another hand." He put his hands in his pockets and bounced on his toes. Looked out the window and went on, "Max is dead. He jumped three of them but didn't see the fourth one in time. Took them all out before succumbing to injuries, losing your arm and half a face will do that."

"The ladies, bless 'em, fared better," he continued. "They encountered a bunch of corrupt police who hesitated over shooting women." We both smiled at that, the amateurs. "They disabled another four and then picked up their blasters to keep the remaining idiots busy. Thulani lost one crewman, the damn fool followed Thulani in a charge towards the villains when they realised we were amongst them. Thulani caught one in the arm but he'll recover."

The door burst open and my lovely Lydia bounded into the room. It was a repeat of the smothering given to me by Layla. Again, I struggled to breathe but not too much. Lydia and I have been seeing a bit of each other. Quite a bit of each other. And all her bits are fabulous. We stopped when the deafening silence in the room reminded us of our visitors. When we disentangled, I caught a very censorious look from Layla who had a hand in her pocket while giving Lydia judgemental glances. I knew that hand was grasping a knife.

"Layla," I croaked, still a little out of breath, "This is Lydia. She's my ..." I paused; we had never formally identified our relationship.

"... Main Squeeze," finished Lydia. "And he's my little snookums."

"I may just throw up," said Right Honourable.

Layla shrugged, the teenager's natural defence. Just sayin', you know, who cares. "Yeah. Hi," she said. "I'm ..."

"You're his **Bodyguard**," said Lydia, emphasising the last word. "I am forever grateful; you are one brave lady. I think I love you."

Something passed between them, and suddenly they were best friends. Both sat on my bed while Lydia said, "I've just come from the children's ward. All your charges are fine, Val. No long-term damages. We've flushed the remaining nanobots out of their systems. Now we just have to wait and see what to do with them."

I fell asleep during the resultant conversation and did not surface until the next day. Layla was still at my bedside with a nervous Greenash beside her.

"Greenash, you horrible NightWatchman," I said, "What are you doing here?"

"I, er, I wanted to see how you were feeling, Val," he said.

I raised an eyebrow, "Sure you did," I said. "And the real reason is ..."

"Val," he said, "It's awful down there! They ask questions, play with my stuff and then they," he gulped, "make suggestions for improvements. "

"This would be the kids?" I asked. He nodded. "Get Wallace and H'Nuth involved, they seem to like them."

His eyes goggled, "They're already there, the worst of the lot! They play silly games involving hiding from each other, or some form of throwing competition. This morning they were trying to see how many children could balance on a chair! On a single chair! What about Workplace Health and Safety!"

He took a breath and dragged control back into his life, "But I did want to see how you were doing. I jiggled your nanobots a little and wondered if you felt any changes?"

Blood drained from the Valentine visage. "You 'jiggled' my wee beasties, Greenash? What does 'jiggled' mean?" My voice may have begun to increase in volume, I could tell by the way Greenash was shrinking back into the wall. Layla grabbed her knife and stood before me, ready to rip and rend. "What have you done to me, Greenash? I don't want to become another zombie!"

He patted the air but kept his distance from me, "No, no, no, nothing like that," he said. I noticed he was also edging towards the door, sliding along the wall to keep as far away from Layla as possible. "I just turned on the full capacity of the translation programming, you should be able to read text now."

That didn't sound so bad, I put a consoling hand on Layla's arm and gently guided her back to a seat. "Okay," I said. "That makes sense." I pursed my lips, looked into space and muttered, "Thank you." Grace above all, that's my motto.

"And, er," began Greenash, "I also added a routine to assist your body's healing ability." He was almost at the door, almost free.

I erupted up from the bed, "WHAT?" I bellowed. "What do you mean, you 'added a routine'? Stay out of my stuff, Greenash!" Various wires and tubes prevented me from leaving the bed, another example of modern medicine prolonging life.

In this case, the life prolonged belonged to Greenash.

Chapter 55

He opened the door, preparing to bolt through but ran into the rather large figure of Thulani, complete with a bandaged arm. He came into the room, pushing Greenash ahead of him. Behind Thulani came my gang, Swim Girl herded them in where they took up positions around the room, Jeremy and Justine were brave enough to come over and give me a hug. I didn't see Nashwa anywhere. Thulani had a paw on Greenash's shoulder. I was hoping he could squeeze it a little. Or a lot.

"Greenash has been telling you about his nanobot tinkering, I see," said Thulani. "When he told me he was going to inform you of the changes, I just had to come and watch. Found this gaggle of reprobates cluttering up the corridors looking for your room. Have I missed much?"

I sat up in the bed; my teeth may have been grinding. "I'm a sick man, Greenash. Very Poorly. Now is not the time to suck blood out of my body and perform your arcane and mysterious rites. I do not want any changes made to these horrible things infesting my body. I can feel them crawling around, I know they nest in my skull. Sometimes, I think I catch a glimpse of one of them skidding across the surface of my eye. Do not, let me make this perfectly clear, do not play with my inner monsters."

In fact, I was feeling pretty good. I did a mental check of my various injuries – bruises from beatings, loss of fingernails and toenails, assorted burns and abrasions, some cuts and slashes, a nasty knife wound in my shoulder and whatever damage the darts had done. Probably other things as well but the cup was already full. I should be moaning. "Why aren't I moaning?" I asked.

"Ahh," said Greenash, "So, you're not feeling at death's door?" he bravely approached my bed and looked into my eyes, I graciously allowed him to live. "Can I see your shoulder, the one with the knife wound?" he asked.

Talk about a weird scene, I uncovered my wounded shoulder for an assessment and, as I did so, everyone in the room stepped in for a look. I mean, they crowded around, bumping heads, craning necks over each other. I only got to see it because I was attached to the arm. I think Jeremy ended up on my lap with Layla leaning over my head, peering down to inspect the damage. Greenash unwrapped the bandages.

My shoulder looked good. There was a deep cut, looking very clean and tidy. It didn't seem too deep, no blood or other yucky stuff lying about. I flexed it a few times, the kids laughed when I made the shoulder dance. There did not seem to be any loss of motion or degradation of power. "I guess the stab wasn't as bad as I thought," I said.

"What about the other injuries?" asked Greenash. I held up my fingers and rolled one foot out from underneath Jeremy. All had the nails back in place. Okay, now it was getting freaky. I shifted Jeremy and Layla, lifted the neck of my garment, and peered down the length of my body. And it was just me peering, there are things down there not meant for the eyes of mortal man. No bruises, no scars. Well, well, well.

"What's going on, Greenash?" I asked. "Choose your words wisely and you may yet live to see another dawn." Layla stayed close to me but the rest backed away to give us all some breathing space. Thulani leaned against the door, effectively blocking any rash exits.

"Well," said Greenash, "Your nanobots are experimental, the guy who designed them was a genius."

"I held up a hand, "that 'guy', was Layla's father," I said. "She needs to know how special her dad was." I squeezed her shoulder; she fixed her gaze on Greenash.

"Oh," he said, "okay. Well. Slynkor was experimenting with nanobots that could be programmed. Programmed after they were inserted into the host." My stomach gurgled at the word 'host'; I didn't like the sound of that. "Nanobots are programmed before they go into a body, nothing can change their initial instructions. But Slynkor worked out a way to do it. Your nanobots, as well as those in all the NightWatch, can be re-programmed. On top of that, they can carry two functions, not just the normal single function."

"Currently," he went on, "if we wish to change instructions, we have to reprogram them all. One of the glitches in the technology is the aversion one set of nanobots has for another set with different programming. They tend to fight which," he tapered off as he watched my face, "is not good. Usually, an agonising sickness followed by death."

He picked up my hand and looked at it as if seeing the little buggers inside. "The work he was doing is beyond genius," he whispered, then shook himself and returned to normal-sounding Greenash. "Magic has mandated that communication is one of the programs with the other one up for consideration. For you, Sergeant Valentine, I set yours to be healers. Sicknesses will be much reduced or even eliminated and they will repair your body faster, if it becomes damaged in any way."

Thulani laughed, "Not a huge conceptual leap, Val, given the way you attract damage." He wiped his eye, "Oh, dear. IF it becomes damaged! Hah!"

"There are some side effects," continued Greenash. "In fact, there are a lot of side effects so they cannot be used by most of the population. It would appear that humans from technologically backward planets and certain pre-pubescent children have the smallest adverse reactions."

"Layla has the nanobots in her as well," I said. "What happens when she hits puberty?"

Greenash looked with renewed interest at Layla, "Does she now? How fascinating," he said. "Your father was brilliant, Layla. Absolutely brilliant, a wonderful mind. I would love to track your health, especially as you approach puberty. Perhaps I could assist if things ... become... difficult?" Layla's face gave nothing away. She could be on any world-level poker team.

Someone tried to enter but encountered Thulani's bulk. A peremptory rapping noise followed, accompanied by much swearing about closed doors. Thulani opened the door to a tense Frenzek. The man took in the room, pushed his way in and asked, "What the hell is going on here? Who are these people? Why are there children in your room, Valentine? All of you," he swept the room with an arm, "Get out." Everyone ignored him.

You had to admire his resilience. This guy was one of the movers and shakers of the planet, a heavy hitter in the security forces and a big deal used to issuing orders to unpleasant people. Unpleasant people who then jumped when being told how high. He was, therefore, somewhat taken aback when no one moved. No one except Swim Girl, she stepped up to the big man and poked him in the chest. She had to reach up.

"Back off, pal," she said. "Wait your turn and show some respect to MR Valentine."

Well, this was a sight. The gang coalesced behind Swim Girl, she formed the apex of a solid group of children, they reeked of competence, confidence and implacability. I thought they were great.

"I've heard about you," said Frenzek, "Valentine's little mobsters."

"Frenzek," I said, "Meet the gang. The feisty one out the front is Swim Girl, the rest are just plain mad, bad and dangerous to know. "Gang," I continued, "meet Sergeant Frenzek, he's a Big Deal around here. Also, he's on our side."

"Your name is Swim Girl?" asked Frenzek, going right to the critical issue.

"No," said Swim Girl. "That's the name Mr Valentine gave me when we were escaping; I wanted to swim across a river. My real name's Emilii."

I gulped. "Did you say, 'Emilii'?" I asked. What were the chances? Surely not. "You wouldn't happen to know someone named Amadi, would you? Is Sefu your father?"

She looked over at me, eyes a little wide. "Amadi's my cousin," she said. "Sefu is, or was, my father. Before he sold me. Now he is nothing to me. I like Amadi, I think he's in prison."

"Yeah," I said, not anymore. "He asked me to rescue you from the Syndicate." Her eyes became moist, we looked at each other for a few more heartbeats. And then I said a stupid, stupid thing, "You can't go back to Sefu, he'll just sell you again. How about you join the NightWatch?" I am sure that somewhere in my brain, alarm bells were going off, alarm bells I ignored. I turned to the rest of the gang, "You can all join if you want to. Anyone interested?"

Every hand shot up. Every face glowed with a smile, every eye shone. They positively shone.

"Aw, crap," said Thulani.

"More bloody kids," said Greenash.

We chatted a while longer, the kids turned on a video screen attached to one wall. It seemed to show animals singing and dancing, as well as the odd talking piece of fruit. They all sat on the floor or the end of my bed and watched the shows. Sometimes a real human appeared at a desk and read things which I resolutely ignored. Apparently, I could buy just about anything if I used a communicator to call a certain number. Holidays and gambling seemed to be popular topics.

One by one, each of them made the time to come over and give me a cuddle. They whispered in my ear, "Thank you. Thank you for saving us and keeping us safe." Layla kept a close watch on their behaviour, ensuring they performed their obeisance with the proper dignity and respect. I choked up, until Emilii saw me and said, "Rule four; Suck it up, Valerie!" Kids these days, have no respect. Some tittering broke out.

When she came over for her turn, she said, "We're changing Rule Five."

Rule five, rule five. Wait a minute, that was the one about me, the one they all ignored. Oh, well, it made sense. "Dropping me out of it, eh?" I said. "Very wise. What is it now?"

She hugged me and said, "It's now the Valentine Rule." She turned to the juvenile mobsters and said, in her parade ground voice, "What is the Valentine Rule?"

They all turned to me and yelled, "Fall down seven times, stand up eight!"

Damn, must have something in my eye.

Layla stayed within arm's reach, she had extended her circle of protection to Lydia who sat on my bed and ran her fingers through my hair. I had a question for Lydia, "I thought you were off somewhere in space? Making sure Magic doesn't crash our ship."

She ruffled my hair and said, "I had to come back. We picked up the vison of your torture. Days of it." She gulped, "Oh, Val! You poor thing, Magic raged through the ship, the rest of the team became surly and picked fights. I couldn't think straight. I was able to get on a small shuttle and return here." She grabbed Layla in another hug, "And this wonderful, wonderful girl saved you."

Layla blushed, smiled and leaned into the hug. My girls.

Frenzek and Thulani pulled up chairs and we chatted off and on about the world. "What about Louise? Is she going to do a deal?" I asked.

"Yes," said Frenzek. "We have the video of her torturing that guy. She knows she is dead in the water. We'll put her in witness protection and drain every bit of information out of her. Mr Grey survived, he has proven to be another rich resource, especially with his knowledge of their procedures. Don'elk is also giving evidence, I suspect his sister had a lot to do with his decision to leave a life of crime. The Syndicate is finished on this planet."

This was good news; it should mean I could walk around and not get shot or stabbed too often. No more than two or three times a week, at least.

"Pity we couldn't identify 'Ghost,'" said Thulani, extending an olive branch to the group. "Would have been the cherry on top." We all murmured agreement, the tension level continued to drop, Lydia even smiled.

I was watching the video screen; the program was another one of a man at a desk but then changed to someone being interviewed. It looked like they were in a hospital. Emilii turned back to us and said, "They're doing a story about you, Mr Valentine. About your nanobots, the healing and everything."

"Who's that?" I asked. On the screen, a man was being interviewed. A thin, ascetic man, a man I knew.

Thulani peered and said, "That's the Chief Surgeon of this hospital. He's also a minor royal."

"About twelfth in line to the Emperor," said Frenzek. "Has his own space yacht, flits about doing good deeds and opening things. Does some surgery here but seems to be mainly interested in children's health."

"Is that right?" I said.

I looked at the screen and said, very softly, "Hello, Ghost."

THE END

Don't miss out!

Visit the website below and you can sign up to receive emails whenever Terry Hornby publishes a new book. There's no charge and no obligation.

https://books2read.com/r/B-A-ZYBAB-SUBSC

BOOKS 2 READ

Connecting independent readers to independent writers.

About the Author

Terry is married to Glenda, a beautiful lady of infinite patience. They have two sons who allow him to tell them stories over and over again. He lives on the Sunshine Coast of Queensland which explains his self-satisfied smile. He may be contacted at hornbywriting@gmail

www.ingramcontent.com/pod-product-compliance
Lightning Source LLC
Chambersburg PA
CBHW030646260626
47157CB00007B/2510